Carrie listened attentively while a man with a very deep voice invited listeners to call Maeve Elliot and tell her about their problems. Maeve rested her head in her arms and groaned. Jonathan shushed her irritably. The next advertisement was a young woman saying much the same thing. He stopped the tape. 'The idea is to appeal to all age groups,' he explained. 'Now, our next job is to come up with topics for each of the shows until Christmas.'

Karl frowned as he consulted his diary. 'That's thirty-five shows, Jonathan.'

Maeve raised her head and stared at them. 'We've to come up with thirty-five topics now?'

'I'd certainly like some ideas today,' Jonathan said firmly. 'You've had three days to think about it.'

'I've been trying *not* to think about it,' Maeve retorted.

Jonathan threw down his pen. 'Fine, Maeve. If you want me to get someone else to do the show then that's what I'll do.'

The silence was electric as they stared at each other.

'A superb read' *OK Magazine* on *On Too Little, Too Late*

Also by Colette Caddle

Shaken and Stirred
A Cut Above
Too Little, Too Late

About the author

Colette Caddle's first novel, *Too Little, Too Late*, was published to enormous success in Ireland in 1999, becoming a No.1 bestselling success. She lives in Dublin with her husband, Tony, and her son, Peter.

COLETTE CADDLE

Forever FM

CORONET BOOKS
Hodder & Stoughton

First published in Great Britain in 2002 by Hodder and Stoughton
A division of Hodder Headline

A CIP catalogue record for this title is
available from the British Library

ISBN 0 340 79288 4

Typeset in Plantin Light by
Palimpsest Book Production Limited, Polmont, Stirlingshire

Printed and bound in Great Britain by
Clays Ltd, St Ives plc

Hodder and Stoughton
A division of Hodder Headline
338 Euston Road
London NW1 3BH

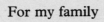

For my family

I

Linda tilted the mirror and examined her expression. Her blue eyes were large in her small oval face. They looked back at her shocked rather than angry. The fine lines around her eyes and at the edges of her mouth were more pronounced. She put her hand up to her dark blonde hair – she needed some highlights. She made a mental note to call her hairdresser. There were no grey hairs yet but that might change before the day was out. She readjusted the mirror as the traffic lights changed and guided the car along the Clontarf road. For once, morning traffic in Dublin suited her. It gave her time to think, time to try to figure out what had happened. There must be some mistake. It was laughable really. No one would ever have thought it – least of all Linda. But then she was nearing forty and Patrick was older – maybe that was it. She started as she realised she'd nearly missed the turn. She drove up towards Raheny village wondering what he'd say. She slowed as she neared the shops, quickly turned into a spot outside the florist's and turned off the ignition. She sat staring for a moment at the windows of Patrick's office. What would he say? she wondered as she grabbed her bag, got out of the car and straightened the narrow skirt of her suit.

'Good morning. Jewell's Surveyors. Can I help you?' Carrie Lambe looked up and smiled at her boss's wife. 'Oh, hi, Linda.'

Linda nodded tersely. 'Is he in?'

'Yes, go on in.'

'Thanks.' Linda strode past her and into the office without knocking.

Carrie frowned as she went back to her phone call. It wasn't like Linda to be so abrupt. Still, she supposed as she listened to the salesman drone on, everyone had off-days.

Patrick looked up and smiled at his wife. 'Hello, love, what brings you here so early?'

Linda clenched her hands together to stop them trembling. 'I suppose the usual story would be that when I was sending your suit off to the dry cleaners, I checked the pockets and found something.'

'Sorry, dear, I don't understand.' He chuckled. 'I take care of the dry cleaning in our house, remember?'

He was going a bit grey, Linda noticed, as Patrick ran a hand through his thinning hair.

'Yes, that's right, you do. You take care of a lot of things, don't you, Patrick?'

Patrick started to nod benignly and then stopped, realising that there was something distinctly odd about his wife. 'What is all this about, Linda?'

'It's about rings.'

'Rings?'

'One ring in particular.'

'Linda, I really don't know what you're talking about . . .'

'No, of course you don't. I should explain. You see, a very nice gentleman from Weirs called looking for you this morning. He'd tried your mobile number but couldn't get through. Anyway, he left a message.'

Patrick's pale blue eyes wavered and his thin, bony fingers tightened around his pen.

'He said that the ring was ready and he hoped I'd be happy with it.' She smiled at him.

He smiled back. 'The stupid man, it was supposed to be a surprise.'

'Oh, it was a surprise all right.'

'I was going to give it to you for our anniversary.'

'Our anniversary is three months away.'

'Yes, I know, but I saw it and couldn't resist—'

'Shut up, Patrick! Shut up, do you hear me? I don't want to hear any more lies. That ring isn't for me. I checked the size with the salesman. Her fingers are a lot slimmer than mine.'

'They made a mistake. I'll call them—'

She glared down at him, willing the tears not to spill over on to her cheeks. 'I told you to shut up. He was an extremely chatty salesman. He said that he was sure I'd be pleased with the ring. It had looked so well on my finger that day when I tried it on and – oh yes – how it was unlucky for anyone other than a Libran to wear an opal. Pity I'm a Gemini, isn't it?'

Patrick stood up and came around the desk. 'Oh, Linda, this isn't how I wanted you to find out.'

Linda gulped. That wasn't what he was supposed to say. That wasn't in the script. She preferred his denials.

Patrick's face was twisted in anguish. 'I've been trying to work up the courage to tell you for months.'

'Tell me what, exactly?' Linda thought that the icy calm that had descended on her must be shock. Why wasn't she hitting him, kicking him, crying?

'It's over. I'm moving out.'

'You're moving out,' she repeated stupidly.

'It can't be that much of a surprise, Linda. Things haven't exactly been great between us for a long time. There's no excitement any more. No fun.'

Linda stared at him. Excitement. Fun. In all the time that she'd known Patrick she would never have associated either of those words with him. He was kind, gentle even but very serious and straitlaced. 'When were you ever interested in fun? With you it's always been work, work, work.'

Patrick sighed. 'That's true but you have to take some responsibility too, Linda.'

'Responsibility for what?' Linda spluttered. She'd just discovered that her husband was having an affair and suddenly she was to blame?

'It takes two to make a good marriage,' he said gravely. 'You weren't there for me when I was getting the business on its feet.'

Linda stared at him astounded. 'That's because I was working my butt off to keep a roof over our heads!

You have a very interesting way of rewriting the past, Patrick. Who paid the electricity bills, the phone bills, the insurance?'

'I know you helped out financially—'

'Helped out?' she screeched. 'I carried you for five years. Five bloody years, Patrick, and you say that I didn't put enough into our marriage.'

'Not in the emotional sense, no.'

Linda blinked. Was this really her husband talking to her about emotions? The man whose idea of romance was to send her a birthday card through the post?

'You never listened to me.'

Linda smiled bitterly. 'Ah, I see. And now you've found someone who does? Did you tell her your wife didn't understand you?'

'Stacey isn't like that.'

Stacey. Somehow hearing her name made it seem horribly real. 'Isn't like what?'

'She wasn't out to catch a married man, to break up a marriage. It just happened.'

Linda looked at her husband's receding ginger hairline, his pale blue eyes and his slight frame. 'She just couldn't help herself?'

He nodded, missing the note of sarcasm. 'But she won't have anything to do with me until I leave you.'

'But she was happy to take your ring.'

'We got engaged. I wanted to prove to her that I was serious. That I would marry her some day.'

Linda gasped, more taken aback by his bluntness than anything else. 'But you're already married, Patrick. You have been for fifteen years, or had you forgotten?' She shook her head in bewilderment. 'Was it all so bad?'

'No, love, of course not, but it wasn't . . .' He shrugged, unable to find the right words.

'Special?' Linda volunteered, her voice barely a croak.

Patrick nodded enthusiastically. 'That's it. I suppose we were like a pair of old slippers – comfortable. Let's face it, Linda, we've gotten into a terrible rut.'

Linda couldn't even answer. She felt numb. Somehow she'd always thought that if anyone broke up their marriage it would be her. Not that it had ever been a serious consideration, of course. It's just that she'd always believed that if she hadn't married Patrick, no one would. His attractions weren't immediately obvious. He was shy really, lacking in confidence – damn it, how dare he dump her? It was bloody insulting! 'What's she like?'

'Sorry?'

Linda sank into a chair not trusting her legs, which seemed to have turned to jelly. 'This Stacey. What's she like? Younger, I suppose.'

'Well, she is a bit . . .'

'How old?' Linda barked.

Patrick studied his shoes. 'Twenty-five.'

'Twenty-five! Jesus, Patrick, you're old enough to be her father!'

'Don't be ridiculous. It's only eighteen years of a difference. And she's very mature.'

Linda smiled slightly, though she felt quite ill. 'I

thought it might be something like this. It's a mid-life crisis, isn't it?'

He shook his head impatiently. 'Of course not. Don't try and make it sound sordid, Linda, because it's not. What Stacey and I have is very pure and beautiful . . .'

'Oh, spare me, Patrick! You've been screwing around. Here's a newsflash for you. That *is* sordid.'

'I have not screwed around. There has never been anyone else. Stacey is different.'

'How long has it been going on?'

Patrick went behind the safety of his desk. 'A while.'

'How long?'

'Just over three years.'

'God! You've been lying to me for three years and you have the nerve to call this relationship pure.'

'I only stayed because I was sorry for you. I didn't know how to break it to you.'

'How very big of you.'

'Still, it's done now. I'll leave today.'

Linda looked at the almost relieved expression on his face. He was delighted that she'd found him out. 'So that's it?'

Patrick shrugged uncomfortably. 'Sorry.'

Linda shook her head in bewilderment. He was ending their marriage not even bothering with the pretence that there was a hope of saving it. She was dumped. Well and truly dumped. 'Right, then. I'd better get to work.'

Patrick reached out to her, his eyes full of concern. 'Will you be okay?'

Linda shrunk from him. Pity. God, she couldn't handle that. 'Sure. I'll be fine.'

When she thought about it afterwards she couldn't remember the journey from Patrick's office to Reeve's Recruitment in the centre of Dublin. She'd been oblivious to the blasting horns and the perennial road works. She was on automatic pilot – probably not even safe behind the wheel. She entered the office quickly and quietly and made a beeline for her desk in the corner. She sank into her chair with a tremulous sigh, grateful for the protective screen that hid her from the rest of the staff. She hadn't cried yet, although the tears had been very close while she was in Patrick's office, but for some reason she couldn't stop trembling. Her whole body seemed to be shaking uncontrollably. She must be in shock. Maybe she should make a cup of sweet tea. But that would involve shaking hands and boiling water and it would also mean she'd have to cross the room to the little kitchen, past Cheryl and Marie. She wasn't ready to talk to anyone, least of all Cheryl. She wasn't even sure that her voice still worked.

'Linda? Can I just check some of these letters with you?' Marie stood smiling nervously at her. 'Your voice was a bit muffled on the dictaphone and I'm not sure I got everything right.'

'Just leave them there, I'll check them later,' Linda said abruptly. Well, that answered that question. Her voice did still work, although it sounded odd even to her ears.

Marie looked worried. 'But you did say they were to go out today . . .'

'They can wait, Marie,' Linda said through gritted teeth. 'I'm busy.'

'Oh. Right then, sorry.'

Linda sighed as Marie shuffled back to her own desk. Now the girl would be afraid to say boo to her for days. She decided to risk the tea after all and, taking a deep breath, stood up and made her way briskly across the room. As she was putting on the kettle, Cheryl appeared at her side.

'Oh, good, I could murder a coffee. Did you tell our little Marie off then?' she murmured, nodding towards where the young girl sat trying to hide behind her PC.

Linda groaned inwardly. 'No, of course not.'

'Well, she's definitely upset about something. It must be a man.' She chuckled. 'Or the lack of one! Lord, it's hardly surprising. Did you see what she's wearing today?'

'I never noticed.' Linda spooned coffee into a mug and shoved it into Cheryl's hand. Sometimes she really felt like telling Cheryl not to be so bloody nosy, but she was the boss's wife so Linda held her tongue.

Cheryl babbled on. 'Thanks. Oh, no, she'll never get a fella if she keeps dressing like that. I've tried to drop her some gentle hints but she seems to be a bit slow on the uptake.'

Linda had heard Cheryl's 'hints' and thought that Marie would want to be downright thick not to pick up on them – and certifiable if she heeded any of them. Cheryl had told her to wear shorter skirts, tight blouses – although she probably would need a padded bra for it to make any difference – and skyscraper-high shoes. In effect, copy Cheryl's own inimitable style. Linda suppressed a shudder as she dangled a teabag in her mug. Cheryl and style were two words that did not go together. Mutton dressed up as lamb, Linda's mother would have said. It wasn't that Cheryl was that old – she was only forty-six – or even that ugly. But she insisted on wearing clothes that only a confident, beautiful teenager would get away with. And the thickly applied make-up and peroxided big hair didn't help. Marie might be a little on the frumpy side but Linda was grateful that she hadn't taken any of Cheryl's 'hints'.

'Are you okay, Linda?' Cheryl poured milk into her coffee and added two sweeteners. 'You're very quiet and pale. Have you got that bug that's going around? Apparently it's a terrible dose.'

'I'm fine.' Linda smiled shakily and hurried back to her desk. If Cheryl probed any further, there was a very strong chance that she would burst into hysterical tears and never stop.

'Linda? Jonathan Blake is on line two,' Marie called to her.

'Tell him I'm on a call and I'll get back to him,' Linda said hurriedly. There was no way she could focus on work and she certainly wouldn't be able to handle Jonathan's flirtatious banter. Not today.

Marie eyed her nervously as she put down the

phone. 'He says he's out for the rest of the day but you can call him tomorrow.'

'Fine.' Linda stared at the CVs in front of her and tried to look as if she were engrossed. But when a big fat tear plopped on to the page, she picked up her bag and stood up.

'Actually, Cheryl, I think I might have that bug after all.' She paused briefly at the other woman's desk and sniffed convincingly. 'Maybe I will go home.'

'You do that, Linda. And tell Patrick I said he was to look after you.' Cheryl winked broadly.

'I will,' Linda gasped and shot out of the door.

2

'I'm very sorry, Patrick, but I've made up my mind.'

Patrick looked at his secretary as if she were mad. 'But, Carrie, this has nothing to do with you!'

Carrie pulled herself up to her full five feet, five inches and watched him steadily, her large brown eyes dark with disappointment. 'No, maybe not, but I can't work for you after what you've done.' The walls in the tiny office were thin and Carrie had heard the whole miserable exchange.

'You're being ridiculous. Marriages break up every day.'

'And lots of married men have affairs,' Carrie agreed shakily as she piled her personal effects into a box. 'But it doesn't make it right.'

Patrick shook his head in frustration. 'You're not even Linda's friend. You only know her through me!'

'Yes, and I know what a lovely woman she is and that she deserves better treatment than this. Goodbye, Patrick.'

And she'd taken her belongings and stumbled out of the office without a backward glance. On the bus home she'd had time to reflect on her rash behaviour. Declan wouldn't be impressed, she realised as she

pulled her raincoat close around her slim shoulders.
She'd been working as Patrick Jewell's assistant now
for nearly two years – the longest she'd been in a
job yet – and had recently got a salary increase. She
finished every day at five on the dot, which Declan
particularly liked because it usually meant dinner was
on the table when he arrived home at seven. No, her
beloved boyfriend would be furious, especially as they
were saving for a new telly. One of these wide-screen
ones that they'd always wanted – well, Declan had
always wanted. Carrie was just as happy curled up
with a good book. She sighed heavily. Maybe she'd
stop off at the butcher's on the way home and get a
couple of steaks. Declan always took bad news better
after a good dinner. Not that it was bad news, she
reminded herself. She'd easily find another job.

'You did what? Are you mad, Carrie? That was a very
cushy number you had. Not many people work a nine
to five job any more. You don't know when you're
well off.'

Carrie placed another beer by his plate and said
nothing.

Declan tore the ring from the can and took a gulp.
'What did he do that was so bad anyway?'

'He left his wife.'

'What?'

'He left his wife,' Carrie repeated patiently. 'He's
been having an affair for three years and now that
Linda's found out he's leaving her and going to live
with this other woman.'

Declan's brow wrinkled in confusion. 'But what has that got to do with you? You just work for him.'

'Not any more I don't. I couldn't work for someone like that. It would be very disloyal of me to stay there another minute.'

'But you hardly know her!'

Carrie shook her head sadly at his lack of understanding. 'That's not the point, Declan. Anyway, I've made up my mind. More gravy?'

Linda sat staring at the television screen, not even trying to absorb the storyline of the soap. She had been sitting here since she'd gotten in from work. It was like she was frozen, unable to move, to talk – even to think. No, that wasn't true, she couldn't stop thinking. What had happened? Had her husband really just told her that he was leaving? Her quiet, reserved Patrick. Had he really told her that he was going to marry someone else? Someone much younger than she was? What did the girl see in him? That thought made her feel slightly disloyal, which in turn made her laugh mirthlessly. She felt disloyal when he was the one who'd been seeing another woman for months – no, years. God, she was a fool. How had she not seen the signs? Things had been fine between them. Okay, they didn't make love that often but then their marriage had never been that passionate. Patrick wasn't really the passionate sort. Neither was she, if she were honest. She was just as happy with a kiss and a cuddle. Sex was a very overrated activity as far as she was concerned. She never believed these articles in magazines that went into gross detail about how to improve your sex life. She was sure most people only had a quick romp once a week and then rolled over and went to sleep. But the thought of Patrick with another woman – she closed her eyes tightly – oh, how could he? They were partners, best friends, they were a team – he must realise that he'd made a terrible mistake. He was probably regretting telling her already.

She jumped as she heard his key in the door. Oh, thank God . . .

'I thought you'd be still in the office,' Patrick mumbled apologetically. She often worked late these days. He stood in the doorway looking awkward and embarrassed.

Linda smiled thinly. 'For some reason I was finding it hard to concentrate.'

'I just came to pick up a few things. I'll get the rest at the weekend, if that's all right?'

If that's all right? Of course it wasn't bloody all right! He wasn't supposed to be leaving. He was supposed to be on his knees begging for forgiveness. 'Sure. Do it on Saturday. I won't be here.'

He sat down suddenly and took her hands in his. Linda looked at him hopefully. 'I'm sorry about today, Linda. I never meant to just blurt it all out like that.'

She slumped back in the chair. No change of heart then.

'Carrie tore strips off me after you left.'

Linda stared at him in surprise. 'Did she?'

'Absolutely! And I always thought she was such a quiet little thing.'

'I like her,' Linda said absently.

'She's a bloody nutcase! She walked out on me just like that. Told me I could keep this month's salary, that she couldn't stay another minute.' He shook his head in exasperation. 'Crazy kid!'

'Isn't she the same age as your girlfriend?' Linda retorted harshly.

Patrick dropped her hands and stood up. 'I'll get my things.'

As she heard him packing a bag upstairs Linda wondered vaguely what had prompted his little secretary to take such drastic action. It was nice to know that someone supported her but a phone call or a note would have done just as well. Maybe she'd just acted on impulse and would be back in the office in the morning all embarrassed and apologetic. Yes, that's probably what would happen. She'd tell Patrick to pretend it had never happened. It was the least he could do under the circumstances. He'd already screwed up one life today.

Carrie was in the kitchen washing up when the phone rang. After a few minutes of muffled conversation, Declan called her. 'It's for you.'

'Oh, Carrie, what have you done?'

Carrie sighed. Declan had lost no time in informing her sister of her irresponsible behaviour. She shot him a dirty look before taking the phone out to the kitchen. 'It's no big deal, Helen. I fancied a change anyway.'

'But it was a great job.'

Carrie chuckled. 'That's the first time you've said

so. If my memory serves me right you thought I was wasting my talents.'

Helen sighed irritably. 'Well, you were – you are. You're a clever girl. You could be much more than just a secretary.'

'You know someone has to do the ordinary jobs, Helen—'

'Oh don't start all that again! You're avoiding the subject. All I'm saying is that if you insist on being a secretary, you could do a lot worse than Jewell's Surveyors. Why on earth did you hand in your notice?'

'I'm not sure. I suppose I just don't like my boss any more.'

'You're not supposed to like him,' Helen said impatiently. 'He's the boss.'

'I don't agree at all. Much more can be achieved in a harmonious atmosphere.'

'You sound like a hippy. Have you told the folks?'

Carrie winced. 'No, why bother them? I'll have found something else in a few days. I can tell them then.'

'Your optimism is admirable.'

'Thank you.'

'Or else you're just kidding yourself.'

Carrie grinned. She was twenty-four years old and her sister still treated her like a child. 'Thank you, dear sister, for your support.'

'Sorry. How are things with Declan? He didn't sound too impressed with your decision.'

Carrie lowered her voice even though there was zero chance of her boyfriend hearing anything over the football match blaring from the television. 'He'll be fine once I've found something else. He's just worried, that's all.'

'Worried that you won't be bringing in any money,' Helen retorted.

'Don't start, Helen,' Carrie said mildly. 'He's not like that.'

'Yeah, right. Listen, I'm going to have to go. I promised Lily I'd read her a bedtime story.'

'How is the little angel?'

Helen laughed. 'Behaving like a little devil, but I've bribed her to be good with the promise of a story and some chocolate.'

'That would work for me,' Carrie laughed.

'As you're a lady of leisure, why don't you come over tomorrow for lunch?'

'Aren't you working?' Helen was a physiotherapist and had her own practice in the local GP's clinic.

'I just have a couple of appointments in the morning. I'll be home by twelve.'

'Okay then, you're on. I'll be over around one.'

'Great. See you then. 'Bye, Carrie.'

'Seeya, Helen.'

Declan looked up as she came back into the room and sat down beside him. 'Well? Did your sister manage to talk some sense into you?'

'She didn't even try,' Carrie said.

He shook his head. 'I find that hard to believe. I really do think you're making a big mistake, Carrie. Would you not consider phoning Patrick and apologising?'

Carrie ignored his wheedling tone. 'No, Declan, I'm sorry. Look, please don't worry. I'll bet you I'll have a new job by the end of the week. A better one, with more money too!'

'I hope you're right. My salary won't be able to support us both for very long.'

Carrie leaned over and planted a kiss on his cheek. 'It won't have to. Trust me, love. Everything's going to work out for the best. You know what they say. Every cloud has a silver lining.'

'And it's probably lightning,' he grunted.

Carrie laughed at his miserable expression. 'I'm going to have a bath and a root through my wardrobe. I need to dig out my interview clothes.' Her smile faded as she went upstairs to escape. Why was it that she was always disappointing people? Her boss, her family, even her boyfriend. Everyone seemed to know what she should be doing with her life. They were all experts at pointing out her mistakes. But the thing was Carrie didn't really want to be successful. No, she corrected herself as she rummaged through her wardrobe, she had a different view of success. Someone to love, a nice home and cash in her pocket – that was enough for her. But her family had always been baffled by her attitude. Her parents, both doctors, couldn't understand why she wouldn't go to university.

'I'm not clever enough,' Carrie had pointed out. She wasn't dumb but she knew that when the brains were being doled out in her family she was at the end of the queue. Her brother was a successful vet, Helen a brilliant physiotherapist, but she had been happy to plod from one office job to the next. It wasn't that she was thick – she'd managed to get through her final exams without failing a subject. But in the Lambe household one didn't pass exams, one got straight A's. Carrie giggled. 'But not this "one".'

Her brother and sister accepted her decision not to go on to third-level education although she knew they didn't really understand it. But her parents had taken the whole business very personally and still looked at her reproachfully when they discussed her brother and sister's success. But she'd got used to that. It was a bit of a disappointment though to see Declan hop on the bandwagon. But then he was probably just worried about her. She shouldn't be too hard on him. It probably had been a bit silly of her to throw in her job just like that. But something else would turn up, it always did.

3

'Sod off, you dirty perv,' Maeve Elliot muttered and pressed the button to cut off the caller. This was the worst about doing a nighttime spot. You got all sorts of weirdos ringing in. She liked working for Forever FM but she'd like it a lot more if she didn't have to do the *Dream-time* easy-listening show. Not only was it lousy hours, it didn't present any kind of challenge. She should be on prime time running a current issues chat show, or interviewing politicians. As the song ended, she leaned forward. 'And that's it for tonight, listeners,' she purred into the mike. 'Sweet dreams.' She pulled off her headset, threw it on the desk and stood up, stretching her long neck. 'God, I need a drink.'

'What hot spot are you hitting tonight? Or should I say who are you hitting on?'

Maeve shot her producer a smouldering look. 'Poor Karl, are you jealous?'

He grinned. 'Nah, I never liked cats.'

Maeve scowled at the Australian who never let her away with anything. 'You'd better watch it or I might just scratch your eyes out!'

Karl laughed. 'I'm not into that kind of thing, even if you are.'

'Nice to see a good relationship between a DJ and her producer,' Jonathan said from the doorway.

'Hey.' Karl nodded at his boss.

Maeve grinned. 'Hi, Jonathan, did you catch the show?'

'Just the last five minutes. I thought it was a bit . . . dead.'

Maeve's eyes narrowed. 'What the hell do you expect? It's eleven o'clock at night and the only calls we get are from people who don't have a life!'

'Yes, I've been thinking about that. I think it's time to make a change.'

Maeve and Karl exchanged worried looks.

'What do you mean?' Karl asked.

'I'm not sure,' Jonathan murmured. 'But I think we need to liven things up a little.'

'I've told Karl that.' Maeve grinned at the murderous look from her producer.

'I must have been out that day,' he drawled.

'Okay, children, let's remember we have to work together. Any ideas, Karl, on beefing up the ratings?'

Karl shrugged. 'There's not much you can do with a nighttime music show. We could start interviewing bands, something like that.'

Jonathan shook his head. 'That corner is catered for already. The one market niche that we aren't covering, however, is these phone-in talk shows.'

Karl nodded gravely. 'That would be quite a big change. Are you talking about going head-to-head with the other stations?'

'Those shows are ridiculous,' Maeve protested. 'As

if we don't have enough perves phoning in – no, thanks!'

Jonathan watched her steadily. 'Well, you wouldn't have to deal with them, Maeve.'

'What do you mean?'

'I mean I'd bring someone else in to run the show, of course. It's not your area. You're a DJ.'

'Are you firing us?' Karl asked quietly.

'Of course not. Your show would just go back an hour or so.'

Maeve paled. 'Jonathan, you can't do that.'

'It is still my station, I believe.'

Karl shot her a warning glance. 'Hey, you're the boss, Jonathan, but there's no need to rush into anything.'

Jonathan shrugged casually. 'Who's rushing?'

'I'm sure that Karl and I could come up with something,' Maeve said hurriedly.

Jonathan smiled. 'I thought you might say that. Well, I'll look forward to hearing your ideas at the meeting on Friday morning.'

'That's not a lot of time . . .' Karl started.

'I'm sure you can rise to the challenge. I'll leave you to it. Night, guys.'

'Night,' Maeve said miserably, sinking back into her chair.

'Well, I don't suppose we should be surprised,' Karl said philosophically as he lit a cigarette.

Maeve stared at him. 'That we're losing our jobs?'

'Don't exaggerate. You heard him, he'll just move our show out. Anyway . . .'

'Yes?'

He smiled at her. 'We're going to do that talk show.'

'Why don't I just change my name to Geraldine Springer,' Maeve muttered.

'You always said you wanted a talk show,' he reminded her.

'I wanted to interview interesting people,' Maeve retorted. 'Not listen to a bunch of low-life losers who want to tell all the world their problems.'

Karl chuckled. 'That's your fellow Dubliners you're talking about.'

'Losers are losers and every city, every country has them. Anyway, why are you so cool about all this?'

He shrugged. 'Jonathan's right. Our show is jaded. It's time you and I had a change. But we need to put a different slant on it if we're to beat the other stations.'

'I don't see how.' Maeve stared at him moodily.

'Look, Maeve, Jonathan is expecting ideas from us in two days' time. I suggest that you stop moaning and get on with it. This could be the end for us both or it could be a great opportunity.'

'I suppose you're right,' Maeve admitted. It was true that this would be a step closer to her dream but at the same time if the show bombed, she'd probably go down with it. She'd just have to make sure that didn't happen. She stood up. 'Okay, then. I suggest that we both catch a show tonight and we can talk again tomorrow.' It was only eleven and their two biggest rivals had chat shows running until midnight.

She could listen to the show in her car and still have a drink in her hand by midnight. 'I'll take Dublin FM. You cover City Live.'

Karl nodded and slung his jacket over his shoulder. 'That's more like it. See you tomorrow.'

Maeve made her way to the ladies', pulled out her make-up bag and examined her reflection in the grubby mirror. Despite the late hour, she still looked fresh and her blue eyes were bright. She released her long blonde hair from the tight ponytail and shook it out then took off her shirt to reveal a thin black vest. A touch of lip-gloss and some eyeliner and she was ready to face her public. She hurried out to her red MG, tuned her radio into Dublin FM and guided the car out into traffic and towards the city centre.

'It's a fucking disgrace, that's what it is,' a woman with a voice like a pneumatic drill was saying. 'Lettin' a bugger like that walk the streets, it's not right.'

'And what do you think the police should do?' the presenter asked.

'Lock the bastard up and throw away the key!'

'I don't agree with that.' Another male voice chipped in. 'We need to rehabilitate drug-pushers.'

A reasonable attitude, Maeve thought with a wry grin. That was novel.

'Rehabilitate me arse!' the woman replied.

Maeve laughed out loud. 'Charming.'

'Cut the balls off him, that's what they should do. That'd make him think twice before sellin' his filth to innocent young kids.'

Maeve pulled neatly into the car park of the Burlington

Hotel; the security man waved her towards the underground car park and she gave him a dazzling smile.

'If we don't try and help these people the problem will only get worse,' the man argued.

'You're fighting a losing battle,' Maeve told him as she pulled into a parking spot and switched off the engine.

'And ye think the problem's going to get better if we mollycoddle the thugs who're killin' our kids?' the woman screeched.

'How do you respond to that, sir?' The presenter sounded bored.

Maeve turned off the radio. Oh, God, she'd die if she had to do a show like that – if not of boredom then of embarrassment. She'd have to talk Jonathan out of this but she already knew what he'd say. 'Come up with a better idea.'

She swung her long legs out of the car and stood up. After smoothing down her top and locking the car she walked into the hotel and headed for the nightclub. There were bound to be some interesting faces here this evening. She paused in the doorway and glanced around.

'Maeve, over here.'

She smiled as she spotted the tall, slim redhead waving at her and moved through the throng to join her. 'Hi, Julie.' She air-kissed the girl's cheek and nodded around vaguely at the people she was with. Julie Rose was a model whose aim in life was to find a rich husband before she had to retire. She was now thirty-two and though still beautiful the phone didn't ring as much as it used to. She and Maeve never shared men but all other husbands and boyfriends were fair game. In fact, Julie rarely dated a single man.

'If he's over thirty and still single there's a reason for it and I don't want to find out what that is,' she said matter-of-factly.

Maeve agreed, although because she was in the public eye she only dated married men who were officially separated or divorced. She also kept her distance from men with children. She didn't need to take on extra baggage and she certainly didn't see herself entertaining another woman's kids.

'Maeve, do you know Paul Riche?'

'I don't think so.' She smiled into the eyes of the man with the flashy tie and expensive suit. 'I'm sure I'd remember that name.'

'And I definitely wouldn't forget you,' he replied, looking her up and down. 'Can I get you a drink?'

'Tequila on the rocks, please.'

'Coming right up.'

'What does he do?' she asked Julie when he'd moved away.

'Something in banking,' Julie said vaguely, 'but rolling in it. He's been going on about his yacht all evening. A bit of a bore, but then you can't have everything.'

'Married?' Maeve asked, studying him intently as he stood at the bar. He wasn't bad looking. A bit on the heavy side and not as much hair as she'd like but his eyes were intelligent and he moved with authority.

'Separated,' Julie whispered.

'Excellent.'

Paul returned and smiled warmly as he handed her the glass. 'Cheers, Maeve.'

She took her drink, allowing her hand to brush against his.

'Cheers. Lovely to meet you.'

'The pleasure is all mine.'

'Hello, Maeve.'

Maeve groaned inwardly as another man appeared at her side. 'Hi, Vince.' He bent to kiss her and she turned her head so that he caught her on the cheek.

He frowned. 'I didn't think you'd be here tonight.'

She shrugged. 'My plans changed.'

His eyes shifted to Paul. 'Aren't you going to introduce me?'

'Vince McHugh this is Paul Riche. Paul, Vince.' Maeve put down her drink. 'Now, Paul, what about that dance?'

Paul smiled politely at Vince. 'If you'll excuse us.' He led her on to the dance floor. 'Someone you wanted to escape from?' he enquired as they swayed to the music.

'Let's say he's a little too persistent.'

'And don't you like that?' Paul pulled her closer.

Maeve smiled lazily. 'It depends on the man.' They danced together for a couple of songs before returning to the bar for another drink. She smiled and nodded as Paul talked about his job and his boat and then she set her barely touched drink down on the bar. 'I must be going.'

'Let me see you home,' Paul murmured.

'I'm driving.'

'Can I see you again?'

'I'll probably be in the Pod on Tuesday.'

He took out his Palm Pilot and switched it on. After scanning it for a few seconds, he shook his head. 'I have to attend a function on Tuesday.'

'Some other time then,' Maeve said coolly and headed for the door.

Paul hurried after her. 'How about lunch on Friday?'

Maeve's eyes twinkled. 'I don't eat lunch.'

He looked at her, frustrated. 'Maybe I'll be able to get out of the other function.'

She leaned up to kiss his cheek, letting her long hair brush against it. 'I'll see you in the Pod then.' She walked away, aware that he was watching her every move. Paul Riche was a good replacement for Vince. He didn't move in media circles but he would have contacts and she had no doubt that she would find a use for them.

4

Linda sat in the car and stared at herself in the mirror. She was doing a lot of this lately. Searching her face for the reason why her life had fallen apart. The way she looked this morning she could understand Patrick leaving. She looked every one of her thirty-eight years and more. Her hair was lank and dull, her skin pasty and her eyes lifeless. It had taken a great deal of willpower to get out of bed this morning. She'd spent most of her time in bed since Patrick had left, with the exception of Saturday when she'd dragged herself around town while he packed his belongings. It would have been too painful to watch and she was afraid that she'd throw herself at his feet and beg him to stay. That would be the final humiliation. No, she'd get through this and if she had moments of weakness, she would have them in private. No one was going to look at her with pity, certainly not Patrick Jewell.

She hoisted herself out of the car and started the short walk to Reeve's Recruitment. She dreaded the thoughts of work and having to listen to Cheryl prattle on. And what would she say when Cheryl started to interrogate her about her weekend? Would she tell them about Patrick? Exactly how did you go about telling people that your husband had left you for a young girl? Maybe she should send out cards. *Mrs Linda Jewell regrets to inform you* . . . Linda laughed, but there was a slightly hysterical edge to it. 'Pull yourself together, Linda. Remember it's a brave face for the world. There's plenty of time to cry when you're all alone in your king-size bed every night.'

Marie was the only one in the office when she arrived. 'Are you feeling better, Linda?' she asked with a timid smile.

Linda took off her coat and hung it on the stand inside the door. 'Yes, thanks, Marie, I think I had that awful flu bug that's doing the rounds.'

'My mother had that. She was in bed for two weeks. Are you sure you should be back so soon?'

'Oh, yes, I'm fine.' Linda smiled brightly and walked briskly down to her desk.

'I'll make some tea,' Marie called after her.

'Lovely.'

'Did I hear someone mention tea?' Cheryl bustled in, her husband in her wake.

'Honestly, Bill, I don't know why you don't change that car. It's not as if you can't afford it.'

Linda smiled sympathetically at her boss. 'Did you have a breakdown?'

'Just a flat tyre. There's nothing wrong with that car, Cheryl, and I do not intend to change it. It's only three years old.'

Cheryl tut-tutted. 'He can be so mean,' she murmured as she hung up her jacket and then tottered down to Linda's desk. 'He won't take me on holiday either.'

'We were in London last month,' Bill retorted before retreating into his office.

'Hah! That was only for three days and you only agreed because Ryanair were running a twenty-five-pound special. Honestly, Linda, I don't know what to do with the man. Maybe I should ask your Patrick to have a word. Didn't he bring you to Austria last Christmas?'

'Switzerland.' It seemed like years ago. Linda cringed as she realised Stacey was around then. He'd probably been calling her every day. He'd probably been thinking of her when they—

Cheryl sighed. 'You're lucky, Linda, not many men are so romantic.'

Linda wished the phone would ring so that Cheryl would go away. She could be here all morning once she got talking.

Bill stuck his head out of his office. 'If it's not too much trouble, *dear*, we have interviews starting in ten minutes.'

'All right, all right, I'm coming. Honestly, Linda, the man's a slave-driver.'

Linda breathed a sigh of relief as Cheryl tottered off to join her husband. When Marie brought her tea, she thanked her and asked her to hold all her calls for the morning. 'I have to go through the papers and then check through our files again to see if I can find a researcher for Forever FM,' she explained unnecessarily.

'Okay, Linda.'

After an hour, Linda was regretting getting out of bed. It was almost impossible to concentrate. All she had to do was look at a girl's photo on a CV and she'd start to wonder if Patrick's new love was dark or fair. Every candidate seemed to be twenty-five. God, what would a girl of that age see in Patrick? There had to be something wrong with her. Why wasn't she dating – no, married – to someone her own age?

By the time Cheryl emerged from her meeting, Linda was totally depressed and racking her brains for a reason to leave the office. It would only be a matter of time before Cheryl picked up on her mood. 'I'm going over to Forever FM,' she announced, springing to her feet.

Cheryl looked faintly surprised. 'Oh?'

'Yes, I need to discuss some candidates with Jonathan. There's no point in me dragging them in here first. He's so fussy and difficult to please.' She grabbed a handful of files and stuffed them into her briefcase.

'I'd be happy to try and please him any day,' Cheryl murmured, smacking her lips. 'The man is gorgeous.'

'Is he?' Linda shuffled into her coat.

'Oh, come on, Linda, you know he is!' Cheryl eyed her suspiciously. 'I hope you're not up to anything you shouldn't, Mrs Jewell.'

'In comparison to the women Jonathan usually dates I'm just about ready for my pension,' Linda said with an edge to her voice.

'He does seem to like them young,' Cheryl agreed wistfully.

'I'm off, then. 'Bye.' And Linda hurried out of the office before Cheryl could ponder any more on Jonathan Blake's love-life. She decided to walk the two miles to Forever FM's offices, she needed the air. She was sorely tempted not to go at all but Jonathan Blake called her nearly every Monday and if he phoned when she was supposed to be with him, there would be a lot of awkward questions. But how was she going to face him of all people? He was a year older than she, divorced and he dated girls barely out of the classroom. She wasn't sure she could be civil to him today. Somehow, like Patrick, he was now the bad guy and she had a sudden empathy with his ex-wife. She strode up Harcourt Street, oblivious to the rain that had started to fall and the light wind whipping her hair into her eyes. Why was it always the men that did this? You rarely saw a forty-year-old woman going around with a twenty-something guy – what on earth would they talk about? But then conversation probably wouldn't play a major part in such a relationship. She smiled grimly as she bowed her head into the wind and felt a cold trickle of rain slide down the back of her neck. When an older man looked at a young girl he wasn't wondering what they'd talk about. He was looking at her firm young boobs, tight bum and long legs. If she could string an intelligent sentence together, it would be a bonus. As the light rain turned into a deluge, Linda quickened her pace, but by the time she reached Ranelagh and stumbled through the door of Forever FM she resembled a drowned rat.

'Oh, Linda you're soaked!'

Linda smiled grimly at the receptionist that she'd placed here less than a month ago. 'Hi, Karen.'

'Are you here to see Mr Blake?'

'Yes, but he's not expecting me. It's no problem if he's busy.'

'I'll check.'

Linda nodded. 'Great, but can I go somewhere and dry off first?'

'Straight through there.' Karen pointed her towards the ladies' and Linda went in and stripped off her sodden jacket. Apart from a few marks around the collar, her blouse was miraculously dry, but her skirt was drenched. She hitched it up around her waist and held it under the hand-dryer. Then she bent her head and started on her hair. It would look like a bush as a result but there was no alternative. She didn't have one of these sexy, sleek hairstyles that looked good wet or dry. Stacey probably did. Stacey's hair was probably always perfect. 'Oh for God's sake, pull yourself together,' she said aloud and then cringed as she heard the toilet flush in one of the cubicles. A young girl emerged, hurriedly washed her hands and left. Linda sighed and rummaged in her bag for some make-up but as it was 'one of those days', she had left it at home. She smoothed down her hair with her hands and used some toilet roll to wipe the mascara stains from her cheeks. She prayed fervently that Jonathan Blake would be unavailable. She'd hate him to see her like this.

But as she emerged she saw the man himself waiting for her in reception. 'Linda, what a nice surprise! God, what happened to you? You look terrible.'

Linda noted his dark shiny hair, immaculate suit, sensuous lips and the faint smell of expensive cologne. She was dismayed to find her eyes were filling with tears. 'In case you hadn't noticed, Jonathan, it's raining.'

His eyes narrowed. 'Is it? Karen, make us some coffee, will you? Come into my office, Linda.'

Linda wiped surreptitiously at her eyes. 'Are you sure you have the time? It's no problem if you don't. I just happened to be passing . . .'

Jonathan took her by the arm and propelled her along. 'So what's wrong?' he asked when they were sitting in his large office.

Linda took a deep breath and assumed a professional expression. 'I'm having some problem finding a suitable person for the research position . . .'

'Forget that. Tell me what's really wrong.'

Linda looked at him wide-eyed. 'Sorry?'

'Oh, come on, Linda. I don't usually manage to reduce you to tears.'

She tugged at her right eye and laughed nervously. 'Oh, I just have something in my eye. It's terribly windy out. Crying! My goodness, why on earth would I be crying?'

Jonathan didn't look totally convinced, but he didn't pursue it. 'Okay, then. You were saying?'

She looked blank for a moment and then remembered the reason for her visit. 'Oh, yes, the position of researcher. I just wondered if I could go through a few possible candidates with you.'

'Sure.' Jonathan broke off as Karen tapped on the

door and brought in their coffee. 'Thanks, Karen. Hold my calls, will you? Now, Linda, what have you got?'

Linda went through the files that she had brought with her but Jonathan wasn't happy with any of them. 'Yes, Linda, they have great qualifications, but this job requires a bit more than that. The position needs someone interested in people, downright nosy, in fact. They have to be able to draw people out, home in on the interesting stuff.'

'What kind of work will this person be doing, exactly?' Linda asked wearily.

'A bit of everything at first,' Jonathan admitted. 'But I'm planning a talk show and we need a researcher who will be able to spot good guests, ones with personality and attitude.'

'Sounds interesting,' Linda said doubtfully.

Jonathan laughed. 'Liar. It's not really my kind of show either but if it helps the ratings . . .'

'Are ratings so important to you?'

'They are to our advertisers.'

'Oh, I see. Well, I think it's time to go back to the drawing board. Can you leave it with me for another few days?'

'Sure but I'd need someone to start by the middle of October at the latest.'

'I'll get right on it,' she promised, piled the files back into her briefcase and stood up to leave.

He stood up too and looked at his watch. 'Come on, I'll buy you lunch.'

Linda looked at him, so handsome and confident,

and then down at her damp, creased skirt. She didn't even try to imagine the state of her hair. 'I don't think so.'

'Oh, come on, Linda.'

She smiled. 'It would ruin your reputation being seen out with me in this state.'

'I know a restaurant with very dark corners,' he assured her.

True to his word, Jonathan took her to a dimly lit Indian restaurant and asked for a corner table. There were only a few other diners – all couples. Somehow the romantic lighting and soft music didn't suit business lunches. This was the ideal place for illicit meetings between lovers. Linda studied Jonathan covertly as he ate his starter. How many girls had he brought here? she wondered. He certainly seemed to be known to the staff. They must be in shock at his companion today, although they didn't show it.

'Great food, isn't it?' Jonathan popped his last prawn into his mouth and sat back.

Linda smiled politely. 'Lovely.'

He frowned. 'You've hardly touched it. Is there something wrong?'

She shook her head. 'No, honestly, it's fine. I'm just watching my weight at the moment.'

He groaned. 'Why do women go on about their weight all the time? You're fine as you are.'

Linda shot him a look of total disbelief. 'Yeah, fine, sure.'

'I refuse to feed your ego,' he told her with a grin. 'You're just angling for compliments.'

'You're a client, Mr Blake. I'm interested in your business not your compliments.'

'Rubbish! There isn't a woman alive who isn't interested in compliments.'

Linda laughed. 'You're probably right.' As he topped up her glass she was glad she'd phoned the office and said she wouldn't be back. There had been only one message. Carrie Lambe had returned her call. It took her a moment to register the name. Ah, yes, Patrick's secretary. She had left a message with the girl's boyfriend suggesting that Carrie come in for an interview. The least she could do was find Carrie a new job as she'd left the old one because of her.

'Linda?'

'Sorry, what was that?'

'I was just asking if you prefer radio or TV.'

Linda considered the question. 'It depends on the time of day really. I love to listen to the radio when I'm driving. I'm sure there'd be a lot more road rage if it weren't for radio. And if I'm reading, I put on the radio or a CD. But in the evenings I'm afraid I'm the original couch potato.'

Jonathan sighed and patted his flat stomach. 'Aren't we all?'

'I don't think so! I can't imagine you ever settling down with a TV dinner to watch *East Enders*.'

He laughed. 'No, you're right, I don't. But I do watch the football.'

'I'd have thought you were out every night of the week.'

'In my job it's necessary to attend a certain amount of functions,' he conceded.

'My heart bleeds for you,' Linda said drily.

'Don't you and your husband socialise?'

Linda stiffened. 'Not much.'

'He's a surveyor, isn't he? That must mean long hours.'

'Oh, yes, he puts in plenty of long hours.'

Jonathan looked at her curiously. 'Have you two had an argument?'

'No, now can we leave it please? I don't want to talk about my private life.'

Jonathan inclined his head. 'Of course, I'm sorry.'

Linda sighed at the coldness that had crept into his voice. He was so nice and a very important customer; the last thing she wanted to do was offend him. 'I'm sorry too, Jonathan. I didn't mean to bite your head off. You're quite right, we have had a row.'

'I'm sure it will all work out, Linda,' he said kindly. 'He'll turn up with a large bunch of flowers and a bottle under his arm, you'll see.'

Linda's smile was forced. 'I'm sure you're right.'

5

Carrie finished the ironing and made another cup of coffee. She carried the clothes upstairs and put Declan's shirts in their tiny wardrobe and her tops and trousers in the chest of drawers. There was no room for both their stuff in the wardrobe and Declan hated it when his clothes were creased. She went back downstairs and took her coffee and a chair out to the garden. Well, it wasn't so much a garden as a tiny paved square that she'd tried to liven up with some potted plants, but it still looked a little sad. She held her face up to the sun, although there wasn't much heat left in it. But at least, after a disgustingly wet August, it had made an appearance for a brief interlude before the leaves started to fall and the mornings turned dark. As she was off work, she'd suggested to Declan that they go away for a few days. Nowhere fancy, just a guesthouse down in Wexford or something. If there was any sunshine to be had in Ireland, you could depend on it being in Wexford. But when she'd mentioned it last night he had looked at her as if she'd lost her mind.

'There's only one salary coming in with no prospect of another and you want to go on holidays?'

'Just a few days, Dec, and I told you I'd have a job sorted before the end of the month.'

'No, actually, initially you said you'd have one by the end of the week. Have you even applied for anything?' he demanded.

'Well, no, but I've been keeping an eye on the situations vacant columns . . .'

'For God's sake, Carrie, you need to be a bit more proactive. And what about Patrick's wife? Have you spoken to her yet?'

'No, I did call but she wasn't there.'

'So phone her again.'

'I don't like to bother her.'

Declan threw up his hands in exasperation. 'God give me strength! She works as a recruitment consultant, Carrie, she's paid to get people jobs.'

So Carrie had promised him, before he left for work this morning, that she would call Linda again. But she kept putting it off. She didn't really want to talk to Linda Jewell. The woman had to be terribly upset and talking to Carrie would only be a reminder of what her husband had done. She finished her coffee and went back inside to do the hoovering. One thing Declan couldn't complain about since she was off work was the house – it had never been so clean. He hated untidiness and he was always giving out about the way she left old magazines lying around and didn't hang up her clothes at night. So to keep him off her back about getting a job Carrie had the place as neat as a new pin. She should invite their parents around to see it. Both families had always looked down on their little

home. But Carrie loved it. Messy or not it was hers –
theirs. And she hadn't needed a degree in order to be
able to fork out her half of the mortgage repayments.
She hoovered away energetically and was just tugging
the heavy machine out into the hall when she realised
the phone was ringing. She switched off the vacuum
cleaner and made a dash for the phone. 'Hello?' she
said breathlessly.

'Carrie?'

'Yes.'

'It's Linda here, Linda Jewell.'

'Oh, Linda, hi.' Carrie wound the flex nervously
around her finger. 'How are you?'

'Oh, you know, coping.'

'Good. That's good.'

'Listen, Carrie, I wonder if you'd like to come in
and see me. There are a few positions on the books
at the moment that might suit you.'

Carrie stared at the phone in disbelief. 'Really?'

'Yes, I'm sure I can find you something. Have you
an up-to-date CV?'

'Yes, yes I do.'

'Good, bring it along. How about three o'clock?'

'Today?'

'Well, if that doesn't suit . . .'

'Oh, no, that's fine. Thanks, Linda. I'll see you at
three.' Carrie put down the phone and did a little dance
around the hall.

Wearing her nun's outfit – that's the only way she
could describe her black, sensible, interview suit –

Carrie knocked nervously on the door of Reeve's
Recruitment and waited. Marie hurried to open the
door and smiled at her.

'Can I help you?'

'I have an appointment with Linda? My name's
Carrie Lambe.'

'Mrs Jewell will be with you in a minute. Would you
like to take a seat?'

Carrie sat down on the two-seater sofa in the corner
and looked around her with interest. She could just
see into the office across the room where a man
was talking loudly into the phone, his feet on the
desk. The woman sitting at the desk just outside
his office was also on the phone and painting her
nails a vivid plum colour at the same time. The
girl who had let her in sat at a desk in the centre
of the room surrounded by a fax machine, photo-
copier and printer. Carrie could just see Linda's dark
blonde head peeking out from behind a screen at the
far end of the room – she appeared to be on the
phone too.

Carrie picked up a copy of the *Irish Times*.

'Hi, Carrie, thanks for coming in.' Linda stood
smiling down at her.

Carrie jumped up and shook her hand. 'Thanks for
asking me.'

'The least I could do,' Linda said over her shoulder
as she led the way back to her desk. 'Have a seat. Did
you bring your CV?'

Carrie quickly opened the folder she was carrying
and handed over her résumé.

Linda ran an expert eye over the five-page docu-
ment. 'You need to condense this into two pages,' she
said when she'd finished.

Carrie looked bewildered. 'You mean drop some of
my jobs?'

'No, no, but you only need to write a couple of lines
about the first positions you held.'

Carrie nodded. 'Oh, I see. I always thought it would
look better if I put in everything I did.'

'There's no need. A good employer will be able to
read between the lines. So all of your experience has
been in general office work, has it?'

Carrie made a face. 'Not very exciting, is it?'

'Nonsense,' Linda said briskly. 'We can't all be brain
surgeons.'

Carrie grinned delightedly. 'That's what I always
say.'

Linda smiled back. She really was a lovely girl. It
would be wonderful if she could find her a nice job.
And it would be a bonus if it paid better than Patrick's
budget had allowed. Still, that was a question that she
must deal with first. 'Carrie, Patrick tells me that you
only left your job because of me. Is that true?'

Carrie reddened. 'Not exactly.'

'Could you explain, then? If I'm going to place you
I need to know what you didn't like about your job.'

'Oh, I liked everything about my job,' Carrie assured
her.

'I'm sorry, I don't understand . . .'

'I just couldn't work for a man like that. Oh, I
know you probably think I'm mad – my boyfriend

and my sister do and God help me when my folks find out.'

'But Patrick treated you fairly, didn't he?' Linda asked nervously.

'He treated me just fine, Linda, but it's the way that he treated you that's the problem. Oh, I know people split up, I know people divorce, I'm not that naïve, but he deceived you and for so long too. I thought he was the most honest, straightforward man in the country but I was wrong. And I think he must be a bit mad, Linda, I mean how could he leave you like that? You're pretty, you're intelligent and you're great fun. So,' she said finally, 'I don't want to work for him any more.'

Linda stared in astonishment at the bright red spots on Carrie's cheeks. And she'd thought this girl was timid and shy? 'Well, I appreciate what you're saying, Carrie, but Patrick seems to have fallen in love.'

'Rubbish! I give it six months – no, less. It's easy to be in love when you've a nice wife and a nice house to come home to. It's a different story when you have to give up your whole life and get used to someone else's habits, especially someone so young. God, can you imagine her dragging him along to nightclubs?'

Linda laughed, despite her misery. 'He'd hate it. He never liked dancing, even when we were dating.'

'There you go then,' Carrie said triumphantly.

'You seem to have very strong opinions on the subject,' Linda remarked.

Carrie looked down at her hands. 'I had a friend

whose husband left her. She was devastated. They had only been married three years.'

'That is sad. How's she doing now?'

Carrie shrugged. 'No idea. She moved away. When he first left, though, Mel went on a serious drinking binge for a couple of months – I was really worried about her.'

Linda thought of the amount of wine she'd been drinking lately and laughed shakily. 'Well, I don't plan to do that.'

'No, of course you don't.' Carrie looked at her sadly. 'And you mustn't let him destroy your life.'

Linda felt a tide of depression threaten to engulf her.

'You need to talk about it, Linda,' Carrie urged. 'That was the mistake Mel made. She kept it all inside.' She looked around the office. 'Still, you've got plenty of people to confide in, haven't you?'

Linda shuddered at the thought of Cheryl finding out. 'I haven't told anyone yet,' she admitted, to her surprise. Why was she talking to this girl? She was practically a stranger.

'Oh, Linda, you poor thing! Now, you have to realise that none of this is your fault. You can't take responsibility for Patrick's actions. You get out there and tell everyone what a complete bastard he is.'

Linda looked shocked. 'I'm not sure I'm ready to do that yet.'

'Trust me, Linda, you'll feel better the moment you've opened your mouth. You need to talk these things through. You need to talk to other women who've been dumped. What do you say?'

Linda nodded but her mind was on other things as she looked at Carrie perched on the edge of her chair, her eyes bright and passionate. 'Carrie, would you excuse me a moment?' She walked out of the cubicle and across the room. 'Marie? Would you get Jonathan Blake on the phone, please?'

6

Maeve pulled herself up, grimacing as she felt the gorse tear at her leg, and reminded herself that she went climbing in this disgusting weather for fun. But even in this weather the Wicklow Mountains looked beautiful in a wild and abandoned sort of way.

'Come on, Maeve, get a move on. I'd like to get back to Dublin before dark.'

'Piss off, Craig, I'm going as fast as I can.'

'Ah, all these late nights are finally catching up on you. Or maybe it's old age. You're nearly thirty now, aren't you?'

Maeve gave the rope a vicious tug and it tore at Craig's hands. 'Bitch, I'll get you for that.'

Maeve chuckled, her face pressed close against the cliff face. 'You'll have to catch me first.' She levered herself up and reached for the slim ledge above her. The wind whipped tendrils of hair into her eyes and the rock grazed her cheek but this was, for her, the perfect way to relax. There were now twenty-three people in FECC – Freddy & Eamonn's Climbing Club. Freddy Cashman and Eamonn Rose had originally set it up two years ago but Eamonn had since emigrated. Maeve had heard about it through

Fergus, a cameraman in RTE that she used to date. Fergus had left the club months ago when he started to do more location work but Maeve was well and truly hooked now and looked forward to all the challenges that Freddy threw at them. And it wouldn't be as much fun if Craig Prentice wasn't shooting smart remarks at every turn. 'Are you all right down there, Craig?' she called now. 'Or do you need to stop for some cocoa?'

Craig pulled himself on to the ledge she'd just vacated. 'I think I can hang on for another few minutes. Mind you, having to look at your butt is turning my stomach.'

'There are men that would kill to be in the position you're in,' she promised.

'What, under your feet? Isn't that where they all are anyway? Mind you, I'm sure they'd prefer your climbing boots to those ridiculous shoes that you wear.'

'How do you know what I wear?' she asked, genuinely curious.

'Because my sister reads all those stupid social columns that you get your silly mug in and she insists on keeping me the cuttings.'

Maeve laughed, delighted. 'Do you keep them under your pillow?' she purred.

'No, I use them to line the dog's kennel,' he said honestly. 'It seems only right to put you with another bitch.'

'Would you two cut it out?' Freddy called. 'This isn't an easy climb and you need to concentrate.'

Maeve swung herself up on to the top beside him

and grinned. 'It was a doddle, Freddy, but I don't know about this guy. I think he's finding the going tough.'

Aoife, the other woman in the team, glared at her as she wound up her rope. 'Don't you ever get tired of being so bitchy?'

Maeve put her head on one side. 'Er, no, now that you mention it.'

Craig's head appeared in front of them. 'She does it for a living. No, that's not true, I forgot. She runs after rich, influential men for a living. She's only a bitch on the side.' He hoisted himself up and started to wind up the rope.

'Well, the men wouldn't be so keen if they saw her now.' Aoife looked scathingly at Maeve's jeans and stout oilskin jacket. Her beautiful blonde hair was scraped back under a woolly hat and she wore not a screed of make-up.

'Now who's being bitchy,' Maeve said with a wink at Craig. He laughed and held out a hand to pull her to her feet.

Aoife shook her head as she scrambled up unaided.

'Shall we take a break here or do you want to do Charlie's Wall?' Freddy asked as he checked the gear.

'Let's rest,' Aoife said.

'Keep going,' Craig and Maeve chimed and then grinned at each other.

Freddy shot Aoife a sympathetic look. 'Sorry, love, the ayes have it. It's getting late so we'll use Mona's Route – it's quicker.'

'Fine by me,' she sniffed and strode ahead of them towards the next cliff face.

Three hours later they were back at Freddy's jeep at the base of The Scalp, drinking hot coffee from his large Thermos and eating chocolate biscuits.

'So what have you got planned for this evening, Maeve?' Craig asked.

'Oh, I think I'll have a quiet night,' she said, playing along. 'A little dinner, a couple of clubs.'

Aoife rolled her eyes. 'I don't know how you can live like that. It's all so fake.'

'Fake? How so?' Maeve asked calmly.

'Well, I know Craig is only joking, but let's face it, you're photographed with a different man nearly every week. Are you trying to tell us you're in love with them all?'

Maeve looked horrified. 'God, no! I don't believe in love.'

'Do they know that?' Craig asked quietly, his eyes serious.

Maeve looked away. She hated it when Craig got all holier-than-thou. 'Believe me, it's all just a game and everyone knows the rules.'

Freddy looked at them bemused. 'Well, I'm going home to a nice fish supper and then I'll watch the football.'

'What are you doing, Craig?' Aoife gazed up at him.

Maeve groaned at the blatant adoration in her eyes.

Craig smiled at the girl. 'I'll probably get a video and order a curry.'

'Exciting stuff,' Maeve murmured. 'What about you, Aoife?'

'Oh, I've nothing planned. I wouldn't mind watching a film—'

'And eating a curry?' Maeve jeered.

Aoife's cheeks reddened. 'No, that is, I didn't mean . . .'

'Leave her alone, Maeve.'

'Don't mind me, Aoife. PMT.' Maeve flashed a false smile.

'Mother of God,' Freddy muttered and threw the dregs of the flask into the bushes. 'I think we should make a move. Who's coming out tomorrow?'

Craig shook his head regretfully. 'I'm working.'

'I can't make it either,' Maeve told him.

'Aoife?'

'Yes, if you can get a group together, you can count me in.'

'Right, then, I'll phone round the others and let you know in the morning.'

Maeve shot the other girl a pitying look. Aoife was always free. It must be depressing to lead such a boring life. Didn't she have any friends? She turned her attention back to Craig. 'So another exciting day at the garden centre?' she said with a wide yawn.

'Fresh air and healthy living,' he countered. 'And the beauty of being surrounded by nature all day.'

Maeve laughed. 'In the heart of suburbia, I don't think so!'

'It doesn't matter where it is,' he replied calmly. 'It's still a haven from the madness of city life.'

'I think it's lovely, Craig,' Aoife simpered. 'You're so wonderful with your hands.'

Maeve opened her mouth to respond but obediently shut it when she saw the look on Craig's face.

'Thanks, Aoife, but you know you're clever too. I don't know how you make all those curtains. It must take a lot of concentration.'

'Oh, it's not that hard.'

Maeve glowered at her. She hated it when women denigrated what they did. Was it a Stone Age kick-back, or something? Always make the man feel better, cleverer, and more successful? Bloody rubbish.

'You're too modest,' Craig was saying and Maeve noted with satisfaction the irritation in his voice.

Freddy pulled up outside the shopping centre in Bray where they had left their cars. 'Is anyone coming for a pint?' he asked hopefully.

'I have time for a quick one.' Aoife looked at Craig expectantly.

'Yeah, me too.'

Maeve checked her watch. It would take her at least thirty minutes to get home. 'I'm afraid I must drag myself away from your exhilarating company.' She grinned at them as she pulled her backpack out of the jeep. 'I have to get back to the real world.'

'Poor you,' Craig called after her, but when she looked back to make a suitable retort she noticed he was looking a bit miserable.

'I'll call you during the week,' she told him.

A smile returned to his lips. 'I'll make sure the answering machine is on.'

Maeve laughed as she climbed into her MG and drove away. The traffic was heavy but she'd still be at home and in a hot bath within the hour. That was the wonderful thing about Dublin. You could be at the seaside, up a mountain or in the heart of the countryside within minutes. It suited her perfectly. She loved the beautiful scenery of Wicklow but would feel isolated if she lived there permanently. Thanks to FECC, she had the best of both worlds. Though she had a few aches and pains and she was wet through, she felt exhilarated after the climb. The air had cleared her head and the mindless jibes that she shared with Craig had cheered her up. And she needed cheering up because despite her and Karl's pleas, Jonathan was still hell-bent on introducing this new show. She'd told Karl the gist of the first programme that she'd listened to the night Jonathan had broached the subject.

'That's nothing,' he'd drawled. 'On City Live they were talking about falling in love with your pet.' And so, in a rare show of solidarity they had begged and pleaded with Jonathan to change his mind. But his answer was always the same. Until they came up with a better idea, they had to go with this one. And if they weren't up to it, he'd find a team that were. They had assured him there was no need for that and he'd agreed to give them a go. 'But if the ratings don't go up, you're out,' he'd warned bluntly. Now they had to decide on a title for the programme and hire a researcher to help dig up people to take part in the façade. The first show was to air on Monday, 5 November, and Maeve dreaded it. How could it possibly help her career? She wanted to be considered a candidate for serious talk shows or current affairs programmes not an Irish version of Ricki Lake. But the alternative was to be demoted – a show after midnight was definitely a step backwards – and Jonathan would find a new star. She couldn't let that happen. She'd worked too long and too hard for this. It was time that the years standing on cold Dublin streets doing vox pop – finding out public opinion on the silliest subjects – and the hours spent editing paid off.

Maeve pulled her car into a parking spot outside the Willows apartment block, just off the coast road in Sandymount. She took her backpack and went inside, taking the lift to the top floor. When she opened the door of her apartment, she got the same feeling of satisfaction that she had the day she bought it. Everything about it spelled success. Maeve had decorated it in pale colours; the paintings were modern and the ornaments few and carefully chosen. There were no family photos. She had no brothers or sisters, she didn't talk to her mother, and her father had died when she was still a baby. She hardly remembered him, but she could recite practically every detail of his life off by heart – particularly his sporting achievements. After he'd died her mother had turned their home into a shrine. It was impossible to have a conversation without some reference being made to him. It was 'Andy would have said' or 'Andy always thought'. As she got older Maeve started to resent her dead father for his interference in her life. In an effort to get closer to Laura, she had tried to be the perfect child. She'd worked hard at school, helped around the house, did the shopping and tried to look after the garden that her mother neglected. But Laura had seemed oblivious to her efforts and retreated into her own private world of grief. By the time she was fifteen, Maeve had realised that she was just an addendum to her mother's life. It was her aunt Peggy who showed an interest in the subjects she chose for her leaving cert. Peggy who took her shopping, Peggy who teased her about boyfriends. Sometimes Maeve wished that Peggy and not Laura was her mother. As soon as she finished school, she left home, moved into a bedsit and focused all of her attention on the media studies course that she'd secretly applied for months earlier. Laura reacted with vague surprise. This was the final nail in the coffin of their relationship. Maeve had hoped her mother would beg her not to leave home but the woman didn't seem to care. Maeve's heart hardened the day she walked out of that house swearing never to return. Of course, she had and she phoned every so often but it was clear that Laura wasn't that interested in her life. When Maeve accepted the position as a DJ on Forever FM she had called excitedly to tell Laura. Her mother had sounded almost pleased for her but soon lost interest in the conversation and found some reason to bring it around to her father. Maeve had hung up in defeat. How did you compete with a corpse?

Maeve went into the bedroom, decorated in soothing tones of grey and white, and took off her coat. It was only seven and there was plenty of time for a long soak in the bath. She never went anywhere before ten unless she had a dinner engagement. Even then she would turn up about thirty minutes late. But tonight there was no dinner date. Her perfect eyebrows were knit together in a worried frown as she went into the tiled bathroom and turned on the taps of the enormous pedestal bath. It didn't look good to be without a date on a Saturday night. Maybe she'd call Vince, although it would be impossible to get rid of him if she gave him any encouragement at this stage. It was too soon to phone Paul Riche. She had been pleased when he'd turned up at the Pod on Tuesday night but she'd still kept him at a distance. Her next encounter with him would be at a book launch on Thursday. Before she got into the bath, she went to get the phone, dialled the number and started to undress as she waited for an answer.

'Hello?'

'Julie? Hi, it's Maeve. I'm at a loose end. Is there anything on tonight?'

'There's a film première at the Savoy. I'm not going to the film but the reception afterwards is in the Clarence.'

'Sounds good. Do you have a date?'

Julie laughed. 'Yes and no. There are a couple of agents over from Paris that I promised to show around. Fancy a foursome?'

'Sounds good,' Maeve agreed. 'Give me some background on these guys.' After she hung up she sank into the bath and closed her eyes. These friends of Julie's were of no use to her but it was good to arrive at the best parties on a man's arm. And with Julie in the party, they would definitely be in the social columns on Sunday. That would keep Paul Riche on his toes.

7

Jonathan flicked through Carrie Lambe's CV. 'I really don't think so, Linda.'

'Trust me, Jonathan, she's perfect for the job.' Linda crossed her fingers and hoped she was right. Bill would be very annoyed if she got this one wrong. Forever FM was one of Reeve's Recruitment's oldest customers. It had been a long time before he had trusted anyone else in the company to deal with Jonathan Blake and now Jonathan would only deal with Linda. It would be a major blot on her copybook if she screwed up, although Cheryl would be delighted – she'd always resented that her husband had bypassed her and given the account to Linda.

'But she's no experience in this area, Linda,' Jonathan was saying. 'She's been a filing clerk, a secretary and a receptionist.'

'With extensive experience on the phone and dealing with people's problems,' Linda pointed out. 'At least meet her. She has that spark you were talking about.'

'And what does your husband think of all this?'

Linda stared at him. 'Patrick?'

'Well, she works for him, doesn't she?'

'Oh! Eh, no, well; that is, she did.'

Jonathan frowned. 'And?'

'Carrie decided that it was time for a change.'

Jonathan put down the CV and stared at her. 'Linda, why do I get the feeling that you're not telling me everything?'

Linda flushed. 'I'm sorry, Jonathan, you're right. But there is no mystery here, I promise you. Carrie left her job for personal reasons and I can assure you that Patrick will give her a glowing reference.'

Jonathan looked dubious.

'Have I ever let you down before?' Linda demanded and prayed that this wouldn't be the first time. 'Just meet her, Jonathan. There's no harm in that, is there?'

'Okay, then. Tell her to come by this afternoon at two.'

Linda beamed at him. 'She'll be there.'

As soon as Jonathan had left her office Linda picked up the phone and dialled Carrie's number. 'Carrie, I've got you an interview to go to. Two o'clock today.'

Carrie laughed delightedly. 'You're kidding! Where? What's the job?'

'It's a little bit different to the jobs you've done before. I'd like to come over and talk to you about it, if that's okay. Then I could drop you there on my way back to the office.'

'Well, that's very kind of you, Linda, but there's really no need—'

'It would be my pleasure,' Linda said quickly. 'Give me directions.'

*   *   *

Carrie hung up the phone mystified. Why on earth did Linda need to talk to her before the interview? It wasn't as if she were applying for chief executive of Bank of Ireland! She went upstairs to fetch the skirt of her nun's suit and a white blouse. As she ironed, she hummed happily to herself. Declan would be thrilled if she got this job and it would be a relief if the atmosphere around here improved. He had been a terrible grouch since she'd walked out of her job and hadn't stopped talking about money – or the lack of it. Carrie didn't understand why it was such a big deal. Even if she had to go and work in McDonald's, they'd get by. It wasn't as if they had a hectic social life to support. A trip to the cinema followed by fish and chips on the way home was the highlight of the month. Not that it bothered Carrie. She and her friend Orla went clubbing occasionally and that was more than enough excitement for her. Once she had Declan she didn't need anything or anyone else. She chuckled. At least when he was in a good mood!

'Hi, Linda, I'm all ready.'

Linda looked worriedly at Carrie's suit. 'We've got some time. Why don't I come in and tell you a bit about the job?'

'Oh, yes, of course, sorry.' Carrie stepped back to let her in and then led the way into the small kitchen. 'Would you like a coffee?'

'I'd love one.'

Carrie put on the kettle and fetched two mugs. 'I think there are some biscuits somewhere.'

'Not for me, thanks.'

Carrie spooned coffee into the mugs and then drummed her fingers on the counter as she waited for the kettle to boil.

Linda smiled at her. 'You must be wondering why I'm making such a big deal about this interview.'

Carrie giggled nervously. 'A bit.'

'It's just that this job is a bit different, and hopefully you'll agree, a bit more exciting and challenging.'

Carrie nodded enthusiastically as she poured the water into the mugs. 'Sounds great.'

'It's in the radio station, Forever FM.'

Carrie slopped coffee all over the table. 'Damn. Sorry.' She mopped up the mess with a dishcloth. 'Forever FM, are you kidding me?'

'No.'

'But that's my favourite station, I listen to it all the time.'

Linda smiled. 'I'm sure that will impress Jonathan Blake.'

Carrie gaped at her. 'Is he the one who's interviewing me? I'm being interviewed by the owner of Forever FM?'

Linda nodded. 'Jonathan takes a very hands-on approach with the station and this particular position is quite important to him.'

Carrie pushed away her mug and stared at her. 'Please tell me what it is, Linda.'

'Oh, I'm sorry. I am making a meal of this, aren't I? They want a researcher for a new programme that they're launching in November.'

Carrie looked bemused. 'Researcher? But I wouldn't

know where to begin. I have no training, I never went to university . . .'

'Calm down, Carrie. I know all that. I read your CV, remember? Look, it's not research in the real sense of the word. Your job would be talking to listeners on the phone, listening to their tales of woe and deciding whether or not they'd make good guests for this radio show.'

'Oh. That doesn't sound too complicated, but why me? I still don't have any experience. Does Mr Blake know that?'

'He does, but I persuaded him that you had something more than that.'

Carrie was looking very worried now.

'When you talked to me the other day about Patrick and the way he'd behaved, well, you were wonderful. You were so sympathetic and supportive. I think people would feel able to open up to you.'

'Really?'

'Yes. Do you think it's something you'd enjoy?'

'Well, yes, of course. What could be more interesting? Getting a peek into other people's lives – it sounds fascinating.'

Linda smiled. 'That's what I hoped you'd say. There's only one problem.'

Carrie looked worried. 'Oh?'

'The suit. It's not exactly the kind of funky, young image that a radio station – or Jonathan Blake – expects.'

Carrie laughed delightedly and jumped to her feet. 'Give me ten minutes!'

When she reappeared, Linda blinked at the trans-
formation. Carrie had not only changed into a slinky
cerise top and tight black leather trousers, she'd also
reapplied her make-up. Her dark eyes were lined with
kohl, making them look huge in her tiny heart-shaped
face. Pink eye-shadow added to the trendy look and
she'd finished it off with pink glossy lipstick. She'd
also combed wax through her short dark hair and it
looked like she'd stepped straight off a catwalk.

'You look amazing,' Linda breathed.

Carrie blushed under her make-up. 'I usually only get
the chance to dress up like this when I'm going out with
my friend, Orla. Patrick preferred skirts and blouses.
This isn't quite the image for a surveyor's office. Do
you think Mr Blake will think it's too much?'

'I think Mr Blake will love it.' Linda hoped fervently
that Jonathan wouldn't add Carrie to his long list of
conquests.

'Then let's go,' Carrie said, feeling a lot more
confident than she had in her nun's suit.

Jonathan's eyes widened when Karen led Carrie Lambe
into the room. She was beautiful. Not the sort of
woman he usually went for – he liked blondes with
curves. But Carrie was lovely in a coltish sort of way
with amazing bone structure and beautiful eyes. But
he wasn't hiring her for her looks. He stood up to
shake hands and then asked her to sit down. 'Thanks
for coming in at such short notice, Carrie.'

'No problem.'

'Has Linda told you about the job?'

'Yes, it sounds great.'

'Not what you're used to, though, is it?'

Carrie clutched her bag nervously. 'Well, no.'

'So why do you think you're the right person for the job?'

'I don't, but Linda's convinced that I am.'

Jonathan's lips twitched at her honesty. 'And why do you think that is?'

'She says I'm a good listener and that I can draw people out. She thinks they'd tell me things that they wouldn't ordinarily talk about.'

'If she's right, then that's quite an accomplishment.'

'I suppose,' Carrie said doubtfully. 'But it's just human nature, isn't it?'

'What do you mean?'

'Well, isn't everybody interested in other people's problems? That's why all these talk shows on television are so popular.'

'That's true, Carrie, but how do you think you'd be able to tell a good guest from a bad one? Do you think you'd be able to pick out the troublemakers? Would you know the ones who are going to clam up once they're on air?'

'Probably not.'

Jonathan blinked. This girl was too honest for her own good.

'That's the kind of thing I'd get to know with experience. Probably the way to go about it would be to talk to the person for a while before they went on the show so that by the time the interview started they'd have relaxed and forgotten that they're on air.'

Jonathan nodded in agreement. 'That sounds like a good idea. How it will probably work is we will advertise the topics of various shows in advance and ask people to write in with their stories. Your job would be to go through these letters and bring the best of them to a meeting with myself, the producer Karl Thompson, and Maeve Elliot who will be presenting the programme.'

Carrie's eyes widened. 'Maeve Elliot, she is *so* cool!'

Jonathan grinned. 'She'll be delighted you think so. Okay, then, Carrie, let's give it a go.'

'I've got the job?'

'For a three-month trial period – that should be ample time for you to settle in. The salary is twenty thousand Euros a year with twenty-two days' holidays.'

Carrie's eyes widened. 'Great.'

'The show will go out from ten until eleven week nights, and you'll be expected to be there for the show and a couple of hours before it to line up the calls.'

'Of course.'

'How soon can you start?'

Carrie blinked. 'As soon as you like.'

'Okay, then, Monday, nine o'clock.' He stood up, walked around the desk and held out his hand.

Carrie jumped up and grabbed it eagerly. 'You won't regret it, Mr Blake. I'll work really hard.'

'Believe it, Carrie. Working in radio may seem like a glamorous occupation but I expect everyone in Forever FM to give one hundred per cent.'

'You won't be disappointed,' she assured him and practically floated out of his office.

8

The first person Carrie had to tell was Linda Jewell. If it weren't for her, she'd never have got the job. She hopped on a bus and fifteen minutes later was in Reeve's Recruitment. 'I got it, Linda, I got it!' she said excitedly before Linda had even crossed the room to meet her.

Marie smiled up at her as Linda led her back to her desk.

Carrie took the seat Linda indicated and put down her bag. 'And he's going to pay me much more than Patrick did.'

'Yes, well, you know you're going to have to put in some late hours.'

'I don't mind.'

Linda looked at the girl's outfit. 'What about your nights out with Orla?'

Carrie giggled. 'Oh, they only happen once a month, if we're lucky, and we usually go out on a Saturday night anyway.'

'And you don't think your boyfriend will mind?'

'Mind?' Carrie laughed. 'He'll be over the moon. He's been very worried since I left Jewell's. And if I'm out late he'll be able to watch football all night every night!'

Linda smiled. 'Well I'm very happy for you, Carrie, I hope it all works out.'

Carrie leaned forward, suddenly solemn. 'Thanks a million, Linda. I know Mr Blake wouldn't have given me the job if it weren't for you. I hope I don't let you down.'

Linda smiled confidently at this lovely, bubbly girl. 'You won't, Carrie. You'll be marvellous. Good luck.'

Carrie left the office and headed for Henry Street. If she was going to be working with the gorgeous, sophisticated Maeve Elliot she needed to get some decent clothes. And now that money was no longer a problem, she could really push the boat out. And to top it all she could even afford a nice roast for dinner. Declan was going to be over the moon when she told him the news. She decided not to phone him. It would be a nice surprise when he got home tonight. Carrie tripped her way from Wallis to Sasha to Principles, having a whale of a time picking out more daring clothes than she would usually go for. But she was going to work for Forever FM. She had to fit in with their trendy, young image. Maybe she should get a belly ring? She'd discuss it with Orla. She checked her watch and realised it was still only five o'clock. Declan wouldn't be home until after eight so she had time to drop into Orla on the way home and give her the news. Orla would be dead impressed. She thought Forever FM was brilliant and that Maeve Elliot was the sexiest, most beautiful woman in Ireland.

*   *   *

When Orla opened the door, she had her son, Ethan, in her arms. 'Cawie, Cawie.' He reached out chocolate-covered hands to her.

Orla kept him well out of reach. 'Don't you dare touch your aunty Carrie, you little monkey and she dressed up to the nines. Where are you off to?' she asked as she led the way back to the kitchen.

'It's not where I'm going it's where I've been.' Carrie put one of her bags in Orla's fridge and dropped the rest in a heap in the corner.

Orla scrubbed her son's hands and face with a cloth before allowing him to run and hug Carrie.

'Oh, hiya, buster. How are you?'

'So, where have you been?' Orla asked curiously. 'Apart from buying out half of the town.'

'I've been to an interview.'

'Dressed like that? What was it for? A lap dancer?'

'No, cheeky, actually it's for a job at Forever FM.'

Orla looked at her wide-eyed. 'You're kidding.'

'I'm not. Ask me if I got it.'

'I don't have to.' Orla went to hug her. 'Oh, congratulations, Carrie, I'm delighted for you. Wow, how exciting is this? What are you going to be doing there? Tell me everything.'

'My want hug too,' Ethan demanded and Carrie and Orla obediently hugged him.

Orla winked at Carrie over his head. 'Now, Ethan, time for your nap.' She scooped him up into her arms.

'No, Mummy.'

'Yes, Ethan, you can play with Aunty Carrie later. Say bye-bye.'

'Bye-bye, Aunty Cawie,' he said, sticking his thumb into his mouth and resting his head on his mother's shoulder.

'Back in a minute. Make some tea, would you?'

When Orla returned, the table was set and Carrie was looking for some biscuits.

Orla made straight for the fridge. 'I've got some cheesecake, we can celebrate!'

Carrie laughed. 'Oh, Orla, I cannot believe it. This morning I was doing the ironing with no prospect of a job and now here I am working for Dublin's hippest radio station!' Orla cut two large slices of cheesecake and slid one plate across to Carrie. Then she fetched some Twix Bars from the cupboard.

Carrie licked her lips. 'You knew I was coming.'

'Please put me out of my misery and tell me what you're going to be doing,' Orla said before tucking into her cheesecake.

Carrie was only too happy to comply and filled Orla in on all the details from the phone call with Linda to the interview with Jonathan Blake.

'Wow, you met Jonathan Blake. Is he as gorgeous up close?'

Carrie wrinkled her nose. Unlike Orla she wasn't really into dark, sultry good looks. She quite liked Declan's fair hair and skin and blue-green eyes. 'He's nice,' she said finally.

'They say he's a real ladies' man. Did he come on to you?'

'No, of course not, Orla. I was there for an interview, after all.'

Orla giggled. 'So he didn't have a casting couch, then?'

'Well, if he did, I didn't see it. Maybe he didn't fancy me.'

Orla rolled her eyes. 'Yeah, right. So what does Declan think?'

'I haven't told him yet. It's going to be a wonderful surprise. I'm going to do him a gorgeous roast beef dinner – God, don't let me forget the meat, it's in your fridge. We'll have a nice few drinks and then I'll tell him the good news.'

'He may not be happy with you working so late at night,' Orla warned.

Carrie shrugged. 'You can't have everything. Forever FM will be paying me more than I've ever earned before and he kept nagging me to go out and get another job.'

Orla frowned. 'It's only been a couple of weeks.'

Carrie sighed. 'I know, but Declan is a terrible worrier what with the mortgage and everything. But he'll be fine now. He'll be happy for me.'

Orla smiled, nodded and said nothing.

They chatted on over their tea until Carrie glanced at her watch, jumped up and grabbed her bags. 'Crikey, we won't be eating until midnight if I don't get a move on.'

Orla kissed her cheek. 'I'm really happy for you, Carrie, you're going to be great. Give me a call next week and we'll arrange a night out. We have to show off some of those gorgeous clothes.'

*　　*　　*

At home, Carrie put the roast in the oven and ran upstairs to change into jeans and a T-shirt. Then she went back downstairs, peeled some potatoes, set the table and mixed up some gravy. The beef would be ready about nine, just time for Declan to kick off his shoes and have a beer first. She switched on the radio and hummed along happily to Forever FM as she prepared the carrots and peas. She still couldn't believe it. Next Monday she would start work there. How amazing was that?

Declan didn't get in until nine but Carrie was too excited to be annoyed with him. He sniffed the air appreciatively. 'Beef? Smells good, but burgers would be cheaper.'

Carrie kissed him. 'It doesn't matter, Dec, we can afford it. In fact, you can have roast beef every night if you want to.'

Declan disengaged himself and took off his jacket. 'What are you on about and why have you all that muck on your face?'

Carrie touched her cheek self-consciously. Damn it, she'd completely forgotten to take her make-up off. Declan hated her wearing too much. 'I went for an interview today.'

'Oh yes?' He perked up a little at that.

Carrie hurried to the fridge and came back with a can of beer for him and a bottle of Guinness for herself. 'At Forever FM.'

'The radio station? What's the job, receptionist?'

Carrie shook her head, her eyes dancing. 'No, researcher on a new show.'

'But you don't know anything about research,' he pointed out. 'They'll never give a job like that to someone with no experience.'

'They already have, Dec. I start Monday.'

He took the can down from his mouth. 'Really?'

She nodded. 'And what's more the salary is great.'

'How much?'

'Twenty thousand.'

Declan sat up in his chair. 'That's over two thousand more than you earned in Jewell's. That's great, Carrie.'

'I knew you'd be pleased.' She hopped up to carve the meat. 'Isn't it exciting?'

'What hours will you work?'

'I'm not too sure,' she said, keeping her head bent over the joint. 'The show is on between ten and eleven at night—'

'What?'

'Only from Monday to Friday, Dec, and for that kind of money . . .'

'I suppose,' he agreed reluctantly.

'From what I can gather, I'll work mornings, get a few hours off and then come back in a couple of hours before the show starts.'

Declan brightened. 'So you'll still be able to cook – I mean we'll still be able to eat together?'

Carrie smiled at him affectionately. 'You're so romantic. Yes, of course we will and then you can settle down to watch the football and I'll be home before you know it.'

'That's not so bad.' He tucked into the plate of food she'd placed in front of him.

'I just can't believe it, Dec.' Carrie took her seat opposite him. 'Isn't it great? Wait till I tell everyone.'

Declan snorted. 'Don't expect your family to be pleased for you.'

Carrie sighed. 'Oh, I know the folks probably won't approve but Helen will think it's great.'

Declan laughed. 'I doubt that. She'll think it's just another one of your weird jobs. The fact that it's in a two-bit radio station will probably shock them more than anything.'

'It's not a two-bit radio station,' Carrie protested.

'It's not RTE either.'

Carrie pushed away her plate and sipped her Guinness.

'Don't worry about it, Carrie. You're old enough to live your own life. You don't need their approval.'

Carrie nodded, but it occurred to her that he was singing a different tune from the one when she'd left Jewell's. Then, he couldn't wait to tell Helen what she'd done and ask her to try and talk her out of it. But then this was different. If she went to work for Forever FM she'd be earning real money and money was important to Dec. He was very insecure really, Carrie mused. Material things were important to him. But then as he so often told her, he'd come from a poor background and had to work hard to get to where he was today. Carrie just wished sometimes that he'd acknowledge her contribution too.

'Here's to you, Carrie. Well done.'

She smiled guiltily. 'Thanks, Dec. Cheers.'

9

Linda scrubbed the kitchen floor as if her life depended on it, rejoicing in the feeling of total exhaustion that was beginning to creep up on her. Maybe tonight she'd sleep. The weekends were the worst. She'd always enjoyed her weekends with Patrick. It wasn't that they ever did anything wildly exciting. Just lounged around reading, eating too much and going out for a few drinks alone or with another couple. She sat back on her heels and sighed. Not only had she lost Patrick she'd lost her life. There would be no more cosy foursomes; in fact she'd probably never get invited anywhere again. A woman on her own would upset the numbers and make everyone feel uncomfortable. She had become a social pariah. It was a punishment for something that was not her fault. Tears of self-pity rolled down her cheeks. She threw the scrubbing brush into the bucket and stood up. Damn it, it was six o'clock on a Saturday evening and she was washing the bloody floor. And what for? No one else had stood in this house since Patrick left. Despite Carrie's advice, Linda had still told no one what had happened. The thought of even having such a conversation was too humiliating. She went to the fridge and took out a bottle of wine. After opening it she got the largest wine glass she could find and took it and the bottle into the living room. Without bothering to even wipe away her tears she poured a full glass and toasted the empty room. 'Cheers.' The sound of her voice was strange in the empty house. It sounded weak. 'Cheers!' she shouted and took a long drink. That felt better. 'Bottoms up!' She downed the rest of the glass and poured another. 'Here's to those that wish us well and those that don't can go to—' She paused, the glass halfway to her lips as the doorbell rang. Who could it be? Patrick? No, he'd use his key – except he didn't have one any more. She ran out to the hall and flung the door open.

'Good God, what's the matter with you?'

Linda slumped against the wall and stared miserably at her sister. 'Hi.'

Viv pushed past her and walked into the living room. Linda closed the door and followed slowly.

Viv looked from the wine back to her sister's tear-stained face. 'Are you going to tell me what's wrong? Is it Patrick? Is he sick?'

Linda's laugh sounded slightly hysterical, even to her ears. 'I hope so.'

Viv led her to the sofa. 'Linda?'

'He's left me, Viv.' She put her head in her hands and burst into tears again.

Viv sank to her knees and threw her arms around her. 'Oh, Linda, I'm sorry. Oh, you poor thing. When did this happen? Is he just gone?'

Linda shook her head and wiped her face on her sleeve. 'Three weeks ago.'

Viv stared at her. 'And you didn't tell us?'

Linda's shoulders started to shake once more. 'I didn't want to tell anyone. Then it would seem too real. Oh, Viv, what am I going to do?'

'You'll be fine, Linda. You're tough, you'll get through this. But tell me . . .' She sat up on the sofa beside her sister. 'What happened?'

Linda took a long drink. 'I got a call from Weirs saying that my ring was ready.'

'What ring?'

'*Her* ring.' Linda's voice started to wobble again. 'He's been seeing another woman – no, a girl, she's only twenty-five.'

'Wow.'

'Indeed. And he bought her this ring. He tried to tell me it was for me but it wasn't even my size. Then he admitted it all. He bought it for her as an engagement ring, Viv. He wants to marry her.'

'I can't believe it. Patrick just isn't the type. It must be an ego thing. He'll be back, I'm sure of it.'

'I don't think so.'

'I know things may seem very dark right now, Linda—'

'He's been with her for over three years.'

Viv stared at her. 'Bloody hell.'

'Exactly.'

'Still, he never made any move to leave you until you found out, that must mean something.'

Linda shrugged. 'Only because he's a spineless wimp.'

'I'd love to meet her.'

Linda stared at her in disbelief.

'Just to see what she's like,' Viv assured her hurriedly. 'I mean, twenty-five and she's dating a man, of average looks it must be said, eighteen years her senior.'

'I know. It's not as if he's even young in spirit. He's always been middle-aged, even when we first met. I kind of liked that. He seemed so solid and reliable. It made me feel safe. Maybe that's why Stacey fancies him.'

'Stacey?'

'Yes. It doesn't really sound like the name of a mistress, does it?'

Viv gave her sister a hug. 'Poor Linda. I wish you'd told me sooner. The last thing you should be doing is sitting here on your own wallowing in self-pity.'

'And what should I be doing?' Linda demanded.

'You should be changing the locks, talking to a solicitor, getting a new hairdo and buying a new wardrobe. All on your joint credit card, of course.'

'And do you think that would make me feel better?'

Viv shrugged. 'If nothing else it will take your mind off things. Has Patrick talked about divorce?'

Linda gave a mirthless laugh. 'Well, he's talked about marrying Stacey so I suppose I can assume he wants a divorce. Oh, Viv, I feel like such a fool. I can't believe he's been seeing someone else for three years and I never noticed anything different about him. I mean, they say, don't they, that there are always signs.'

'Maybe you weren't looking for signs,' Viv said shrewdly.

'What do you mean?'

'Well, maybe you didn't care one way or the other.'

Linda blinked, completely at a loss for words.

'How long have you been married?' Viv asked gently.

'Fifteen years.'

'And do you feel the same about Patrick as you did the day you married him?'

Linda drained her glass. 'Well, no, probably not, but that's normal. Isn't it?'

'Hey, don't ask me, what would I know?' At thirty-three Viv was still a free agent and was determined to keep it that way. 'Tell me, how was the sex? Could he still make you—'

'Enough, Viv!' Linda jumped to her feet and took the empty bottle and glass to the kitchen. Viv followed, circumventing the bucket in the middle of the kitchen floor.

'Well at least let me help you drown your sorrows.' She opened the fridge and stared at all the bottles. 'No chance of you running out, is there?'

'Don't nag me,' Linda warned.

Viv took out a bottle and opened it. 'I wouldn't dream of it. But don't forget to buy some food occasionally, okay?'

Linda fetched her a glass and Viv poured them both some wine.

'Okay, here's to the future.'

Linda sank into a chair and stared at her sister. 'You have a very sick sense of humour.'

'No, I'm serious, Linda. Everything happens for a reason. This starts a whole new chapter in your life – maybe even a better one. I mean, come on admit it. Weren't you getting just a teeny bit bored with Patrick?'

Linda looked shocked. 'Of course not.'

Viv watched her closely. 'Don't believe you.'

'We had got into a routine. It's hard not to when you're together so long. It was comfortable.'

'Boring,' Viv retorted.

'To you maybe, but I've never been like you, Viv. I don't want excitement. I'm perfectly happy with safe.'

'Boring,' Viv repeated. 'When are you going to tell Mum?'

Linda rested her head on her arms. 'I don't know. She'll probably take the news very badly.'

'Oh, I wouldn't say so. She never liked Patrick all that much.'

Linda sat up and stared. 'She never said anything.'

Viv chuckled. 'Well, she was hardly going to tell you, was she?'

'Why didn't she like him?'

Viv scrunched up her nose in concentration. 'I can't really remember. I think she thought he was too quiet.'

Linda sighed in exasperation. 'How can someone be too quiet? That's ridiculous.'

'I think she thought that he didn't always say what he thought,' Viv explained.

'You mean he was diplomatic,' Linda said flatly. 'And he kept his mouth shut when she was holding forth with her rather Left-wing views.' Rosemary Taylor was not an average housewife or mother. In fact, there was nothing average about her at all. She was an eccentric, opinionated and vivacious woman. Viv was very like her, but Linda seemed to have inherited all of her late father's characteristics.

'That's probably it,' Viv agreed with a grin.

Linda frowned. 'Did you like him? Apart from the fact that he was—'

'Too boring? Yeah, Patrick was all right. But maybe our dear mother had a point. I mean, this is one hell of a secret he's been keeping and for a very long time.'

'Yes.'

'I tell you what. I'm on my way over there for dinner.' She rolled her eyes. 'She's doing one of her stir-fry thingies. Come with me. We'll pour some wine into her and tell her the news.'

'I'm not sure.'

'Why, have you got something else to do?' Viv challenged.

Linda didn't. She obediently climbed into Viv's jeep and they drove to Rosemary's house in Howth. Linda always thought of it as 'Rosemary's House' and not home. When they'd moved out she had put her own stamp on it, redecorating it with dramatic colours and tactile materials that would have made their dad cringe. Linda often wondered how their marriage had worked so well, they were completely different people. The only interest they'd shared was reading, a passion they'd passed on to their daughters. Although Viv had taken it a step further and was now a successful novelist.

'Here we are.' Viv swung into the driveway, switched off the engine and turned to look at her sister. 'You okay?'

Linda nodded. 'Yeah, but promise me you'll let me do the talking. I don't want to talk about Stacey, so don't say a word.'

Viv held up her hands. 'Not a word. It's going to be fine, Linda. Don't worry.'

Linda smiled as her mother threw open the door. 'Linda! This is a surprise.'

'Sorry, Mum, Viv said it would be all right.'

'Well, of course it's all right! I've cooked enough to feed an army. Come on in. Where's Patrick?'

'I'm not sure,' Linda mumbled, climbing on to a stool and shooting Viv a beseeching look.

Rosemary shook the wok and some mushrooms hopped precariously into the air. 'Open some wine, Viv, would you?'

'Sure.' She smiled encouragingly at Linda.

Linda watched as Viv took down her mother's largest wine glasses. She fiddled nervously with the colourful tablemat in front of her. 'He's left me, Mum.'

Rosemary turned the gas off under the wok, walked over to the table and sat down.

'Oh, my darling, are you okay?'

Linda gulped at the tender concern in her mother's eyes. 'Not really,' she admitted with a giggle before dissolving into tears.

Viv set two full glasses of wine down beside them and took hers into the other room.

'What happened?' Rosemary asked as she stroked her daughter's hands.

'I found out he was seeing someone else.'

Rosemary looked startled. 'Patrick?'

Linda dabbed at her eyes with a tissue. 'Yes, it took me by surprise too.'

'Do you want to talk about it or shall I mind my own business?'

Linda was taken aback by her mother's discretion. 'I'd, ah, like to talk,' she surprised herself by saying.

Rosemary pushed her glass towards her and took a sip of her own. 'Go on then.'

Linda told her mother the whole story, not holding back on any of the painful details; despite the warning she'd given her sister. 'So it's over,' she said finally.

'I'm so sorry, my darling, it must have been such a shock. It won't last, of course, although I don't think that matters to you, does it?'

'No, I wouldn't take him back.'

Rosemary squeezed her hand. 'I'm so glad.'

Linda raised an eyebrow. 'You're not supposed to say that, Mum.'

Rosemary shrugged. 'I never say what I'm supposed to say.'

'True. Viv said you didn't like Patrick.'

'Rubbish, of course I liked him. Patrick wasn't

the worst – well, not until now. But he wasn't your type.'

Linda pulled her hand away irritably. 'We've been together fifteen years.'

'Yes, you have,' Rosemary agreed.

Viv appeared in the doorway. 'Can I come back in now?'

'Yes, Vivienne, I'm just about to serve up. Get some plates, would you?'

Viv did as she was told and then topped up their glasses. Linda put a hand over hers. 'I think I'll have some water.'

Rosemary smiled her approval as she served the meal. 'Good idea, darling. I don't believe there are any answers at the bottom of a bottle.'

'Only oblivion, which can be quite attractive occasionally,' Viv pointed out.

'Thank you, Vivienne, but that's exactly the kind of help Linda does not need.'

'Sorry.' Viv winked at her sister.

Linda smiled back. She was so lucky to have these two. She'd be able to cope with all that was to come with them by her side.

The next morning she wasn't so sure. Despite her switch to water she had a dreadful hangover and the depression and sadness had descended again like a heavy blanket that she was too weak to shrug off. She sipped a strong cup of coffee and stared at the clock. Eleven thirty. Normally she and Patrick would have been for their walk by now. Then they'd have gone to the Spar on the corner, bought fresh croissants and all the papers and returned to read them at the kitchen table, a large pot of coffee between them. She jumped to her feet, went in search of her hiking boots and a rain jacket and made for the door. She could still go for a walk without Patrick. She didn't have to let life grind to a halt because of him. She'd drive down to the beach. It was windy and the clouds looked ominous but she could do with a bracing walk. It would clear her head and put in a couple of hours.

As she stepped out of the car she wondered if it had been such a good idea. The waves were lashing the shore, and the wind whistled through the few dinghies tied up in the bay, making them bob up and down precariously. The beach was deserted except for the occasional hardy walker with a dog or loving couples bent against the breeze and huddled together for warmth. She didn't have anyone to cling to. She zipped her jacket to her chin, jammed her hands in her pockets and set off. She kept her eyes firmly on the horizon when she passed the first couple – it was best not to look. Instead, she went back over last night's conversation in her head. After they'd finished eating they'd sat at the table until late talking about anything and everything but mainly about Patrick. While she was glad of their support, Linda was depressed that her family didn't think Patrick was worth fighting for. Fifteen years down the drain, just like that. Was she supposed to forget that it ever happened? Behave like he'd never existed?

'Linda!'

She looked up startled to see Patrick standing in front of her, his arm protectively around the slip of a girl at his side. 'Patrick!'

'What are you doing here? I didn't think . . .'

'No, you didn't, did you? How could you bring her here?' For years they had walked this stretch of beach together. It was the ultimate betrayal.

'I'm sorry.'

'So you're the little bitch who's been screwing my husband.'

'Linda, don't!' Patrick glared at her and turned to the girl. 'Go back to the car, Stacey, I'll be with you in a minute.'

Stacey hesitated for a moment, but after a murderous look from Linda, turned wordlessly and left.

'There's no need to talk to her like that,' Patrick said when they were alone.

'Oh, I'm so sorry if I upset her. How insensitive of me. I should be more considerate of her feelings, should I? Maybe you'd like us to be friends!'

'This is no time for sarcasm, Linda. I know it's a difficult situation but you'll get used to it. I'm sorry for coming here, it was a bad idea.'

'You bastard, it was a lousy idea. What are you trying to do, rub my nose in it? Humiliate me?'

'Of course not, don't be silly.'

Linda glared angrily at him. 'I am not being silly and if I'm sarcastic, angry or bitchy I think I have every right to be, don't you?'

Patrick shifted from one foot to another and looked longingly back at his car. 'Of course, I'm sorry. I know you must be very hurt and upset. But one day you'll meet someone too.'

'Already have,' Linda flung at him. 'In fact, Patrick, you're fooling yourself if you think you've been the only one all these years.'

He studied her closely. 'What do you mean?'

Linda laughed harshly and pulled her hair out of her eyes. 'Like you said, Patrick, there haven't been many fireworks for us lately. So I've been finding them elsewhere.'

'Are you telling me you were unfaithful?' he asked slowly.

She smiled, her eyes hard. 'Unfaithful is such an old-fashioned word. Let's say I've been having fun.'

'So there was more than one, is that what you're saying?'

'I don't think that's anything to do with you any more, Patrick. We're history.' And she strode off down the beach aware that he was standing staring after her.

10

Carrie rushed around the kitchen like a headless chicken.

Declan watched her, amused. 'Calm down, Carrie. They're not going to eat you.'

Carrie finally found her earrings behind the toaster. 'Oh, I know, it's just first-day nerves. How do I look?'

Declan frowned at the tight yellow jeans and cropped black top. 'Fine,' he said grudgingly, 'but you've too much make-up on.'

'It gives me confidence,' she said lightly. The last thing she needed this morning was a silly row. 'Right, I'd better make a run for my bus.'

'What time will you be home?'

'Not sure. I'll call you. Wish me luck.' She bent to kiss him.

And she was out of the door and running down the road to catch the bus that would take her to Forever FM. As she looked at the other people at the bus stop, she wondered did any of them have a job that was even half as exciting. She couldn't help smiling. Even if her parents seemed totally unimpressed by her new position she was over the moon about it. Thankfully the rest of the family were assembled in the large house when Carrie had told them. Her sister-in-law, Jill, bless her, had been very enthusiastic.

'Good on you, Carrie, it sounds like a great opportunity.'

'Is there any prospect of promotion?' her brother Andrew had enquired.

Jill had rolled her eyes and then turned to smile at Carrie. 'You'll probably end up with your own show.'

Carrie had laughed. 'No way! I'm much happier staying in the background.'

'As usual,' her father had muttered.

Helen had shot him a dirty look and turned to quiz her sister about Jonathan Blake and Maeve Elliot.

Carrie had told her all she knew about the crew and about her job. 'There's a wonderful buzz about this new show,' she had said finally.

'I suppose if it makes you happy, dear, then that's all that matters,' her mother had said with a long-suffering smile. 'What does Declan think?'

Carrie had lifted her chin defensively. 'He's thrilled for me.'

'Well, he'll be happier about the extra money.' Her father had never liked Declan and didn't miss an opportunity to get a dig in.

Carrie had left shortly after that and returned home to find Declan engrossed in the afternoon football. 'How did it go?' he'd asked, not taking his eyes off the TV screen.

'Okay.'

He flashed her a grin. 'That bad, eh?'

She smiled. 'Andrew, Jill and Helen were there. They were nice about it.'

'But your folks weren't impressed?'

She shook her head. 'But at least it distracted them. They never asked once when we were getting married.'

Carrie wondered about that now as she got on the bus. While her parents obviously disapproved of Declan, they still wanted her to marry him. But then anything was preferable to her 'living in sin' – they hated that. 'Hypocrites,' Carrie muttered, getting a worried look from the lady beside her. They only went to Mass at Christmas and Easter. And weddings, she thought wryly. If ever she were to finally make them proud it would be the day when she walked up the aisle – even if it was with a serial killer.

Carrie was jerked back to reality as she saw her stop flash past. 'Blast!' She rang the bell and hurried down the bus. Luckily, it was only eight thirty and it wouldn't take her that long to walk back. Only she didn't want to arrive all hot and bothered and she'd intended to be early. First impressions were important, after all.

Twenty minutes later, she took a deep breath and pushed open the door of Forever FM. The receptionist looked up and smiled. 'Carrie, isn't it?'

'That's right.'

'I'm Karen. Linda got me the job here too.'

Carrie smiled, relieved to be greeted by a friendly face. 'She's great, isn't she?'

'The best,' Karen confirmed. 'I'll be looking after you this morning, Carrie. I'll show you where you can put your things, where you will sit and I'll bring you around and introduce you to everyone, although you won't meet Karl or Maeve until this afternoon. Just let me get someone to take over here and I'll be right with you.'

While she made a call, Carrie wandered around the reception area studying the photographs that covered the walls. She gasped at some of the famous faces. Imagine, she might actually get to meet some of these people.

Another girl wandered into reception and took Karen's position behind the desk.

'Jackie, this is Carrie Lambe the new researcher. Jackie takes over reception for me when I'm on lunch or break,' Karen explained.

'Hi, welcome to Forever FM,' Jackie said without much enthusiasm.

Carrie smiled brightly at her. 'Thanks, it's great to be here.'

Jackie picked up a magazine and started to leaf through it.

'This way, Carrie,' Karen said and opened the door that Jackie had just come through. Carrie hurried after her. Ten minutes into Karen's rather hasty tour Carrie was trying to hide her disappointment. Forever FM looked like every office she'd ever worked in. Except for the two studios. But even these small glass cells weren't that impressive. The only buzz Carrie got was when a producer barked at them to be quiet and the

'On Air' sign flashed on. There weren't many staff either, which surprised her. There were only three people in the newsroom, but Karen explained that a lot of the reporters were freelance or out on jobs. As she led Carrie up- and downstairs, through the green room, up to sales and marketing and back down CommProd – a dimly lit studio where they made commercials and jingles and stings – Karen reeled off names of people that would appear later in the day. 'Ant Preston – the presenter of our afternoon show – won't be in until twelve,' she explained. 'Jackie mans the phones for his show.'

'Oh, so the calls don't come through reception?' Carrie asked, slightly disappointed.

Karen shook her head. 'Listeners phoning in about competitions and that sort of thing go straight through to the show. The calls that come into reception are just for the general office.'

'So I probably will just be working evenings,' Carrie surmised.

'No, more like all the hours that God sends!'

Carrie had laughed along with Karen, but she didn't like the sound of that. It had an uncanny ring of truth to it.

'You won't be able to start your real job until they start to advertise for guests for the new show,' Karen explained, 'so for the moment you'll be helping me with the post, reception and switchboard.'

'That's fine.' Carrie tried to hide her disappointment.

'You'll be sitting over here with Jackie and me when

you're not in reception.' Karen led the way to a cluster of untidy desks in the corner. 'I need to find you a chair,' she muttered. 'You can use Jackie's for the moment.'

'Right.' Carrie thought of the tidy little office she'd had all to herself in Jewell's Surveyors.

'That's it for now,' Karen told her. 'If you start to sort through that lot, I'll see you later.'

Carrie panicked at the top-heavy basket of post that had been shoved in front of her. 'But what way do you want it sorted?' she called, but Karen had gone. She sighed and started to open the letters. She'd just have to use her initiative, she told herself firmly. It was hardly rocket science. And though it was a disappointing start to her new job, it was, after all, only a temporary situation.

After a couple of hours, she had finished the job and the post was neatly stacked into bundles. There was no sign of either Jackie or Karen so she made her way to reception to see what she should do next. The two girls sat side-by-side, gossiping.

'Hi.' Carrie smiled grimly. Why did she get the feeling that she'd just done their morning's work for them?

'Finished?' Karen asked.

'Well, I wasn't sure what way you wanted the post sorted so I broke it down into accounts, sales, the different shows and personal. And of course a separate pile for Mr Blake.'

Karen beamed at her. 'That's not quite the way we do it but I'll show you our system later.'

'Fine,' Carrie said tightly.

'But now I need you to do something else.'

'Yes?' Carrie perked up.

'Yes, would you go around and take everyone's order for lunch? Then you can phone the deli – the number's there' – she pointed at a notice stuck on the top of the partition – 'and go and pick it up.'

Carrie blinked. 'But that's not part of my job.'

'It's part of everyone's job, Carrie,' Karen assured her. 'We take turns. I must say I always enjoy getting out of the office for some fresh air.'

Carrie looked out of the window at the rain that had started to come down in a deluge. 'Right.'

'Make sure you get money from everyone before you go,' Jackie warned. 'There are a few people in this place who never pay their debts.'

Carrie's eyes widened. 'Thanks for the warning,' she muttered and went off to fetch her pad and pen before trailing from one desk to the next to take orders.

The day didn't improve with the arrival of the boss. Carrie was alone in reception and after a brief nod and vague smile in her direction, Jonathan had closeted himself away in his office and she hadn't seen him since. At four, she'd asked Karen about Maeve.

'Oh, she won't be in until about five,' she was told. 'Then she works through until the show is over.'

'And her producer? I didn't meet him yet, did I?' Carrie frowned. Surely he would want to talk to her about the job.

'Karl Thompson? He'll be in later too.'

Carrie sighed. 'So I won't meet any of them until tomorrow.'

Karen stared at her. 'No there's a meeting this evening. You'll see them all then.'

'Oh?' Carrie brightened.

'Yeah, they have a meeting every Friday morning at nine and every Monday evening at seven. Jonathan said you were to attend.'

Carrie gawped at her. 'At seven?'

'Oh, don't worry, it will only last a couple of hours. Then Karl and Maeve have to get ready for their programme.'

Carrie closed her eyes and had a mental image of Declan returning home to a cold empty house with no dinner. Still, it would only be one night a week.

11

Carrie would never forget the first time she came face to face with Maeve Elliot. The girl breezed into the meeting room wearing a transparent cheesecloth shirt, denim hipsters and pink kitten-heeled shoes. On her slim brown arms several bracelets jangled and her mass of blonde hair hung loose around a face that with the exception of some pink-frosted lipstick seemed devoid of make-up. Carrie stared openly in admiration. Perhaps she had hitherto undiscovered lesbian tendencies, because she couldn't take her eyes off this gorgeous creature.

Jonathan Blake called the meeting to order. 'Karl, Maeve, I'd like to introduce Carrie Lambe. She's going to be working with us on the new show.'

Karl Thompson smiled. 'Welcome aboard, Carrie, nice to meet you.'

'Yes, welcome to Forever FM,' Maeve murmured, not looking up from the papers in front of her.

Carrie flushed happily. 'Thank you, I'm delighted to be here.'

'That won't last long,' was Maeve's caustic reply.

Jonathan smiled grimly at his sharp-tongued DJ. 'What Maeve means, Carrie, is that this job won't be easy.'

'I'm used to hard work,' Carrie assured him.

'Good. How was your first day? Have you any questions?'

'Well,' Carrie said nervously, 'I did wonder about a job spec.'

Jonathan frowned. 'A job spec?'

'You know, laying out my responsibilities. It's just that today I seemed to be doing a little bit of everyone else's work.'

Maeve sighed impatiently. 'You are new, darling. The best way to find out how a business works is to have a go at everything.'

'It's only until we get started working on the new show,' Karl said kindly. 'Then there won't be time for anything else.'

Carrie smiled gratefully. 'Oh, right, I see.' She turned back to Jonathan. 'And my hours?'

He shrugged impatiently. 'We'll have to see.'

Maeve rolled her eyes and grinned at Carrie. 'You'll be pretty much working a seven-hour day,' she explained. 'That includes the show, so say three to eleven, including an hour for dinner. For now though, you can work nine to five.'

Carrie gulped. 'Oh, I see. I didn't realise . . .'

Jonathan frowned in annoyance. 'Oh, really, Carrie, let's take this one day at a time, shall we? We work flexible hours in Forever FM and I'm quite happy if you need to play around with the timetable – once the work gets done, of course.'

Carrie smiled warily. 'Okay, then.'

Maeve looked pointedly at her watch. 'Can we get on with the meeting now?'

'I have a tape of the advertisement the agency have come up with to get people phoning in,' Jonathan told them, slipping the cassette into the portable stereo on the table. 'Of course, it's only a rough idea at this stage. It doesn't help that we haven't come up with a title.'

'*Slime Time*,' Maeve told him with a wink at Carrie.

Carrie, surprised by this sudden flash of humour, grinned back.

'Serious suggestions only, please,' Jonathan scowled at Maeve.

'I *was* serious,' she muttered.

'What about *Pillow Talk*?' Karl suggested.

Maeve wrinkled her nose. 'That sounds like some kind of sex show.'

Karl grinned. 'Well, that would do wonders for the ratings.'

Jonathan shook his head regretfully. 'I'd do it like a shot but I'm not sure Dublin is ready for blue radio. The show will cover every topic under the sun and the name has to reflect that.'

'What about *Dublin Tonight* or *Dublin Talks*?' Carrie suggested tentatively. She wasn't sure she was supposed to open her mouth but she couldn't help herself. It would be so exciting if she were the one to come up with the name for the show.

Jonathan looked at her thoughtfully. 'Not bad.'

Karl shrugged. 'Either would do. Let's pick one as a working title and ask the rest of the staff if they've any better ideas.'

'*Dublin Tonight*,' Maeve said decisively.

'Okay.' Jonathan was relieved that they'd finally

come to some decision regarding the show. He'd met with nothing but resistance from Karl and Maeve about the new show and he was beginning to wonder if he should shelve the whole project. 'Let's listen to the tape.'

Carrie listened attentively while a man with a very deep voice invited listeners to call Maeve Elliot and tell her about their problems. Maeve rested her head in her arms and groaned. Jonathan shushed her irritably. The next advertisement was a young woman saying much the same thing. He stopped the tape. 'The idea is to appeal to all age groups,' he explained. 'Now, our next job is to come up with topics for each of the shows until Christmas.'

Karl frowned as he consulted his diary. 'That's thirty-five shows, Jonathan.'

Maeve raised her head and stared at them. 'We've to come up with thirty-five topics now?'

'I'd certainly like some ideas today,' Jonathan said firmly. 'You've had three days to think about it.'

'I've been trying *not* to think about it,' Maeve retorted.

Jonathan threw down his pen. 'Fine, Maeve. If you want me to get someone else to do the show then that's what I'll do.'

The silence was electric as they stared at each other. 'I'll do it,' Maeve said finally.

Jonathan nodded curtly. 'Right, now that that's sorted, has anyone any topics? Karl?'

'We need to be careful that we come up with some good stuff for the first few shows – subjects that will appeal to most people. The obvious ones are relationship issues.'

'Like?' Jonathan prompted.

Karl sighed. He didn't like this show any more than Maeve did. 'I slept with my brother-in-law/sister-in-law—'

'Mother-in-law!' Maeve chipped in.

'Good, that's good!' Jonathan drummed his fingers on the desk. 'What else?'

Karl looked distinctly uncomfortable. 'My partner isn't the father of my baby.'

Jonathan grinned delightedly. 'These ideas are great, Karl, where did you get them?'

'*Geraldo*,' Karl admitted.

'What about "My wife doesn't know I'm gay"?' Maeve suggested.

'Good, Maeve, now you're getting the idea. Carrie, are you getting all this?'

Carrie nodded and scribbled frantically on her pad.

'Shouldn't we go for some light-hearted stuff too?' Karl asked. 'I mean, all of this stuff is pretty depressing.'

Jonathan frowned. 'I think we have to be either serious or funny, we can't be both.'

Maeve perked up at the idea of a comedy show. 'We could do a send-up of all the real shows,' she said excitedly. 'We could have fake guests with outrageous problems.'

'The listeners would probably believe it,' Karl said drily.

'It could be controversial,' Jonathan mused.

'It would get talked about,' Maeve pointed out. 'We would get lots of media coverage if we were risqué.'

'True, but there would be an awful lot more work and cost involved, Maeve,' Jonathan said. 'You're talking about a *Scrap Saturday* type of show. We're not equipped for that and you've no experience.'

Karl looked enquiringly at Maeve.

'Before your time,' Maeve explained. 'Dermot Morgan used to have this amazing show on RTE on Saturday mornings, basically sending up anyone and everyone.'

'Mainly politicians,' Jonathan added. 'Completely out of our league unfortunately.'

She sighed. She knew he was right but she'd try anything to avoid presenting the kind of show he wanted.

'So it's going to be serious?' Carrie asked, her pen poised over her pad.

'Yes, definitely,' Jonathan said firmly. Karl shot Maeve a sympathetic look.

'What about some heavier topics like "I don't know how to tell my wife I've only got three months to live"?' Carrie suggested.

Jonathan nodded. 'That's not a bad idea at all, Carrie. Maeve?'

Maeve was looking slightly surprised. 'It's a bit more upmarket,' she admitted.

Karl banged the table excitedly. 'I've got a title.'

'We've moved on from titles, Karl,' Maeve drawled. 'Try and keep up.'

'No, listen, let's call it *Confessions*. We could make every subject about people admitting things to their loved ones.'

Maeve shook her head. 'That's totally *Jerry Springer*.'

'Not *Confessions*,' Carrie said, her eyes dancing. '*Secrets*. The guest tells Maeve what the secret is but remains anonymous. They could be admitting to her that they're alcoholics, gamblers, adulterers, transvestites even!'

Maeve scowled. 'Oh, great, thanks! I think you've just managed to beat Jerry on the sleaze scale.'

Carrie's face fell. Her first day and she'd already managed to annoy her heroine. 'Sorry.'

'No, I think Carrie's got something there.' Jonathan drummed the table even harder and stared up at the ceiling. 'But,' he said slowly, 'instead of having several guests, Maeve, you could have just one. There would be no slanging matches, no hair flying and no bad language.'

Karl scratched his head. 'I thought the whole point of these shows was that everyone ended up killing each other. That's how our competition works.'

'But we need to be a little bit different,' Jonathan pointed out. 'We need to get their listeners to switch channel.'

Maeve stared thoughtfully at her boss. 'I think you've got it, Jonathan. When I listened to the shows on Dublin FM and City Live I had to switch off after a while because I couldn't make out what anyone was saying. There was absolutely no control and everyone was talking at the same time. It got really irritating after a while. I'm sure I'm not the only one who switched stations.'

'But their ratings are still higher than ours,' Karl said wearily.

Jonathan's eyes twinkled. 'Because the listeners want a talk show and don't have a decent alternative.'

Carrie nodded. 'But now they have Maeve Elliot listening to Dublin's secrets.'

Again, Maeve looked at her in surprise. 'I think you should be working for our ad agency.'

'Yes, that's a good line, Carrie, write it down.' Jonathan turned to Karl. 'Have we convinced you?'

Karl nodded slowly. 'Let's go over it one more time.'

It was nearly ten o'clock when Carrie left the office, high as a kite. She couldn't believe that not only had she been included in a meeting with Jonathan – stop calling me Mr Blake, Carrie – Karl and Maeve, but they'd listened to and welcomed her ideas. Karl was lovely, really kind and sincere. Maeve could be quite cutting but funny with it and there was no doubting that she was good at her job. Carrie didn't blame her for being negative about the programme. At the end of the day, the public would blame her if it didn't work. But if it did, she'd be an even bigger star than she already was. Carrie had been lost in admiration just listening to her ideas once she'd come around to the idea that *Secrets* might be a success. She sighed as she hopped on a bus and slid into a seat at the back. She knew that she'd be useless at it but she did envy Maeve her job. In fact, secretly she envied almost everything about Maeve. She was clever and funny and free to go to all the hot nightclubs with any man she wished. And having seen her in the flesh Carrie could understand why the men were queuing up. Crikey, why was she thinking like this when Declan was waiting for her at home? Oh, God, Declan! He must be sick with worry. She had meant to phone but there just hadn't been an opportunity. It would be another thirty minutes before she was home. At times like this, she wished she had a mobile. Then she could at least put his mind at rest.

'Where the hell have you been?' he barked, looking more angry than worried. 'I had a lousy day at work and came home to an empty house, no dinner and not even a phone call to explain why.'

Carrie threw her bag on a chair and pulled off her jacket. 'I'm sorry, I didn't get a chance to phone. I'll make us something now.'

'Don't bother, I've eaten.'

'So you have,' Carrie murmured when she saw the Chinese cartons littering the table, soy sauce dripping on to the floor.

'But I'll have another beer,' he called grumpily from his chair in front of the TV.

Carrie fetched two beers and went in to join him. She was too excited to be annoyed about the mess. And she didn't want to argue when she had so much she wanted to tell him. 'Oh, Dec, I'm sorry I was so late but Jonathan called a meeting with the producer, and Maeve Elliot – there was nothing I could do.' This was not the time to tell him that the meeting would be a regular thing. 'I couldn't just walk out on them, it was my first day. Oh, please, Dec, don't be like this.'

'You should have called, then I could have stopped by my mother's for dinner.'

Carrie stared at him. God, all he was worried about was his bloody dinner. 'I'm going to have a bath.'

She went upstairs fuming. How could he be so horrible? He hadn't even asked her how her first day had been. She asked him every bloody day how work was going for him. Admittedly, she usually tuned out to the details of selling ink cartridges and zip drives to outlets that didn't know what they wanted and knew nothing about computers. But at least she asked. She filled the bath, tugged off the yellow jeans and black top – they'd been a good choice – slipped out of her bra and panties and climbed into the hot water. She closed her eyes and smiled as she thought back over the day, although all she really wanted to think about was the meeting. She'd never felt so fired up or enthusiastic about anything in her life. And she'd certainly never seen herself as an ideas person. But that's what Jonathan Blake had called her.

'Well done, Carrie, you're going to fit in very well here,' he'd told her after Karl and Maeve had hurried off to the studio. 'You've got the right attitude and curiosity for the job. Linda Jewell was spot on as usual.'

She'd blushed like a schoolgirl. 'I'm really enjoying myself, although I didn't realise that I'd be doing so much work on reception and switch as well.'

Jonathan had looked totally confused. 'Karen and

Jackie look after the phones and reception, Carrie. Of course, it would be nice if you could help out occasionally if we're stuck and you're not busy.'

Carrie's smile was grim. 'I must have got the wrong end of the stick.' It was clear that Karen and Jackie had been trying to take advantage of her and while she wanted to put a stop to it she didn't want to alienate them either. After all, they had to sit together in that poxy little corner. She sipped her beer and gazed at her crimson toenails peeping out of the water. There must be a way to deal with the matter discreetly. She'd just have to think of it.

12

Linda sat perched on the edge of a chair in Bill's office. Her boss sat opposite sifting through papers and trying to look busy. Linda suppressed a smile. He obviously thought she was here to ask for promotion or a salary increase. But she'd decided it was time to tell her boss about Patrick. Then he would tell Cheryl and she would tell the world and that would be that.

'Now, Linda, what can I do for you?' He sat back, twiddling a pen between nervous fingers.

'I thought you should know that Patrick and I have separated.'

Bill dropped the pen and stared at her. Linda was sure the main emotion in his eyes was interest. 'Oh, Linda, I'm sorry.'

Linda shrugged. 'These things happen.'

'I must say you're taking it very well.'

Linda bristled. He'd already assumed that the separation was Patrick's idea. Bloody men. 'We both agreed it was for the best,' she said smoothly. 'There's no point in flogging a dead horse, is there?'

'Eh, no, indeed, but still, Linda, I'm sure Patrick will be back. What possible future could he have with her?'

The colour drained from Linda's face. 'You know?'

Bill shifted uncomfortably. 'Cheryl and I saw them in The Westbury on Friday night,' he admitted. 'We were a bit shocked, I can tell you – didn't think Patrick was the sort. It seemed odd that he'd taken her to such a public place, but now it all makes sense.'

'Yes.' Linda managed a thin smile.

'But like I say, Linda, I'm sure he'll be back.' He leaned over and patted her hand kindly.

Linda flashed him a brilliant smile. 'Oh, but Bill I don't want him back. You see, well, we've been pretty much living separate lives lately – if you know what I mean.' She did her best to look coy when all she actually wanted to do was escape to the loo and cry like a baby.

Bill looked totally flummoxed. 'Oh! Well, I must say this is all very . . . civilised.'

'Yes, isn't it? Unlike Patrick, I'm keeping my private life private for the moment, Bill, so if you wouldn't mind keeping it to yourself . . .'

'Of course.' He nodded vehemently.

Linda figured it would be teatime at best before Cheryl had wormed all the details out of him. She stood up. 'Well, then, I'd better get back to work.'

Bill was around the desk in a flash with a hand on her arm. 'I'm glad you're okay about all of this but I still think Patrick's a very foolish man.' He looked down at her, his eyes warm.

Linda swallowed hard and smiled. 'That's sweet of you, Bill,' she said and escaped out of the door.

*   *   *

As she sat back down at her desk, the phone rang. 'It's your sister,' Marie told her.

'Hi, Viv. How are you?' she said when Marie had put her through.

'Not as well as you, by all accounts,' Viv replied.

'Sorry?'

'Don't play the innocent with me, Linda, Patrick told me everything.'

Linda closed her eyes. 'When were you talking to Patrick?'

'He called me this morning wanting to know all about your love-life.'

'What did you tell him?' Linda whispered.

'There was nothing I could tell him now, was there? Do you know, I think he's jealous.'

'More likely his ego is dented,' Linda said coldly.

'I can't believe you have another man tucked away somewhere and you never told me.'

Linda sighed. There was no way she could have this conversation on the phone. 'Are you free for lunch?'

'I certainly am! Once you promise to spill all the gory details.'

'I promise. Kingsland at one, okay?'

'I can't wait.'

Linda put the phone down. Already this was getting complicated. She couldn't believe that Patrick had called Viv. Mind you, she couldn't believe that he was already parading Stacey around the city like some kind of prize – the bastard! God, what was she going to do? She'd have to confide in her sister – she needed advice. And surely she would know what to do; she was a writer, after all.

Viv burst out laughing. 'What on earth did you do that for?'

'It's not funny, Viv.'

Viv looked penitent. 'No, sorry. But why did you tell him there had been other men?'

Linda shook her head impatiently. 'Oh just to shut him up. He kept telling me I'd get over him, that I'd meet someone else one day. Sanctimonious shit.'

Viv sighed. 'I think you're the one who should be writing fiction. And you're quite sure there's no truth behind this?'

'No, I told you, I made it all up. I just wanted to claw some dignity back. I can't tell you how good it felt when I told Patrick. The look on his face.' Linda smiled at the memory.

'I wish I'd been there,' Viv said wistfully. 'But what are you going to do now?'

'I don't know. It was a brief triumph. If Patrick starts telling everybody, my name will be mud. I'll look like a complete slapper and he'll end up the good guy. You know, that pisses me off more than anything.'

'But you don't want to be pitied,' Viv reminded her. 'The poor little wife.'

'No.' Linda was vehement.

'I think you did the right thing,' Viv told her. 'It's much more exciting to be the scarlet woman. All the guys will be looking at you in a totally new way. Gosh, this is better than a novel.'

Linda's look was withering. 'This is my life, Viv!'

'Sorry.' Viv signalled the waiter and asked for a bottle of house white.

'I can't drink,' Linda protested. 'I've got a lot of work to do this afternoon.'

'Rubbish, this is more important. Call them and say you won't be back.'

'You're right.' Linda took out her mobile and phoned Marie. The wonderful thing about her job was that as it was commission based and because she was so good at it she could pretty much come and go as she pleased. It annoyed Cheryl, but there was nothing she could do about it. Every month it was Linda that had the highest number of placements and Bill would do anything to keep her happy.

When the wine arrived, Viv took a long drink and gazed thoughtfully at her sister. 'Let's talk about all these lovers you've had.'

'There haven't been *any*!'

Viv wagged a finger at her. 'That's not what you told Patrick and hinted to Bill Reeve. Too late to change your mind now.'

Linda ran a hand distractedly through her hair. 'This is such a mess.'

'Nonsense, it's going to be great fun.'

Linda glared at her. 'I can assure you that there is nothing remotely funny about this situation.'

'Sorry,' Viv murmured.

'I've made a total fool of myself. Who'd ever believe that I'd had a string of lovers?'

'Patrick obviously did.'

'When he has time to think about it he'll realise that I was lying and then he'll think I'm pathetic.'

Viv's eyes narrowed. 'You shouldn't care what he thinks. You don't, do you, Linda?'

'I don't bloody know what I think. I wish I could just hop on a plane and get the hell out of here for a while.'

'You need a man,' Viv said calmly.

Linda stared at her. 'Have you listened to a word I've said? A man is the last thing I need. God, the thought of going through all that dating crap again.' She shuddered.

'But if you were seen around town with another man it would shut everyone up and no one would think you were pathetic.'

'No,' Linda agreed, 'they'd think I was a tart. I think I'll just tell Patrick the truth and get it over with.'

Viv stared at her over the rim of her glass. 'Really?'

Linda grinned reluctantly. 'No. Let him wonder.'

'Good.' Viv paused as the waiter brought their food. 'So what next?' She started hungrily into her beef chow mein.

Linda stared at her prawn curry. 'I wait for the divorce papers, I suppose.'

'I mean, what are *you* going to do.' Viv tossed her head impatiently.

'Dunno.'

'Oh, come on, Linda, pull yourself together.'

Linda's fingers tightened around her knife. 'One more platitude out of you and you're dead.'

Viv made a face. 'Sorry, I just hate to see you

so defeatist. The best thing you've done so far is telling Patrick you were unfaithful too. I think that was brilliant – in fact I wish it were true.'

'Me too.'

Viv looked at her curiously. 'Have you ever been tempted?'

Linda looked at her exasperated. 'Of course I've been tempted, Viv, I'm married not dead! I look.'

'Yes, but did you ever want to do more than look?' Viv persisted.

'Of course not.'

'But it's a bit odd that you never realised that Patrick was playing around.'

Linda pushed away her plate and sat back. 'What exactly are you trying to say?' Viv's amateur psychology could be very annoying.

'Just that maybe you weren't too bothered what he was up to,' Viv carried on blithely.

'Ah, right, why didn't I think of that?'

Viv flashed her a wicked grin. 'Because I'm the genius in the family.'

'True.'

Viv inclined her head modestly. 'So what do you think? Are you going to find yourself a man? I could fix you up, if you like.'

Linda scowled. 'No, thanks.'

'I'm telling you, if you want to get out of this with your head held high you need a man.'

'I was quite happy with the one I had,' Linda murmured.

'It's just for show – a business arrangement. You

could hire one of those escorts.' Viv's eyes twinkled excitedly. 'What do you think, Linda?'

'I think I need another drink.'

13

Maeve hummed as she stood on the balcony watering her plants. Craig would fall around the place laughing if he could see her. She'd always scorned gardening and all those who indulged in it. She bent to sniff a rose and smiled. Her apartment was very cool, very modern, very minimalist, but on her balcony she indulged her softer side – although Craig probably didn't think she had one. She sat down on the wrought-iron bench and stared across Dublin bay. Sometimes she wished she didn't have this tough-as-nails image. Sometimes she thought it might be nice to be completely open with someone. To open up about her insecurities, her hopes, and her fears, but there was no one that she trusted enough to do that. She had no female friends – Julie didn't count – and the men in her life were not interested in her feelings. But then she didn't pick men for their sensitivity. She was only twenty-nine and there was plenty of time to find Mr Right. For now what she needed were partners who could either help further her career or increase her visibility. As it turned out Vince had fulfilled neither role. He had seemed the perfect escort – funny, intelligent and well connected in the industry – she had grown quite fond of him. But unfortunately Vince couldn't make the final break with his wife and Maeve couldn't risk being seen around town with a married man. Hopefully Paul Riche's personal life was more straightforward. She had deliberately brought him to places where they'd be photographed, and so far he'd seemed very comfortable about it. Jonathan loved it when she was in the papers, especially if she was with someone important. Maeve photographed arm-in-arm with the occasional rock star or actor was excellent for Forever FM's image. It was important to keep Jonathan happy, Maeve thought with a worried frown. He was a nice enough guy but he was a businessman and if Maeve no longer appealed to the listeners, he wouldn't think twice about dropping her. She was very lucky that he was giving her a chance to host *Secrets*, but she knew if she didn't perform, she'd be out. She had to make sure that didn't happen. She wanted to be number one in Forever FM because that was the only way she'd be able to move on to better things. She was beginning to feel quite excited about the show now. Thanks to the new format they'd come up with, it might actually be something to be proud of. At least there was no longer a chance of any slanging matches on air, with her playing referee. The phone ringing broke in on her thoughts and she reluctantly went back inside. 'Hello?'

'Maeve, it's Craig.'

'Hey, Craig.'

'Are you coming to the meeting this afternoon or do you have to sharpen your claws?'

Maeve grinned. 'I've just finished. I'll be there. The Purty Kitchen at four?'

'Yeah, see you then.'

'I didn't think you were going.' Craig was always telling them that Sunday was his busiest day.

'Debs is looking after the shop,' he told her. 'See you later.'

''Bye.' Maeve hung up and went back outside. These club meetings were just an excuse for an afternoon piss-up, Freddy being the only one who took it seriously. He would tell them the events he'd lined up for the month ahead and after they'd signed up for the various activities they would get down to the serious business of drinking. Maeve kept her distance from most of the club members but she'd grown quite fond of Freddy, and Craig was the only one who seemed to share her sense of humour. She always teased him when he missed a climb, saying that he was losing his nerve.

'If your programme aired on weekend afternoons you wouldn't be a member of FECC at all,' Craig would retort.

Maeve was scornful. 'It's not the same at all, anyone can sell a few plants.' That was one of the few occasions she'd ever seen him really lose his temper. After hurling a string of abuse at her he'd stormed out of the pub and she hadn't seen or heard from him for over a week. It had bothered her because she'd only been having a laugh and he'd always given as good as he'd got in the past. When they finally called a truce – Maeve had managed a stilted apology – she was careful not to go too far again. His business obviously meant more to him than she'd realised.

Maeve took a last look at the view, breathed in some sea air and went inside to shower and dress. When she'd finished the onerous task of drying her long hair, she pulled on her jeans and red fleece and slipped her feet into tan, leather boots. After a moment's hesitation, she applied some foundation, mascara, and lip gloss. She fluffed up her hair and looked around for her mobile phone and car keys. Within minutes she was driving along the coast heading for Dun Laoghaire and the pub where FECC usually met – mainly because it was Freddy's local. Maeve was glad that Craig was coming. It was always more fun when he was there. Everyone liked him and he could defuse most situations with one of his dry quips. Not that there were ever any real arguments to avoid, Maeve admitted to herself as she flew through Blackrock. Only occasional quibbles about the locations of the climbs or, from the hardened veterans, complaints that the climbs were too easy. Maeve smiled. She was the one who usually complained about that, much to Aoife's disgust. But as the only other two women in the club, Niamh and Valerie, agreed with her, there wasn't much Aoife could do about it. Except bat her eyelashes at Craig and wonder aloud if it would be too much for her. Craig fell for it every time.

'You'll be fine,' he'd say kindly. 'Just stay close to me.'

And Aoife would be grinning for the rest of the

evening, like the cat that got the cream. God, but the girl was annoying. Maeve slowed as she came into Dun Laoghaire and swung the car into a parking spot. She stepped out of the MG, flashed a coquettish smile at two teenagers who were torn between staring at her and the car and walked into the pub, her hips swinging gracefully.

'Hey, Maeve, what are you having?' Freddy was at the bar, ordering.

Maeve wrinkled her nose. 'A bottle of Miller, please.'

Freddy raised an eyebrow. 'No tequila?'

Maeve laughed. 'It's a bit early for tequila and I'm driving.'

'Fair enough. Take those two pints over to Craig and Ken, would you?'

Maeve obligingly carried the two pints of Guinness to their usual table at the end of the room. 'Hi, guys.'

'Maeve! You've never looked as well.' Craig licked his lips as he eyed the pint in her hand.

Ken relieved her of the other. 'What's the difference between a pint and a woman?'

Maeve shook her head.

'You can't beat a pint!' Ken laughed uproariously at his own joke.

Maeve rolled her eyes. 'Pathetic. With comments like that you could be a guest on my new show.'

'What's this, Maeve?' Craig set down his glass and looked at her curiously. 'Are you leaving Forever FM?'

'No, I'm going to host a new talk show.'

Craig raised an eyebrow. 'That's great, congratulations.'

Maeve smiled. 'Yeah, thanks, I'm really looking forward to it.'

Ken looked dubious. 'Is it going to be a show where everyone screams at each other? I can't stand that rubbish.'

Maeve's eyes were cool. 'Funny, I would have thought that would be right up your street.'

Craig hid his smirk behind his glass. Ken was a good laugh and an excellent climber but he was one of those people who had something bad to say about everything and everyone from politicians, to priests, to refugees. Craig had nearly pulverised him the last time he'd started spouting his racist views, but Maeve had put a warning hand on his arm. 'He's not worth it,' she'd murmured.

'No,' she continued now, 'there'll be no screaming or shouting on my show. I'll only have one guest a night. And they'll be ordinary people with ordinary lives.'

'Sounds boring,' Ken muttered.

Craig smiled encouragingly at Maeve. 'I'm sure it will be a great success.'

'I think so.'

Ken shook his head. 'No, you should have more than one guest on. You need a good argument if the programme's to succeed.' He drained his glass and went off to get a refill.

Maeve shook her head. 'Am I going mad, here?

He started off the conversation giving out about programmes where everyone screamed at each other.'

Craig grinned. 'Don't mind him. Ken's only happy when he's contradicting someone.'

'He's an idiot,' Maeve muttered. 'How did Freddy let someone like him into FECC anyway?'

Craig bent his head closer to hers. 'He's his brother-in-law, but don't say anything. Freddy isn't exactly proud of the fact.'

'I'm not surprised.' Maeve watched as Ken paid for his drink and went over to talk to some of the rest of the group. 'Miserable bastard didn't even get us a drink.'

Craig stood up. 'I'll get them in.'

Maeve shook her head. 'No, I'm driving.'

'You should take the DART. It's only a couple of stops.'

'I haven't used public transport in years.'

'You should try it, it's great. And you can get plastered if you feel like it.' He grinned at her and went off to the bar.

'Are you telling me you're not driving?' she said when he returned.

'Nope.'

'But you must have to take two buses to get to Blanchardstown.'

He looked amused. 'But I don't *live* in Blanchardstown.'

Maeve frowned. She'd always assumed that because he worked there he also lived there.

'So where *do* you live?'

· 'Sutton.'

Maeve's eyes widened as he named one of the more salubrious suburbs of Dublin. 'I didn't know that.'

His eyes twinkled at her over his pint. 'There's a lot you don't know about me, Maeve.'

Out of the side of her eye, Maeve saw Aoife looking longingly at Craig. 'There's a lot I know that you don't,' she retorted.

'Like what?'

'Like Aoife O'Hanlon has the hots for you.'

Craig's smile faded. 'Rubbish.'

Maeve grinned at his discomfort. 'It's true. In fact, I bet you a fiver that if I go to the ladies' she'll be over here in a flash.'

'No, don't,' Craig begged as she stood up.

Maeve sat down again, laughing.

'You're a horrible, nasty, person,' Craig complained. Maeve started to get up again. 'No, no, sorry, you're wonderful.'

'That's more like it. I should be charging you protection money. She won't come near you as long as I'm around.'

'I'm not surprised. You're horrible to her.'

'No, I'm not,' Maeve said defensively. 'I just slag her the way I slag everybody.'

'Not everybody can take it, Maeve.'

Maeve shrugged. 'If you can't stand the heat . . .'

Craig shook his head sadly and stood up. 'You shouldn't feel that you always have to be a smart-arse.'

Maeve's eyes widened. 'I beg your pardon?'

He looked uncomfortable. 'I'm just saying that

there's nothing wrong with being nice to people occasionally. You should try it sometime.' And with that, he left her and went to sit between Valerie and Freddy.

Maeve slammed down her glass angrily and went out to the ladies'. After a few deep breaths, she came back inside, took her drink and sat as far away from Craig as possible.

14

Orla carried their coffees back to the table where Carrie sat watching Ethan guzzling up his yoghurt. 'Sure you don't want a cake?' she asked before she sat down.

Carrie grimaced. 'No, I don't feel great. I cooked breakfast for Declan – bacon, egg, sausage, the works – but he didn't fancy it. So I ate it.'

Orla scowled. 'I'd have thrown it over him!'

'I should have asked if he wanted it first,' Carrie pointed out. 'It's just that I wanted to make up for all the TV dinners lately.'

Orla added two spoons of sugar to her coffee and stirred vigorously. 'You've spoiled that man, Carrie.'

'But I like cooking. And it's not like it's just for him. I like sitting down to dinner together in the evening. It's romantic.'

'I bet he eats in front of the television most nights,' Orla said shrewdly.

Carrie sighed. 'Yeah. Still, he's entitled to relax after a long day.'

'So are you,' Orla pointed out.

'Want some choclat.' Ethan smiled angelically at Carrie.

'Ask properly,' Orla said automatically.

'May I have some choclat, please, Aunty Cawie?'

Carrie kissed the top of his head. 'Of course you can, darling.' She went to the counter, glad that Ethan had interrupted the conversation. She didn't want to listen to another one of Orla's sermons on Declan, she knew that he could be a selfish sod sometimes. She'd been disgusted with him this morning for not eating the breakfast and told him so. He'd flung out of the house and she'd sat down and stuffed herself and felt sick since. She should never have mentioned it to Orla; her friend didn't like Declan. Carrie vowed to keep her mouth shut about her private life in future. What went on at home was their business and no relationship was perfect. It couldn't be easy for Declan, they'd hardly seen each other since she'd started her new job. Still, at least some mornings she could prepare something for him to eat in the evening. It wasn't the same and he particularly hated it when she left him salad, but it was the best she could do for now. She paid for the chocolate and brought it back to the table. 'Here you are, Ethan.'

'Thank you, Aunty Cawie.'

'You're welcome, pet.'

He giggled. 'I'm not a pet, I'm a lickle boy.'

Carrie laughed. 'Of course you are, sorry.' She looked tenderly down at the little boy's mop of blond hair, his incredibly long lashes and clear blue eyes. 'Oh, Orla, you're so lucky.'

Orla smiled at her son. 'Yeah, I am. Will you and Declan have kids, do you think?'

Carrie shrugged. She'd been thinking a lot about babies recently, although she'd said nothing to Declan. And then she'd got the job with Forever FM. 'There's plenty of time.'

'What about marriage?' Orla asked.

Carrie raised her eyebrows. 'What is this? Has my mother been talking to you?'

Orla laughed. 'Your mother would never deign to talk to the likes of me.'

Carrie flushed with embarrassment. Her mother had been completely horrible when Orla had found herself pregnant and the father was nowhere in sight. It had made things worse – as far as Mrs Lambe was concerned – that Orla had decided to have the baby.

'How can she give a child a decent life? She should have an abortion and forget it ever even happened.'

Carrie had shuddered at her mother's coldness. She was full of admiration for Orla. Imagine having the courage to go through pregnancy and bring up a child alone. And, she looked affectionately at Ethan, to do such a great job too. 'Sorry. Mum's a bit old-fashioned.'

Orla shrugged. 'Don't worry about it. A lot of my mum's neighbours and relations reacted like that. It used to bother me when I was pregnant but once Ethan came along it was like water off a duck's back.'

'I think you're both great,' Carrie told her affection-ately. 'And old biddies like my mother should mind their own business.'

Orla looked at her in mock horror. 'Carrie Lambe!

I've never heard you talk about your mother like that before.'

Carrie's eyes were sad. 'I'm fed up defending my parents, Orla. I thought they'd be happy about this new job but even that isn't good enough for them.'

Orla patted her hand sympathetically.

'The only thing that would make them happy now is if I gave up work, married Declan and started a family.'

'But I thought they didn't like him?'

'They'd prefer us to be married than living together.'

'Is that why you haven't?' Orla probed. 'Married Declan and started a family, I mean.'

'Well, I'm not married because Declan hasn't asked me,' Carrie admitted sheepishly. 'And as for a baby – well, if we're not committed enough to get married, how can we even think about children?' She sniffed and scrambled in her bag for a tissue. So much for her keeping her private life to herself.

Orla busied herself scraping chocolate off her son. 'You okay?' she asked when Carrie had tucked her tissue into her sleeve.

'Yeah, don't mind me. I just hate it when Dec and I fight.'

'Isn't he happy about the new job?'

'He's happy that I'm earning some money, but he hates the hours. I suppose I should be glad that he misses me.'

Orla said nothing.

'Things will get better.' Carrie forced a smile. 'Once the show has started it won't be quite so hectic.'

Orla frowned. 'But won't you be working even later then?'

Carrie nodded. 'But I'll probably be able to take a break before the show starts. I could nip home some nights and we could have dinner together. Declan would love that.'

'I'm sure he would,' Orla agreed and avoided eye contact.

After Orla had left to take Ethan home for his nap, Carrie wandered around the shops. She had an hour to kill before she was due into work. She should really be at home cleaning the house but after the row with Declan she'd just dumped the dirty dishes in the sink and got a bus into town. Thankfully, when she'd phoned her friend, Orla had been only too delighted to come in and meet her. She hadn't meant to blurt out all that stuff to Orla. What on earth had gotten into her? She hadn't thought about marriage and kids in ages. She wasn't sure she wanted either any more. Forever FM was the best thing that had happened to her and she wanted to make a go of it. It seemed ridiculous to call it a job, as she was having so much fun – and getting paid for it too! Since the research work had started she was on a high. It was so incredibly interesting. She couldn't believe the things people were willing to talk about over the phone. The ad campaign had started, inviting people to write in if they were interested in taking part in shows about: Secret children – did you give up your child? Have you a secret addiction? Are you being abused? The last one had resulted in a flood of letters, many of which reduced Carrie to tears.

Later at the Monday evening meeting, she produced some of the more serious letters.

Maeve frowned as she read out passages. 'We should pass these on to the police.'

'No way!' Jonathan grabbed a couple and read avidly. 'This is going to be great radio.'

Carrie looked at him in dismay. 'Oh, for God's sake, Carrie, don't look at me like that.'

She bent her head. 'Sorry.'

'Look,' he said more reasonably. 'These people are looking for help. Maeve will be able to give it to them.'

Maeve looked startled. 'I will?'

'Yes, of course you will. What they need is someone to listen to them. The police would probably only make things worse. And they don't like interfering in a family dispute.'

'So why are we?' Karl asked quietly.

Jonathan sighed impatiently. 'Because the people concerned will remain anonymous, of course. What's got into you lot tonight? Are you getting cold feet?'

Maeve gazed at him solemnly. 'No, but some of these letters concern very serious situations. These people should be talking to a proper counsellor.'

Jonathan placed his hands on the table, palms down and looked steadily around the table. 'Let me make something very clear. We are not setting ourselves up as counsellors. The listeners are telling their story and

Maeve is going to ask questions. No one is going to offer advice and no one is going to pass judgement.'

Karl shook his head. 'That's rubbish. Advice, insults and abuse will flood in – they always do.'

Maeve looked at him worriedly. For all their wrangling, she trusted Karl's judgement. He had nearly twenty years' experience in radio in Australia and he was very broadminded. If he wasn't happy about this then Maeve would have to back him up. 'Let's rethink the format,' she suggested gently to Jonathan. There was no point in antagonising him or he'd just dig his heels in.

'You're both overreacting.' Jonathan stood up and started to pace.

Karl and Maeve exchanged worried looks.

'Er, I agree with them,' Carrie said tremulously.

Jonathan looked amused. 'Do you now? Oh, well, in that case I'd better pull the plug on the whole show.'

Karl sighed. 'All I'm saying, Jonathan, is that we need to be careful. If we rush into this show unprepared we could do real damage to Forever FM and screw up people's lives too.'

Jonathan looked irritated. 'I can't believe you're losing your bottle, Karl.'

Karl watched him steadily. 'I take chances, Jonathan, but I don't put my head in a noose.'

Jonathan flung his pen across the table, making Carrie jump. 'You have twenty-four hours to come up with alternatives.' He stood up and glared at the three of them. 'Otherwise we go with the existing format.'

He strode out of the room, not bothering to shut the door after him.

Carrie smiled nervously. 'Would anyone like coffee?'

Karl nodded grimly. 'Get some for us all, Carrie. I think it's going to be a long night.'

15

Linda took her mug of tea back upstairs to bed and found the remote control before climbing into bed. She flicked through the channels on the tiny portable on the dressing table – Patrick would probably want that – finally settling for Kilroy. There were a number of middle-aged women talking about their toyboys. Maybe she'd end up like that. She sipped her tea and listened as a young girl told the women they were pathetic and disgusting. It was so easy for the young to be judgemental. She should really shower and get up. Lying here wasn't helping her mood. But somehow – she snuggled further under the covers – it was preferable to facing the world. Usually when she took a morning off she cleaned the house from top to bottom, went shopping, or got her highlights done. This morning none of these things held any attraction. She'd just stay here all morning, watch rubbish and feel sorry for herself.

Patrick had called last night, which was one of the reasons she was feeling so down. He'd been so business-like, coldly polite, like a total stranger. He'd been that way since the day on the beach. He'd called a few times trying to get more details about her adultery, but she'd refused to tell him anything. That was, of course, because there was nothing to tell. Patrick stopped trying to be considerate and sensitive after that. She was no longer the injured party. There was no reason for him to feel guilty any more. It must be like someone had lifted a huge weight from his shoulders, Linda realised. She'd made it easier for him to walk away. Last night he'd called to discuss the contents of their house. Well, actually, he'd just told her what he wanted and as it was quite a modest list, Linda hadn't argued. He'd also given her the name and address of his lawyer whom she'd be hearing from quite soon. It was the first time she'd known him to act so quickly. Patrick was the kind of man who liked to weigh up all the pros and cons before making any decisions, he didn't like to be rushed. Obviously, Stacey had changed all that. They said goodbye and Linda had felt totally bereft when she hung up. She'd thought it couldn't get worse but it had. Every week brought a new aspect to their split. Every day she realised how different her life would be from now on. The doorbell interrupted her thoughts, but she ignored it. It rang again and Linda pulled herself up to take a peak out of the window. She groaned when she saw her mother's car. She'd have to answer, her own car was in the driveway and Rosemary wouldn't go away. She shrugged into her dressing gown and hurried barefoot down the stairs.

'Oh, sorry darling, did I disturb you?' Rosemary asked innocently as she eyed her daughter's dishev-elled appearance. 'You're not sick, are you?'

Linda stood back to let her in. 'No, I'm fine. Just a bit tired.'

'And feeling sorry for yourself,' Rosemary guessed, as she peeled off her white wool car coat.

Linda smiled weakly. 'Something like that.'

'Then hanging around the house will make you feel worse. Why don't I make us some coffee while you go and dress?'

'I don't feel like it,' Linda said, feeling like a narky teenager. 'Okay, okay,' she said when her mother gave her 'that look'.

As usual Rosemary was right. Linda felt much better when she was dressed in clean jeans and a soft pink top. She scraped her hair back into a neat ponytail and went back down to rejoin her mother.

'Better,' Rosemary pronounced as she pushed a mug of strong coffee towards her.

Linda sipped her coffee and studied her mother. Her black hair was pulled back into a bun, her make-up was perfect and she was wearing one of her flamboyant knitted cardigans over black trousers. Linda always thought she looked like a ballet teacher. She certainly had the figure and poise for the job. 'You look well, Mum.'

'I wish I could say the same for you,' Rosemary said, her eyes travelling over Linda's strained, white face.

'Thanks.'

'What you need is a distraction. Why don't you come out with me tonight? I'm going to a rally and then me and a few of the girls are going for a meal.'

Linda smiled. 'What's the worthy cause this time?'

'It's nothing to smile about, I can assure you. It's about all these poor kids who end up back on the streets because there's no suitable place to put them.'

'You mean kids who've committed crimes?'

'Don't look at me like that, darling,' Rosemary chided, 'they're hardly likely to change their ways if they end up on the streets.'

'That's true, I suppose.'

'So how about it?'

'I don't think so, Mum. I really need to start dividing up the spoils.' Linda gestured at the furniture and ornaments around her.

'Oh, you poor thing. I wish there was something I could do to make this easier for you.'

Linda squeezed her hand. 'You are helping, believe me, you *and* Viv. I don't know what I'd do without you both. Especially now.'

'What do you mean? Has something happened?'

Linda sighed. 'I met Patrick and Stacey last week. They were out walking on Sandymount beach – the exact same walk that we took every Sunday.'

'Oh, Linda!'

'I just couldn't believe my eyes. And I'm afraid I got a bit . . . upset.'

'I'm not at all surprised. I'd have hit him,' Rosemary retorted.

'I didn't do that – it might have been better if I had. Instead, I called his girlfriend a few names and I told him—'

'Yes?' Rosemary prompted, her eyes alive with curiosity.

'I told him I'd been unfaithful too. In fact, I led him to believe that it had been a regular occurrence.'

Rosemary stared at her stunned for a moment and then threw her head back and laughed.

'Mum!'

Her mother wiped her eyes. 'Oh, I'm sorry, darling, but that's priceless. I wish I'd been there.'

Linda grinned. 'That's what Viv said.'

'How did he react?'

'Totally disgusted. He's been pestering me about it since, but I've told him I don't owe him any explanations any more.'

'Darling, you're brilliant! I'm so proud of you.'

Linda made a face. 'I don't know why. Now he thinks he's off the hook and he'll probably waste no time telling everyone.'

Rosemary's eyes narrowed. 'I wouldn't be so sure about that. No man likes to admit that his wife was playing away. It doesn't exactly reflect well on him.'

Linda brightened. 'I hadn't thought of that.'

'So, did you? See other men, I mean.'

Linda's eyes widened. 'Mum!'

Rosemary rolled her eyes. 'Just asking. I wouldn't blame you if you had.'

Linda eyed her curiously. 'Did you ever . . . ?'

It was Rosemary's turn to look shocked. 'Of course not! I was always faithful to your father.'

Linda sighed. 'Me too, but unlike Daddy, Patrick didn't deserve such devotion. I tell you, Mum, I've had it with men. I wouldn't go through this again if my life depended on it.'

'You won't always feel that way,' Rosemary said equably.

'Don't count on it. Just take note. I don't want you trying to fix me up with anyone. And that goes for Viv too, so keep her under control.'

Rosemary arched her eyebrows. 'When have I ever been able to keep your sister under control?' She stood up and reached for her coat. 'You're sure I can't persuade you to come along this evening?'

Linda hugged her. 'No, I'm not in the mood for socialising, but thanks for asking.'

Feeling remarkably cheered by her mother's visit, Linda gave the kitchen a good clean and then went to get ready for work. She applied her make-up carefully, brushed her hair till it shone and put on her black and white hound's tooth suit with a thin black top – that always made her feel good. When she walked into the office an hour later, Marie gazed at her in admiration. 'You look lovely, Linda.'

'Thanks, Marie.' She was delighted to see that Cheryl was not at her desk and Bill's office was empty.

'There are some messages on your desk,' Maria told her, 'and Jonathan Blake is on his way over.'

Linda stopped in her tracks. 'What?'

Marie's smile faltered. 'Well, I checked your diary and you've no other appointments. I'm sorry, I didn't mean—'

Linda forced a smile. 'No, that's fine, Marie, you did the right thing.'

Marie visibly relaxed. 'Can I get you some coffee?'

'Oh, yes, please,' Linda said fervently. 'What time are Bill and Cheryl due back?' she added casually.

'Cheryl said something about shopping, so I'm not sure if they'll be back at all.'

Linda let out a sigh of relief. If Cheryl had managed to persuade Bill to go shopping she wouldn't stop until the shops shut. Which at least meant she wouldn't have to put up with Cheryl's curious glances. She pulled out the Forever FM file and glanced through the page Marie had neatly stapled to the inside cover. It had all the names, positions, and salaries of the people she'd placed with Jonathan since she'd taken over the account. She was quite proud of that list. It had resulted in two salary increases for her, and Bill had handed over two other major accounts that were very lucrative. She wondered what Jonathan wanted to see her about. Did he want someone else? She had only just placed Carrie with him. She hoped that he wasn't going to complain about the girl. She'd had a gut feeling that Carrie Lambe was made for that job. Hopefully her instincts weren't being affected by her personal problems. That would definitely be the final straw. 'Did Jonathan say what time he'd be in?' she asked as Marie set the coffee down carefully on her desk.

'Just that he was having lunch nearby and that he'd drop in afterwards.'

Linda smiled. Given the long lunches that he indulged in that could mean five o'clock. Still it would force her to sit at her desk and do some

work for a change. And it was an added bonus that
neither Bill nor Cheryl was around. She pulled out
the job specification that had arrived from a major
software company this morning. They were looking
for a systems analyst and she thought that she had
just the man for the job. But she trawled through
the database anyway, determined to give her client
a reasonable selection. She was on the phone to the
third candidate she'd found when Jonathan arrived.
She smiled and waved him to a chair before signalling
to Marie to bring him a coffee.

'Okay, Fran, I'll talk to the company concerned
and check that out for you. Right, fine, I'll call you
tomorrow. 'Bye now.' She put down the phone and
scribbled a note in the file in front of her before closing
it and putting it to one side. 'Hello, Jonathan, how
are you?'

He grimaced. 'Fed up. And you? You seem busy.'

'Not too bad. Why are you fed up?' She prayed that
it had nothing to do with Carrie Lambe.

'Oh, it's this damned show we're starting next
month. It's proving very messy.'

Linda frowned. 'That's the show you hired Carrie
to work on?'

'Yes, unfortunately.' Jonathan smiled his thanks as
Marie set a mug on the desk in front of him.

Linda felt her stomach churn. 'Isn't she working
out?'

Jonathan laughed. 'Oh yes, too bloody well! She's
only ganging up with my producer and presenter and
telling me how to do my job. Underneath that quiet

exterior lurks a strong-minded, stubborn crusader. God, as if I need another one!'

'So are you going to fire her?'

Jonathan looked surprised. 'Lord, no, she's great!'

Linda breathed a sigh of relief. 'I'm afraid you've lost me.'

He grinned at her. 'Oh, don't mind me, Linda. I'm actually here to talk to you about hiring another recruit for the show.'

Linda brightened and picked up her pen. 'Really?'

'Yes. We need someone with experience. This show is turning out to be an ethical, not to mention legal, quagmire. I want someone on the team who knows the pitfalls.'

Linda frowned. 'Are you talking about another researcher or producer?'

He shook his head. 'No, the title I've come up with is Programme Co-ordinator. I'm doing my best to be politically correct.'

'That's not like you.' Linda laughed.

'No,' he agreed, 'but like I say, the troops are turning nasty. Now, the kind of person I'm looking for isn't going to be on your books.'

Linda put down her pen. 'You have someone specific in mind?'

Jonathan's eyes twinkled. 'Ben Donnelly is his name. He works for the talk show on Dublin FM.'

Linda scribbled down the name. 'I'll need a job spec and terms from you.'

Jonathan produced an envelope from his breast pocket. 'Everything you need to know is in there.'

'Great. I'll get right on it.'

Jonathan glanced at his watch. 'It can wait until tomorrow. Let's go for a drink.'

'I'm sorry, I can't. I've got a mountain of work to do.' Her voice trailed off as Cheryl and Bill arrived back into the office.

'Jonathan, good to see you.' Bill came over to shake hands.

Cheryl tripped after him and shot Jonathan a flirtatious look. 'I hope Linda has been looking after you.'

'As always.' Jonathan smiled politely. 'In fact I was just trying to persuade her to join me for a drink. She's been working way too hard.'

'Of course you must go, Linda,' Bill said expansively. 'It's nearly five o'clock.'

Cheryl smiled eagerly at them. 'We could all go.'

'I'm afraid not, dear,' Bill said firmly and rolled his eyes at Jonathan. 'We've spent the afternoon looking at curtains.'

'Hardly all afternoon,' Cheryl protested, looking cross.

'Nevertheless we need to make up the time. But please, Linda, you go on.' He smiled kindly and patted her hand. 'It will do you good.'

'That's settled then.' Jonathan handed her her coat. 'Let's go.'

16

'Do you always get your own way?' Linda asked when they were sitting in the corner of a wine bar in Dawson Street.

'Pretty much,' Jonathan said cheerfully. 'Except when my staff gang up on me.'

Linda saw the look of exasperation that crossed his face. 'What's the problem?'

He sighed. 'They're worried that we're getting in way above our heads.'

'And are you?'

'Possibly,' he admitted. 'Karl Thompson, our producer, has a lot of experience in radio. When he gets worried I get worried.'

'And that's why you want to hire Ben Donnelly?'

He nodded. 'The Dublin FM talk show covers some extremely controversial topics.'

'I see. Do you think he'll be willing to jump ship?'

'For the money I'm offering, absolutely. They haven't looked after him very well over there. He doesn't even have a proper title, although he seems to pretty much run things.'

Linda sipped her Chardonnay. 'You seem to be very well informed.'

Jonathan smiled. 'It's important to know your competition.'

'And would your competition put on a show like this one?' she countered.

He frowned. 'They haven't so far, but we have to take a chance. The only way to beat them in the ratings is to do something radical.'

'You're making me very curious. What exactly is this show about?'

Jonathan gazed at her solemnly. 'I could tell you, but then I'd have to kill you.'

Linda laughed. 'But I'm your recruitment consultant. You must treat me like a priest. You can tell me anything and I will take it to the grave.'

Jonathan studied her intently. 'Anything?'

Linda shifted uncomfortably. 'Well anything relating to your business. I'm not sure I could handle the rest.'

Jonathan threw back his head and laughed. 'Are you afraid I might shock you?'

'I'm too old to be shocked by anything,' Linda assured him.

'How are things at home?' he asked gently.

Linda stared into her glass. 'What do you mean?'

'Well, the last time we talked you and your husband had quarrelled.'

Linda laughed shakily. 'No, actually, the last time we talked my husband had just walked out on me.'

Jonathan's eyes darkened with concern. 'Linda, I'm sorry. Why didn't you say something?'

Linda looked at him, her eyes bright with tears. 'That wouldn't be very professional now, would it?'

'What happened? I'm sorry,' he added quickly. 'You probably don't want to talk about it.'

Linda shrugged nonchalantly as the wine started to take effect. 'I don't mind. It's a story you'll probably be familiar with. Patrick has traded me in for a younger model.' She stared at him, her eyes cold. 'You two have quite a lot in common.'

Jonathan watched her steadily. 'You shouldn't believe everything you read in the papers.'

Linda laughed. 'Oh, come on, Jonathan. You hardly live like a monk. And most of the girls you're photographed with don't look old enough to vote.'

'I work in the media, Linda. People look at me and see Forever FM. It's the same for Maeve Elliot. That's why I fork out an outrageous amount of money on her wardrobe. The young people want to see her out on the town, meeting celebrities – that's what it's all about.'

'And you too?' she said quietly.

'And me too,' he agreed.

'And God forbid if you were photographed with someone your own age.' Her look was withering.

'I know you've been hurt, Linda,' he said patiently. 'But why are you attacking me? I thought we were friends.'

Linda banged down her glass, slopping wine across the table. 'Because you're all the bloody same,' she cried and grabbing her bag she ran to the ladies' room before she broke down and made a complete fool of herself. She locked herself in a cubicle, had a good cry and then emerged, still shaking, to study her sad, blotched face in the mirror. God, what would Jonathan think of her? Of all people to preach to she had to choose her best client. She wondered if he'd left by now or was he waiting for her to return so that he could tell her she was fired. She opened her bag and took out her make-up bag. She would only be able to deal with this if she was looking her best – although that wasn't exactly possible with puffy, bloodshot eyes. She took slow steady breaths as she carried out the repair work and after brushing her hair and dabbing on some perfume she went back outside with her head held high.

Jonathan stood up as she approached. 'Feeling better?'

Linda nodded warily and sat down. 'I'm sorry. I had no right to speak to you like that.'

Jonathan groaned. 'Oh, God, no, not formal civility, I don't think I can handle that!'

Linda grinned. 'Sorry.'

'If you apologise one more time you're not getting another drink,' he warned her.

Linda sighed. 'Then I'll shut up right away because I could really use one. I'm turning into a terrible lush, Jonathan. I hate to think how much wine I've got through since Patrick left.'

'And are you doing all of this drinking alone?' he asked gravely.

It was Linda's turn to groan. 'Oh, don't you start. I'm getting plenty of lectures from my mother and sister.'

'Okay, my turn to say sorry.' He smiled as the

waitress appeared with another bottle. 'Now, let's get drunk.'

Linda raised an eyebrow. 'Am I allowed to?'

'I only object to you drinking *alone*,' he said solemnly. 'I'm quite happy to keep you company any time.'

'As long as there are no photographers around,' she retorted and then stared at him, crestfallen. 'Oh, sorry, that just slipped out.'

He shook his head, a sad smile playing around his lips. 'I had no idea that you had such a low opinion of me.'

'I don't!' She stared at him in dismay. 'Oh, God, maybe I should just go home.'

'And leave me drinking alone? What about my image?'

'You wouldn't be alone for long,' Linda said drily.

'You're doing it again,' he warned. 'Casting aspersions on my character.'

'No, actually, I'm paying you a compliment. You attract women like flies, you must realise that.'

'Not always necessarily a good thing,' he muttered, 'but thanks for the compliment. I think.'

'Why did your marriage break up?' she asked curiously.

Jonathan looked off into the distance. 'I'm not sure I remember. It was a very long time ago.'

'Rubbish,' Linda retorted, swinging her glass around precariously. 'No one forgets something like that.'

'You're more perceptive when you're sober, Linda. I'm trying to tell you that I don't want to talk about it.'

'Oh.'

'Let's talk about Patrick instead. Tell me about this new woman in his life.'

Linda snorted. 'Woman! She's only a kid – eighteen years his junior. It's disgusting.'

'Indeed.' Jonathan nodded gravely.

'Don't laugh at me,' Linda warned.

Jonathan leaned across and brushed her fringe out of her eyes. 'Oh, believe me, Linda, I'm not laughing at you.'

Linda sat perfectly still, conscious of the light touch of his fingers that were now stroking the side of her cheek.

'He's a stupid man,' he murmured.

Linda moved self-consciously away from his touch. 'So everyone keeps saying, but he seems to be having a ball.'

'At the moment. It will take him a while to realise his mistake.'

'Is that the voice of experience talking?'

'Stop probing, Linda,' he said easily. 'You're wasting your time. Let's order some food.'

'I'm not hungry.'

'You'll need some food inside you if you're going to keep up with me,' he assured her.

'Two bottles of wine? That's nothing,' Linda scoffed.

'And champagne to follow.' He stopped a passing waiter and asked for the menu and wine list.

'This is hardly a celebration.' Linda cupped her face in her hands and looked glum.

'Of course it's a celebration,' he insisted, thanking the waiter as he was handed the menus. 'There's always something to celebrate.'

Linda eyed him stubbornly. 'Like what?'

He shrugged. 'Like the fact that I've asked you to hire another employee for me, which means a nice fat juicy commission for you.'

'Why aren't you going to talk to this guy direct?' she asked suspiciously. 'Are you just feeling sorry for me? Giving me this job out of pity?'

Jonathan chuckled. 'You really can't hold your drink, Linda, can you? If you think about it you'll realise that I asked you to talk to Ben *before* I knew anything about your circumstances.'

'Oh. Right.' Linda shot him an embarrassed smile but he was engrossed in the wine list.

'Look at your menu,' he instructed without looking up.

'You really are very bossy,' she complained.

He shot her a beguiling smile. 'Masterful, I think you mean.'

'I know what I mean,' she told him and turned her attention to the menu. As she scanned it she realised that she was actually very hungry. And some food might avoid a horrendous hangover in the morning.

'What's it to be?' he asked.

'I haven't decided yet.'

'I'll order for us both.'

'You most certainly will not. I'm not one of your brainless bimbos. I'm quite capable of making my own decisions.'

'Well, could I ask you to make them tonight?' he drawled.

She closed the menu with an angry snap. 'Mussels followed by chicken.'

He beamed at her. 'Excellent choice. I think I'll have the same.'

Linda gazed at him mystified as he ordered the food and a bottle of champagne. The man was a mass of contradictions; she didn't know where she was with him from one minute to the next. But he certainly wasn't boring. Now that she'd had a cry and a few glasses of wine, she was feeling better. Maybe she should just relax and enjoy his company. God only knew when she'd be out with a man again.

'You've got that faraway look in your eye again,' he commented.

'I was just thinking that it will probably be a very long time before I go out to dinner with another man,' she answered honestly.

'I don't see why.'

'Unattached men of our age are hardly numerous,' she pointed out. 'And unlike you, I prefer the company of my own age group.'

'I think that's a very blinkered attitude. You might meet a wonderful octogenarian with a nice smile and a big wallet.'

Linda watched him carefully, trying to figure out if he was serious. She was finding it harder to tell the more she drank. 'I don't need money,' she said with dignity.

'Lucky you,' he said cheerfully. 'You see, I told

you there were things to celebrate. You're a self-made woman and indispensable to Bill Reeve.'

'No one is indispensable as I've just found out.'

'Oh, here we go again. You know, I really hate self-pity.'

'Sorry for boring you,' she said, hurt.

He leaned across the table and kissed her cheek. 'You're not boring me, Linda. I'm just trying to make you see that it's not the end of the world. You're successful, young—'

'Not by your standards!'

'And you're beautiful,' he finished, ignoring the barb.

Linda blushed. 'Save your chat-up lines for your girlfriends, they're wasted on me.'

He looked at her reproachfully. 'I was just trying to cheer you up.'

Impulsively, Linda leaned over and hugged him. 'I'm sorry, Jonathan. I'm being an awful cow.'

'Well, well, well. Look who's here.' Linda looked up to see her mother standing over them. 'Aren't you going to introduce me?'

17

Linda sat fidgeting, trying to ignore the fact that her mother was staring at them from the table across the room.

'Are you going to tell me what that was all about?' Jonathan asked when the waiter had poured their champagne and left. 'She seemed to think that you and I were an item.'

Linda laughed nervously. 'Oh, you know mothers.'

'I think there's more to it than that.'

Linda pushed away her mussels. 'This is so embarrassing.'

Jonathan took a piece of French bread and dipped it into his sauce. 'I'm really curious now.'

'I met Patrick with his new girlfriend last week. They were walking along the beach – the same stretch where Patrick and I always walked.'

'Oh, poor Linda,' he murmured and took her hand.

'It really got to me. I couldn't believe he'd do that. Anyway, I hurled some abuse at Stacey and then we had a bit of a quarrel and then I—'

'You?'

She sighed. 'I told him that I'd been unfaithful too.

I hinted that it was a regular thing and I'd been at it for years.'

Jonathan arched an eyebrow. 'Linda Jewell, I'm shocked.'

'It wasn't true,' she protested. 'Anyway, it's Taylor,' she added grimly. 'It's going to be Linda Taylor from now on.'

'So, does your mother think I'm your lover?'

Linda reddened. 'Probably. I mean, I told her that none of it was true but then I also told her I didn't want anything to do with men from now on. And . . .' She sighed.

'And?'

'She asked me to come out tonight and I told her I wasn't in a sociable mood.'

Jonathan chuckled. 'And then she comes in and sees you sitting drinking champagne with me. She'll never believe you now. Who else knows what you told Patrick?'

Linda shrugged. 'Whoever he's told – oh, and my sister.' She groaned. 'Viv will be convinced there's something going on.'

The waiter cleared their starters away and another appeared with two plates of chicken. Linda doubted she could eat anything at this stage.

Jonathan helped himself to some vegetables and cut into his chicken. 'Oh, come on, it's not the end of the world. You really should eat something. This chicken is gorgeous.'

Linda obediently put a tiny piece of chicken into her mouth and chewed mechanically.

'So what are you going to do now?'

'Firstly, tell my mother that she's got the wrong end of the stick.'

Jonathan glanced over at her mother's table and raised his glass in a toast when he caught her staring back at him. 'Why don't you just brazen it out? Let her and everyone else think that we're an item.'

Linda gasped. 'You are joking.'

He shrugged. 'It's an obvious solution.'

'But who's going to believe us? You're always out with different women.'

'Which is an excellent cover if I've been seeing a married woman,' he pointed out.

'But isn't there anyone special that's going to get hurt?'

Jonathan shrugged. 'I haven't had a steady relationship since I split up with Alison.'

'But why?' Linda asked curiously, forgetting her own problems for the moment.

'Because that's the way I want it,' he said briskly and Linda realised he did not intend to tell her any more.

'What about your son?'

'Daniel? What about him?'

'Won't he be upset?'

Jonathan laughed. 'Daniel and I have a deal. I always tell him the truth and he promises to ignore any gossip he hears about me.'

'So what would you tell him about me?'

Jonathan smiled. 'I would tell him that you're a very dear friend that I've known for a long time. I would tell him that you've recently split up with your husband, that you're very sad and that you need someone to look after you for a while.'

Linda swallowed back the tears. 'It's very good of you, Jonathan, but I really don't see how we can carry this off. It's one thing convincing a child but we'll never be able to convince anyone else.'

'I never had you down as such a defeatist,' Jonathan murmured.

'I'm not but this whole stunt is ridiculous. I should never have lied to Patrick in the first place.'

'Don't be so hard on yourself,' Jonathan said gently, taking her hand. 'You've had a rough time and it's natural to hit out when you're hurt.'

'That's no excuse. No, I've made up my mind. I'm going to put a stop to this before I make an even bigger fool of myself.'

'No, you can't do that. I won't let you.'

Linda raised an eyebrow. 'You won't let me?'

He grinned. 'No. I refuse to be jilted. We've only just got together.'

'Only in my mother's imagination,' Linda pointed out.

Jonathan's eyes twinkled back at her. 'Oh, I don't know. I think you've always secretly fancied me.'

'Then I must need a lobotomy,' Linda said drily.

'You really know how to hurt a man's feelings,' Jonathan sighed.

Linda smiled. 'I don't think anyone is capable of hurting Jonathan Blake's feelings.'

He looked thoughtful. 'Everyone gets hurt sometime, Linda, and I'm no exception.'

'I'm sorry.' Linda reddened. God, he was being so nice to her and all she'd done in return was put him down. 'I appreciate what you want to do for me but I don't think it would work.'

'Tell you what. Let's eat our dinner, enjoy the rest of our evening and worry about it tomorrow. We've had way too much to drink to discuss it sensibly now, anyway.'

'Fair enough.' Linda moved her food around the plate half-heartedly.

'You know, you don't look like a woman in love,' Jonathan teased.

'Which proves my point. How am I going to convince anyone that we're having an affair?'

'Now, now, we said we weren't going to discuss it any more.'

'You brought it up,' she retorted.

He leaned across and took her hand. 'No, I just said that you don't look like a woman in love. So for your mother's sake, why don't you try and look at me as if I'm important to you?'

Linda looked at his black eyes, dark, tightly cropped hair – there was a definite resemblance to George Clooney and thought that it would be very easy to care about Jonathan Blake. And very unlikely that he would care about her in return. Still, he'd been wonderful this evening and she wouldn't forget that. She smiled at him and leaned forward to kiss his cheek. 'Is that better?' she murmured.

Jonathan, looking slightly startled, said, 'It's a good start.'

Linda grinned. 'Maybe I should go into acting.'

Jonathan's smile faltered. 'Yes, maybe you should.'

They finished their meal and while Jonathan was paying the bill, Linda crossed to her mother's table to say goodnight.

'Not interested in men, eh?'

'It's not what you think, Mum.'

'You keep telling me that, darling, but I think you protest too much.'

Linda kissed her cheek. 'I'll call you tomorrow.'

'Make sure you do. I want to know everything. Who'd have thought it? Jonathan Blake of all people.'

Linda glanced at the other women at the table, who were doing their best to appear engrossed in conversation and listen in at the same time. 'Not now, Mum. We'll talk tomorrow. 'Bye.'

She rejoined Jonathan, who waved at her mother and escorted Linda to the door.

'You shouldn't encourage her,' Linda complained.

He took her arm and steered her towards a taxi rank. 'So do you think she'd like me for a son-in-law?'

'I think she'd approve of anyone after Patrick.'

'Thanks a lot,' Jonathan said drily.

Linda laughed. 'Sorry.'

'So she didn't like your husband?'

'She just didn't think we were suited. My sister, Viv, says that it was because he was too quiet and secretive.' She gave a hollow laugh. 'It looks like she was right. He managed to keep his girlfriend a secret for three years.'

Jonathan stopped. 'Three years!'

Linda nodded and tugged him on down the street. 'Now do you understand why I feel so humiliated?'

Jonathan hugged her against him and kissed her hair. 'Poor Linda.'

'Oh, don't say that,' she wailed. 'That's exactly what I don't want to hear. Poor Linda. Poor *old* Linda.'

Jonathan stopped again and turned her to face him. 'Exactly how old are you?'

'Thirty-eight,' she murmured.

'Right, well, I'm a year older than you so no more derogatory comments about age.'

'It's different for men,' Linda assured him. 'You're seen as more attractive, more intelligent, more bloody everything the older you get. Women are on the scrap heap once they pass thirty-five.'

'What about Madonna, Sharon Stone, Tina Turner, for God's sake.'

Linda gave him a withering look. 'I'm a recruitment consultant, not a celebrity.'

Jonathan allowed her to pull him towards a waiting taxi. 'I think it's all in your mind. If you think you're old and you keep telling people that you're old then that's exactly what they'll think. Go and get your belly button pierced, dye your hair red, get a tattoo. You need to snap out of this.'

She turned to smile at him before climbing into the car. 'Do you know, you'd get on really well with my little sister.'

18

Maeve rested one booted foot on top of the other on the edge of Karl's desk. 'Any other ideas?' she asked without much enthusiasm.

Karl screwed a page into a ball and tossed it into the bin. 'Nope.'

'So what now?'

He shrugged. 'We go along with Jonny boy's idea.'

'But it's madness.'

'It's all we've got,' he pointed out. 'And now that the advertising has started there's no way out.'

Maeve groaned. 'God, this could finish us both in radio for good.'

Karl lit a cigarette and grinned at her through the smoke. 'You'll live to fight another day, Maeve. And you've got to remember that you're still going to be the one in control.' Karl stubbed out his cigarette and stood up. 'And now, after such a hard day's work, I'm going to the pub.'

'It's only twelve o'clock,' Maeve said drily.

He grinned down at her. 'So I'll have a sandwich and call it lunch. Good day!'

'Well, at least when we do a show on alcoholics we'll have a resident expert,' Maeve called after him.

Karl waved without turning round, swung out the door and down the narrow corridor.

Maeve laughed and picked up the page with the first ten show titles on it. As she scanned it she realised that Karl was right. She was in control. It was important to get the first show right to get the listeners – and Jonathan – on side. The more she thought about it the more she was sure the one to go for was the young girl with HIV. Though a controversial topic, the girl had got the disease through no fault of her own. Her mother had been totally out of her head one night and left a needle lying around. The girl – then only five – had decided to play doctors and nurses and accidentally pricked her finger. At the tender age of thirteen, she had been diagnosed as HIV positive. Now, at seventeen, she was afraid to tell anyone her secret for fear of being shunned by her friends – especially her boyfriend. Maeve was convinced it would be a riveting show. It showed that they could deal with serious topics.

She turned to her PC and quickly typed up a memo to Jonathan and Karl, putting forward her proposal.

When she'd finished, she checked her watch and on impulse picked up the phone and dialled her aunt Peggy.

'Hello?'

'Peggy, it's me.'

'Maeve, love! Lovely to hear from you.'

'Sorry it's been so long, I've been up to my eyes.'

'With this new show? I'm so excited about it. I've told all my friends to listen in.'

'I hope they're not disappointed.'

'You're on it: how could they be disappointed?'

Maeve smiled. If only her mother was as affectionate as her aunt.

'I was over with your mother this morning,' Peggy said as if reading her thoughts.

'Oh, yeah? How is she?'

'Oh, fine. You should call her.'

'Yeah, I will. Listen I'd better go, Peggy. I have a meeting.'

'Okay, love. Thanks for the call. Take care of yourself.'

Maeve hung up the phone with a sigh. She'd enjoy her conversations with her aunt a lot more if they didn't have to discuss Laura every time.

She put her mother to the back of her mind and went to find Carrie. The girl, as usual, was buried under a mountain of post. 'Hey, Carrie.'

Carrie glanced up. 'Hi, Maeve.'

'I need you to do something for me.'

'Sure.' Carrie nodded eagerly.

'I want you to pull out any letters relating to AIDS. Bring them to me at six o'clock and I'll pick the ones I want you to follow up.'

Carrie's smile faltered.

Maeve frowned. 'Is that a problem?'

'No, no problem,' Carrie said brightly.

'Fine. I'll see you later then.'

★   ★   ★

'Why didn't you tell her you were going home early?' Karen asked. 'She uses you, you know that, don't you?'

Carrie laughed. 'That's good coming from you!'

Karen looked suitably shamefaced. 'Don't start that again. I told you that Jackie and I were just having a laugh. You have to expect that kind of thing on your first day.'

'I know.' Carrie smiled. It had been a great relief when she'd found out that Jackie and Karen had just been pulling her leg about the extent of her duties. Since then the three of them had got on just fine although, privately, Carrie thought that Jackie was terribly lazy. She did as little work as she could get away with and was always on the phone to her friends.

'This show sounds like heavy stuff,' Karen said, dragging her back to the present.

'Yes.' Carrie kept her head down. Karl had warned her not to discuss the programme but it wasn't easy around someone as curious as Karen.

'It sounds like Maeve is setting herself up as another Miriam O'Callaghan.'

Carrie smiled. She knew Maeve would be thrilled to be compared to the presenter of RTE's current affairs programme. 'Maeve's great. I think she'll really go places. It's one thing to be clever, but with her looks as well . . .' Carrie had successfully diverted Karen's thoughts from the *Secrets* programme.

'Yeah, she is gorgeous, isn't she? But she's such a bitch.'

'I don't think so,' Carrie said loyally.

'You don't know her as well as I do,' Karen warned. 'I'm telling you she's only interested in Number One.'

'I suppose you have to be like that if you want to make it to the top.'

Karen shrugged. 'I don't understand it myself. I don't care how much money she earns, I wouldn't want her job.'

Carrie suppressed a grin. 'No?'

'No way.' Karen was emphatic. 'Talk about unsociable hours.'

'It doesn't seem to stop her socialising.' Carrie nodded at the copy of *VIP* on the desk. As usual, Maeve's face was splashed all over the social pages.

'Yes, but that's just it. She's always on show. She couldn't go out with the girls on a Friday night and get sozzled now, could she?'

Carrie couldn't imagine Maeve wanting to, but Karen wouldn't want to hear that. 'I suppose.' She stood up and put on her coat. 'I'm going for a sandwich. Do you want anything?'

'Ooh, yes please.'

After Karen had given her order, Carrie went up and knocked on Karl and Maeve's office door. Maeve was alone and on the phone. 'Want anything in the shops?' she whispered.

Maeve shook her head and covered the mouthpiece with her hand. 'No, thanks, Carrie; I'm going out to lunch.'

Carrie nodded and closed the door gently. Of course, she was off out to lunch. To some very exclusive restaurant with another gorgeous man, no doubt.

Carrie sighed as she turned up the collar of her coat and went out into the cold. She wasn't sure that she shared Karen's feelings. She wouldn't mind stepping into Maeve's shoes for a while. Her life seemed very glamorous when compared to her own. Not that she was unhappy, Carrie quickly reminded herself. She had a great job, she was well paid, what more could she want? A partner who smiled occasionally, she thought as she trudged on. Declan had been getting more and more moody lately and he was going to be furious when he heard that she wasn't coming home today. He was finishing work at five and Carrie had promised that they would have the whole evening together and she would cook them something special. But now that she had to meet Maeve it was unlikely she'd be home before eight. Oh well, he'd just have to make do with takeaway. Again. Carrie went into the shop and joined the queue at the deli counter. She wasn't looking forward to giving Declan the bad news. He probably wouldn't talk to her for days. Maybe she should work late and let him eat his pizza alone. She was getting heartily sick of the arguments. Declan did nothing but complain about the hours she worked and he'd no interest in how she was doing. Any time she tried to talk to him about her day he either cut her off because he wanted to watch something on TV or his eyes glazed over with boredom. It hurt. Carrie had always tried to show an interest in his job, surely he could do the same? They were a couple, after all. Isn't that what couples did? Discuss their day, their dreams, their future? Carrie gave her order to the girl behind the counter and watched as she slapped turkey and mayonnaise on to a baguette. Why had she got so down? She could be serving behind that counter, buttering endless rolls for an ungrateful public, whereas instead she had this fantastic job. She paid for the food, thanking the girl profusely. She should stop feeling sorry for herself and be grateful for her good luck. It was just that it would be nice if Declan shared her happiness. Orla was always asking her about Forever FM and Helen seemed interested too, but it wasn't the same. Sometimes she found herself deliberately avoiding talking about the radio station with Declan because it usually resulted in a row. That wasn't right. If he loved her he wouldn't make her feel like that. He'd be happy for her even if it meant making a few sacrifices. 'Ah, there's the rub,' she murmured to herself. Did he love her? In fact, did she love him? It was a question she usually avoided asking herself. They suited each other, they were comfortable together, they wanted the same things – well, most of the time. But was that enough? At the moment, Carrie admitted, her personal life was miserable, but had it ever been fantastic? Had it ever been what she'd dreamed of? Had the earth ever moved? Carrie groaned as her thoughts turned to their sex life. It had never been wild but it was pleasant enough. But nowadays she often made excuses not to have sex. And, she realised, that was another thing. She used to think of it as making love. Now it was just sex. That had to mean something. She reached Forever FM and pushed open the door.

Karen was sitting at the desk. 'Oh, goody, I'm starving.'

Carrie took a sandwich and Mars Bar out of the bag and handed it to Karen with her change. 'See you later.' As she headed back to her desk, Maeve sailed by her with a casual wave. 'See you this evening.'

Carrie smiled. 'Have a nice lunch.'

Paul came back into the bedroom, sat down beside her and trailed kisses down her back. Maeve smiled lazily and turned around. 'I don't usually indulge in dessert after lunch.'

'A little of what you fancy does you good.' Paul's voice was muffled as he buried his head in between her small breasts.

Maeve pushed him off and sat up. 'And you've had more than a little. Time to get back to work.'

Paul kissed her soundly on the lips, snaking his hands through her hair. 'We've got plenty of time yet.'

Maeve pulled away reluctantly. 'Sorry. I've really got to go.'

Paul rolled out of bed and started to dress. 'How about dinner?'

Maeve slipped on her bra. 'I'll be in the office all evening.'

'Then lunch again tomorrow?' He winked at her in the mirror as he put on his tie.

'I'll check my diary.' Maeve put on her jeans and pulled a T-shirt over her head.

Paul frowned. 'Not getting tired of me, are you?'

Maeve pulled him to her and pushed his shirt open again. 'What do you think?'

19

'I'll see you at one then.'

Linda sighed. 'There's really no need, Jonathan.'

'Of course there is. I want to see Cheryl's face.' He chuckled.

'You're not supposed to be enjoying this so much,' Linda complained.

Jonathan had already left three messages that morning, two of them with Cheryl. Linda had spent her morning avoiding her. As she put down the phone she saw Cheryl bearing down on her.

'Well, you're a dark sheep and no mistake.'

'Horse,' Linda corrected automatically.

'Whatever.' Cheryl waved her red talons around and perched on Linda's desk. 'So how long has this being going on? Tell Aunty Cheryl everything.'

'There's nothing to tell.'

'Oh, come on, Lin, this is no time to be coy. How long have you and Jonathan been seeing each other?'

'Not long.'

Cheryl's eyes widened. 'Gosh! Were you seeing him while you were still with Patrick?'

Linda looked away. 'Cheryl, please.'

'My God, it's true, isn't it? Does Patrick know?'

'There's nothing to know. Anyway, Patrick isn't exactly sitting at home pining, is he?'

Cheryl's eyes sparkled. She was never happier than when she was gossiping. 'No, I couldn't believe it when I saw him with that Stacey. She's very pretty, isn't she?'

'I can't say I noticed.'

'Oh, she is. I wonder what she sees in him?'

'Thanks for your sensitivity, Cheryl.'

Cheryl slapped her hand playfully and laughed. 'Oh, what do you care, Lin, when you've got a fine thing like Jonathan Blake? You're the envy of every red-blooded woman in the country!'

Linda smiled weakly. If they knew the truth she wouldn't be envied, she'd be a laughing stock.

'But they won't know the truth,' Jonathan had pointed out over an alcohol-free lunch the day after they'd bumped into her mother.

Linda had been adamant they forget the whole thing. 'No one is ever going to believe it. We are the most unlikely couple.'

'I don't see why. We're the same age, we come from similar backgrounds, and we have lots in common.'

Linda had blinked. 'Name one thing.'

'We're both good liars.'

'But that's just it. I don't think I'm good enough to pull this off.'

'Sure you are. Aren't you always telling silly sods like me that you've got the perfect candidate for the job?'

'And I usually do,' Linda had protested.

He had grinned at her. 'Ah, usually, but not always. Oh, come on, Linda, it will be a laugh.'

'This is my life, Jonathan, not a sitcom!'

His smile had disappeared. 'I'm just trying to help.'

'I know and I really do appreciate it. I just don't think it's going to work.'

'Of course it will,' he'd said confidently and Linda found herself caving in.

'So where's he taking you?' Cheryl was asking now.

'What? Oh, the Chilli Club.'

Cheryl giggled. 'Nothing like a bit of spice, although I would have thought you two would have enough of that.'

Linda dived under the desk for her bag. 'I'd better go and get ready, he'll be here in a minute.'

'I have a new red lipstick if you'd like to try it,' Cheryl offered.

'Eh, no, thanks all the same, red doesn't really suit me.'

Cheryl scrutinised Linda's pale face with a practised eye. 'No, I suppose not. You go ahead and make yourself beautiful. Take your time. I'll keep Jonathan entertained.'

You wish, Linda thought with a wry grin as she went out to the ladies'. When she returned, Jonathan was sitting on the edge of her desk and Cheryl was sitting in her chair fluttering her considerable eyelashes at him.

Jonathan stood up. 'Linda, hi, are you ready to go?'

'All ready.'

Cheryl looked disappointed. 'Oh, there's no need to rush off.'

'Sorry, Cheryl, but we're meeting my sister.'

Jonathan smiled apologetically. 'Don't want to keep family waiting, you know how it is.'

Cheryl smiled back. 'Of course, you two go and have fun. No need to rush back, Linda. I'll square it with Bill.'

Linda gasped as Jonathan steered her out of the office. 'God, the effect you have on some women!'

'Cheryl's not so bad.'

Linda raised an eyebrow. 'Is that why you looked so relieved when I came in?'

Jonathan laughed. 'All right then, she scares the living daylights out of me. How on earth did someone as quiet as Bill end up with her?'

'I have a theory about that,' Linda told him as they walked up Grafton Street. 'I think she must have proposed one night when he was drunk and she never shut up long enough for him to refuse ever since.'

'Sounds reasonable. So what have you told Viv about us?'

'The truth. I couldn't handle lying to her.'

'Will she like me?'

Linda looked at him in surprise. 'Does it matter?'

'Well, no, I don't suppose it does.' He looked slightly flushed. 'It would just be a lot easier if she did.'

'I'm sure she'll like you,' Linda assured him as they turned the corner and she saw her sister standing outside the restaurant. 'Viv!'

Viv turned and smiled.

'You're early,' Linda accused.

'Well, it's not every day I get to meet your lover.' She held out a hand to Jonathan and smiled. 'Hi.'

Jonathan took it. 'Nice to meet you, Viv.'

Linda looked from one to the other and thought what a good match they would make. It would be nice if something real came out of all this make-believe, and nothing would make her happier than to see her sister settle down with a nice man. Jonathan wasn't exactly reliable, Linda was the first to admit, but Viv could well be the woman to tame him.

After they'd ordered, Viv took charge. 'So, Jonathan, how exactly did you get roped into all of this?'

Jonathan explained about the night they'd bumped into Rosemary.

Viv watched him suspiciously. 'Are you sure that's all there is to it?'

Linda groaned. 'Oh, don't you start, Viv.'

'Well, it's just that you seem very comfortable together.'

'Jonathan and I have known each other for over two years,' Linda pointed out.

'So you're friends.'

Jonathan nodded. 'I'd like to think so.'

Linda smiled nervously. 'Of course – well, most of the time. When he isn't complaining about my commission.'

They laughed and Viv watched them. 'Okay, then. So what did you tell Mum?'

Linda rolled her eyes. 'I didn't get much of a chance

to say anything. She put two and two together and came up with five the minute she saw us together.'

'And Linda was in no condition to explain,' Jonathan added.

'I wasn't that drunk,' Linda objected.

Jonathan grinned at Viv. 'Pissed as a newt.'

Viv grinned back, warming to him more by the minute. 'And have you talked to her since?'

'I've been avoiding her,' Linda admitted.

Viv shrugged. 'Well, that's not such a bad thing. She'd expect you to be embarrassed.'

'True,' Linda agreed. 'Listen, can we order? I'm really hungry.'

'Me too,' Viv agreed and studied her menu. 'But remember, this is a working lunch.'

Linda nodded wearily. 'I thought it might be.'

When they had ordered and were sipping their wine – Linda stuck to water – Jonathan studied the two sisters. 'Explain to me again why you're keeping your mother in the dark.'

Linda and Viv looked sheepishly at each other. 'She'd be disgusted with me,' Linda said at last.

'She would,' Viv assured him.

'But why? She seemed pleased enough to see us together that night.'

'That's because she thought it was for real,' Linda explained. 'She'd be horrified if she knew the truth.'

'Mum is a bit of a feminist,' Viv chipped in. 'She doesn't believe you need a man for anything. She'd be disgusted at Linda going out with you just because she's been dumped.'

'Thanks,' Linda said glumly.

Viv patted her hand. 'And if she thinks Linda has in fact been having a bit of nooky too, she'll be delighted.'

'Rosemary's not your typical Irish mother,' Linda told him.

'I think she's great,' Jonathan replied. 'And I've only met her once.'

'Yes, well, she is of course, just not very . . . conventional.'

He grinned. 'That's probably why I like her.'

'So we're agreed. Mum is to be kept in the dark?' Viv looked at her sister.

'I think so. But it will only work if this relationship breaks up very soon. My nerves won't hold out much longer.'

'Wimp,' Viv said affectionately and turned her attention to the food that was being set out in front of them. 'Oh, yum, this looks gorgeous.'

After they'd piled food on to their plates Viv returned to the subject. 'When you break up Linda should dump you.'

'Fine,' Jonathan said through a mouthful of spicy chicken.

Linda looked at Jonathan's handsome features and sighed. 'Not very likely, is it?'

Viv scowled at her. 'Oh, for God's sake, Linda, don't be such a doormat.'

Linda glared back. 'I'm just stating the obvious. Everyone knows the kind of women Jonathan usually dates. They're never going to believe that I dumped him. They're going to think that he's finally come to his senses. We should forget the whole thing. We'll tell Mum the truth. I'll call her as soon as I get back to the office.'

'And what about Bill and Cheryl?' Jonathan asked.

'And Patrick,' Viv added, helping herself to more lamb.

Linda sat back in her chair and closed her eyes. Viv and Jonathan exchanged worried looks. He stood up. 'Excuse me for a moment.'

Viv pushed her plate away and looked at her sister. 'Are you okay?'

'No. Whatever happens I'm going to look pathetic. I mean, what must Jonathan think of me?'

'From where I'm standing, I'd say he really likes you. Everyone likes you, Lin. You're strong, pretty, clever—'

'And alone.'

'There's nothing wrong with being alone, take it from me.'

Linda sighed. 'It's not the same – you're alone by choice. I've been half of a couple for fifteen years. All of my friends are Patrick's friends too. And they're all couples.'

'So now you can bring Jonathan along instead of Patrick.'

'And sit opposite him and Stacey, very cosy.' Linda's voice was flat and cold.

'Oh, come on, Linda, you've still got me and Mum.'

Linda smiled sadly. 'Yes, and I wish I'd remembered that before I told Patrick that stupid lie.'

'It wasn't your best move,' Viv agreed. 'In fact it's more the kind of thing I'd do.'

'Except you and Jonathan would pull it off no problem.'

'And so can you. All you need to do is change your attitude.'

Linda looked longingly at the bottle of wine and took a sip of water. 'Really.'

'Yes, it's a case of nerve, of bravado, of sheer hard neck.'

Jonathan rejoined them and sat down. 'Someone talking about me?'

'I'm trying to persuade Linda that you two can carry this off if she's just more . . . more . . .' Viv waved her hands around in exasperation as she searched for the right word.

'Bolshie?' Jonathan suggested.

Viv beamed at him. 'Exactly!'

Linda abandoned her good intentions and reached for the wine. 'You're both wasting your time. This isn't going to work.'

'Sure it will,' Jonathan said easily. 'Just relax and have a bit of fun with it.'

Linda shook her head and smiled. 'I don't know why you're going to all this trouble for me, but thank you.'

He shrugged. 'We're friends, aren't we? Anyway, I've figured out how we can mix business with our so-called pleasure. From now on any meetings we have about work we'll hold in a well-known pub or restaurant. That way we can kill two birds with one stone.'

'Very romantic,' Viv murmured.

'It is only an act, Viv,' Linda pointed out. 'I think that's a great idea, Jonathan.'

'Good, I'm glad we've got that sorted.' He leaned over and kissed Linda gently on the lips. 'Well, Viv, was that convincing?' he murmured.

Viv looked at Linda's flushed cheeks. 'Very.'

20

Maeve turned the car into Blanchardstown and headed for Craig's garden centre. She had missed a couple of meetings – things were really hotting up for the start of the new show – and she wanted to check what was happening with the club. Of course, she could have phoned Freddy but she had nothing better to do on this gloomy Sunday afternoon so it was more fun to go and annoy Craig. With a bit of luck she'd be able to tempt him out for a pint. She wasn't seeing Paul until nine so there was plenty of time to kill. Traffic was heavy and it looked like parking would be a nightmare. Finally, she squeezed the car into a space a couple of hundred yards away and walked back. Judging by the number of people pushing trolleys around it looked as if business was very good in the Prentice Garden Centre. God, what a way to spend your Sundays, she mused, looking at the couples of all ages shuffling around the centre. But then she had nothing to do this afternoon either, she thought with a wry grin. And nobody to do nothing with either. Paul spent most of his weekends with his kids, but even when he was free, Maeve wouldn't see him. That was a little too personal and Maeve didn't want to get to that level with Paul Riche – at least not yet.

'Maeve?' She swung round to see Craig walking towards her, carrying several bags of manure.

'They're not for me, are they?'

He laughed. 'You don't need them. So, what are you doing here? Have you come to find out what it's like to do a real job?'

'This isn't a job, it's a charity,' she murmured as an elderly couple paused beside them. 'It's depressing that all of these people have nowhere else to go.'

Craig sighed irritably as he dumped the bags against a wall in the corner and started back for some more. 'Did it ever occur to you that they might be enjoying themselves? Planting things, watching them grow, it can be very rewarding.'

'If you say so.' Maeve thought guiltily of the plants on her balcony.

'Look how much enjoyment we get climbing,' he continued.

She waved a dismissive hand at him. 'That's different.'

'Not really. It involves fresh air and a challenge. Not everyone is up to climbing the Scalp, Maeve.' His tone was reproachful as a thin old woman with a walking stick tottered by.

Maeve scuffed the ground with her boot. 'Okay, okay, sorry.'

He smiled. 'You don't always have to pretend you're a hard-hearted bitch.'

Maeve raised an eyebrow. 'Who's pretending? Anyway, according to you I don't have a heart.'

'Oh, I was just kidding. I'm sure it's in there . . . somewhere.'

'Excuse me, have you got any slug pellets?' An elderly man peered solemnly into Craig's face.

'Yes, in here.' Craig led the customer into the shop and Maeve followed slowly. She watched as he patiently explained the merits of the various brands of slug pellet to the man, who then decided they were all too expensive and left.

'How do you put up with that?' Maeve said when he rejoined her.

'It's part of the job. About seventy per cent of the people here today won't buy anything.'

'So how do you make a living?'

'Ah, well, luckily the other thirty per cent spend lots,' he said with a wide grin.

Maeve shook her head. 'It would drive me mad having to be nice to stroppy customers all the time.'

'This from the woman who's going to present a chat show.'

'It's not your average chat show,' Maeve said darkly, 'and most of the time I won't have to be nice.'

'Sounds intriguing, tell me more.'

Maeve shrugged. She wasn't supposed to discuss the show with anyone, but it was unlikely that Craig would leak anything to the press. Besides, she'd like to get his reaction. 'Well, you know the programme is called *Secrets*?'

Craig nodded.

'Well, I'm going to be interviewing people who've kept secrets over the years about really terrible things.'

'Like what?'

'Robbery, vandalism, drugs,' Maeve said vaguely. She didn't want to get into specifics – that would be revealing too much.

Craig looked unimpressed. 'Is it a serious show or one of those exploitative jobs?'

Maeve flushed. 'Hard to say. Obviously, it has to be entertaining, but there will be only one guest on each show, so it won't turn into a slanging match.'

'And you'll be the one running the interrogation?'

'I'll only give them a hard time if they deserve it,' she said quickly.

'And who decides if they deserve it?'

'Oh come on, Craig, don't be so bloody pious. These people deserve what they get. Especially if they volunteer to come on the air.'

'Do you pay them?'

Maeve shook her head vehemently.

Craig looked at her mystified. 'Then why would anyone want to come on and tell you what they've done just to be abused?'

'Maybe that's the reason. Maybe they feel guilty and they *want* to be abused. Maybe they've lived with it for so long they're dying to tell someone. And of course their anonymity is assured.'

Craig frowned. 'So even if someone comes on and admits to murder you won't tell the police?'

Maeve laughed. 'Don't be ridiculous, Craig, we're not going to have a murderer on the show. Just petty criminals, people who've had affairs, stuff like that.'

'Ah, so it's sensationalism.'

'No,' Maeve said shortly, 'it's not like that at all.'

Craig grinned. 'Sounds like it.'

Maeve gritted her teeth. 'It's just a conversation between two adults.'

'So you're not taking any calls.'

'Well, yes, but I'll relay the questions – and only those that are reasonable.'

'I'm surprised. From what I've heard of your boss I would have thought he'd be an all or nothing kind of guy.'

Maeve looked away. Craig was much too shrewd. 'Well, I've told him I just won't do that kind of a show.'

'Good for you,' Craig said, genuine admiration in his voice.

Maeve looked surprised. 'Anyway, tell me what climbs are on in the next few weeks.'

Craig glanced at his watch. 'I've got a schedule in the van. Give me a minute and I'll tell Debs I'm nipping out for a while. We can go for a pint.'

Maeve wandered around the centre while Craig went to check on his assistant. He really had an amazing range of plants and flowers and Maeve was studying a dwarf tree that would look wonderful on her balcony when he returned.

'It's yours for a fiver,' he said chuckling.

'Okay.' Maeve rummaged in her bag for the money and then picked up the tree.

'You're kidding.' He stared at her.

Maeve reddened. 'It's a present. I have a friend who's into this sort of thing – God knows why. The only flora I'm interested in are delivered wrapped in cellophane with a large bow.'

Craig laughed. 'I should have known.' They went back into the shop where Debs checked the bar code on her tree and took the money. Then Craig got the FECC schedule out of his van and they strolled up the road to Hartstown House, Maeve stopping on the way to place the tree carefully in her boot. When they got to the pub, they sat at the bar and Craig ordered a pint of Guinness, a bottle of Miller and two packets of peanuts.

'Not for me.' Maeve pushed them away. She had taken to eating a lot of junk food since joining FECC and it wasn't good for her skin. She'd have to start drinking more water.

Craig started to wolf down his nuts and, as they talked, Maeve absently started to nibble hers. She studied the schedule with increasing disappointment. 'What is all this? There seems to be nothing but hikes planned between now and Christmas.'

Craig shrugged. 'With the dark evenings it's the best we can manage.'

'We could do some early morning climbs,' Maeve insisted.

'Frost,' Craig told her. 'Oh, it's not written in stone, Maeve. If the weather permits we'll go up the Scalp, but these are the fallback plans.'

'Oh.' Maeve was slightly mollified. 'But couldn't we

go somewhere other than Wicklow? I'm getting a bit bored climbing the Scalp.'

Craig laughed. 'Oh, Maeve, you haven't even done half of the climbs on the Scalp yet. Anyway, the only other decent climbs are down the country. We'd have to stay overnight.'

'So how many climbs are there on the Scalp?' Maeve asked, ignoring his suggestive wink.

'At least twenty.'

Maeve's eyes widened. 'I didn't realise.'

'The ones we haven't tackled are a bit more challenging. Freddy didn't think the group was ready for them yet.'

Maeve scowled. 'The likes of Aoife may not be, but that shouldn't stop the rest of us. Let her and the other wimps do the Barnaslingan walk and let us get on with the real challenge.'

Craig shook his head and smiled. 'You're so tough, aren't you, Maeve?'

'I just like a challenge,' she said defensively. 'I don't see anything wrong with that.'

'I think the walks are nice too. The sea views are incredible.'

Maeve shrugged. 'I can look out my bedroom window if I want to see the sea.'

'Lucky you,' he said drily. 'I'll talk to Freddy. If there's enough interest we'll organise a climb up the Welsh Rarebit.'

'Where's that? Is it hard?' Maeve's eyes flashed with excitement.

'It's on the west side and it's very difficult. It

wouldn't be a good idea to have a late night beforehand and I doubt very much if you'd be up to hitting the clubs after it either.'

'Count me in,' Maeve said without hesitation.

'Like I say, it depends if there's enough interest.'

'But you and I could do it,' Maeve pointed out.

Craig shook his head. 'No way, I wouldn't go without Freddy – he knows the west face a lot better than I do.'

'I'll talk to him.'

21

Carrie pulled on her jeans and a black top. Her
mother would not be impressed. Sunday lunch was,
in her view, a formal occasion. A skirt would be more
appropriate. But not the ones that Carrie now had in
her wardrobe. She'd bagged all of her old office gear
and sent it off to a charity shop and now the only
skirts she wore to work were long, floaty numbers
or short tight minis. Neither style would be suitable
for a Lambe family meal. She'd come up with several
excuses why she and Declan couldn't go to Helen's for
Sunday lunch, but her sister had cut through all her
blubbering. 'You're coming, Carrie, and that's final,'
she'd said and hung up.

Declan was more than happy to go. Her sister was
a good cook and always laid on a huge spread with
all of the trimmings. Once there was enough alcohol
to allow him to tune out of the conversation, Declan
could handle the Lambe family gatherings. Carrie
hated them. Though Declan only ever drank lager, he
insisted on drinking wine when he was at Helen's. Not
being used to it, it made him very silly or aggressive,
either way he was no match for her family. Her dad
was the worst, although Andrew had his moments.

Her mother would just stare blankly at Declan or throw Carrie a 'couldn't you do any better than this?' look. Helen would try to keep the conversation light but it rarely worked and Carrie was usually the first to leave, dragging an oblivious Declan with her. These occasions always left Carrie feeling furious with her family – Helen and her wonderful husband, Oscar, being the exception – and irritated by Declan.

As she applied her eyeliner, Declan came into the bathroom. 'Where's my blue shirt?'

'In the wash.'

'Oh, Carrie.'

'Wear the black shirt. It looks great on you,' she said quickly.

'Okay, then.' Mollified by the compliment he went back into the bedroom.

Carrie sighed and rooted in her make-up bag for mascara.

'Should I wear the black jeans?' Declan called.

It was like this every time they met up with her family. Declan turned into some kind of fawning child, eager to please. It drove Carrie nuts. 'Black or blue are fine,' she assured him now. She put the mascara away and applied a thick layer of red lipstick.

'That's a bit much for this hour of the day, isn't it?' Declan was watching her, his face full of disapproval.

Carrie shrugged. 'I need plenty of make-up when I wear black.'

He grunted and splashed on some aftershave. 'We'd better get a move on. We have to pick up a bottle of wine on the way.'

'Oh, I picked up a bottle yesterday in the super-market.'

'What did you get?'

'That French white that Helen loves,' Carrie said lightly.

Declan tut-tutted. 'You should have stuck to the German stuff, Carrie. Everyone prefers it.'

No, only you, Carrie fumed inwardly. Declan always insisted on buying German wine, and her brother and father, who saw themselves as connoisseurs, refused to drink it every time. Declan didn't seem to notice or else he did it deliberately because there was more left for him. 'Sorry,' she murmured now. She wasn't going to argue with him or the afternoon would be even more intolerable.

An hour later, they pulled up outside Helen and Oscar's house. Carrie was relieved to see that neither Andrew nor her father's car was there yet.

'Hi, Carrie.' Oscar was at the door with Lily clinging to his leg and smiling shyly at her aunt.

'Hi, Oscar.' Carrie hugged him affectionately and then bent down to scoop her niece up into her arms. 'Hello, Princess, how are you?'

'I'm fine.' Lily beamed at her.

'Hey there.' Helen emerged from the kitchen, rubbing her hands in her apron. 'You're the first to arrive.'

'Great, that means at least five minutes of civil conversation,' Carrie muttered.

'Now, now, Sis, don't be like that. This is going to be a nice, friendly family lunch.'

Carrie shook her head but she was smiling. Helen never gave up. She seemed convinced that if she kept bringing her family together, one day they'd actually have a good time. Not a chance. 'Just set up a barrel of Guinness beside me and I'll be fine,' she said, allowing Lily to drag her inside to play with her dolls. Having locked the car, Declan joined them. 'Hello, Oscar, Helen, good of you to invite us.'

'Not at all, Declan, you're welcome,' Helen said politely. 'Would you like a beer to keep you going?'

'That would be grand.'

'Wine for you, Helen?' Oscar asked.

'Yes, please.'

Helen and Declan followed Carrie into the living room and sat down.

'So, Declan, how are things?'

'Oh, busy as always, Helen. I'm under an awful lot of pressure at work.'

'Really?' Helen nodded gravely.

'Oh, you wouldn't believe it. The competition in the computer supplies industry is incredible. Someone is going to go to the wall soon, mark my words.'

Carrie frowned. 'I thought you said that your company were hiring people at the moment.'

'Well, yes, but that's because we're the best in the business.'

Carrie tuned out as Declan droned on. Oscar had arrived back with the drinks and Helen had excused herself on the pretext of checking on lunch. Carrie sighed. She knew Declan could be a bit of a bore when he talked about his job but most men were like that. When Andrew and her dad got together, they went on and on as well. Oscar was different though. Carrie watched her brother-in-law nod enthusiastically as Declan talked – he really was a nice guy. Probably the most hardworking GP in Dublin, he hardly ever talked about work. And any time his father-in-law tried to draw him out about his practice he'd put a speedy end to the conversation. 'My wife has to put up with my dreadful hours. I don't think she should have to listen to me talk about work when I am at home.'

Helen would always flash him that special, secret smile – the one that always made Carrie envious. She and Declan didn't have a secret code. If she tried to flash him a message with her eyes, you could bet he'd be looking the other way.

'Any chance of watching the match?' he was saying now to Oscar, having exhausted the topic of work.

'Oh, Declan.' Carrie stared at him in dismay.

'No, it's okay, Carrie,' Oscar assured her. 'I wouldn't mind seeing a bit of the game myself. We can switch it off when the others get here.'

Carrie smiled gratefully and went out to join Helen in the kitchen. 'Can I do anything to help?'

Helen shook her head as she mashed potatoes. 'No, it's all ready. So how are you? How's the job going?'

Carrie brightened. 'Great, I'm really enjoying it.'

Helen grinned. 'So now maybe you can understand Andrew and me a bit better.'

'What do you mean?'

'Oh, come on, Carrie, you thought we were both nuts going to uni.'

'No, I didn't,' Carrie protested. 'It just wasn't something I could have done.'

'But we had to do it to get where we are now.'

'I know that, Helen. For the first time I actually understand the concept of job satisfaction.'

Helen chuckled. 'Oh, well, I suppose that's progress.'

Carrie glanced at the clock. 'Where is everyone? You did say half past two, didn't you?'

'I told them all to come about three.' Helen pushed the door closed. 'I wanted to talk to you before they got here.'

'Oh?' Carrie stiffened. When her big sister wanted to talk it usually meant a pep talk.

'Don't look like that. Aren't I allowed some time alone with my sister?'

'It depends.'

Helen sat down on a stool opposite Carrie. 'It's about Declan.'

Carrie scowled. 'Oh for God's sake, what is it now?'

'Look, you obviously aren't getting on as well as you used to.'

'I wouldn't say that.'

'You're always snapping at each other, Carrie, and that's in public. What's it like at home?'

Carrie refused to look at her.

'Look, I can understand what it's like to get into a rut. And I know it's hard to walk away from a steady relationship. But you've got this wonderful new job now. This is a chance for you to make a fresh start.'

Carrie stared at her. 'Well, don't beat around the bush, will you?'

'I won't. Look, Carrie, you're nearly twenty-five – too old to be wasting time on a guy who's obviously wrong for you.'

'You don't know that,' Carrie retorted hotly.

'I know what I see and I know what you tell me,' Helen persisted. 'Come on, Carrie, be honest. You know that you don't love the guy.'

'Has Mum put you up to this?'

'No, of course not, although I know Andrew and Jill are worried about you too.'

'Darling Jill maybe but my brother?' Carrie's eyes widened in disbelief.

'Look, I know he can be a pain and he gives Declan a hard time, but behind all of that he really does care.'

Carrie looked doubtful. Her brother wasn't the greatest communicator in the world and she couldn't imagine him talking like this about her to Helen, never mind even taking the time to think or worry about her. Carrie gazed silently into her Guinness. Maybe she'd underestimated him. After all, he must have something going for him if Jill loved him – she was such a great girl. And he was a good dad too. *And* he'd been very nice about her new job, she realised guiltily. In fact, the only thing that they didn't agree on was Declan. Andrew couldn't abide him. It annoyed Carrie because she knew it was pure snobbery. As a mere computer peripherals salesman, Declan wasn't good enough for his sister.

It had made Carrie more determined than ever to move in with her boyfriend when he'd suggested it a couple of months after they met. It hadn't been the most romantic proposal, Carrie remembered. Declan had just pointed out that two could live as cheaply as one and she spent most nights in his flat anyway. And so, they'd bought their little townhouse in Terenure. Carrie had loved it from the moment she set eyes on it. Granted it was small but they didn't need much space. And it was so pretty and in a tiny little square with a small green in the centre. Carrie felt more grown up since she'd moved in there. It was a good idea to live together before you married, she decided, although two years on, the prospect of marriage seemed unlikely.

'Aren't you going to say something?' Helen was looking at her anxiously.

Carrie sighed. 'Look, I appreciate your concern – and Andrew's – but everything's fine between me and Declan.' She smiled lamely. 'Okay, we're not as lovey-dovey in public as you and Oscar but we're quite happy in our own way.'

'And is quite happy enough?' Helen asked.

'Yes, it's fine,' Carrie insisted crossly and drained her glass. 'Please tell me that the lecture is over.'

Helen patted her hand but her smile was unconvincing. 'Sure, sorry. I'll get you another drink. The folks should be here soon.'

Carrie looked miserable as she held out her glass. 'Goody, goody, I can hardly wait. Why do you insist on having these dinners, Helen?'

'Because family is important.' Her sister refilled her glass.

'What, it's important that we get together to back-bite, bitch and nag?'

'It doesn't have to be like that, Carrie. Please, make an effort for my sake. Oscar doesn't have any family and you lot are the only relatives Lily has.'

Carrie softened. 'Yeah, okay, I promise not to flick peas at Andrew.'

'Good, because despite what you think, he's very fond of you. He's just a bit overprotective.'

Carrie found that hard to believe, but she said nothing. Poor old Helen so wanted everyone to get on and she promised herself that she would behave. She wouldn't react no matter what little gems her family came out with.

'So, Carrie, how's the little job going?' her father asked, his smile patronising.

Carrie's fingers tightened around her knife. 'Great.'

'They have her working ridiculous hours,' Declan grumbled.

Carrie flashed him a look. How could he let her down in front of her parents? 'We're starting a new show and there's a lot to do.'

He laughed. 'You're only the researcher on the show – the gofer. The way you talk you'd think you were running things.'

Helen glared at him as her sister reddened. 'From what I hear they work very much as a team, isn't that right, Carrie?'

Carrie nodded, trying to smile.

'If the hours are too long, why don't you keep an eye out for another little job? There are plenty of companies looking for general office workers.'

Carrie stared at her mother. 'The rest of this family all work odd hours, why shouldn't I?'

Her father chuckled. 'Hardly the same thing, Carrie.'

'Not at all,' Declan agreed.

Andrew glowered at him. 'Do you like the job, Carrie?'

'I love it, Andrew.'

'Then stick with it, Sis. There's nothing better than doing something you enjoy.'

Helen shot her a 'told you so' look and Carrie smiled shyly at her brother. 'Yeah, I will.'

Jill nodded enthusiastically. 'I think it's perfect for you, Carrie,' she said, taking a break from the onerous task of trying to persuade Bobby and Sam to eat their vegetables.

'Thanks, Jill.' Carrie watched the twins as they tried to hide their peas under the edge of their plates.

'More wine?' Oscar held up the bottle.

'Yes, please,' Carrie's dad held out his glass. 'That's a rather nice Sancerre, Oscar.'

'Declan and Carrie brought it,' Helen told him.

Eugene Lambe raised an eyebrow. 'That must have cost you.'

Carrie avoided Declan's eyes. 'It was on special in

Tesco's. Any more of those gorgeous garlic potatoes, Helen?'

'Plenty.' Helen stood up to fetch them from the sideboard.

Annabel Lambe looked approvingly at her eldest daughter. 'What a pretty dress,' she said and then stared pointedly at her younger daughter's jeans and jumper.

Helen sighed as she saw the hurt in Carrie's eyes. 'Thanks, Mum, although I wish I was as slim as Carrie and could fit into tight jeans.'

Carrie smiled tightly but even Helen's kindness could never make up for her mother's caustic comments.

'I prefer Carrie in a dress too,' Declan told Annabel. 'Though not those tight little minis that she insists on wearing to work.'

Carrie pushed back her chair and stood up. 'Right! I'll make a start on the washing-up.'

Oscar looked around in confusion. 'But we haven't had dessert yet.'

Helen sighed as her sister almost ran from the room. '*And* we have a dishwasher.'

22

Linda finished the ironing, put the board away and carried the clothes up to her bedroom. She looked around the blue room and wondered how many more nights she would spend here. She and Patrick had finally decided to sell the house. At first when he'd broached the subject she'd baulked, but soon after she'd slammed down the phone she realised that she didn't really belong in this house any more. Most of the furniture in it they'd bought together and though she'd always chosen the wallpapers and carpets, she'd always discussed the colours and patterns with Patrick. As for their bed – Linda looked at it reproachfully – it just reminded her of all the lies. How could he have cuddled up with her every night for three years when he was seeing someone else? It sickened her and she was finding it very hard to sleep here now. So she'd agreed to put the house on the market and had started looking for a flat near the office. Patrick had assumed she'd be moving in with a boyfriend and she'd let him. He didn't know about Jonathan yet. Surprisingly it was taking a long time to leak out. Typical. If she'd really been having an affair with him, you could bet that everyone would have known within days. But despite several lunches and dinners in prominent places and moonlit walks down Grafton Street and through Temple Bar, no one had written a word about the new woman in Jonathan Blake's life.

'They probably look at my lines and dismiss me.' She'd laughed when Jonathan had phoned earlier.

'You really annoy me when you talk like that,' he'd said.

'It's just as well we're not really going out together then, isn't it?' she'd retorted.

'I think we should go out with some of my friends,' he'd said as if she hadn't spoken.

'I don't think so—'

'Linda, we need to get this out in the open.'

Suddenly Linda realised that what had been fun to him at the start was probably getting rather tiresome. 'What do you want to do?'

'I'll call you tomorrow, but keep Saturday night free.'

And that was now, tonight. Linda opened her wardrobe and stared gloomily at the contents. She didn't believe she owned anything that suited such an occasion. There was her long black skirt and the high silver sandals but any of the tops she normally wore didn't seem appropriate. Jonathan's usual partners wore tops that were transparent, cropped or barely there. Even if she possessed such an item in her wardrobe, she'd never have the courage to wear it. She picked up the phone and called her sister.

'I'll be right over,' Vivienne said and hung up.

Linda went downstairs and opened a bottle of wine. She didn't know why she'd called Viv. It was highly unlikely there was anything in her wardrobe that Linda would wear. Their styles were very different. Linda lived in suits or dresses. Viv floated around in layers of different fabrics and bright colours. The addition of a headscarf worn gypsy style and large gold hoops in her ears made her look like an exotic Romany. Still, a couple of glasses of wine and a laugh with her sister would calm her down and prepare her for the night ahead. Jonathan had promised it would be all very casual but when he'd mentioned the restaurant they were going to she knew different.

Twenty minutes later, the bell shrilled and Linda hurried to answer the door.

Viv stood there triumphantly, a suit carrier dangling from her bejewelled fingers.

'Behold your fairy godmother.'

Linda grinned and stood back to let her in. 'You don't have to bother with a coach and horses, Jonathan's picking me up in his BMW.'

'Nice.' Viv hung the carrier carefully on the banister and followed her sister into the kitchen. Linda took the wine out of the fridge and poured them both a glass.

'Let's take these upstairs.'

'But there's plenty of time,' Linda protested, looking at the clock.

'Rubbish. We have a lot to do. You bring my bag.'

Linda lifted Viv's voluminous bag and obediently led the way upstairs. 'What on earth have you got in this thing?'

Viv grinned as she balanced the suit carrier in one hand and her glass in the other. 'Everything a girl could ever need.'

Linda climbed up on the bed as Viv hung the carrier on the back of the door. 'Right, first we'll tackle your skin.'

'It's only dinner,' Linda protested.

Viv stared at her. 'Only dinner? My dear, you could end up in all the papers tomorrow.'

Linda's eyes widened. 'Do you really think so?'

'Well, that's the plan, isn't it?' Viv pulled bottles and tubes out of her bag. 'First a face mask and while that's working its magic I'll paint your nails.' She grabbed one of Linda's hands and peered at it. 'You need to use hand cream more often. Hands always give away your age,' she said wisely.

'I thought the hulking great crevices under my eyes did that,' Linda retorted before gulping down some wine.

Viv paused and looked up into her face. 'You are very pretty, Lin, I wish you'd remember that.'

Linda's eyes were sad. 'It's not easy.'

Viv squeezed her hand. 'It will be once I've finished with you.'

Two hours later, Linda stared at her reflection in the mirror. 'I hardly recognise myself.'

'You look beautiful.' Viv beamed at her.

'Are you sure you don't mind me borrowing this?' Linda fingered the silk black dress with reverential fingers.

Viv shrugged casually. 'No, it's probably more you than me anyway. I bought it for my UK launch last year. You know, everyone wears black in the publishing industry.'

Linda twisted left and right. The dress was certainly very subtle for Viv. A slim-fitting cocktail dress, it reached just below the knee. But thanks to the plunging v-neck and the slit up the side, it was very sexy. After her face mask, Viv had slobbered on several different creams and then insisted on applying her sister's make-up. Linda had fully intended to wash it all off again, but when she saw the result of Viv's handiwork she was delighted. Viv had used dark brown shadow and eyeliner to emphasise her hazel eyes. She'd also – despite much screaming from Linda – plucked her eyebrows into a narrow line that somehow had opened up her whole face. The final touch was the dark plum lipstick that made Linda look almost vampish. Viv had used the same colour on her nails and with a long plum-coloured chiffon wrap the outfit was complete.

Viv stared at her thoughtfully. 'You need some jewellery with that hairstyle.' They had pulled Linda's hair up into a knot on the top of her head, leaving soft tendrils to frame her face.

Linda shook her head. 'No. Everything I own Patrick bought for me. I won't wear it.'

'You must have something,' Viv insisted, going to her sister's jewellery box.

Linda followed reluctantly. 'Only some costume pieces, nothing that would go with this outfit.'

Viv pulled the coloured bangles off her own arm. 'Well, you can have these.' She went back to rummaging in the box as Linda slipped the bangles on. 'Oh, here we go. This is perfect.'

Linda looked dubiously at the necklace of coloured stones that looked like a cobweb. 'I don't think so.'

'Try it on,' Viv insisted.

Linda struggled with the clasp and then turned to study herself in the mirror. Viv was right. It was lovely. The delicate threads of the piece were almost luminous against her skin and it dipped into her cleavage provocatively.

'You look hot, kid.' Viv nodded with approval.

Linda's eyes shone. 'I think I might actually enjoy myself after all.'

'Of course you will! Now, let's go downstairs and have another drink while we wait for Prince Charming.'

He arrived twenty minutes later and stopped in his tracks when he saw Linda. 'Wow!'

Linda twirled around self-consciously. 'Will I do?'

'You'll be the most beautiful woman in the room,' he said gallantly.

'There's no need to go overboard,' Linda said drily. Somehow, his compliment had dulled her excitement. There was no way she could compete with some of the beautiful women he dated and she'd prefer it if he didn't pretend otherwise. 'Shall we go?'

Jonathan shot Viv a bemused look. She shrugged.

'Have a lovely evening, Sis.' She kissed Linda

affectionately. 'And he's right. You're going to knock their socks off!'

Linda smiled. 'Thanks, Viv.'

'There will be four other couples here this evening,' Jonathan explained as he drove into town. 'Maeve Elliot and her latest boyfriend.'

Linda swallowed hard. The beautiful DJ?

'Doug Hamilton, and his wife Pamela. They run CML.'

Linda nodded, she'd heard of them too.

'Joe Lane and his girlfriend.'

'The newscaster?'

Jonathan nodded. 'He's an old friend. And Sally Keating and one of her toyboys.'

Linda gasped. 'The singer? Good God, what am I going to talk to these people about? Couldn't we have gone out with a more normal gang?'

Jonathan grinned. 'If we did that, we wouldn't get in the papers.'

Linda closed her eyes, suddenly feeling sick.

Jonathan reached over and squeezed her hand. 'You're an intelligent woman, you're very good company, everything's going to be just fine.'

'I'll try not to embarrass you,' Linda promised.

'For God's sake, Linda, you don't have to impress anyone. Just relax and enjoy yourself. Now after dinner we'll go on to a club and that's where the photographers will be snapping. So it would be better to stay sober until then.'

Linda nodded vehemently. She wouldn't let Jonathan

down. He was going to all this trouble to help her and she would do her best to play her part.

When Jonathan stopped the car outside the restaurant the doorman hurried out to open Linda's door and once they were both on the pavement, he drove the car away. Jonathan tucked her arm into his and kissed her forehead. 'Good luck.'

As they walked through the restaurant, Linda drew herself up to her full five feet, four inches – six if you took into account her sandals – and smiled calmly. She was immediately aware of the looks they were getting. Or the looks Jonathan was getting, she amended. Even if he weren't famous, he'd get those looks. He was a very handsome man, in a dark, foreign kind of way. Of course there was Greek blood in the family, she remembered. It was always a surprise to anyone meeting him for the first time to hear the lilting Dublin accent. The other guests were already at the table when they arrived.

'Hello, everybody, I hope you haven't been waiting too long.'

Doug stood up and shook his hand. 'Only just got here, Jon, how are you?'

'Great. Let me introduce Linda Taylor.'

Linda smiled at the use of her maiden name. 'Lovely to meet you.' She shook the man's hand.

'What on earth is a lovely lady like you doing with a scoundrel like Jon?' he demanded, his eyes twinkling in his handsome face. He definitely lived up to the photographs she'd seen in the papers.

'You'll have to forgive my husband, Linda, he's a consummate flirt. I'm Pamela.' She reached up to shake Linda's hand. 'Forgive me for not getting up but it's a bit difficult these days.'

Linda smiled as she realised the other woman was heavily pregnant – and blooming too. Linda admired her wonderful skin, the brightness of her eyes and the shine of her beautiful blonde hair. 'Nice to meet you.'

'Linda this is Maeve Elliot, and . . . ?' He looked curiously at the man next to his DJ.

'Paul Riche,' he introduced himself, standing to shake hands with Jonathan and Linda.

Maeve was looking curiously at Linda. 'Hi.'

Linda smiled back amazed that the girl looked even more beautiful in person – all that amazing hair.

'And, this is Sally Keating.'

Sally smiled thinly and inclined her head towards the man beside her. 'This is Kevin.'

Linda nodded at them both. Jonathan had been right. Kevin was at least fifteen years younger than Sally.

'And this is Joe Lane,' Jonathan said as they turned to the last couple at the table.

Joe smiled at her. He didn't look half as scary as he did on television. 'Nice to meet you, Linda. This is my fiancée, Fiona.'

Jonathan pumped his hand. 'You've finally done it, congratulations! But, Fiona, are you sure you know what you're doing marrying this grizzly old bachelor?'

'I hope so,' she said laughing, but her eyes rested lovingly on Joe.

Linda felt a pang of envy. What would it be like to be starting out again?

Jonathan pulled back a chair for her and she found herself with Doug on her left, Jonathan on her right and Maeve opposite.

'What do you do, Linda?' Maeve asked once they were all settled again.

'I'm a recruitment consultant.'

'Oh, you work for Reeve's, don't you?' Maeve said with sudden recognition.

'She runs Reeve's Recruitment,' Jonathan corrected with a loving smile at Linda.

Maeve watched them curiously, eyebrows raised.

'How's business, Doug?' Jonathan quickly changed the subject.

Linda sipped her drink gratefully and took a few deep breaths. She felt relatively protected between the two men but she knew that it would be different in the club. Mindful of what was ahead she took a drink of water too. It was going to be a long night.

23

'Linda, have you seen the papers?'

Linda rubbed her eyes and looked at the clock. It was just gone eleven and she'd only got to bed at six. 'Oh, Viv, can I call you later? I'm so tired.'

'Linda, did you hear me? You're in all the papers,' Viv repeated.

Linda shot up in the bed and then winced as a drum started to beat loudly in her head. 'Oh, no. What do I look like? Am I a mess?'

'You look great,' Viv assured her. 'There's one of you and Jonathan and you can almost feel the electricity between you.'

Linda smiled. Viv's speech was as colourful as her prose. 'Don't be silly, Viv. It was all an act. Though, I must say, once I relaxed, I really enjoyed myself.'

'I can't believe you met Sally Keating and Joe Lane. What were they like?'

Linda propped up the pillows behind her, resigned to the fact that she wouldn't be getting any more sleep. 'Sally is only interested in number one,' she reported. 'If the conversation wasn't about her, then she wasn't interested. And I'd swear she was on something. She had this slightly dazed look in her eyes.'

'Stretched look, you mean,' Viv said shrewdly. 'Rumour has it she got a face lift in the Blessington Clinic last month.'

'That explains it.'

'And what about Maeve Elliot? Is she a total bitch?'

'Not at all. I'd say she doesn't suffer fools easily but she's a good laugh. We really hit it off.'

'Did she try and worm information out of you about you and Jonathan?'

'No, Fiona, Joe Lane's fiancée, did that. She was nice, but such a gossip. She gave me a blow-by-blow account of Jonathan's ex-girlfriends and told me how happy she was that he'd finally settled down with someone his own age.'

Viv groaned. 'What did you say?'

Linda smiled. 'I told her I was recently separated and Jonathan and I were just—'

'Good friends!' Viv laughed.

'So tell me what the papers say? Which ones are we in?'

Viv spent the next thirty minutes reading out the snippets of gossip until they were interrupted by Linda's doorbell. 'Oh, I bet that's Mum. I'll call you back, Viv.'

Linda pulled on her dressing gown and ran downstairs.

'Jonathan!' She pulled the belt tighter. 'What on earth are you doing here?'

'That's a lovely way to talk to your boyfriend,' he said reproachfully.

Linda laughed. 'Come in then. I suppose you can

have a cup of tea.' She stepped back to let him in, conscious of his size and proximity in the narrow hall.

'I thought you'd like to see the newspapers.'

'Yeah, great. Look, why don't *you* make the tea and
I'll go and put on some clothes?'

'This way?' He pointed towards the door at the end
of the hall.

'Yep. Won't be a minute.' Linda ran upstairs to her
room and closed the door. She looked in the mirror
and groaned. God, why did he have to drop in now?
The remains of last night's mascara was on her cheeks,
her face was shiny and her hair was tousled. 'Oh, God,'
she moaned. This was a very different image from the
glamorous one of last night. It was just as well this
wasn't a real romance or Jonathan would run a mile.
She went into her bathroom and scrubbed her face
clean, pulled on a pair of brown jeans and an orange
jumper that she knew flattered her colouring and then
pulled a brush through her hair. She still looked lousy.

'Tea's ready,' Jonathan called.

'Coming.' Linda hurriedly brushed her face with
some bronzing powder – at least she didn't look like
death warmed up any more – and ran downstairs.
'Sorry about that.'

Jonathan grinned. 'No problem, I found some para-
cetamol. I thought you could use a couple.'

'So I do look as bad as I feel.'

'You look fine.'

For the first time, Linda noticed how fresh and
bright he looked in his jeans and rugby shirt. 'How
come you're so chirpy?' she complained.

'I was driving, remember?'

She put a hand tentatively to her head. 'I think I'll drive the next time.'

'Oh, so there is going to be a next time?'

Linda took a sip of her tea and nodded dubiously at the newspapers. 'It depends on them.'

Jonathan flicked through them and pushed them towards her open at the relevant page.

Linda stared in wonder at the glamorous woman with the large dark eyes staring back at her. 'Gosh. I clean up okay, don't I?'

Jonathan laughed. 'You certainly do, Ms Taylor.'

'Oh, I meant to thank you for that,' she said shyly. 'We hadn't discussed it but I would have hated it if you had introduced me as Linda Jewell.'

'Well, you're not Linda Jewell any more, are you?'

'I suppose not.' Linda tried to imagine how Patrick would react when he saw these pictures. Would he be jealous? She read the snippets of gossip greedily. '*Who is the new mysterious brunette in Jonathan Blake's life?* Bloody cheek! I'm not a brunette – at least, not when I've had my highlights done.'

'Read this one.' Jonathan pointed to another.

'It looks like Jonathan Blake may finally be ready for wife number two. There was no denying the chemistry between him and his new, sophisticated amour, Linda Taylor.'

She gasped. 'How did they get my name?'

'I gave it to them.'

'You didn't!' She burst out laughing. 'You're incorrigible, you know that?'

'It's fun though, isn't it?'

'Well, yes, I suppose it is,' she admitted. 'I've never been a celebrity before. And I certainly have never been described as mysterious or sophisticated before.'

Jonathan picked up another paper. 'There's one here somewhere that calls you sexy.'

'Sexy! Now that's a bit much.'

Jonathan gave her a long look. 'I wouldn't say that. You looked amazing last night.'

'Thanks to my sister and her magic bag.' Linda laughed off his compliment.

'Has your mother called yet?'

Linda groaned. 'No! Oh, God, I'd forgotten all about Mum.'

'Why don't you call her?'

Linda shook her head. 'No, I think this calls for a face-to-face.'

'I'll come with you, if you like.'

'Oh, you don't have to do that.' Linda looked alarmed.

He shrugged. 'It's up to you but Daniel is going to a birthday party this afternoon so I'm at a loose end.'

She took a deep breath. 'Okay then. Let's do it. Just let me take those tablets first.'

When they arrived at Rosemary's house, all was quiet.

'She's probably gone out,' Linda said as Jonathan switched off the ignition.

He looked at her his eyes full of amusement. 'A forty-year-old still afraid of her mother.'

'I'm only thirty-eight!'

'Whatever. Let's go.'

Linda got out of the car reluctantly. She hadn't even got halfway up the path when Rosemary threw the door open. 'Well, well, well. If it isn't the happy couple.'

Linda made a face.

'Hello, Mrs Taylor.'

'I suppose you'd better call me Rosemary.' Her eyes flashed in amusement.

Linda sighed. 'Any chance of a coffee?'

Rosemary led the way through to her large kitchen. 'Oh, it's after twelve. Let's have Bloody Marys instead.'

'Excellent idea,' Jonathan agreed. 'It will make you feel better, Linda.'

'Several hours' sleep is the only thing that's going to make me feel better.'

'So the night was as good as it looked in the papers?' Rosemary splashed generous helpings of vodka into three glasses.

'It was very enjoyable,' Linda agreed reluctantly.

Rosemary rummaged in a cupboard for Worcester sauce and Tabasco. 'Afraid there's no lemon.' She fetched a large carton of tomato juice from the fridge.

Linda glanced at Jonathan who gave her an encouraging nod. 'Look, Mum, I'm sorry, but I wasn't exactly honest with you.'

'There's a surprise.' Rosemary handed them their glasses and then perched on a stool.

'But I didn't lie either,' Linda said quickly. 'I have been faithful to Patrick – that bit was true.'

Rosemary glanced down at the intimate photograph of Jonathan leaning close to Linda, his hand caressing the small of her back. 'Really?'

'Really,' Jonathan told her. 'You see, Rosemary, Linda and I were just friends while she and Patrick were together. Maybe we would have liked it to be more but—' He shrugged.

'But now that Patrick has left there's nothing to stop you two getting together,' Rosemary surmised.

Linda reddened, conscious of Jonathan's eyes on her. 'Something like that, Jonathan thought that it would teach Patrick a lesson if we went out publicly and it would save people from pitying me because he was the one who walked out.'

'How clever of you, Jonathan. You've certainly shown Patrick. So will this be an exclusive relationship or do you plan to keep seeing your other little friends?'

'Mother!'

'No, it's a fair comment,' Jonathan said. 'Linda isn't like the others, Rosemary.'

'Obviously not. You two must be almost the same age.'

'Mother, please!' Linda was mortified. 'Enough of the third degree. I'm old enough to take care of myself. Jonathan and I are having a bit of fun which is exactly what I need right now. I would have thought you'd be happy for me.'

Rosemary studied them for a moment and then lifted her glass. 'Of course I am, darling. As long as you know what you're doing.'

Linda avoided her eyes and glanced briefly at Jonathan. He smiled reassuringly at her before turning to Rosemary. 'We do.'

'That went well,' Jonathan said when they were back in the car.

Linda was slumped in her seat, her eyes closed. All of this acting was exhausting. 'I suppose so.'

'Let's get some lunch.'

'We can go back to my place. I'll make you a sandwich.'

'No way, I'm starving. We'll go to Roly's.'

Linda's eyes flew open. 'Oh, Jonathan—'

'No arguments.' He swung the car around and headed for Ballsbridge and Linda closed her eyes again. She was too tired to argue.

The restaurant was buzzing when they arrived but somehow Jonathan managed to secure a table. 'How do you do that?' Linda asked when they were seated at a table in the centre of the room.

'I tip heavily.'

Linda laughed. 'I should really go out to the ladies' and touch up my make-up. We're bound to meet someone you know.'

'You look fine, Linda, stop fussing.' He took her hand and stroked it.

Linda stiffened. Her instincts were to pull away but then Jonathan was just acting and she'd have to get used to that. He was much better at it than she was, but then he'd had a lot more practice. She forced herself to leave her hand where it was and smiled at him. 'This still seems a little weird to me,' she admitted.

'What's that?'

'Our so-called relationship. Only a few weeks ago you were just a customer.'

Jonathan's eyes were reproachful. 'And I thought you cared.'

'Nut.' Linda ,laughed, relaxing. She'd have to remember that this was the same old Jonathan and nothing had really changed. He was her friend. It was just that when he touched her or looked at her in that intimate way, her heart started to race. She'd have to learn to lighten up a little.

'Are you hungry?' Jonathan asked as he scanned the menu.

'Do you know, I think I am,' Linda said, realising that her stomach was indeed rumbling. She'd hardly eaten a thing at dinner last night, mainly because guiding her trembling hands towards her mouth had proven quite a challenge.

'The fish is always good here.'

'I have been here before, you know. I may not be in the papers every week but I do go out occasionally.'

Jonathan held his hands up. 'Sorry.'

Linda looked shamefaced. 'Me too, I'll be okay when I've got some food inside me.'

'Would a glass of wine help too?'

'I think I could manage something.'

When the waiter arrived to take their order, Jonathan asked for some bottled water. 'And a bottle of Dom Perignon.'

Linda gasped as the waiter departed. 'What's that for?'

'In case we're seen, of course.' He winked at her.

'Surely the house sparkling would have done.'

Jonathan looked shocked. 'I couldn't be seen buying you the cheap stuff!'

Linda threw back her head and laughed. 'Oh, this is great fun. But how am I ever going to cope when we break up? I'll have no one to spoil me any more.'

Jonathan gave her an enigmatic smile. 'Then we'd better not break up.'

24

Maeve made her way to the meeting room, a large file under her arm. *Secrets* was due to start in just three weeks' time and she was beginning to feel quite excited. As long as Jonathan was happy with the format that she and Karl had come up with everything should work out fine. 'Hi, Carrie.' She smiled at the girl who was already sitting at the table sifting through letters.

'Hi.'

'Have you got those scripts typed up for me?' Maeve didn't believe in wasting time on small talk.

'Yes.' Carrie passed a sheaf of pages over. 'They're the five scripts for the first week.'

'Great. Do you have copies for Jonathan and Karl?'

Carrie nodded. 'And I've selected out some new letters that came in that I think might interest you. God, there's an awful lot of misery in Dublin, if you can believe the half of them.'

'And misery means listeners,' Maeve said drily.

'Won't we be doing some happy shows?'

'The show's called *Secrets*, Carrie. And secrets are rarely about something pleasant.'

'Keeping a pregnancy secret can be pleasant,' Carrie ventured.

'A secret like that is unlikely to hold the listeners' attention for an hour.'

'I suppose not.'

Maeve frowned. 'Are you having second thoughts, Carrie?'

'No, of course not! I'm really enjoying the work. It's just that it's a bit depressing sometimes.'

'After a couple of weeks it will all wash over you,' Maeve assured her. 'You can't afford to get personally involved in a show like this. It would end up destroying you.'

Karl and Jonathan arrived so Carrie didn't have time to reply.

'Okay, troops, how goes it?' Jonathan took his seat at the head of the table and looked around.

'Fine,' Maeve said confidently. 'The first week of shows is sorted. Carrie has the scripts.'

Carrie obediently handed them each a copy and they sat in silence while Jonathan scanned them. Karl already knew the content.

'This seems okay,' Jonathan said slowly. 'Although not very controversial.'

'HIV, adoption, affairs – seems pretty controversial to me,' Karl replied.

Jonathan drummed his pen against the pages. 'I think we need a fresh perspective. I've hired someone to join our team that should be able to steer us in the right direction.'

Maeve's eyes widened in alarm and Karl stared at him coldly.

'Oh, don't worry, your jobs are safe.' Jonathan's

laugh was slightly forced. 'But we need someone with experience of this type of show to oversee the whole programme.'

'I oversee the whole programme,' Karl said.

'Yes, mate, and you do a great job, but there is a lot of content in this show and I think we need a co-ordinator as well.'

Maeve breathed a sigh of relief. 'The show on Dublin FM use a co-ordinator,' she acknowledged.

Jonathan grinned. 'Funny you should mention that.' He picked up the phone and tapped in a number. 'Karen? Would you bring Ben Donnelly up to the conference room, please?'

'Ben Donnelly!' Karl exclaimed.

'Who's Ben Donnelly?'

'The man behind *Pillowtalk* on Dublin FM.'

'I see.' Maeve shot her producer a sympathetic look.

'He's not coming in to take over the show, Karl,' Jonathan said. 'You'll work as a team.'

'Who will have the final word?' Karl asked, not one to beat around the bush.

Jonathan held his gaze. 'He has more experience in this type of show.'

'Right.' Karl stood up and left.

Jonathan turned back to Maeve. 'I expect you to work with Ben, Maeve. I hope you understand what I'm saying.'

Maeve stared at him sullenly.

Karen knocked on the door and looked uneasily around the room. 'Eh, Jonathan, I've brought—'

'Yes, Karen, bring him in.' He stood up and held out his hand. 'Ben, welcome to Forever FM. Meet Maeve Elliot and Carrie Lambe.' Maeve nodded coolly and Carrie flashed him a feeble smile. 'Take a seat. I'm afraid Karl Thompson had to rush off.'

'So I noticed.' Ben's lips twitched and Maeve glowered at him.

Jonathan shot her a warning look before pushing a file over to Ben. 'Let's dive right in then.' He nodded to Maeve who briefed Ben in clipped tones. He stopped her every so often with a question. Carrie glanced nervously at the three of them. You could cut the atmosphere with a knife. Even Jonathan seemed gloomy. But then, from what Carrie could gather, Karl and he had always been good mates.

'I'm not sure you've got the right slant on this show,' Ben said when she'd finished. He ran a sharp eye over the first script. 'It needs to be more "in your face".'

'I don't agree.' Maeve's voice was coldly polite. 'I think the story is a strong one and speaks for itself.'

'Your listeners need to be led a lot more than you realise.'

Maeve bristled at his patronising tone. 'I think I know my listeners.'

Ben sighed. 'A talk show is a little bit different to an easy-listening show, Maeve.'

'I am aware of that, thank you, Ben.' Maeve's voice dripped with sarcasm.

'Good, then I'm sure that together we'll manage to put a show together that will knock the socks off the other stations.'

'That's what I like to hear.' Jonathan was slightly too hearty and he looked away from Maeve's accusing glare. 'You can meet up with Karl tomorrow and talk about your ideas. I've no doubt that *Secrets* is going to be something very special.'

'Something very special,' Maeve spat angrily as she paced her small office. 'It's going to be a disaster if Ben Donnelly has anything to do with it.'

'Maybe he's not so bad,' Carrie said hopefully. 'He was probably just putting on a show for Jonathan.'

'Oh, he did that all right. I can't believe that Jonathan would hire him behind our backs. He's such a little weasel.'

'I thought he was kind of cute,' Carrie said honestly. Ben had curly fair hair and pale blue eyes and the few times that he'd smiled at Carrie his whole face had lit up.

'His eyes are too close together. Never trust a man whose eyes are too close together,' she warned Carrie.

'I'll bear that in mind.' Carrie frowned. Declan's eyes were quite close . . .

'Karl won't stand for it,' Maeve continued. 'He'll leave, I know he will.'

'Then we have to talk him out of it.' Carrie's mouth settled into a determined line. It didn't matter how nice Ben's smile was, she owed her loyalty to Karl.

Maeve looked at the little researcher in surprise, her lips twitching. 'We?'

Carrie reddened. 'Well, yes, we're a team, aren't we?'

Maeve grinned. 'Right, grab your coat.' She put on her leather jacket and headed for the door.

'Where are we going?' Carrie hurried after her.

'I think I just might know where to find Karl.'

As Maeve had suspected, Karl was sitting at the bar in O'Brien's on Leeson Street, sipping moodily on his pint. Usually, he got talking to the barman or one of the locals, but not tonight. He couldn't believe that Jonathan Blake, of all people, had shafted him. Perhaps it was time to move on. He looked around the smoky pub mournfully. This was the first place he'd felt at home since he'd left Australia. And though it hadn't cost him a thought to walk out of any of the jobs he'd picked up since, he really didn't want to leave Forever FM. Especially like this. It looked like he'd failed. It looked like Jon didn't trust him to do the job. If he left, he knew he would leave the country too. There was nothing to keep him here. He had lots of mates, but as usual, he hadn't allowed anyone to get too close, but he liked it here and the thought of going back on the road didn't appeal.

'I knew I'd find you here.' Maeve plonked her bag down on the bar and sat up on a stool. Carrie stood awkwardly behind them.

Karl got off his stool and shoved it towards her. 'What can I get you, ladies?'

'Miller,' Maeve said.

'A glass of Guinness, please,' Carrie said shyly.

Karl smiled warmly at her. 'A real drink, good on ya, Carrie.' He turned to the barman and ordered their drinks. 'And another pint of Guinness for me.'

'So why the hell did you go storming off like that?' Maeve said without preamble. 'If I did that you'd be calling me a Prima Donna.'

Karl massaged the bridge of his nose. 'Yeah, I know, but I was so pissed off with Jon.'

'You're not alone. As for that little asshole, Donnelly – God, how are we going to work with him?'

'I'm not,' Karl lit a cigarette and inhaled deeply.

Carrie's eyes widened with dismay. 'You can't leave.'

He smiled at her. If they didn't work together, he'd be very tempted to—

'You're not leaving,' Maeve told him.

'Hey, Maeve, I didn't know you cared.' He handed over the money as the barman brought her beer, his tongue hanging out.

Maeve flashed the man a flirtatious smile before turning back to Karl. 'You can't walk out now, you dag.'

Karl laughed. 'I've told you before, Aussie slang don't work with a Dublin accent.'

'Oh, come on, Karl, we can handle Ben Donnelly.'

The barman delivered the Guinness and Carrie sipped hers in silence.

'So you can't do it without me, Maeve?' Karl teased, as he watched his pint settle. If he left he would miss sparring with Maeve.

She made a face at him. 'I want this show to be a

success and I don't think it will be if Ben is calling the shots.'

Karl nodded. 'From what I've heard of Donnelly he doesn't worry too much about ethics.'

'Well, after what he said today I'd say he wants to turn *Secrets* into something very sordid and nasty. Come on, Karl, you're not going to give up without a fight, are you?' Maeve taunted him.

'Okay, I'll stay but I won't accept Donnelly as my boss.'

'Jonathan says he's just part of the team,' Carrie pointed out.

Maeve shot her an incredulous look. 'You are so naïve.'

Carrie reddened. 'But I believe him. He wouldn't want to lose you, Maeve, and he knows that if Karl left you would too.'

Maeve avoided eye contact with Karl.

He chuckled. 'Well, we are a team, I suppose. I think it's time we made it clear to Jonathan that he can't have it all his own way.'

Maeve's lips twitched. 'Sounds good.'

'Are you with us, Carrie?' Karl looked at their researcher.

Carrie had no idea what she was getting into but she wouldn't dream of letting either Karl or Maeve down. 'Sure.'

25

Jonathan, oblivious to his staff's rebellion, was planning his weekend. His ex-wife, Alison, was going away and he'd have Daniel from Friday night until Sunday evening. He was excited at the prospect. It was a long time since they'd spent so much time together. Jonathan particularly enjoyed bedtime. Even now, he still missed tucking his son in and kissing him goodnight. Daniel pretended disgust when his father kissed him, but Jonathan would tousle his hair and remind him that he had Greek blood in his veins and Greek men weren't afraid to show their emotions.

Jonathan had gone to a lot of trouble to secure tickets for the Ireland v. England rugby match in Lansdowne Road on Saturday. Before that, he'd bring Daniel to Planet Hollywood for lunch – he'd love that. On Sunday, they might visit the zoo if the weather held and then go and have tea with Jonathan's mother. Daniel loved to visit his nan. Given the spread that she usually laid on and the money that she slipped to her grandson when she thought his father wasn't looking, it wasn't surprising. He took a few hours off on Tuesday morning to tidy the apartment. He would leave the shopping until Friday morning – the only time the fridge was ever full of food was when Daniel visited. Jonathan wasn't interested in cooking for himself. One of the things he missed about married life was the three of them gathered in the kitchen while he made dinner. He was a good cook but only enjoyed it if he'd someone to cook for. Nevertheless it wasn't a good enough reason to stay married to a woman he couldn't love any more. No matter how much she apologised, how often she'd told him that her affair had meant nothing, he couldn't forgive or forget. Eventually he had left. Of course, he was immediately cast as the bastard who'd walked out on his wife and child but his pride wouldn't allow him to admit the truth. It wasn't easy to let Alison get off scot-free but it was Hobson's choice as far as he was concerned, and he was prepared to live with the consequences. Alison still hadn't given up on him unfortunately and she begged him, on a regular basis, to come home. He'd wavered occasionally when she said that Daniel needed him but he knew that his son didn't need his parents living together like strangers. That couldn't be good for him. When Daniel asked why he'd left, he just told him that Mummy and Daddy couldn't be happy together any more. The one thing he'd made Alison promise was that she would always give him the same story. But Daniel, a very quick-witted ten-year-old, was well aware that his mother would love her husband to come home. It bothered Jonathan that one day he might have to tell his son the truth. If he didn't, he might lose him for good. He'd heard all about the dreaded teenage years. Even when you were the best parent in the world your children apparently hated you. Jonathan sighed. He should stop worrying about the future and enjoy their time together now. And that meant making this weekend one to remember.

Linda smiled brightly at Cheryl as she breezed into the office on Friday morning. 'Morning. Beautiful morning, isn't it?'

Cheryl eyed her suspiciously. 'Ask me again after I've had my coffee. You're very chipper this morning. Were you with the boyfriend again last night?'

Linda laughed. 'Actually I had an early night.'

'That doesn't answer my question,' Cheryl said with a knowing grin.

'Cheryl, really!' Linda tried to look shocked, but the truth was she was enjoying herself enormously. Being Jonathan Blake's 'girlfriend' had done wonders for her street cred. She hadn't seen him since Sunday lunch – although they'd talked on the phone a couple of times – but it didn't seem to make a difference to the gossip circulating about them. The highlight of her week had been a call from Patrick. Ostensibly, it was to discuss the offer that had been made on the house, but it didn't take long for Patrick to ask about Jonathan.

'Were you seeing him when we were together?' he had asked in clipped tones.

'No.'

He had given a muffled snort. 'So there were others?'

'Oh, Patrick, leave it. You're happy with Stacey, can't you be happy for me?' She had been glad he couldn't see her face because she couldn't suppress the wide grin spreading across it.

There had been a short silence. 'I'll tell the estate agent that we'll accept that offer, okay?' he'd said finally.

'Fine by me, I can't wait to see the back of this place.' Linda's smile had faded as she looked around her small but compact kitchen. Up until a couple of months ago she'd loved her home. Now it was just a cruel reminder of her old life.

'Are you moving in with Blake?'

On the verge of hotly denying it, Linda bit her lip. 'I don't think that's any of your business, do you?' she'd said instead. 'Goodnight, Patrick.'

'It must be wonderful to go out with a man like Jonathan,' Cheryl was saying dreamily, having followed Linda to her desk. 'He reminds me of George Clooney. All broody, and then he switches on that sexy smile.'

Linda laughed. 'You think so?'

Cheryl nodded. 'Oh, yes. I don't think you realise how lucky you are, Linda. I mean, you're not a teenager any more and you've landed one of the most eligible men in the country. He could have anybody.'

'You're great for my ego.'

Cheryl grinned. 'Oh, you know what I mean.'

Linda nodded. It had been the main flaw in this

whole plan – as she'd pointed out to both Viv and Jonathan.

'Still, you're looking great these days.' Cheryl's eyes were taking in her neat bob, perfect make-up and manicured nails. 'And you've lost weight.'

'Have I?' Linda said lightly. She had lost a few pounds, although it hadn't been easy. But she figured it was the least she could do if she was going to be hitting all the hot spots in town on Jonathan's arm. Having got back down to a size twelve she'd gone out and spent a ruinous amount of money on clothes and had her hair coloured so it was a rich golden halo around her face. That comment in the newspaper about her being a brunette had touched a nerve. She was relieved when the phone rang and Cheryl reluctantly went back to her desk. The morning flew and at one o'clock she slipped out of the office afraid that Cheryl would suggest a cosy lunch. She believed in long lunches on Friday, mainly because Bill was usually off playing golf. She didn't see anything wrong with leaving Marie to answer the phones while she dragged Linda off to the nearest wine bar. Linda usually agreed. Cheryl was a pain in the neck but she was the kind of person who was better with you than against you. But these days all Cheryl wanted to discuss was Linda's love-life and she needed a break from it today. She hurried up Grafton Street towards Marks and Spencer's. She could pick up a low-fat sandwich there and a TV dinner for tonight. There was a good film on so Linda was looking forward to settling down for a relaxing evening with a glass of wine.

'Linda?'

She swung round as she heard her name called. 'Gwen! How are you? Long time no see.'

The other woman's smile was cool. 'That's not my fault now, is it?'

'Sorry,' Linda said lamely. Gwen Harper and her husband Brian were old friends and since she and Patrick had broken up Gwen had left a number of messages for her on the answering machine. 'I wasn't ready to see anyone.'

Gwen's eyes were shrewd. 'You seemed to be enjoying plenty of company the last few weekends, if one can believe what it says in the papers.'

Linda sighed. Gwen was obviously furious with her, but it was impossible to tell her the truth. 'I'm getting back on my feet now,' she explained feebly, 'but it hasn't been easy.'

The other woman's mouth settled in a grim line. 'From what I've heard, you weren't the only injured party. But that's your business, Linda, nothing to do with me. I just don't understand why you've dropped your friends. Sally says she hasn't heard from you in weeks.'

'Like I say, it's been difficult.'

Gwen's eyes raked her new suit, high shoes and immaculate hair. 'Really? Look, I must go. It was nice to see you at last. I was worried.'

As she turned to leave, Linda put a hand on her arm. 'I'm so sorry, Gwen. I'll call you.'

'Whatever.' The other woman pulled away and marched off with her head in the air.

'Shit.' Linda fought her way through the lunchtime

crowds into the department store, her earlier good mood forgotten. She should have called Gwen and Sally but when Patrick had first left, she was too miserable to talk to them. And after she'd started this charade with Jonathan she was afraid to in case she tripped up on all the lies. Now, it looked like she'd lost two valuable friendships – ones she'd sorely miss when she was alone again. She went back to the office, nibbled on her sandwich and ploughed through her workload, resolutely ignoring any of Cheryl's attempts at conversation.

'Somebody must have had a tiff this lunchtime,' Cheryl said in a loud whisper to Marie. The girl shot Linda a sympathetic smile but Linda was beyond caring. At five o'clock she refused Cheryl's invitation to go for a drink, pleading a headache. She couldn't wait to get home so that she could be miserable in peace. Although, it didn't feel much like home any more, she realised when she got there and looked at the boxes lining the hall. There weren't that many really. It was kind of sad to think that fifteen years of her life could be condensed into just a few boxes.

She went into the kitchen and made herself a cup of tea. She was just sitting down to drink it when the phone rang. She was tempted to let the machine pick up but it was probably Viv. They were supposed to be going shopping tomorrow. 'Hello?'

'Hi, Linda.'

'Hi, Viv.'

'What's wrong?'

'Nothing.'

'Liar.'

Linda sighed. 'Oh, I'm just a bit fed up.'

'Why?'

'I met Gwen. She was pissed off with me because I haven't returned any of her calls.'

'What did you tell her?'

Linda snuggled up on the sofa and tucked the phone under her chin. 'Oh, that I'd needed to be alone, that I was sorry. But I don't think she bought any of it.'

'Well, she doesn't know the truth.'

'And I can't tell her, can I? I should never have got myself into this mess.'

Viv groaned. 'Oh, not again, Lin. If she's really your friend she'll get over it.'

'I suppose.'

'Are we going shopping tomorrow?'

'I don't think so.'

'But you're moving into your new flat in a week's time, Linda. You need to buy the basics.'

'I could always order from Argos.' Linda was finding it very hard to get enthusiastic about kitting out her new home.

'You can't kit out your new home from a catalogue.' Viv was disgusted. 'Oh, come on, Lin, it'll be fun.'

'Okay, then,' Linda agreed, just to get her sister off the phone. 'I'll meet you outside the Stephen's Green Centre at ten.'

'Righto, byee!'

Linda put down the phone and picked up her tea. She winced. It was stone cold. She went back out to the kitchen, poured it down the sink and took a bottle of wine from the fridge. Well, it was Friday, she reasoned, and if she'd gone to the pub with Cheryl she'd probably be on her third drink by now. She took her wine back inside and switched on the TV. As she flicked through the channels the tears started to flow. Was this all she had to look forward to? Nights alone with a bottle, a takeaway and the TV, while Patrick took his girlfriend to posh restaurants with their friends. After all, Linda wasn't bothered, so why should they be? It seemed she'd succeeded in her plan. No one was wasting any sympathy on her. In fact, if anything, they seemed to be more outraged by her so-called behaviour than Patrick's. 'There's equality for you,' she muttered. The phone rang again. 'What is it now, Viv?'

'Eh, it's Jonathan, actually.'

'Oh, sorry, Jonathan. I thought you were Viv.'

'So I gather. What's wrong?'

'You see, you even sound like her,' Linda sniffed.

'Having a bad day?' he said softly.

'No, yes, oh, it's nothing, don't mind me.'

'But I do mind you. Look, would you like to come over? I can't come to you because Daniel is here. But he's fast asleep,' he added hastily.

'I'm not very good company tonight, Jonathan, but thanks for the invitation.'

'Well, I can't see you tomorrow, I'm afraid, Daniel and I have a hectic day planned.'

Linda's eyes filled up again. 'That's okay, Viv and I are going shopping.'

'Then you must come to the zoo with us on Sunday,' he said decisively.

'Oh, I don't think so.'

'I won't take no for an answer. It's about time you and Daniel met. We'll pick you up at twelve.'

Linda blinked as she realised she was listening to the dial tone. Oh, God, this was all she needed. Perhaps she'd have flu by Sunday.

26

Freddy grinned down at Maeve. 'Well, is this difficult enough for you?'

Maeve nodded, too breathless to reply. She pulled herself up on to the top of Welsh Rarebit, one of the more difficult climbs on the Scalp. Craig followed suit and sat down heavily beside her.

'It's a good job we started early.' Freddy frowned as he looked up into the sky. It was only three but with the heavy rain clouds, it was ominously dark. 'We'll have a short break and then we should head back down.'

Maeve rummaged in her pack for the water. After drinking thirstily, she handed it to Craig.

'So, Maeve, would you do this again?' He drank and then passed it on to Freddy.

'Oh, yes,' she said her eyes sparkling. 'It was brilliant.'

Craig smiled. 'You're a glutton for punishment, aren't you?'

'Well, I think we'll all sleep well tonight,' Freddy observed. 'Now come on, you two. I want to get home. Eileen is making one of her curries for dinner tonight.' He licked his lips in anticipation.

Maeve watched him in amusement. While he

sprawled on the sofa tonight with his wife, she'd be making a flying stop at a cocktail party before heading on to dinner with some of Paul's more affluent clients. 'What are you doing tonight, Craig?' she asked curiously.

'I've got a hot date.' Craig winked as he stood up and reached out a hand to help her up.

Maeve laughed. 'Oh, yeah? With one of your customers?'

'No, actually. I'm seeing a model at the moment. Who knows, we might even bump into you later, I fancy a bit of clubbing.' He turned and followed Freddy.

Maeve stared after him, lost for words. Craig Prentice seeing a model? It seemed ludicrous. What on earth would they have to talk about? He was always scathing about Maeve's social life and the shallow people she mixed with and he was dating a model! 'What's her name?' she asked casually when she'd caught up on him. 'Maybe I know her.'

'I don't think so.' Craig didn't break his stride.

Maeve scowled. 'Oh, come on, don't be so coy.'

'Not all of us like to tell the world about our love-lives, Maeve. Sometimes it's nice to keep your private life private. You should try it sometime.'

Maeve went to retort but he'd already started down the incline. She followed him silently – this descent was too tricky to indulge in idle chitchat. Maeve tried to put the image of Craig slow dancing with a beautiful model out of her mind but it stubbornly refused to go away.

'Hey, are you going to be all night?' Craig hollered. Lost in thought, she'd fallen behind and now Freddy and Craig were standing on the rough pathway below. 'Freddy wants to get home to his curry, remember?'

'And you want to get home to your model,' Maeve roared back. 'Probably a model car,' she muttered to herself as she searched carefully for footholds.

'Mind that last stretch, Maeve, it's slippy,' Freddy warned.

'Yeah, I'm fine, aargh—' Maeve's feet went from under her and she slid down the last few feet, landing in an ungraceful heap at their feet.

'Jesus! Are you okay?' Craig crouched down beside her.

'Yeah, sure.' Maeve managed a shaky smile.

'Don't move,' Freddy instructed, kneeling down on her other side. 'Does anything hurt?'

'I think you mean does anything *not* hurt,' she joked as she tried to sit up. Craig put a steadying arm around her shoulders and she leaned against him gratefully.

'Take it slowly,' Freddy remonstrated. 'Get your breath back.'

'Really, I'm okay. There's no need to fuss, Freddy.' She went to stand up but as she put her weight on her right foot, she screamed and slipped back down again.

'Okay, let's have a look.' Craig gently removed her boot, pulled down her sock and examined her ankle. 'Can you move it at all?'

'Yes, but it hurts like hell.' Maeve looked down and watched as her ankle began to balloon.

'A bad sprain, I'd say,' Craig mused.

'You two wait here,' Freddy said. 'I'll go and get a bandage.'

When he'd left, Craig tried to make her more comfortable and then sat down beside her. 'Here, have some of this. Sugar's good for shock.' He opened up a bar of chocolate and handed her a chunk.

'I'm not in shock,' she told him, taking the chocolate anyway. 'Just pain.'

Craig eyed the swelling ankle with a wry grin. 'I don't think you're going to be doing much dancing for a while.'

'As long as I'm able to hobble as far as the bar.'

Craig frowned. 'Eh, I don't think you realise how serious this is, Maeve. You're going to have to go to hospital for an x-ray and at the very least they'll bandage it up and send you home to rest for a few days.'

'But I can't rest,' Maeve wailed. 'My new programme starts in a couple of weeks.'

'Stop panicking,' Craig said easily. 'I'm sure you'll be fine by then. Anyway, you're not going to do your shows standing up, are you?'

Maeve's lips twitched as she looked up at him. 'Depends on the guest.'

He leaned closer and stroked her cheek.

Maeve flinched. 'What are you doing?'

'Relax, I'm not going to jump on you! There was some dirt on your face.'

'Oh.' She looked away, embarrassed.

'So tell me more about your show.'

'I can't.'

'Oh, come on, Maeve. Will you tell me if I cross my heart not to tell another living soul?'

Maeve grinned. 'Oh, well, okay. The first show is about a girl who is HIV positive.'

Craig listened intently as she told him the young girl's story.

'Poor kid,' he said when she'd finished. 'I can't understand why she's telling you her problems. No offence, but going on a talk show about something so personal, so serious . . .' He shook his head, bemused.

Maeve wasn't in the least offended. Being a private person, she understood Craig's viewpoint. 'Well, remember she will be anonymous. And it must be very hard to keep something like that to yourself. From the few conversations we've had so far I think she's just bursting to tell her whole story.' She shivered.

'Are you cold?' He looked at her worriedly. 'It could be the shock.'

'Don't be silly. I've just hurt my ankle, for God's sake.' She flexed it gingerly and whimpered as the pain shot up her leg.

'Yes, you're obviously fine.' He looked worriedly at the sky as fat raindrops started to plop on them. 'Get a move on, Freddy,' he muttered.

Maeve blinked the rain out of her eyes and gritted her teeth against it. 'He's probably forgotten all about this and gone home for his curry.'

'No, he's coming,' Craig said and she breathed a sigh of relief. 'We'll have you in hospital within the hour.'

*   *   *

They were actually sitting in A & E forty minutes later, but it looked like they were going to be there for quite some time. When Craig had seen Freddy's crestfallen expression, he'd sent him home. 'There's no point in the three of us sitting here, I'll take care of her.'

'I don't need to be taken care of,' Maeve told him when Freddy had left. 'Go home.'

'There's gratitude.'

'Sorry,' Maeve said grudgingly, 'but we could be here for hours and you've a date tonight.'

Craig shrugged. 'Don't worry about that.'

Maeve sighed. 'I'm not a child.'

'No, but not only have you got no way to get home—'

'Oh, bloody hell, my car!' she wailed.

'It's okay, I'll go and get it after I've dropped you home.'

Maeve flashed him a guilty look from under her lashes. 'I'm an ungrateful cow, aren't I?'

'Absolutely. Now, how about a cup of coffee?'

'I think I'd prefer a diet Coke.'

'You should have an ordinary one. You need the sugar—'

'For the shock, yes, you said.' She smiled as Craig headed off down the corridor. She was lucky to have such a good mate. Craig was the kind of reliable bloke that was handy to have around in a crisis. He always seemed to know what to do and was completely unflappable.

He returned with two Cokes and a couple of Mars Bars.

'You know what I'd really love now?' Maeve told him as they ate. 'A bacon sandwich.'

Craig laughed. 'Afraid that's a little beyond the hospital's capabilities.'

'Maeve Elliot?' the nurse called.

Two hours later, Craig led the way to his car as Maeve experimented with her crutches.

'Damn things have a mind of their own,' she grumbled.

'Just take it slowly. You'll soon get into a rhythm.' When they got to his van, he slid the crutches into the back and turned to help Maeve.

'I can manage,' she insisted.

'Don't be so bloody stubborn. It's too high.' And before she could reply he'd lifted her up and settled her carefully in the seat.

Maeve smirked down at him. 'My hero.'

Craig bowed slightly and went round to climb into the driver's seat. They drove in silence and half an hour later he pulled into the car park of her apartment complex. 'I suppose you're on the top floor.'

Maeve laughed. 'Yeah, but relax, they have a lift.'

'Thank God for that. I think I did my back in lifting you.'

'Bloody cheek.'

'Give me your keys.'

Maeve fumbled in her bag, handed over the keys. As he got out, she opened the door and swung her legs out.

'Stay there,' he ordered, coming round to help her.

'I'm not completely stupid.' She waited while he fetched her crutches and obediently put an arm around his neck as he helped her down. She hobbled along slowly as Craig went ahead to open the door. 'Thanks,' she said breathlessly and made her way carefully to the lift. Thankfully, the hall was carpeted, which made the journey less precarious. 'I don't know why this is such hard work,' she moaned. 'I mean, I'm fit.'

'You're using a different set of muscles, and like I say, there's a knack involved.'

'That sounds like the voice of experience.'

'I broke my leg playing rugby. I was in plaster for months.'

Maeve looked up in surprise. 'When was that?'

'When I was sixteen. It was great. I got lots of time off school and tons of sympathy from the girls.'

Maeve laughed as the lift opened on the top floor. 'Last door on the right,' she told Craig. He opened the door and turned on the lights. She watched him look around her apartment before turning to take her crutches. He helped her off with her jacket and settled her on the cream sofa.

'Nice place,' he said, looking very ill at ease.

'Sit down.'

'Oh, no, I'm a mess.' He looked down at his dirty boots. 'God, sorry, I should have taken these off.'

'Don't be silly, it's only a bit of dirt.'

'On a cream carpet,' he pointed out. 'Look, is there anything you want me to get you before I go?'

'You're going?' Maeve tried to hide her disappointment.

'I have to get your car, remember?'

'But what about your van?'

'I'll leave it here and get a taxi back to Bray.'

'Okay. You make me a mug of coffee and I'll ring for a taxi. You'll find the coffee in a jar beside the kettle.'

Craig grinned as he looked at the four white doors. 'Great. Just tell me where the kitchen is.'

Maeve laughed and pointed to the one directly behind him. 'That one.'

The taxi arrived just as he set the coffee down carefully on the table in front of her. 'Will you be okay?'

'Fine.' When he'd left, she rested her head back against the cushions and went fast asleep. It was after nine o'clock when the buzzer woke her. It took her a few seconds to realise that it must be Craig. She jumped up from the sofa without thinking and howled in pain as she put her weight on her right foot. 'Come on up,' she gasped into the intercom, opened the door and then collapsed back on the sofa.

Craig came in and frowned at her pale face. 'Are you having a tough time?'

'I was fine until I jumped up to let you in.'

'Sorry. I should have taken a key with me.'

'Don't worry, I'll live – what's that smell?'

Craig produced a large brown paper bag from behind his back. 'Fish and chips. Afraid they didn't have any bacon sandwiches.'

Maeve's mouth watered as the aroma filled the room. 'I think I can just about forgive you. I'll get some plates.' She went to stand up and Craig put a firm hand on her shoulder. 'You stay right where you are. I'll manage.'

Maeve was quite happy to let him. Suddenly she felt very weak and her ankle was throbbing. She had just found a couple of painkillers when he returned with a tray.

'What would you like to drink?'

'Just some milk, please, but there's beer in the fridge, help yourself.'

He returned with her milk and a can of beer for himself and they tucked in hungrily to the food.

'I didn't even realise I was hungry.' Maeve looked in surprise at her empty plate.

'That'll be the shock.' Craig grinned at her.

Maeve rolled her eyes. 'Of course.'

He pushed his plate away and sat back with his beer.

Maeve frowned. His large frame looked awkward in the chair. She moved up on the sofa. 'Would you prefer to sit here? It's probably more comfortable.'

Craig's eyes widened. 'Are you propositioning me, Maeve?'

She looked horrified. 'No, of course not – oh, you!' She broke off as he laughed. 'I just thought that you didn't seem very comfortable in that chair.'

Craig looked down at the spindly arms. 'It's not really built for comfort, is it?'

'You don't like my home, do you?' she accused.

'No, it's nice. Very, er, modern.'

Maeve scowled. 'That means you hate it.'

'It doesn't matter what I think. You're the one who has to live here. Did you decorate it yourself?'

Maeve looked astonished. 'Of course not.'

Craig smiled at her. 'It can be very rewarding, decorating.'

Maeve wrinkled her nose. 'As rewarding as gardening, I suppose.'

'No,' Craig answered seriously. 'Nothing beats planting things and watching them grow.' He stood up and wandered towards the door to her balcony. 'You could probably keep some shrubs out here.'

'No, don't go out there,' Maeve called, but he'd already switched on the light that illuminated the little garden she'd created.

He turned around and smiled. 'Well, well, well. What have we here?'

'The previous owner did it,' Maeve said defensively.

'It's very well kept,' he noted as he peered out.

'Well, I can't afford to let it go. If I ever sold the place it would affect the price.'

Craig looked at her in amusement.

'What?'

He came over and sat down beside her. 'I think, Ms Elliot, that you have a soft side you've been hiding from me.'

Maeve watched him, conscious of his nearness and the faint smell of sweat mixed with cologne. 'Me soft? Never.'

Craig stared down at her. 'I don't believe you.'

Maeve stared back, unable to tear her eyes from his. 'It's late.'

Craig smiled lazily. 'It is.' He leaned closer and kissed her lightly on the lips. Maeve felt a flutter of excitement quickly followed by disappointment as he stood up. 'I'd better go.'

'Thanks for taking care of me,' Maeve said shyly.

'My pleasure. I'll call you tomorrow.'

'There's no need – well, if you like.'

Craig laughed. 'Goodnight.'

Maeve watched him leave. 'Goodnight,' she called softly.

27

Carrie sat on the floor surrounded by straws.

'What will we make now, Aunty Cawie?' Ethan demanded.

'Let's make a star.'

He beamed at her. 'Oh, yes, a star!'

'Only five more minutes, Ethan, then it's time for bed,' Orla warned.

'Okay, Mummy,' he smiled sweetly.

'He's so good.' Carrie caressed his little golden head.

Orla grinned. 'You won't be saying that in an hour when you're still trying to get him to bed.'

'I don't mind,' Carrie said. 'I haven't had this much fun in ages.' She didn't even look up as she concentrated on connecting the straws together.

Orla stared worriedly at her friend. 'I could easily cancel tonight and we could open a bottle of wine and have a good natter instead.'

'I don't like wine,' Carrie reminded her.

'There's Guinness in the fridge too.'

'No, you go out. Ray seems really nice.'

'He is,' Orla said happily.

'Way's nice,' Ethan agreed. 'I like him, Mummy.'

'Thanks, little man.' Orla ruffled his hair. 'So what's Declan doing tonight?'

Carrie shrugged. 'Don't know.'

'I thought he was coming with you.'

'He was supposed to, but he's been driving me mad all day, moaning. I needed some time on my own.'

'What did he think of that?'

Carrie shrugged. 'I don't think he was too bothered. He'll probably order an Indian and spend the evening in front of the telly.'

'Doesn't he have any friends?' Orla said tentatively.

'A few, but he doesn't see much of them outside of work.'

'But doesn't he ever want to go to the pub with the lads? Or go to a match?'

'Not unless it's on expenses,' Carrie told her. 'Declan only enjoys himself when he's spending someone else's money.'

Orla stared at her in surprise.

Carrie smiled. 'Don't look at me like that, Orla, you know you've always thought he was mean.'

'I wouldn't say that . . .'

'But he probably still has his Communion money,' Carrie interrupted.

Orla giggled. 'Well, he's never the first to buy a round,' she admitted.

'Or the second, or the last,' Carrie added, but her eyes were sad.

'What are you going to do?' Orla asked gently.

'What do you mean?'

'Well, you can't go on like this?'

'Why not? So, Declan's not perfect, neither am I.'

'Oh, Carrie!'

'Listen, I wish you would go and get ready. I'm trying to make a star.'

'Yes, Mummy, go away. Cawie's playing with me.'

'Okay, okay, I know when I'm not wanted.'

When Orla and Ray had left and Ethan was asleep, Carrie settled down to watch the video that Orla had rented for her. *Bridget Jones's Diary*. She smiled. Orla was not very subtle. Mind you, looking at Bridget's disastrous experiences with men might have the opposite effect. Maybe Declan wasn't so bad after all. Carrie settled down with a Guinness and popcorn to enjoy the movie. It was halfway through when Ethan woke up crying.

'What is it, pet? What's wrong?' Carrie put a hand down to touch Ethan's face.

'I want my mummy.' He pushed her hand away and started to cry again.

'She'll be back soon. Would you like a drink.'

'Okay.'

Carrie hurried downstairs and came back with some milk in his beaker. 'Here you are, Ethan. Are you going to sit up?'

The little boy pulled his sheet closer around him and shook his head. 'I want my mummy.'

Carrie eyed him worriedly. Usually she could handle Ethan whatever mood he was in, but this was different. She reached down to touch his forehead and was further concerned to find it both hot and damp. She turned on the lamp and smiled down at him in what she hoped was a confident manner. 'Now, Ethan, I think we'll take off your pyjamas. It's very warm tonight.'

'No,' Ethan protested, but he closed his eyes and allowed her to undress him. This scared Carrie even more – Ethan never usually gave in so easily. When she'd stripped him to his nappy, she checked him from head to foot for signs of a rash. Thankfully, there were none.

'I want mummy,' Ethan wailed.

'Okay, Ethan, I'll call her.' She hurried downstairs, grabbed the phone and dialled Orla's mobile.

Twenty minutes later Orla was running up the path, her eyes wide with worry. 'How is he?'

'I honestly don't know, Orla. He won't let me anywhere near him, just keeps calling for you.'

Orla ran up the stairs with Carrie hot on her heels. 'Hey, Sweetie, Mummy's here.'

Ethan burst into floods of tears again and Orla scooped him up in her arms. 'There, there, Sweetie, what's wrong? Have you a pain?'

Ethan shook his head.

'Do you feel sick? Have you a pain?'

He shook his head silently.

Orla frowned. 'Then what is it, love? What's wrong?'

'I'm scared,' he said into her shoulder.

Orla breathed a sigh of relief. 'What are you scared of, Sweetie?'

'The big spider. He's going to get me.'

'What big spider? There's no big spider, love.'

'Eh, maybe . . .' Carrie started.

'Yes, Mummy, there is,' he protested indignantly. 'Aunty Cawie made a big spider.'

Carrie smiled lamely over the little boy's head. 'Guilty as charged.'

Orla laughed. 'Oh, Ethan, that's just a pretend spider.'

Ethan sniffed. 'Pretend?'

'Pretend,' Orla said firmly.

Ethan watched her sleepily, his eyes trusting. 'Mummy, you stay home now?'

'Yes, honey, Mummy's not going anywhere. Now go to sleep.' She put him back into bed and tucked him in. 'Night, night.'

'I am *so* sorry,' Carrie said when they were back downstairs.

Orla laughed. 'Don't worry about it. It's happened to me a few times. I remember one day I was reading the story of "The Three Little Pigs" to him and we were getting very enthusiastic about our huffing and puffing. That night he bawled saying that the wolf was coming to blow our house down. Children have very active imaginations.'

Carrie flopped into a chair weak with relief and took a grateful sip of her Guinness. 'I thought there was something seriously wrong. I mean, he felt so warm.'

Orla nodded. 'I know. The little terror gets worked up into a frenzy. The number of times I've been on the point of calling a doctor and suddenly he's laughing again.'

'It's true what they say then,' Carrie murmured, '"Children can be cruel."'

'Especially to mums and babysitters!'

'But I messed up your date.'

'Don't worry about it. I was a bit bored, to be honest. We were with a bunch of Ray's friends and they were horrible to me.'

Carrie looked shocked. How anyone could be nasty to someone as nice as Orla was beyond comprehension.

'You see, Ray just broke up with one of their friends,' she explained.

'Ah, and you're the horrible, nasty creature that split them up?'

Orla smiled sadly and kicked off her shoes. 'Something like that. Would you like some coffee?'

Carrie jumped up. 'I'll make it. You rewind the tape. This film is exactly what you need.'

Three hours later, Carrie stepped out of the taxi and let herself into the silent house – Declan was obviously in bed. He usually left a light on for her but tonight the house was in darkness. Carrie sighed. It looked like the Cold War was to continue. Taking off her shoes she went upstairs and put her head round the bedroom door. The humped shape under the duvet suggested that she was correct. She went back downstairs, fetched a Coke from the fridge and went in search of the novel she was reading. Half an hour of escapism would help her sleep. Having found the book, she curled up on the sofa. Minutes later she realised that she was still staring at the same page. She closed it and stared miserably at the photo on the fireplace. Helen had taken it at Lily's last birthday party and she and Declan were laughing happily for the camera. It was less than a year ago but it seemed longer. Carrie couldn't remember the last time she and Declan had really laughed together. Maybe it was her fault. Since she'd taken the job at Forever FM, she didn't have much free time. Perhaps Declan was feeling justifiably neglected. She should try and make it up to him. Perhaps a night out next weekend – before *Secrets* started. They could go to Kingsland – his favourite Chinese restaurant. She stood up, pleased with herself that she'd made a decision, and turned off the light. Creeping upstairs she assured herself that everything would be all right once she and Declan had discussed the situation. She stripped her clothes off in the bathroom, ignored her cleansing routine and went into the bedroom. As she cuddled up close to Declan, she kissed the tip of his nose and smiled. Everything would be fine. Declan snorted and turned over, taking most of the bedclothes with him.

28

Linda had tried to call Jonathan a number of times but his mobile seemed to be switched off. She should have called last night but she'd thought her excuse would be more credible if she left it as late as possible to phone. Now it was after eleven and he was probably on his way to collect her. Linda stared miserably out at the bright sunshine turning the leaves in her garden into a golden carpet. She couldn't even use the weather as an excuse not to go. It was a perfect day to wrap up warm and get out and about. She'd always liked going to the zoo – well she'd liked most things about it. She always stayed well clear of the snakes and spiders. But she loved to watch the grace and dangerous beauty of the big cats; the deceptive cuddliness of the polar bears; the awkward clumsiness of the hippos on land and their incredible smooth speed under water. She pulled on a large baggy fleece over her jumper and jeans and sat by the window to wait. What on earth was Daniel Blake going to make of this? She hoped that Jonathan had made it clear that she was just a friend and he had nothing to worry about. A black Volvo jeep pulled silently to a stop outside her gate. 'Who the hell is that?' Linda muttered, peering through the curtains. Jonathan jumped out of the car and walked up the path. Linda was at the door before he could ring the bell. 'New car?' She glanced nervously past him and spotted a small head sporting a baseball cap in the passenger seat.

'Nah, I've had it a while.' Jonathan grinned down at her. 'Ready to go, then?'

'I suppose, if you're sure Daniel won't mind.'

'Of course not.'

Linda smiled bravely. 'Okay then. I'll lock up and be right with you.'

Jonathan went back out to the car and she fumbled with the keys. A BMW and a jeep – how the other half live! When she reached the car, Jonathan was standing beside the open passenger door, glaring down at his son.

'Daniel, I won't tell you again. Get into the back seat now.'

'Oh, that's okay.' Linda smiled at the grim little boy. 'I'll sit in the back.'

Jonathan ignored her. 'Daniel?' The child scowled at him and then crawled into the back. Jonathan stood back and held the door for Linda. 'Sorry about that.'

'No problem.' She flashed an apologetic smile at Daniel as she got in but he just pulled his baseball cap further down over his dark eyes and fiddled with the zip of his jacket. So much for him not minding.

'Let's go,' Jonathan said cheerfully, ignoring her reproachful look and his son's angry silence. 'We're going to have a great day!'

He chatted away to them about previous experiences in the zoo as he drove. Before long, Linda was relating some of her own memories and Daniel was giggling at his father's impressions of the gorillas, but he still studiously ignored Linda. 'He'll be fine,' Jonathan murmured as they got out of the car. 'Just ignore him and enjoy yourself.'

Linda smiled and pretended not to notice his outstretched hand. Daniel would probably feed her to the lions if he saw them holding hands.

'Let's go and see the snakes first!' he was shouting excitedly as he swung from the entrance gate.

'Sure,' Jonathan said and Linda groaned. She should have known the little horror would want to see all the scary stuff.

Jonathan paid for their tickets and they made their way to the reptile house, Linda trailing behind.

Daniel tugged open the door and Linda closed her eyes briefly at the smell.

'Don't you like snakes?' Daniel was watching her, his eyes twinkling with a mixture of delight and mischief.

'Sure.' She smiled brightly, took a deep breath and followed them inside.

'Wow, Dad, look at that. What is it?'

Jonathan looked at the snake as thick as a drainpipe draping from a tree. 'It's a python.'

Daniel pressed his face to the glass and stuck out his tongue. 'Do they bite?'

'No, they crush you to death,' Jonathan said easily. 'Are you okay, Linda?'

'Sure.' She moved to a cage on the other side of the room that seemed to be empty.

'Dad, look at the crocodiles.' Daniel moved on with Jonathan at his side and Linda counted the seconds until she could go back outside and breath in some fresh air.

'Where are the spiders?'

'Over there, behind Linda.'

She stared at him, looked warily to her left and gasped.

'Cool! That's a tarantula, isn't it, Dad?'

'A black widow, I think.' Jonathan moved to Linda's side. 'They mate with the male and then kill him.'

'Sounds like a good idea to me,' Linda murmured, trying not to look at the eight-legged creatures that suddenly seemed to be everywhere.

Daniel eyed her with new respect. 'You like spiders, Linda?'

'Love them,' she lied.

'Mum hates them. She screams at even the tiniest little thing. I have to catch them for her.'

'That's nice of you. Your mum's very lucky to have you around.'

Daniel smiled proudly. 'It's no big deal. I like spiders.'

Jonathan noted Linda's white, pinched face and steered his son towards the door. 'Let's go see the elephants.'

Linda hurried after them. 'Oh, yes, I love elephants.'

They strolled around the zoo in the winter sunshine,

stopping to get drinks and ice cream. Linda laughed as she licked her cone. 'I can't believe I'm eating ice cream at this time of the year.'

'I eat ice cream all year round,' Daniel informed her.

Linda smiled. Once he forgot to be sullen, he was quite a nice kid. And he was going to be a real ladykiller when he was older. Though he had his dad's dark eyes, the hair – possibly inherited from his mother – was golden-blond and when he smiled it was impossible not to smile back.

After a second break for some sausage and chips, they took the little train around the safari section of the zoo. 'It's changed so much since I was here last,' Linda marvelled, clinging to Jonathan as they went round a bend. 'Sorry,' she gasped.

Jonathan grinned down at her. 'Gosh, you just can't keep your hands off me, can you?'

'Silly.' She turned her head and pointed to the zebra in the distance but she was conscious that his arm was still around her. She shot a nervous glance at Daniel but he was too busy to notice.

'It's been a lovely day,' she said as they went back to the car. 'Thank you for inviting me, I really enjoyed it.'

'It's not over yet,' Jonathan told her. 'My mum is expecting us for tea.'

'Oh, no, I couldn't intrude on your parents,' Linda said nervously.

'It's just Mum, my dad died when I was a kid.'

'I'm sorry.'

'Please come, Linda,' he said. 'She wants to meet you.'

Linda gulped.

'Nan's cool,' Daniel told her, 'and she makes great cakes.'

'Lovely,' Linda said faintly.

'More tea, Linda?'

'No, thanks, Mrs Blake.' Linda sat on the edge of the rose-coloured sofa and smiled at the older woman. Round, soft and pretty, Kathleen seemed to be as smart as her son. Her eyes darted from Linda to Jonathan as she asked question after question.

'Oh, Mum, leave Linda alone,' Jonathan had protested.

Kathleen Blake shrugged, not in the least cowed by her son's rebuke. 'I'm your mother, I'm allowed to ask questions.'

Linda decided to move the conversation away from herself. 'I'm fascinated by your Greek background.'

Kathleen laughed. 'Oh, he hasn't been going on about that again, has he? Daniel, what are we going to do with your dad?'

Daniel rolled his eyes. 'Dunno, Nan.'

Kathleen saw Linda's questioning look. 'My grandfather was born in Crete, Linda, but he was brought to Ireland when he was two. He couldn't even speak the language.'

'Oh.' Linda looked reproachfully at Jonathan.

He shrugged and smiled. 'It's still in the blood, Lin, trust me.'

'Dad, you are such an embarrassment,' Daniel complained before turning back to his grandmother. 'Nan, can I have another éclair?'

'Yes, of course, darling.'

Jonathan chuckled. 'If he throws up later, Alison will murder you.'

Kathleen's eyes narrowed. 'I'd like to see her try. So, Linda, you work in the recruitment business. That must be very interesting.'

Linda smiled ruefully at Jonathan. Her diversion tactics hadn't worked for long. 'It has its moments,' she told Kathleen. 'It can be as boring as most jobs but when I manage to fit the right person to the right job it's a wonderful feeling – especially if that person has been out of work for some time.'

'Linda has brought some wonderful people in to Forever FM,' Jonathan said enthusiastically.

'And stirred up some trouble,' she murmured.

'Oh, yes?' Kathleen's interest was roused.

'I've hired a programme co-ordinator for the *Secrets* show and the other staff aren't too happy,' Jonathan explained.

'I'm not surprised. That seems a bit underhand.'

Jonathan laughed. 'It's good for them to have some competition and this guy is really good.'

Kathleen watched Linda shrewdly. 'But you don't agree.'

'I don't really know him.' Then seeing the woman's confusion, Linda explained. 'Ben worked for another radio station. Jonathan asked me to approach him on his behalf.'

'Ah, I see, so he wasn't your choice.'

Jonathan sighed. 'What's your point, Mother?'

Kathleen watched him calmly. 'I think, maybe, you are making trouble for yourself.'

Jonathan looked at Linda and rolled his eyes, but her eyes were grave. Linda had only met Maeve Elliot once and didn't know her very well, but she was sure that sparks would fly when she and Ben clashed. And from what Jonathan had told her, his producer wasn't happy either. 'Your mother may be right,' she said finally.

Jonathan smiled coolly. 'I think that's enough talk about work. Daniel, go and wash your hands and face, you're covered in chocolate.'

'Oh, Dad, we're not going yet, are we?' The mutinous expression returned to Daniel's face.

''Fraid so, son. Linda's got to be somewhere.'

Linda looked up in surprise and Kathleen, seeing the look, shook her head and tut-tutted.

Linda started to pile cups and saucers back on the tray. 'I'll take these outside for you.'

Kathleen followed her into the kitchen. 'My son doesn't like being in the wrong,' she said, closing the door. 'But you're good for him. Sensible.'

Linda sighed. Not the most flattering description. 'Despite what the newspapers say, Mrs Blake, I can assure you that Jonathan and I are just friends.'

Kathleen waved away her excuses. 'Yes, yes, so he says, but he listens to you. Believe me, Linda, there are very few women that Jonathan listens to. How long were you married?'

Linda blinked at the sudden change in tack. 'Er, fifteen years.'

'That's very sad. You must be upset.'

Linda softened at the kind expression in Kathleen's eyes. 'Yes, I am.'

Kathleen patted her arm. 'It takes time. In the meantime, let my son pamper you a little.'

Linda smiled and, on impulse, bent to kiss her cheek. 'Thank you, Mrs Blake, you've been very kind.'

'Are we ready to go?' Jonathan stood in the doorway, jangling his keys.

'Ready.' Linda went to get her fleece as Daniel bounced down the stairs two at a time and launched himself into his grandmother's arms. ''Bye, Nan.'

Kathleen clasped him to her and kissed his cheek. 'Goodbye, my darling, come back and see me very soon.'

Linda was grateful for Daniel's constant chatter in the car on the way home because Jonathan had hardly opened his mouth. Linda wasn't sure what she'd done to upset him – if anything. It all seemed to go pear-shaped when Kathleen started to question Ben Donnelly's appointment. When they arrived at her house, she quickly opened the door and hopped out. 'Well, thanks for a lovely day. 'Bye, Daniel.'

''Bye.' Daniel grinned at her, his earlier animosity forgotten.

'I'll walk you to the door,' Jonathan said, grim-faced.

'There's no need—' Linda started, but he was already leading the way up the path. When she'd opened the door and switched on the hall light she turned back to face him. 'Look, Jonathan, I'm sorry if I've done something to annoy you, it certainly wasn't intentional.'

He sighed. 'It wasn't you. I'm sorry, but my mother has a knack for touching raw nerves.'

'And is Ben Donnelly a raw nerve?' Linda looked at him worriedly. Ben had been his choice but she had been involved with his recruitment.

'No, of course not.' He bent his head and kissed her briefly on the lips. 'Thanks for coming with us today, Linda, we enjoyed your company. I'll call you.'

Linda stood and watched as he drove away, Daniel waving furiously. When they were out of sight she closed the door and went inside. She was glad that Jonathan wasn't annoyed with her. He'd been so kind she didn't want to do anything to upset him. And, she admitted to herself as she kicked off her boots and padded out to the kitchen, he was a very nice man to be around when he switched on the charm. Linda had wondered why on earth he would want to involve her in his personal life like this.

Meeting his son was one thing but being brought home to meet Mother was something else entirely! But having spent the day with the Blakes she was beginning to understand. Jonathan obviously craved some normality in his life and he knew that he could bring her on a family day out without her jumping to the wrong conclusions. Somehow, it wasn't the most comforting thought. Linda put on the kettle and dropped a teabag into a mug. Safe, sensible, Linda –

God, how boring! She'd have to do something to get her life in gear. Otherwise, once Jonathan was out of the picture she was going to slide into a pit of depression. She carried the tea into the living room, switched on a lamp and sat down. The thought of not having Jonathan around any more was a sobering one. She'd got used to him being there, got used to his funny phone calls. He brightened her life and made her forget her problems. And when he held her hand or kissed her – even though it was all an act – she felt an unmistakable shiver of anticipation. She closed her eyes and groaned softly. She mustn't think like that. It wasn't real, of course. She was just vulnerable and Jonathan had been so kind. As long as she remembered that he was just being a good friend she'd be fine. She switched on the TV and curled up on the sofa. After watching two soaps her eyelids started to droop and she almost jumped out of her skin when the doorbell rang furiously. She jumped up and ran outside. 'What the hell do you think you're doing?' She threw open the door expecting to see kids running away giggling but Jonathan was standing there staring at her in dismay. 'I'm very sorry, Linda, it's just that I've been ringing the bell for ages and I was afraid something was wrong.'

Linda flushed and gave the bell a thump. 'It sticks sometimes. Sorry, I thought it was kids messing. What are you doing here?'

Jonathan stood in the doorway looking slightly awkward. 'I took Daniel back to his mother's, fancied a curry and thought that maybe you'd like to join me.'

'You could have phoned,' she pointed out curtly.

'Oh, I'm sorry, I'll go.'

'No!' She stood back to let him in. 'I'm sorry, I didn't mean to snap.'

'So, is that a yes?'

'To a curry? Well, I am hungry but—'

'But?'

Linda's lips twitched. 'Did it ever occur to you that maybe I'd seen quite enough of Jonathan Blake for one day?'

He thought for a moment and then grinned at her. 'No.'

'Idiot! Well, you're going to have to wait until I get changed.'

Jonathan stretched out on her sofa and picked up the remote control. 'No hurry.'

Linda pushed away her empty plate and sank back in her chair. 'I'm glad you came back tonight.'

Jonathan smiled. 'Is that because you enjoyed your dinner or my company?'

Linda smiled shyly. 'Both.' A voice in her head told her to play it cool, told her not to get too comfortable with him, but she tuned out. She was enjoying herself, enjoying him and it had been a long time since she'd felt this happy.

Jonathan stretched out his hand and stroked hers. 'I've really enjoyed today, Linda. I don't think I've ever relaxed with a woman as much as I do with you.'

Linda stiffened. 'That's because we know where we stand.'

'What do you mean?'

'Well, couples are always playing games but as we're not a real couple we don't have that problem.'

Jonathan stopped stroking her hand and looked up into her face.

'What's wrong?'

He hesitated for a moment. 'Well, you see I think I'd like us to be a proper couple.'

Linda stared. 'What? Why?'

He smiled. 'Because, like I just said, I feel comfortable around you.'

'Very flattering.'

'And,' he continued, ignoring the interruption, 'I think you're very beautiful.'

Linda snatched her hands away and glared at him. 'Don't tease me.'

Jonathan glared back. 'I'm not! You just don't know how to take a compliment, do you? Look, I'm serious, Linda. God, even my mother and son like you!'

She laughed.

'So, what do you think?'

'I think you've probably had too much wine,' she said, willing herself not to believe what he was saying.

'It's not the wine, Linda, you must know that. You are a very special lady and I think that we could be good together. What do you think?'

Linda looked away, embarrassed. 'I think you're a very nice man.'

Jonathan winced. 'That doesn't sound promising.'

'I've just never thought of you like that.'

'I see.'

Linda took a deep breath and looked into his eyes. 'But I think that's because I wouldn't let myself.'

'What do you mean?'

She shrugged, embarrassed. 'It never occurred to me that you would be interested in me.'

Jonathan smiled ruefully. 'Oh, Linda, you must be the only person in the city who doesn't know how I feel about you.'

She stared at him, lost for words. Finally she dragged her eyes away from his and glanced at her watch. 'It's late.'

He took her hands in his and looked at her, his eyes dark. 'Come back with me.'

She stared at him. 'I've a very early start tomorrow—'

'Please, Linda,' he said softly. 'Come back with me.'

'This is madness.'

'No, it's not,' he said softly.

Linda looked at him, waiting for him to laugh and say it was just a joke. But he said nothing, just kept looking at her with those dark, liquid eyes and she knew what she had to do. 'Let's go.'

29

'Have I convinced you yet that I'm serious?' Jonathan murmured as he ran his fingers across her stomach.

Linda shivered and turned her head so that their faces were almost touching. 'Not yet.'

He propped himself up on one arm and smiled down at her. 'Ms Taylor, you are insatiable.'

'I know,' Linda said, slightly surprised as she ran her fingers through the dark hair covering his chest. 'I've never felt like that before.' She looked up at him, feeling slightly embarrassed. 'Patrick and I, well our love-life was a little . . . predictable.'

He looked at her curiously. 'And there was never anyone else?'

She shook her head. 'Only the guys I knew before I got married and there weren't too many of them.'

He leaned down to kiss her. 'Then I'm a very lucky man.'

Linda pulled back and looked into his eyes. 'Please don't play with me, Jonathan. If this is just a one-night thing that's fine. Don't pretend—'

He put a finger on her lips and shook his head. 'I wouldn't do that to you, Linda. I told you, I've been pining over you for quite some time.'

She shook her head, afraid to believe him.

'If you don't believe me ask your mother, ask Viv.'

'What do you mean?'

He chuckled. 'They both saw right through me from the start. They knew I had a hidden agenda.'

'I don't think I like the sound of that.' Linda pulled the sheet up over her breasts and tucked it firmly around her.

'Oh, love, when are you going to trust me? I'm saying that I wanted to get close to you. Pretending to be your lover was the next best thing to being your lover. And I hoped that if we spent some time together you might come to feel about me the way that I feel about you.'

She smiled cautiously. 'I'm not sure I'm ready to feel anything yet.'

'Of course not,' he murmured. 'I realise that you need space. But that doesn't mean we can't have some fun, does it?'

Linda closed her eyes as he pushed down the sheet and kissed her breasts. 'No, I suppose it doesn't.'

Maeve swung herself down the corridor and into her office.

'You're getting real good on those things,' Karl drawled.

Maeve scowled as she shoved the crutches under her desk and sat down. 'I don't want to be good, I want to be rid. Although,' she added with a twinkle in her eye, 'they're handy for tripping up Donnelly.'

Karl's smile disappeared. 'Where is he?'

Maeve shrugged. 'No idea. Probably licking Jonathan's boots.'

'Or closeted somewhere with Carrie.'

Maeve looked at him. 'What do you mean?'

'Oh, he's got her working all hours going through all the guests.'

Maeve's eyes narrowed. 'I don't like the sound of that.'

Karl shrugged and lit a cigarette. 'It's hardly surprising. He needs to bone up on the show and as we're not being exactly helpful, Carrie's all he's got.'

'I thought she was on our side,' Maeve said moodily.

Karl grinned. 'She's a junior and she has to do as she's told. Anyway, at least it means we know what he's up to. Carrie reports back every word.'

Maeve brightened. 'Oh, well, that's good, I suppose.'

'Yeah. I'm going to talk to her before tonight's meeting to see if she's got anything we can use.'

Maeve sighed. 'And if she doesn't?'

'We sit back and let Ben run the show – he is the co-ordinator, after all.'

Maeve grinned. 'And the one with the experience.'

'He's very eager to impress,' Karl mused. 'Maybe he'll trip himself up in his own enthusiasm.'

'Let's hope so.'

'You're very quiet,' Paul said over lunch.

Maeve pushed her Caesar Salad away and smiled. 'Sorry.'

'Tell me about it.'

Maeve looked at his eager face and wondered why she wasn't in love with this man. Unlike his predecessors, he was always attentive, good in bed *and* he had introduced her to some very influential people. But it was the very fact that he was so nice that turned Maeve off. She'd never let him or any other partner close to her and she didn't like the way he was trying to push his way into her life. He'd even suggested joining FECC! She could just imagine how Craig Prentice would react to that!

'Maeve?' Paul was looking at her expectantly.

'It's just a few teething problems with *Secrets*,' she said at last.

'Are you nervous?'

Maeve laughed. 'Of course not!'

Paul's eyes were full of admiration. 'You're something else, you know that, Maeve?'

She forced herself to smile. 'Yeah, that's me.' No wonder she liked sparring with Craig. Paul's compliments and adoration were enough to put her to sleep.

'Will I see you tonight?' He stroked the inside of her wrist.

'I'm not sure. I have to work late.'

'Call me as soon as you finish, I'll collect you and take you back to my place for a massage.'

Maeve smiled slowly as she remembered his last 'massage'. 'It might be very late,' she warned.

'You're worth waiting for.'

At exactly seven o'clock, Jonathan breezed into the

meeting room with Ben hot on his heels. Karl slipped further down in his chair and lit a cigarette, Maeve concentrated on the papers in front of her and Carrie fidgeted with her pen. Jonathan glanced around.

'Evening, everyone, are we ready to begin? Ben, why don't you start?'

Ben cleared his throat and smiled around the table. 'Well, firstly, I think we should deal with Monday's show. It's important that we get it right.'

'Tell us something we don't know,' Maeve murmured.

Ben's smile remained firmly in place. 'As I see it our first problem is our guest.' He stood up and began to pace the room, tapping his pen thoughtfully against his fingers. 'She's too quiet, too retiring. It would be so much better if she was angry with her lot, bitter about what happened to her.'

'I think she's very brave,' Carrie blurted out. She'd got to know Ann quite well over the last few weeks and didn't like Ben's tone.

Ben sighed dramatically. 'Maybe, but that doesn't make for good radio. Maeve, can I ask what questions you plan to ask her?'

Maeve frowned. 'You've seen the list. I take her through her story and then throw the show open to the public.'

Ben shook his head. 'I'm not sure that will work.'

Karl inhaled deeply and blew smoke into the other man's face. 'So what do you suggest?'

Ben waved the smoke away and continued to smile. 'I'm glad you asked, Karl. I think we need to have some tough questions ready in case we don't get good calls. On the first night we won't know what to expect. We must be prepared.'

'I agree,' Jonathan said firmly.

'I've come up with some questions that should liven things up,' Ben continued.

Maeve glared at him. 'I'm quite capable of coming up with my own script, Ben.'

Ben nodded patiently. 'Of course you are, Maeve, but there's a technique that comes with experience if you want to enflame the guest and the audience.'

Karl shook his head in disgust. 'We don't want to do that, do we?'

Jonathan shrugged. 'If that's what it takes. Let's hear some of your ideas, Ben.'

'Well, we need to ask about her sex-life – if she's done anything to put others in danger – that kind of thing.'

'Maeve?' Jonathan turned to her.

'Well, of course I'll ask her about that.'

Ben looked unhappy. 'Yes, but it's how you ask, Maeve. You have to create some tension.'

Maeve looked from him to Jonathan. 'With the questions I plan to ask there will be plenty of tension, believe me.'

Jonathan nodded in approval. 'Good girl.'

'But—' Ben started.

'Maeve's going to take care of it,' Karl said steadily. 'Let her get on with it, okay, Ben?'

By the time they'd thrashed out the details of the

other four shows for the week and who was going to be responsible for what, Maeve was exhausted. Her ankle, which had seemed to be on the mend while she lounged around the apartment, was now throbbing painfully. She made her way slowly back to her office and sat down.

'Are you okay?' Karl asked from the doorway.

Maeve shook her head. 'No.'

'You handled it well, don't worry.'

'But what exactly have I got myself into? Ben and Jonathan obviously want me to go in for the kill.'

Karl shrugged. 'You're still the one in the driving seat.'

Maeve rubbed her eyes wearily. 'And I'm beginning to wonder if I want to be. I can't help thinking that *Secrets* is going to be a disaster.'

'It will be fine once we keep a tight rein on Donnelly.'

'And what about Jonathan?' Maeve remained unconvinced.

'He'll be fine once he sees that it's working.'

'I wish I had your confidence – or is it blind faith?' Maeve muttered.

Karl grinned. 'A bit of both. See you tomorrow.'

''Bye.' Maeve looked up at the clock. It was nearly ten and the thought of going over to Paul's was no longer appealing. She'd be much happier with a nightcap and an early night. But Paul had other ideas when she phoned. 'Fine, I'll meet you at your place. I'll even bring dinner.'

'I'm really very tired.' Maeve groaned inwardly. Why were men so lousy at taking a hint?

'Then we'll have an early night.'

Maeve closed her eyes at the obvious meaning in his words. 'I'll see you later.'

She had just changed into her silk pyjamas and poured herself a large drink when the buzzer rang. 'Hello?'

'Hi, Maeve, it's me.'

'Craig?' Maeve frowned in confusion.

'Er, yeah, just thought I'd drop by and see how you were.'

'Oh! Come on up.' She opened the door and seconds later Craig emerged from the lift laden down with carrier bags. 'I thought you'd like some Chinese for a change.'

'Oh.' Maeve was still staring at the bags when the buzzer went again. 'Hello?'

'Hi, honey, let me in. I've got dinner courtesy of L'Ecrivain's and a bottle of champagne to wash it down.'

Craig's smile froze. 'Sorry, I should have called first. I'll go now—'

'Oh, no, Craig, wait—'

'I don't think Chicken Chow Mein can compete with L'Ecrivain's,' he joked awkwardly. 'I'm glad you're feeling better.'

Maeve watched from the doorway as he strode briskly to the lift. 'Thanks for coming. It was very thoughtful.'

The doors opened and Paul bounced out with a

covered tray and a bottle in his pocket. 'Here we are – oh, hello.' He looked curiously at Craig, who nodded and got into the lift without another word. 'Who was that?' Paul asked as he came in and kicked the door closed behind him. 'And what the hell is that smell?'

'A friend,' Maeve said faintly. 'He brought me some Chinese food.'

Paul laughed. 'Well, I think I can do a little better than that!' He pulled off the cover with a flourish. 'What do you think?'

'I'll get some plates.'

Much later, when Paul was snoring quietly beside her, Maeve lay thinking about Craig. She still couldn't believe he'd come all the way over here to see how she was. And despite the excellent dinner Paul had brought, she had a sneaking suspicion that she'd have had a nicer evening with Craig. It was probably because she was so tired. It was hard to be the woman that Paul expected her to be when she felt so low, whereas Craig had seen her at her worst. He knew what she was like and she didn't have to pretend with him. He was a friend. The realisation took Maeve by surprise. She didn't really have any friends – at least she didn't think so. There were a couple of girls in school that she'd been close to but once she'd left home she'd left them behind too. At college, she'd gone out with a crowd but she'd never got close to any one person. And since then, well since then, there hadn't been time. She'd had a goal to reach and was only interested in developing relationships with people who could help her. Her time spent with FECC was the only treat she permitted herself. Apart from Craig and Freddy she'd maintained a detached relationship with the rest of the members. She was also wary of so-called friends exploiting her celebrity. But neither Freddy nor Craig would ever do that. It wouldn't occur to either of them to treat her differently to anyone else. She smiled, closed her eyes and snuggled under the covers. She would call Craig tomorrow and thank him. Maybe she'd even arrange to meet him for a drink. Maybe there might even be a repeat of that kiss. She shivered at the thought. It had been a very chaste kiss, but it promised so much more. She was imagining it of course. There could never be anything between her and Craig. She sighed and turned over.

'What is it, what's wrong?' Paul murmured into his pillow.

Maeve patted him vaguely. 'Nothing. Go to sleep.'

30

Maeve wasn't the only one lying awake. It was Linda's last night in her home and depression had engulfed her again. She'd fended off her mother and sister's offers to stay, insisting that she was fine, but she wasn't. Despite the lovely time she'd had with Jonathan yesterday – and the amazing night that followed – she felt lonelier than ever. But at least she no longer missed Patrick. One night with Jonathan had made her realise that her marriage had been dead for years. It was hard to come to terms with the fact that she had to make a new start at thirty-eight. She didn't believe that Jonathan would figure in that future for very long – she was a novelty that he'd soon tire of. But the time spent with him and Daniel had triggered something else – envy. Though she and Patrick had discussed having a family from time to time neither of them was that bothered. Linda wondered if subconsciously she'd known there was something wrong with her marriage and that's why she'd put off motherhood. It was unlikely she'd ever be a mother now, she realised, and a tear trickled down her cheek. She sighed, and wiped her face with an impatient hand. She had enough to deal with at the moment without getting all broody.

Jonathan for one. She had to keep him in a very safe compartment of her mind. He was not husband material; he wasn't even steady boyfriend material. He was a wonderful, attractive and sexy companion and when this affair ended – as it would – she would have to let him go, graciously and, even gratefully. He had helped her through such a terrible time and made her feel like an attractive woman again. She felt as if she'd known him forever and he seemed to know instinctively what she wanted. She shivered as she thought of the way he'd made love to her, still not quite able to believe that it had actually happened. She turned over again and squeezed her eyes shut. She had to stop thinking and get some sleep. She was moving into her new apartment tomorrow. Somehow, she didn't think she'd ever call it home.

Carrie twisted awkwardly on the sofa, trying to avoid the spring that kept digging into her back. In future when they had rows she'd make sure she was the one that got the bed, she thought ruefully. Not that Declan would even consider sleeping downstairs. No matter how lousy things were between them, he'd still climb in beside her and fall into a deep sleep. Carrie punched the cushion angrily. How come she was always the one who ended up upset or worried? She spent her life trying to keep people happy – if it wasn't her parents, it was Declan. Even Helen put her under pressure to take control of her life – whatever that meant. If it weren't for her job, she'd crack up. She smiled in the darkness. Carrie Lambe – career woman! It was laughable really. Her parents had always wanted her to be career-minded and now that she was, they still weren't happy. Working on a radio station just didn't live up to their expectations. But then, to be fair, they didn't know how serious this job was turning out to be. They were all in for a shock when *Secrets* aired – if they bothered to listen. She wondered if Declan would. He was already grumbling about the late hours she'd be working but tonight he'd got really angry.

'What kind of life do we have if you're out every night of the week?'

Initally she'd been understanding and patient. 'I know it's going to be hard, Declan, but what can I do?'

'You could refuse. You were hired as a researcher.'

Carrie's eyes filled with dismay. 'Yes, and I'm very lucky that the job has expanded the way it has. I really love it, Declan.'

'You always used to complain about people putting career before family,' he'd said coldly.

Carrie had no answer for that one. It was true that she'd never understood why people were so hung up about their jobs. Until now. 'I'm sorry, Declan,' she'd said finally, 'I didn't plan it this way.'

'I think you should look for another job – something more suitable so that we can get back to normal.'

And that had been the final straw. She'd looked him in the eye. 'I could, Declan, but I have no intention of.' After that, he'd ranted and raved until she could take no more. She'd slammed out of the house and walked aimlessly for hours. When she'd returned Declan was in bed and, unwilling to risk waking him, she'd curled up on the sofa. She probably wouldn't be able to walk tomorrow thanks to that bloody spring. She didn't know about taking control of her life but maybe it was time to buy a new sofa.

Viv staggered in with another two boxes and dropped them in the hall. There was an ominous rattle. 'Oops.'

Linda smiled. 'Don't worry, it's only my bowling trophies.'

'You still have them?' Viv marvelled.

'Of course! My team won three tournaments in a row,' she said proudly.

'But that was years ago when you worked in the bank,' Viv pointed out. 'Still, maybe you should take it up again. It would be a nice little hobby for you.'

Linda gave her a withering look. 'I'm not some sad little deserted wife who needs a hobby,' she growled.

'Sorry. Shall I go back to the house and get the rest?'

'No, I'll do it.'

Viv frowned. 'Is Patrick going to be there?'

'No, he'll collect the last of his stuff tomorrow – not that there's much left. Why don't you make yourself a cuppa, I won't be long. The biscuits are in the box on the counter.'

'Righto, see you later.'

Linda went out to her car and drove the five miles

to the house in Clontarf that soon would belong to
someone else. Already it felt different, she realised
as she opened the door. It was silent and when she
walked through to the kitchen her footsteps echoed
in the empty room. She glanced out of the window
at the little garden, where her roses nodded cheerfully
in the breeze. Patrick had planted them years ago and
she hated leaving them behind, but she didn't even
have a window-box in her new apartment. Anyway,
those roses were part of the past, along with this
house. She went briskly through the rooms, checking
that all the cupboards were empty and the windows
were locked. In the bathroom, hanging forgotten on
the wall, were the prints that her mother had brought
them from France just after they got married. They
were cartoon sketches of a man and a woman with
slightly tongue-in-cheek definitions of their names.
Linda took them down carefully and tucked them
under her arm. She didn't think Patrick would want
his. After checking that the back door was locked,
Linda left all the keys for the house on the kitchen
counter along with instructions for the alarm and the
central heating system. Then she picked up her last
box of belongings, having placed the prints carefully
on top, and opened the front door. She paused to
look back one last time, and then stepped outside,
pulling the door closed after her. She was halfway
back to the new apartment before she realised that
her cheeks were wet with tears – again. She wiped
her face as she sat at the traffic lights and smiled
tremulously at the curious child in the car in front.

'Pull yourself together, Linda,' she murmured. 'Deep breaths.' She couldn't let Viv see her like this or she'd refuse to go home. As it was, she was plagued with her mother and sister doing their damnedest to make sure she was never on her own. It frustrated Linda and at the same time she really appreciated it. But while it was nice to be fussed over and pampered, there was no point in putting off the inevitable. Eventually she was going to have to come to terms with being a single woman again. Jonathan didn't even come into the equation. Linda had decided, as she lay naked in the bed beside him after the best sex of her life, that she must just enjoy him for however long it lasted. It was important that she never thought of them as being a couple and that way she wouldn't get hurt. He would be part of her life but not all of it. She would learn to live alone, of course she would, but it was going to be strange. She'd lived with her mum right up until her wedding day, so she'd never known what it was like to have her own space. She forced a smile to her lips. So now she was going to find out. It would be great. She could eat when she wanted, sleep as late as she wanted, hog the entire duvet and never have to watch a cricket match again. She was going to be fine.

'Everything okay?' Viv asked as she came in with the last box.

'Yes, great,' she said brightly.

Viv looked at her worriedly. 'I think I should stay with you tonight.'

Linda shrugged casually. 'Sure. Why don't we get a video and order in some food.'

Viv grinned. 'Great.'

'Right.' Linda took off her coat and rolled up her sleeves. 'Before I unpack anything I want to give this place a good clean. Grab the Hoover, Viv.'

Her sister groaned. 'I knew offering to help you move was a mistake.'

Linda flung a duster at her. 'Stop moaning and get to work!'

They worked in companionable silence, Forever FM blaring in the background. Linda, always happier when she was working, felt her optimism rise with the dust. After she'd washed every surface in the small one-bedroomed apartment, she got started on the bathroom.

'Ugh, did you pour a whole bottle of bleach down there?' Viv stood in the doorway, her nose crinkled in disgust.

Linda grinned. 'Two. If I decide to stay here I might just treat myself to a new loo.' She peered into it to see if the stains had shifted.

'It's not a bad apartment though.' Viv wandered into the large bedroom and looked out of the window. 'And you can't get more central than this.'

Linda joined her and looked out at the crowds hurrying past, St Patrick's Cathedral majestic in the background. 'The view is great, isn't it?'

'Pity about the bells,' Viv said darkly. 'They don't ring them at night, do they?'

'No, Viv, they don't. But I'm sure it will be pretty noisy anyway. Dublin never seems to sleep any more.'

They went back into the kitchen and Linda put on the kettle.

'Are you going to be okay here on your own?' Viv asked, climbing on to one of Linda's new barstools.

'Of course I will, I'm not a child. And I'll be able to have an extra hour in bed every morning. It should take me, oh, all of three minutes to get to work!'

Viv looked around the bright, but sparse, apartment. Apart from the bedroom and bathroom, there was just one large room, with the kitchen separated by a breakfast bar. Linda had bought a black corduroy sofa bed – in case her mother or sister ever stayed over – two easy chairs and a smoked-glass coffee table. It was simple to the point of boring and, just a little bit depressing. 'It's not exactly what you're used to.'

Linda shrugged. She wasn't that impressed but it was central, came with a parking spot and suited her pocket. 'It's all I need.'

'You'll miss your lovely big kitchen,' Viv persisted.

'I thought you were supposed to be cheering me up,' Linda complained. 'Anyway, I don't need a big kitchen any more, Viv. I won't be cooking that much.'

'I don't think we should stay in,' Viv said suddenly. 'Here we are in the centre of Dublin, let's go out and enjoy it.'

Linda frowned. 'I'm going to have to watch the pennies. I can't dine out all the time.'

'But tonight we're celebrating,' Viv told her. 'Anyway, it's my treat.'

Linda rolled her eyes. 'Now, I don't want handouts from my rich and famous sister. I can stand on my own two feet, thank you very much.'

'Oh, God, you're not going to go all independent and defensive, are you?'

Linda grinned. 'Nope. You can take me out any time you like! So where shall we go?'

A couple of hours later after they'd changed into clean clothes they strolled down Dame Street towards Temple Bar. Linda turned the collar of her coat up around her ears against the biting wind. 'I think there's snow in the air.'

Viv sighed dreamily. 'Oh, wouldn't it be lovely if we had a white Christmas?'

Linda laughed. 'That's weeks away yet and you know it's much more likely to rain.'

'What will you do for Christmas?' Viv asked.

'I don't know.' Linda hadn't thought about it and didn't want to either. She and Patrick had always gone away for Christmas, usually to somewhere hot.

'We should have a traditional family Christmas,' Viv announced.

Linda smirked. 'I can't see Mum bustling around the kitchen in her apron and oven gloves.'

'No, more likely floating around with a cocktail,' Viv agreed. 'Well, we could have it in my house and you could do the cooking.'

'Thanks.'

'Well, come on, you're the best cook,' Viv pointed out reasonably.

'Only because you don't even try.'

'I have to keep all my creativity for my writing,' Viv said cheerfully. 'But I mix a mean martini. And my punch is very good too. Hey, we could have a party.'

Linda stopped to look at her in despair. 'And I suppose you want me to organise that too.'

Viv shook her head. 'No, I'll do it.' She linked her arm through Linda's and dragged her on towards the restaurant. 'We could have it on Christmas Eve. Just drinks and nibbles, nothing complicated.'

'Who would we invite?'

Viv shrugged. 'Mum's cronies, a few of my friends and a few of yours – twenty tops.'

'I can't think of anyone I'd want to invite.'

'Well, there's Jonathan for a start.'

Linda studied the pavement. She wasn't ready to tell Viv about Jonathan yet. 'Oh, I don't think so. I'm sure he'd have plans.'

Viv shot her an impatient look. 'You know what your problem is? You're too bloody considerate.'

Linda smiled at her sister's frustration. 'I didn't know that was a problem.'

Viv shook her head and pulled open the door of the Elephant and Castle restaurant. When they were seated in a quiet corner with a bottle of house wine and the menus Linda took a good look around. 'I've never been here before. It's nice, isn't it?'

'I like it, there's a good buzz.' When they'd ordered Viv turned the conversation back to Christmas. 'We could invite people for drinks on Christmas morning instead of Christmas Eve.'

Linda frowned. 'Mum always does the rounds of the relatives on Christmas morning, doesn't she?'

'Oh, well, they're not coming,' Viv exclaimed. 'It would be more like a wake! I think we shall leave our dear mother off the guest list. She can join us for dinner. We could eat about five and that would give us all plenty of time.'

'You'd have to be the hostess,' Linda warned. 'I can't cook a Christmas dinner *and* entertain all of your friends too.'

Viv frowned. 'There must be *someone* you'd like to invite.'

'I don't think so, Viv, it would be too complicated. I'd prefer to relax, have a drink and enjoy myself.' Linda thought it highly unlikely that she was going to enjoy this Christmas but at least she'd have an excuse for hiding in the kitchen.

'Promise me one thing,' Viv said.

Linda eyed her warily. 'What's that?'

'Invite Jonathan. He can always say no.'

Linda nodded and smiled, 'Okay, then, if it will make you happy.'

Viv beamed at her. 'We'll have a lovely time. Won't Mum be delighted that we're spending Christmas together? It must be the first time in years. And real home cooking too!'

Linda thought guiltily of all the years she'd gone off with Patrick without a thought for her family. Rosemary and Viv usually went to a hotel, sometimes in a group but often alone. It couldn't have been much fun. She vowed to give them a Christmas to remember this year.

Viv touched her hand, her eyes sympathetic. 'We will have a good time, Linda. Life goes on.'

Linda smiled back guiltily and took a sip of her wine. 'Yes, life goes on.'

31

Maeve settled into her chair – thankfully she was now crutch-free – and put on her headphones.

'Can you hear me?' Karl murmured in her ear.

'Loud and clear.'

Ben glanced around the room. 'Is everybody ready?'

Carrie nodded, too nervous to speak. Maeve shook out her hair and took a few deep breaths. Karl nodded curtly. 'Let's go.'

'Okay, Maeve, there's two more minutes of ads and then you're on. You'll have three minutes to explain the show before our guest is in studio. Carrie, go and get Ann, will you?'

Carrie hurried out of the room. Of course, Ann wasn't her real name but they had to call her something. Carrie went nervously down the deserted corridors – she'd never been here so late at night before. Outside the visitors' room she paused, took a deep breath and stuck her head round the door. 'Hi, Ann, we're ready for you now.' The young girl jumped nervously and Carrie's stomach lurched. She looked so miserable and defenceless.

'Oh, Carrie, I'm terrified.'

Carrie patted her hand and smiled reassuringly.

'You'll be fine and Maeve is lovely. She just wants you to tell your story.'

'I did think it would be nice to tell everyone, but it doesn't seem so important any more. I suppose it's because I've spent so much time talking to you. You're a great listener, Carrie.'

'Thanks. Right, we'd better hurry. Do you need to go to the loo first?'

Ann shook her head. 'I wouldn't mind a drink of water though.'

'No problem.'

Carrie brought her through to the dimly-lit studio where Maeve was already in full flow.

'I hope you will join us every night from ten to eleven, listeners, because we have some very interesting and, in some cases, very sad, tales to tell. My first guest is a young girl that we will call Ann. As with all our guests this is not her real name. This programme is called *Secrets* for a reason. Ann has agreed to come on and tell us her story but we will protect her anonymity at all costs. Ann, hello, and welcome to *Secrets*.'

'Hi,' Ann murmured and took a quick gulp of the water Carrie had placed in front of her.

'Ann, maybe we can start with your earliest memory.'

Ann gave a short, harsh laugh. 'I remember lots of shouting, if that's what you mean.'

Maeve watched her intently. 'Who was doing the shouting?'

'My mum. She was always either shouting or crying. If it was quiet it was because she was asleep.'

'How old were you then?'

Ann wrinkled up her nose in concentration. 'I must have been about five – I'd just started school.'

'Where was your father?'

Ann shrugged. 'Who knows? I don't think she even knew his name.'

'Was there anyone else in your life?'

The girl's face softened. 'There was my gran. She used to sing to me.'

Maeve smiled. 'Did you spend much time with your gran?'

Ann's expression hardened. 'No, she and Mum were always arguing. Finally, Gran went away. I didn't see her again until—'

Maeve held up a hand to stop her. She didn't want Ann getting to the main part of the story too quickly. 'Do you know why they quarrelled?'

'I do now,' Ann muttered. 'Mum was an addict.'

'Your mother took drugs,' Maeve said clearly.

'Yes. I suppose that's why she slept so much.'

'And your gran wanted her to stop.'

'Of course, but she didn't. She did try,' she admitted, her eyes suddenly sad and her voice barely a whisper.

'You need to get her to speak louder,' Karl murmured in Maeve's earpiece.

'I know this is hard, Ann.' Maeve reached over and squeezed her hand – 'but could you try to speak up a little?'

'Sorry.'

'No, that's okay. Now, you were saying that your mum did try to stop taking drugs.'

'Yeah, a couple of times. It was great. She was so different when she was clean. She'd take me to school every morning and be waiting at the gate when I came out. And she took me out to different places, sometimes the cinema or the zoo or if she was broke we'd just go to feed the ducks in Stephen's Green.'

'But these good times didn't last,' Maeve surmised.

Ann shook her head. 'No. One day I'd come out of school and she wouldn't be there. After I'd waited and waited, one of the other mothers would take me home. Sometimes Mum wasn't there and I'd be scared that something had happened to her. But it was nearly worse if she was there 'cos she'd be weird.'

'In what way?'

'Oh, she'd be totally hyper, either laughing and talking too much if I was lucky, or screaming and shouting. Then she'd usually pass out. I always felt so relieved when that happened,' she said guiltily. 'Because it was the only time I didn't feel scared of her.'

'What did you do while she slept?' Maeve asked softly.

Ann smiled slightly. 'I played happy families where the mummy and daddy loved their little girl – pathetic, eh?'

Maeve shook her head. 'Of course not. You had to find some way to escape. There's one day in particular you wanted to tell us about, isn't there, Ann?'

Ann sniffed. 'Yeah, well one day I got bored playing on my own: Mum had been asleep for ages. I went into the bedroom to ask her to play with me but though I shook her and shook her I couldn't wake her.'

Maeve heard the tremble in her voice and indicated that she should take some water. Ann obediently took a sip before she continued. 'There was a needle beside the bed and I decided to play nurse – I'd seen the way Mum used it.'

'What did you do with the needle, Ann?'

'I stuck it in my arm. And then I started to cry because it made me bleed. I wasn't expecting that – it had never made Mum bleed like that.'

'Did your mum wake up then?'

Ann shook her head, tears rolling steadily down her cheeks. 'No. So I went into Mrs Flanagan next door – Gran told me that if there was ever anything wrong I should go to her. She came back inside with me and, when she couldn't wake Mum either, sent me back to wait in her house.'

'What happened then?'

'Mrs Flanagan was gone for ages and when she got back she just said that I had to stay with her until my gran came.'

'Where was your mum?'

'She wouldn't tell me.' Ann's shoulders shook with the tears.

'We'll go to break in two minutes,' Karl told Maeve.

'One more question, Ann, and then we'll take a break. Did you ever see your mother again?'

'No,' Ann whispered, then dropped her face in her hands.

'We'll be back after the break to tell you the rest

of Ann's story,' Maeve said into the mike. Then she smiled awkwardly at Ann. 'Are you okay?'

The girl nodded. 'I'm sorry. I didn't think I'd be like this.'

Maeve smiled kindly. 'It's only natural. Do you think you can go on?'

Ann wiped her eyes with a tissue. 'Yeah. That was the worst bit.'

Ben came into the studio and smiled at Ann. 'You're doing great.'

'Thanks.'

He moved closer to Maeve and bent his head to hers 'You need to speed things up.'

Maeve glared at him. 'Thank you, Ben. Now, I think we're about ready to go back on air.'

'In five,' Karl said quietly in her ear.

Ben turned on his heel and went back outside.

'Welcome back, listeners. Tonight, I'm talking to Ann who has a secret to tell. Now, Ann, before the break you were telling us that you didn't know what had happened to your mum. What happened next?'

'A couple of days later my gran came for me. She told me that my mum had gone to live with the angels and that from now on I would live with her.'

'That must have been very hard for you – you were only five.'

Ann shrugged. 'I didn't really understand, but I do remember that I was happy to go to Gran's. Everything was always so normal there.'

Maeve heard Ben's voice in her ear. 'Cut to the chase, Maeve.'

'Do you know now, Ann, why your mum died?'

'It was an overdose, Gran told me years later, when I was thirteen. I told her what I remembered of that last evening and when I told her that I'd hurt myself with the needle she said that I'd need to see a doctor.'

'Did she tell you why?'

'Not then. I was sent for some tests – Gran said it was nothing to worry about, but a couple of months later we had to go back to the doctor again. She came with me.' Ann paused to wipe away her tears and take a drink.

'Take your time, Ann,' Maeve said gently. 'You're doing great. What did the doctor say?'

'He told me . . . he told me that I was HIV positive.'

Maeve remained silent for a moment so that the only sound the listeners could hear was that of Ann sobbing. Karl nodded his approval. 'That must have been a terrible shock,' she said finally.

'I don't think I really took it all in at the time. The doctor gave us the spiel about how it was no longer a death sentence, that sort of thing, but Gran just kept crying.'

'Did you go for counselling?'

Ann shook her head. 'No, I refused to talk about it. Gran seemed almost relieved. I think she thought that if we didn't talk about it, it would just go away.'

'Ben says you need to wind up,' Karl told her.

Maeve ignored him. 'So what did you do?'

Ann smiled bitterly. 'I got angry. With Mum, with life, with everything. Because my mother was weak and took drugs, I had this horrible disease. She had robbed me of a future. So I decided that I would live for the moment and enjoy life – what was left of it.'

'How did you do that?'

Ann laughed. 'I did what most difficult teenagers do. I drank, smoked, skipped school – the usual rebellious stuff.'

'When did this change?'

Ann sighed. 'I met a guy. He was – is – great.'

'Have you told him about the HIV?'

Ann shook her head emphatically. 'No way.'

Maeve let a pregnant pause develop. 'Why not?' she asked finally.

'Because he'd leave me. Even my girlfriends would probably dump me.'

Maeve frowned. 'Not if they're true friends.'

Ann's laugh was cold. 'I've heard them talk. They're not exactly the most open-minded bunch. Some of them don't even know the difference between HIV and AIDS. They'd probably think that they could get it simply by sitting next to me in class!'

'It's time to take another break. Stay with us and we'll hear what you, the listeners, have to say to Ann.'

Maeve smiled at Ann. 'Back in a minute.' She took off her headphones and went out to Karl. 'What kind of calls are we getting?'

'We've one nutter who says this is a message from God that she has to pay for the sins of her mother.'

'Sicko,' Carrie said in disgust. 'But on the bright

side, I've got a guy who says she's got a real sexy voice and he wouldn't mind going out with her.'

'We might use that towards the end,' Maeve said thoughtfully.

'Isn't there anything more controversial?' Ben demanded nervously.

'Nothing,' Karl lied baldly and Carrie kept her head down.

Ben shook his head in disgust. 'Then it's up to you, Maeve. Do you think you can handle it?'

Maeve looked silently from him to Karl and went back inside. 'Are you okay, Ann?'

'Yeah.'

'Right, it's question time now; do you think you're up to that?'

'I suppose.'

'It might get a bit tough,' she warned.

Ann shrugged.

'Back in five, Maeve,' Karl said. 'Five, four, three, two, one.'

'Welcome back, listeners, and thank you for all your calls and e-mails. The lines are open for another five minutes, so if there's anything you want to say to Ann, call now. The number is 1654321. We've had a lot of calls of support, Ann. Mary from Deansgrange thinks that you should go and get some counselling. Do you think you might do that?'

'I don't know,' Ann replied, her expression sceptical. 'Maybe.'

'Vinnie in Swords wants to know if you ever plan to tell your boyfriend the truth.'

'I don't know, I suppose I will some day.'

'How do you think he's going to react if he finds out the truth?'

'Well, if he loves me he'll be okay about it,' Ann said defensively.

'But you've lied to him. Don't you think he has a right to know the truth?'

Ann looked like a rabbit caught in the headlights. 'I, I don't . . .'

Maeve hesitated for a moment when she saw the panic on the young girl's face.

'Maeve?' Karl whispered urgently.

Maeve glanced at him and then turned back to her guest. 'Ann, are you and your boyfriend having sex?'

Ann scowled at her. 'I don't see what that has to do with it.'

'Oh, come on, Ann, get real! It has everything to do with it. Are you having sex?'

'Yes,' the girl answered, her voice barely audible.

'And do you use protection?'

'Of course we do!'

'Condoms?'

'Yes, yes, of course. What kind of person do you think I am?'

'Not a very sensible one,' Maeve said shortly. 'Accidents can happen.'

'We haven't had any accidents,' Ann protested.

'But you might. Don't you think that your boyfriend deserves to have a say in whether or not he wants to take that risk?'

'I didn't get a say, did I?' Ann flung back.

Maeve said nothing, knowing that her silence would speak volumes. 'Is that what all this is about, Ann?' she said finally. 'Are you taking revenge on your boyfriend for what's happened to you?'

'Of course not!'

'But you're angry, aren't you?'

'Of course I'm bloody angry. My own mother gave me HIV and if it comes out no one will want to know me. If there's one thing your listeners have convinced me of, it's that I was right to keep this a secret.'

Maeve groaned inwardly. 'But Ann, you wouldn't want your boyfriend to go through what you've gone through, would you?'

'No,' Ann whispered.

'Wrap it up, Maeve,' Karl said.

'I think, Ann, it may be time you talked about this to people who can really advise you. After the show we can put you in touch with some people that can help. You don't have to face this alone. Will you talk to them, Ann?'

Ann refused to look at her. 'I suppose.'

'Great. Well the best of luck for the future, thanks for being our first guest on *Secrets.* And that's all for tonight, listeners. We'll be back tomorrow night with more secrets. Goodnight.'

32

'That was great, folks!' Jonathan clapped Ben and Karl on the back and hugged Maeve. 'You were fantastic! Is our guest gone?'

'She was out of here before I'd finished talking,' Maeve said grimly.

'Carrie's with her,' Karl told him.

'And we've given the girl all those leaflets,' Ben added.

'Yeah, we're regular Samaritans,' Maeve said drily.

Jonathan frowned. 'Weren't you happy with the show, Maeve?'

'Let's say I don't feel great about myself.' Maeve met Karl's eyes and quickly looked away again.

Ben grinned. 'All part of the job, Maeve. You'll get used to it.'

'Go to hell.' Maeve glared at him and walked out.

Carrie was sitting slumped at the desk outside.

'How is she?' Maeve asked.

'Not great. I tried to talk to her about the counselling services and helplines but she didn't want to know.'

Maeve sat down on the edge of the desk and drummed her nails angrily.

Carrie looked at her with a mixture of disappointment and reproach. 'Did you have to be so hard on her?'

Maeve's eyes flashed. 'This wasn't my idea, Carrie, you know that. That show would have been completely different if Ben Donnelly hadn't interfered.'

'Maybe the listeners will complain about us being too hard on Ann,' Carrie said hopefully.

'Maybe. Goodnight, Carrie.' Maeve stopped by her office for her bag and her coat and went out to the car. She didn't bother turning on her mobile phone. The only person who'd call at this hour was Paul and she wasn't in the mood. Like Carrie, she was disgusted with the way the programme had gone. She felt dirty because though it was Ben's idea to get tough, she'd been the one who'd attacked the poor kid. She sighed, and prayed that Ann would be okay. How could she ever live with herself if she'd sent the girl over the edge?

Carrie called a taxi and went back into the studio to say goodnight. Only Ben and Jonathan were left. Karl had disappeared – presumably to O'Brien's. 'I'm off,' she said, standing awkwardly in the doorway. 'See you tomorrow.'

''Bye, Carrie.' Ben smiled warmly at her and she wondered how he could be so nice sometimes and so nasty at others.

'Goodnight, Carrie, well done.' Jonathan waved at her.

'Thanks.' Carrie went down to reception to wait for

the taxi, feeling deflated, sad and very guilty. She'd been talking to Ann for weeks now, promising her that everything would be fine, telling her how nice Maeve was. What must the girl think of her?

'Hey, Carrie, that was great!' Declan hugged her as she stood in the doorway, her key still in the lock.

'Sorry?'

'Really great show. That Maeve is something else. She didn't let the girl away with anything.'

Carrie winced. 'I didn't think you'd be listening.'

Declan stared at her in surprise. 'Of course I was listening. I've taped it too so that we can listen to it again together.'

Carrie took off her coat. 'I think I'll just have a cup of tea and go to bed.'

Declan looked disappointed. 'Oh, okay then. I'll have a cup with you.' He followed her into the kitchen and leaned against the counter while she filled the kettle. 'So what was she like?'

'Who?'

'Ann, of course.'

Carrie dropped two teabags into the pot. 'Just an ordinary girl who's had a very rough time.'

'Maeve's right, though. She's no right keeping her bloke in the dark.'

Carrie stared at him in dismay. 'But she's afraid, Declan. She's afraid of losing him and being left on her own.'

'She should have told him.'

'I suppose you're right,' Carrie said tiredly.

'I blame the grandmother. She thought if she ignored her daughter's problem and then her grand-daughter's problem they'd go away.'

Carrie set the pot and two mugs on the table and sat down. 'But I felt so sorry for her, Declan.'

'You're just a big softy,' he teased. 'After all, you gave up your last job 'cos your boss left his wife.'

'Oh, don't start that again,' Carrie moaned, but she was smiling. 'Actually Patrick leaving Linda has worked out very well all round. Linda's dating Jonathan now and I'm working for Forever FM.'

Declan grunted. 'And we never see each other.'

Carrie smiled shyly at him. It was nice that he missed her.

'All this takeaway food I'm eating can't be good for my heart,' he continued.

Carrie's smile disappeared. 'You could always cook something.'

Declan stared at her. 'Cooking is women's work.'

Carrie clenched her fingers round her cup. 'Most top chefs are men,' she pointed out.

'Ah, yes, well that's 'cos there's money in it.'

'I'd love to come home to dinner on the table some evening,' Carrie said wistfully.

Declan snorted. 'Then give me a shout that you're on your way and I'll put the chips in the microwave.'

Carrie made a face. 'That would be better than nothing.'

Declan looked slightly shamefaced. 'Sorry, but you're the cook in this house. And you're so good at it.'

'Thanks.'

He pulled her to him and pinched her bum. 'But I'm good at other things. Let's go to bed and I'll show you.'

Carrie sighed wearily. 'Oh, okay, then.'

Linda was sitting at her desk early the next morning when her sister rang. 'Hi, Viv, what's up?'

'Did you listen to your boyfriend's new show last night?'

Linda sighed. 'Yeah.'

'Awful, wasn't it?'

'I wouldn't say awful,' Linda prevaricated.

'Balls! Maeve Elliot made mincemeat of that poor kid.'

'I suppose she was a bit tough on her.' Linda sat back in her chair and stared miserably out of the window. She'd been disappointed when Maeve had started haranguing that girl. She could have made her point without being quite so brutal.

'What did Jonathan think?'

'I haven't been talking to him.'

'Oh, well, enough gossiping, I'd better get to work.'

'How's the book coming along?'

'Don't ask,' Viv said darkly. 'Seeya.'

The rest of the morning flew by for Linda and she didn't get to eat her sandwich until nearly two. As she nibbled on it she flicked through a magazine, looking for ideas to brighten up her new home. Viv had quite rightly described it as anonymous. 'Like a hotel room,' she'd said. But Linda couldn't summon up enough

interest to do anything about it. She looked at the
glossy pages that seemed to favour pale walls, brightly
coloured rugs and lush, vibrant throws. These simple
touches seemed to transform rooms as colourless as
hers. Maybe she'd buy a throw and a rug – a rich
red would be good. That would get Viv off her
back. Her sister was convinced that the reason she
wasn't bothered with her new home was that she saw
it as only a temporary arrangement. 'Patrick's not
coming back,' Viv had said baldly. Linda smiled as
she shoved the magazine in a drawer. As if she'd want
Patrick now. Having sex with Jonathan had changed
her perspective on a number of issues, mainly to do
with her marriage. She sighed as she remembered
the feel of his body pressing down on hers, his lips
tracing kisses across her body and his eyes dark with
passion. Every time with him was different and she
often found herself wondering how long she could
decently wait before jumping on him again. Now that
she'd experienced such passion she could never take
Patrick back – assuming he'd want to come back. But
even if she'd never slept with Jonathan she'd never be
able to kiss Patrick again without wondering if Stacey
had kissed him like that, or, was she better. Linda
shuddered, dumped the remainder of her lunch in
the bin and went back to work. It turned out to
be a terrible afternoon. Two placements that she'd
been sure were in the bag fell through and she had to
phone the unlucky candidates and give them the bad
news. After a long, confidence-boosting session with
the second, she tidied her desk and decided to check

her e-mail one last time before she went home. She cheered up enormously when she found a message from Jonathan.

'*Can I drop around after work? J.*'

Linda was smiling as she tapped in her reply. '*I'll be home by six. Come for dinner.*' Mentally she went through the contents of the fridge and realised she'd need to do some shopping on the way home. She wondered what kind of mood Jonathan would be in – his brief mail hadn't given anything away. He was probably annoyed with Maeve. Oh, well, if Jonathan decided to let her go, Linda could always get her a new job. Despite last night's performance, Maeve Elliot was hot property and wouldn't be out of work long.

Linda hurriedly changed into a black skirt and clingy red top and touched up her make-up. Dinner was simmering on the stove – tagliatelle with chicken in an almond and tomato sauce and there was ice cream to follow. Jonathan was like a child when it came to sweet things. Linda had just opened a bottle of wine and poured herself a glass when the buzzer went. 'Come on up,' she called when she heard Jonathan's voice. 'How are you?' Her eyes searched his face as he came through the door.

'Great.' He bent to kiss her and shoved another bottle of wine into her hand.

'Dinner smells wonderful.'

'It's just pasta.'

'I love pasta. So, did you hear the show?'

Linda nodded hesitantly and poured him some wine.

'Brilliant, wasn't it?'

Linda stopped and stared at him. 'Er, yeah, very sad though.'

'Oh, yeah, right.' Jonathan nodded gravely. 'But a great story for our first show. The phones haven't stopped ringing today.'

'Your listeners liked it?' She handed him a glass.

'Some loved it and some hated it, but everyone's talking about it. I'm amazed you haven't heard anything.'

'I had a busy day.'

'They're saying Maeve's going to be the number one presenter on Irish radio – number one, can you believe it?'

'No, I can't,' Linda said flatly.

Jonathan's eyes narrowed. 'You didn't think she was good?'

'Well, yes, but . . .'

'But?'

Linda sighed. 'I thought she was very rough on the poor girl. Some of those questions—'

'But those questions had to be asked, Linda. Maeve wouldn't have been doing her job otherwise.'

Linda frowned. 'Yes, but she didn't have to be quite so vicious.'

'That's what the public want,' Jonathan said defensively.

Linda's eyes narrowed and her mouth settled into a grim line. 'Oh, I see.'

He groaned. 'Oh, don't look at me like that. God, you women are all the same.'

'Maeve wasn't happy with the show either, was she?'

'She is now. She's never had as much attention as she's had today.'

'So what's tonight's guest talking about?' Linda turned away to stir the sauce.

'Adoption. She had a kid before she got married and gave it away. The husband and family don't know.'

Linda looked at him. 'God, I had no idea this show was going to be so heavy. Is Maeve going to annihilate this girl too?'

'It's a woman in her forties and she wanted to come on the show,' Jonathan pointed out.

'Yes, but I bet you never told her that she was going to be treated like a criminal,' Linda retorted.

Jonathan put down his glass and stood up. 'I think I've lost my appetite,' he said tightly, heading for the door.

'Oh, look, Jonathan, I'm sorry. Please, come back and sit down.'

He paused at the doorway and turned to look at her. 'Can we change the subject?'

'Sure.' She smiled uncertainly at him. 'Let's do that.'

He came back over to her and folded her in his arms. 'Maybe, it would be best if we didn't bring work home with us,' he murmured into her hair.

Linda closed her eyes and breathed in his smell. 'I think that's probably a very good idea.'

33

After a very restless night, Maeve sat drinking coffee and staring into space. The phone was off the hook and she hadn't turned the radio on either. She was convinced that she was going to be public enemy number one after last night. She'd never forget the way Karl had looked at her. She knew that he thought she'd switched sides, but it wasn't true. She still believed that however rough her questions had been, Ben's would have been ten times worse. But the listeners didn't know that, Aunt Peggy didn't know that, Craig didn't know that – God, he'd think she was the scum of the earth. She stood up reluctantly and headed for the shower. It was time to face the music.

Unusually, Karl was in the office before her, looking haggard and red-eyed.

Maeve smiled nervously. 'Have you been on the tiles all night?'

Karl scowled. 'I've been drowning my sorrows.'

Maeve flopped into her chair. 'Don't exaggerate.'

'But why did you do it, Maeve? What was the point in my blocking the nasty calls? I did my part but you played right into Ben's hands.'

Maeve stared angrily at him. 'You were there, Karl. You heard what he and Jonathan wanted. If I hadn't taken control of the situation it could have been a lot nastier.'

Karl laughed. 'You call that taking control?'

Maeve put her head in her hands. 'Oh, give me a break, Karl. If it's any consolation, I feel terrible about it. And Jonathan can find himself a new presenter. I don't want any part in this.'

Karl smiled for the first time. 'Don't be such a drama queen, there's no need for that.'

Maeve shook her head. 'Make up your mind. A few minutes ago it was a disaster.'

'That's when I thought you were happy with last night's little performance.'

'Well, I'm not.'

'Good. Then we can do something about it.'

But they hadn't figured on the reaction *Secrets* would get. It was discussed on several shows during the day and while some listeners were disgusted with Maeve's behaviour, she had a number of supporters too. The final shock was when Karen arrived in after lunch with an early copy of the *Evening Herald*. 'You're a celebrity.'

Maeve stared in shock at the two-page spread, the banner reading '*Queen Bitch of the Airwaves*'.

'Oh, my God.'

The article went on to say that though some people were offended by Maeve's style of questioning, lots of listeners loved this new, hard-hitting show that pulled no punches.

'I can't believe it. Why do people love this sort of thing?' Maeve wailed.

'Voyeurism,' Karl said flatly. 'Or whatever the equivalent term is for listening. Not exactly the outcome we expected.'

Maeve glanced back at the newspaper. 'You don't get a mention. All the credit goes to Ben. Apparently, he's *injected new life into the station* and given me something *to get my teeth into*.' She threw the paper on the desk in disgust. 'This means that Jonathan is going to expect controversy every night.'

'Yep.'

'Bloody hell, Karl, what do we do?' Maeve dragged distracted fingers through her hair.

He shrugged as he stubbed out his cigarette. 'Go along with it or get out.'

'I really had intended to hand in my notice this morning,' Maeve confessed. 'But now—'

'You like the idea of being famous?'

Maeve pulled a face. 'That's awful, isn't it? And I'm not even sure I like this kind of fame. Is there any real merit in being' – she picked up the paper again – '*the queen bitch of the airwaves?*'

'It's a job.'

'I wasn't as tough as they make out,' she protested.

'Oh yes you were,' he assured her.

'Do you think we have any hope of convincing Jonathan that we should tame the show down a little?'

Karl shook his head. 'He's a great guy, Maeve, but even he's not going to walk away from a gold mine.'

'We got *some* negative feedback,' Maeve reminded him.

'Yeah, and those listeners will be tuning in this evening so they can complain about it again. We can't lose.'

Maeve closed her eyes and massaged the bridge of her nose. 'So there's nothing we can do.'

Karl looked at her thoughtfully. 'There's quite a lot *you* can do.'

'Like what?'

'Like changing the tone of your voice, controlling the silences, even injecting some humour on occasion. You can relieve the tension simply by the way you talk.'

She opened her eyes slowly. 'But Jonathan won't go for that, will he?'

'If you're still asking the hard questions, what can he say?'

She nodded thoughtfully. 'It's worth a try.'

'Good girl! Now, tell me, what's tonight's guest like?'

'I've only talked to her for a few minutes on the phone but she seems a sensible sort.'

'How old?'

'Forty-four.'

'And what does she do?'

'She's a civil servant – quite senior, I think.'

'Then it shouldn't be too easy for you to intimidate her.'

'She's probably going to be rattled by last night's show. Maybe I should call her.'

'Let Carrie do it,' Karl advised. 'It would be best if you kept away from the guests before the show.'

Maeve stood up and stretched. 'That suits me just fine. I'm going to grab a coffee, do you want one?'

'Yeah. And then I think we should come up with some questions for tonight.'

Maeve paused in the doorway. 'Before Ben does, you mean. Good idea.'

Karl winked at her. 'I knew you'd appreciate me one day.'

As Maeve made her way down to the coffee machine she thought about Karl's words. He was right, of course. She could change things, but she'd have to be careful to keep Jonathan happy at the same time.

'Hi.' Carrie appeared at Maeve's side as she filled the two plastic cups.

'Hi. Get yourself a coffee, Carrie, we've got a lot to do.'

Carrie glanced around nervously. 'Where's Ben?'

'Gone out. He said he'd be back at nine.'

Carrie got a coffee and followed Maeve down the corridor.

Karl looked up as they walked in. 'Hey, Carrie, are you ready for another evening of cut-throat radio?'

Carrie made a face. 'I'm not sure. Last night left a bad taste in my mouth. I can't believe some people liked it. I was sure they'd be out to hang you, Maeve.'

'Thanks.'

'I'm sorry, but you know what I mean.'

'Yes, I do and I agree. I'm a bit shocked that our

public enjoyed me attacking someone so innocent and defenceless. Have you talked to Ann today?'

Carrie shook her head. 'I did call but her gran said she wouldn't talk to me.'

'Jesus, what if we've really screwed her up?' Maeve chewed on a nail distractedly.

'No time to think about that now,' Karl said abruptly. 'We must concentrate on' – he looked at the page in front of him – 'Therese.'

They worked steadily until ten to nine and then made their way up to the meeting room. Ben and Jonathan were already there. Jonathan glanced at each of them in turn. 'Is everyone ready for another great show?'

Maeve flashed him a brittle smile. 'Sure.'

'So, tell me all about tonight's guest?'

Before Maeve could open her mouth, Ben was on his feet, smiling around confidently. 'Therese is in her forties and is married with two children. She's a senior clerical officer in the Civil Service. She had a brief fling when she was nineteen, resulting in pregnancy. Her folks were shocked but, being devout Catholics, abortion was not an option. Instead, they sent her off to an aunt down the country until she'd had the baby and then they arranged for it to be adopted.'

'She didn't have any say at all,' Carrie interjected. 'The poor woman can't talk about it without filling up.'

Maeve groaned inwardly. 'And she hasn't told her husband and family?'

Ben shook his head.

Jonathan nodded gravely. 'They were different times, I suppose. You were a complete outcast if you had a baby out of wedlock in those days.'

'But it's going to be a lot worse if the kid turns up on the doorstep some day,' Karl remarked.

'No-win situation,' Jonathan agreed. 'I don't think you'll have a shortage of good calls tonight.'

Karl tapped the page in front of him. 'We're all ready, even if we don't.'

Ben looked curiously at him. 'You've changed your tune.'

'What can I say, Ben? You were right. It was a huge success.'

Jonathan eyed his producer suspiciously. 'No surprises, Karl,' he warned.

Karl looked back innocently. 'Of course not, Boss.'

'You've got some questions ready then?' Ben asked.

Maeve nodded. 'Yeah. It was all such a rush job last night we decided it would be a good idea to have something prepared in advance.'

'Good thinking.' Jonathan nodded in approval.

Ben's eyes were watchful. 'May I see them?'

'Carrie?' Karl turned to the researcher.

'Oh, dear, I left the other copies back in the office. I'll drop them up to you before the show.' Carrie stared innocently into Ben's eyes.

'Thanks, Carrie.'

'So what tack are you going to take tonight, Maeve?' Jonathan asked.

She shrugged. 'Much the same as last night. I'll let her tell her story and then ask questions.'

'It could get a bit jaded if you use the same format every time,' Ben cautioned.

'Tell that to Michael Parkinson,' Karl retorted.

Jonathan grinned. 'You're right, Karl, if it's not broke don't fix it.' He turned to Maeve. 'You did great last night, Maeve, you don't need us to tell you what to do. Okay, good luck, everybody. I'll drop by when it's over.'

The atmosphere in the studio was tense and Therese was defensive and wary. Maeve did her best to put her at her ease during the breaks, but Therese just watched her suspiciously.

'I feel terrible,' she moaned to Karl during the final break. 'She's treating me like a Nazi.'

'Can you blame her?'

When Maeve returned to her desk, she smiled reassuringly at her guest. 'We're going to take questions from our listeners now, Therese. Is that okay?'

Therese gave a small shrug. 'I suppose.'

'You don't have to answer anything you don't want to,' Maeve said hurriedly, 'and just give me the nod if you've had enough.'

The woman's expression softened. 'Okay, thanks.'

'Ready to go, Maeve, on five, four, three, two, one.'

'Welcome back, and now it's time for your questions. First, Therese, John in Drimnagh wants to know if you've ever thought about making contact with your daughter.'

'Every day,' Therese said softly. 'But I don't think it would be fair. She may not even know she's adopted.'

'And everyone wants to know, Therese, what will you do if she comes looking for you?'

'I don't know. I'd love it in one way but I don't know how my husband and kids would react.'

Maeve consulted her notes. 'Mary in Cabra thinks you're being very unfair to your family. She says how would you feel if you found out your husband had been lying to you for all these years.'

Therese nodded. 'I'd be devastated. But I think it makes a difference that this baby was born long before I even met my husband. The fact that she exists doesn't mean that I love him or my kids any less.'

Maeve silently applauded this very intelligent woman. 'Sara in Marino wants to know what kind of family adopted your daughter.'

'I don't know. My parents organised everything and they said it would be better for me and the baby if I didn't know anything about them or where they lived.'

Maeve nodded. 'Tell me, Therese, why did you do it?'

Therese frowned. 'What do you mean?'

'Why did you give your baby up?'

'I've told you—'

'But you weren't a child, Therese, you were officially an adult. Your parents didn't have the power to take her away.'

Therese stared at her. 'You don't understand. They were very conservative and very controlling. I was used to doing as they told me.'

'Did they tell you to go out and sleep with a man?'

'Of course not. But haven't you ever made a mistake?'

'Are you really being honest with us, Therese? Are you being honest with yourself? Wasn't it easier to go along with what your parents wanted? Then you could get on with your own life.'

Therese flinched. 'That's not true. I wanted to keep her.'

'Then why didn't you run away?'

'Because I had nowhere to go.'

Maeve said nothing for a moment. 'Tell me, Therese, will you ever try to find your daughter?'

Therese was silent for a moment. 'No, I don't think so. If my daughter comes looking for me then well and good. But if she doesn't, there's no point in dragging up the past.'

'Thank you, Therese. Tune in tomorrow night, listeners, and we'll have another secret. Goodnight.' Maeve looked nervously at her guest. 'Are you okay?'

Therese nodded. 'I'm fine.'

'Did I go too far?'

She shook her head. 'You asked me nothing that I haven't asked myself a thousand times. I think about that child every day of my life.'

Carrie escorted her from the office and Maeve went out to join Ben and Karl. 'Well?'

'It was good,' Karl told her.

Ben frowned. 'Not as good as last night's. You should have followed up on why she didn't leave home.'

Maeve stared at him through narrowed eyes. 'No

way. She told her story well, almost without any emotion. That made clear the hurt that she went through and is still going through. It would have been over the top if I'd gone after her.'

Jonathan walked into the room and applauded Maeve. 'Well done again, it was another great show.'

She looked triumphantly at Ben. 'Thanks, Jonathan. You don't think I was too easy on her?'

He pondered the question. 'I don't think so,' he said finally. 'We don't want you to be too bitchy.'

'Yeah.' Karl glared at Ben. 'It's not that kind of show.'

'She'd better be a bitch tomorrow night,' Ben retorted.

'What's tomorrow night?' Jonathan frowned.

'A guy who's been having an affair for eight years,' Maeve told him. 'And I'll be happy to play the bitch with him.'

Jonathan grinned. 'That's my girl. Come on, folks. I'll buy you all a drink.'

34

Linda leaned back in the comfortable chair and closed her eyes. She was sitting in Viv's sun room relaxing after a rather filling portion of lasagne. It was always either cottage pie, lasagne or some other minced-beef concoction. Linda had tried to expand her sister's repertoire but before she reached the end of a recipe, Viv had lost interest. Linda smiled as she felt the warmth of the sun through the glass. It wasn't surprising that Viv did most of her writing in this room. It was warm, comfortable and relaxing and it would be very easy to fall asleep.

'Your boyfriend's getting very controversial,' Rosemary Taylor remarked after reading the review of the first week of the *Secrets* show.

'Have you heard any of the shows, Mum?' Linda asked.

The older woman lowered the paper. 'Yes.'

'And what did you think?' Linda was curious to hear her mother's opinion – she didn't shock easily.

'Some are better than others. I didn't like the way that interviewer went after that poor girl with HIV.'

'Me neither.' Linda sighed. Her mother was right, some of the programmes had been quite good but others had made her cringe. It hadn't helped her relationship with Jonathan. She wasn't very good at hiding her feelings and they'd got to the point where they just didn't discuss *Secrets* at all. Except for the night Viv dropped in on her way home from a book launch. Linda closed her eyes at the memory. She and Jonathan were having quite a nice evening until Viv arrived. She was slightly tipsy and immediately started to slag off *Secrets*.

'You could be on that show, Linda,' she'd said. 'What do you think, Jonathan?'

He'd smiled coolly and said nothing.

'Do you think Maeve Elliot would take Linda apart too?' she'd carried on regardless.

'Viv, stop it, please,' Linda had hissed.

Jonathan had stood up and shrugged casually. 'Viv's entitled to her opinion.'

'I am, I am.'

'I'll be off.' Jonathan had kissed her cheek perfunctorily and headed for the door. 'Goodnight, Viv.'

''Night, Jonathan.' Viv had waved cheerfully.

The object of Linda's thoughts entered the room. 'Right, the washing up's done, would anyone like a coffee?'

'Lovely.' Her mother smiled.

'Yeah, I'll have one too,' Linda said and followed Viv back out to the kitchen. The three had taken to having lunch together every Sunday, usually in Viv's. Rosemary avoided cooking whenever possible and Linda's apartment was too sterile for her mother and sister's liking.

'How's Jonathan?' Viv glanced guiltily at her sister.

Linda smiled. 'Fine, no thanks to you.'

'Sorry. Was he very annoyed with me?'

'Dunno, he's never mentioned it since.'

'But you have seen him?'

Linda's eyes twinkled. 'Oh, yes.'

Viv, who'd been measuring coffee into the filter, paused. 'Yes?'

Linda said nothing, but continued to grin like the proverbial Cheshire cat.

'Are you two . . . have you?'

Linda nodded.

Viv dropped her spoon and turned to stare. 'You're sleeping with him.'

'I'm not getting much sleep at all,' Linda said smugly.

A flicker of concern crossed Viv's face. 'Is it serious?'

'I don't know and I don't care,' Linda told her. 'I'm having the time of my life.'

'But what happens when . . . ?'

Linda's eyes were sharp. 'A twenty-year-old beauty comes along? I suppose it will be over. So what?'

'I don't want you to get hurt again.'

'This is completely different. Jonathan isn't lying to me or cheating on me. We're two adults who happen to be enjoying each other's company.'

'And you wouldn't mind if he dumped you tomorrow?'

Linda stared at her. 'Of course I'd bloody well mind! But I wouldn't be surprised. It's not going to last, Viv, I'm prepared for that. So I'm going to enjoy the ride – as it were – while it lasts.'

Viv finished preparing the coffee and sat down at the table, her face troubled. 'But that's not you, Lin. I'm the one who lives like that. You – don't.'

'Well maybe it's time I changed. Oh, for God's sake, Viv, can't you just be happy for me?'

'I am, really I am,' Viv said urgently. 'And I do like Jonathan, despite his lousy talk show. I just don't want you to get hurt.'

'I won't.'

'Does Mum know?'

Linda shot her an incredulous look. 'I may be nearly forty but I'm still not ready to discuss my sex life with my mother!'

They were still laughing when they rejoined Rosemary. She put down her newspaper and looked at them. 'What are you two giggling at?'

Linda shot a warning glance at her sister.

Viv grinned back. 'Just one of Linda's dirty jokes.'

Rosemary sighed. 'I don't know why you love that toilet humour, Linda. Your jokes aren't even funny.'

Viv poured the coffee. 'This one was.'

Linda nudged her hard, making her slop some in the saucer. 'Careful there, Viv.'

Viv made a face. 'Are you doing anything exciting this evening, Mum?' She curled up at Rosemary's feet.

'No, not tonight.'

Linda and Viv exchanged glances. 'Are you okay?' Linda asked.

'Of course I'm okay. Can't I have a quiet night in?'

'Well, it's a little unusual, Mum,' Viv pointed out. 'You always go out on Sunday night.'

'And most other nights too,' Linda mumbled. Her mother's social life had never ceased to amaze her.

Rosemary shrugged. 'Well, actually, I've a friend dropping by.'

Though her voice was casual, Viv's ears pricked up immediately 'A man?'

Rosemary looked irritably at her youngest daughter. 'What if it is?'

Linda's lips twitched. 'Have you got a boyfriend, Mother?'

'Don't be ridiculous,' Rosemary replied, but her colour had heightened and she was avoiding Linda's eyes.

Viv stared at her. 'You do, you've got a boyfriend! What's he like? What's his name? When are we going to meet him?'

Rosemary's eyes widened. 'Never! I've told you, he's just a friend and I don't want you scaring him off.'

'It's okay, Mum, I'll keep Viv on a tight leash. But won't he think it odd that you don't want him to meet your family?'

Viv made a ghoulish face. 'Yes, he might think there's something wrong with us.'

'And he'd be right,' Rosemary replied.

'That's very hurtful,' Viv sniffed. 'It's just as well I'm thick skinned.'

'Just thick,' Linda said with a grin. 'What's he like, Mum?'

Rosemary sighed, realising that her daughters wouldn't let her out of the house without some information. 'His name is Liam Kearns, he's a widower and we met at a fundraiser for Children In Need.'

Viv sat at her mother's feet and stared curiously up into her face. 'Where does he live?'

Linda moved closer too. 'How old is he?'

'He lives in Dalkey and he's sixty-three.'

'Dalkey, eh? So he's got a few bob then?'

'I've no idea and I don't care.'

'What does he do, Mum?' Linda asked.

'He was Chief Executive of some insurance company but he's retired now.'

Viv nodded gravely. 'Then he'll definitely have a few bob.'

Linda laughed. 'Since when did you become so obsessed with money?'

'I'm not. I'm just making sure that this man's intentions are honourable.'

'Are you worried about your inheritance?' Rosemary arched an eyebrow.

Viv looked offended. 'Excuse me, Mother dear, but I think that you're forgetting I'm a successful author and don't need your money. You should be grateful that I'm looking after your best interests.'

Rosemary shot Linda an amused look. 'Oh, I am dear, sorry.'

Viv smiled. 'That's more like it. Now what did the wife die of? He didn't top her, did he?'

'Vivienne! I am definitely never going to introduce you to Liam now.'

Viv grinned. 'I might drop by tonight – just to say hello.'

Rosemary's eyes narrowed. 'Don't even think about it or I'll be forced to disown you.'

'Don't worry, Mum, I'll keep Viv out of your way.'

Rosemary smiled gratefully at her eldest daughter. 'Thank you, Linda.'

'That is, if you promise to invite him over for a drink at Christmas,' Linda added.

'Oh, I don't know . . .'

Viv's eyes narrowed. 'Mum?'

'Oh, well, okay then, as long as you promise to behave.'

Viv smiled sweetly. 'We will.'

35

Maeve stood wrapped in a towel in her bathroom, getting ready to go out. It seemed like ages since she'd seen the FECC crowd. Between the show and her ankle she'd missed both the climbs and the social nights. And she hadn't met Craig for that drink either. She frowned at her reflection in the mirror. She'd called him a couple of times but he always seemed too busy to talk – although he made time to criticise her show, she thought wryly. He had been very scathing about the first one and though she'd laughed off his criticism, it hurt. His opinion, she realised, was important to her. Unlike Paul Riche. She sighed. Her relationship with him had been getting more strained, but the final nail in the coffin was the way he'd raved about the first *Secrets* show. Maeve just knew she couldn't carry on after that, so she told Paul that it was over. He hadn't been impressed but he'd get over it. She had been no more than a trophy girlfriend and it wouldn't take him long to replace her. Paul Riche was not the deep, sentimental type and his opinion of her show had confirmed that he wasn't exactly sensitive either. Unlike Craig Prentice. He was a man of integrity and no matter

how successful the show got she would feel a failure
as long as he disapproved. She slammed her mascara
down on the counter and marched into the bedroom
to get dressed. Damn the man, she thought angrily,
as she pulled on her combats. Why did he always get
to her? She tucked a long-sleeved black T-shirt into
her trousers and pulled a large black leather belt tight
around her waist. After another quick appraisal in the
mirror, she decided to pull her long hair back into a
loose ponytail and put on her flat boots. She looked
longingly at her collection of high-heeled boots and
shoes but she'd promised herself she'd stick to flat
heels for one more week – just in case. She grabbed
her bag and headed for the door. It was five thirty and
the gang were meeting at six in Crowes in Ballsbridge,
but she'd decided to walk and it would take at least
thirty minutes at her current speed. She turned up the
collar of her jacket as she wandered up through the
bustling little village of Sandymount. It was always
busy, but on a Saturday evening it was full of locals
doing last-minute shopping and there was a steady
hum from the pubs she passed. Even though it was
still only November there were Christmas lights and
decorations in many of the shop windows and she
smiled at a notice announcing the arrival of Santa
Claus by helicopter the following week. By the time
she'd got to Crowes, Freddy and Valerie were already
there. 'Hi, guys,' she said, taking off her jacket and
climbing on to a barstool.

Freddy looked at her in surprise. 'Hello, stranger.
How's the foot?'

'Fine, thanks. Can I get you a drink?'

'Pint, please,' Freddy said.

'Not for me.' Valerie looked at her watch. 'I should be going.'

Maeve blinked. 'Already?' she said as she signalled the waiter.

Valerie laughed. 'We've been here since four, Maeve.'

'Four? But I thought the meeting was at six.'

Freddy frowned. 'We had to change it. Didn't Aoife call you?'

Maeve grimaced. 'No, she must have forgotten. So has everybody left?'

'Ken's in the loo and Craig just went out to the bank; he should be back in a minute.'

Maeve brightened. 'Oh, well, you can fill me in on the meeting. I don't suppose it matters much, I won't be back in action before January.'

'But you'll come to the Christmas party, Maeve,' Valerie said as she pulled on her coat.

'Yeah, sure.'

'Right, see you then. 'Bye, Freddy.'

''Bye, Val.'

Maeve paid the barman and took a drink of her beer. 'Tell me about this party.'

'It should be a bit of crack. We're going down to some hotel in Kildare.'

'Kildare!'

'Yeah, Aoife organised it. She's hired a mini bus and we're going to stay the night.'

Maeve smiled. 'Really? And is Craig going?'

'I am,' he said from behind her and she swung round. 'Hi, Maeve. How's the foot?'

'Fine. Will I get you a pint?'

'Thanks.' He glanced at the clock on the wall behind the bar. 'You're a bit late.'

Maeve made a face. 'Your little pal, Aoife, forgot to tell me that the meeting was at four.'

Craig met Freddy's gaze, who merely shrugged. 'Oh, well, you didn't miss much.'

'Except the arrangements regarding the Christmas party,' she pointed out.

'Didn't think you'd be interested,' he said nabbing a stool as the couple beside them left. He pulled it in between Maeve and Freddy and sat up, his knees brushing against Maeve's.

'Why wouldn't I be?' she asked casually, trying to ignore the effect his closeness was having on her. He was looking very well tonight, dressed simply in a grey roll-neck jumper and blue jeans, his sleeves pulled up to reveal tanned arms that were covered in fine dark hairs.

He shrugged. 'I just thought that the queen bitch of the airwaves would have better things to do. Like pulling legs off spiders.'

Freddy shook his head. 'Oh, here we go. Don't you two ever stop?'

Maeve bristled. 'I'm just out for a quiet drink with friends – or so I thought.'

Craig looked slightly shamefaced. 'Sorry.'

'That's more like it.' Freddy nodded his approval. 'Now, I'm going for a leak.'

'So are you enjoying it? The show, I mean.' Craig took a sip of the pint that she'd handed him.

'Yeah, it's okay.' She glanced around the pub while she drummed her fingernails on the bar.

Craig raised an eyebrow. 'Only okay?'

'It's fine,' she said irritably.

'I doubt your guests would agree,' he muttered into his pint.

Maeve glared at him. 'What did you say?'

He smiled. 'Nothing.'

Freddy came back and groaned at the loaded atmosphere. 'Oh, lads, can we not have a couple of drinks in peace?'

'Sorry.' Maeve's smile was strained.

'Has Craig told you about his love-life?' Freddy's eyes twinkled.

'Shut up, Freddy.' Craig stared into his pint.

Maeve glanced from him back to Freddy. 'What's this?'

'He's in love with our little Aoife.'

'What?'

'I am not!' Craig flashed Maeve a strange look. 'We've just gone out for a drink a couple of times.'

Maeve forced a smile. 'Well, that's nice, I suppose. If you like that sort of thing.'

Craig frowned. 'Aoife's okay, Maeve. If you took the trouble to talk to her properly you'd know that.'

'She's not my type,' Maeve replied tartly. 'I wouldn't have thought she was yours either.'

'What would you know?' Craig retorted. 'Not all men like to behave like lapdogs.'

'What's *that* supposed to mean?'

Freddy looked at Maeve's flushed cheeks, drained his glass and stood up. 'I think I'll leave you two to it.'

'Sorry, Freddy.' Craig glared at Maeve.

The other man put on his jacket. 'Goodnight.'

''Night.' Maeve watched him as he fought his way through the crowd to the door. She glanced back at Craig. 'So, is it serious?'

He stared back. 'What?'

'This thing with Aoife,' she muttered.

Craig smiled slightly. 'Would it bother you?'

Her eyes widened. 'Why the hell would I care?'

'You tell me.'

She looked away. 'I just don't like to see a mate make a fool of himself.'

'We're still mates then?'

'Of course. Well, you need someone to tell you the truth, don't you?'

Craig laughed, his eyes crinkling at the sides. 'You always do that, Maeve.'

She smiled. He had a lovely laugh and he was good fun. What on earth did he see in that little mouse, Aoife? The girl had nothing to say for herself.

'So will you come to the party?' he asked.

She shrugged. 'Maybe. What night is it?'

'Friday the 21st December.'

She scowled. 'Then how can I come? I'll be working. I suppose it was your girlfriend who came up with that date.'

'It was agreed by the whole gang,' he said quietly.

'Couldn't you get someone else to cover for you for one night?'

Maeve stared at him in disbelief. 'Maybe if the show had been running a few months I'd take a night off, but not after a few weeks.'

'So what shows have you got lined up for Christmas? Are you going to accuse Santa of cruelty to children?'

Maeve shook her head. 'Very funny.'

'Maeve? Hey, I thought it was you.' A silver-haired woman appeared at Maeve's side and hugged her affectionately. 'You look wonderful.'

'Peggy!' Maeve stared at her aunt. 'What are you doing here?'

'I've been shopping all day and I came in for a well-earned drink. Town is mad. I can't imagine what it's going to be like nearer Christmas.' She looked curiously at Craig.

'Oh, this is Craig Prentice. He's just a friend,' she added hurriedly and turned away from Craig's amused look. 'Craig, this is my Aunt Peggy.'

'Nice to meet you.'

Peggy eyed him speculatively. 'Well, if my niece has any sense, you're a lot more than friends.'

'Peggy!' Maeve stared at her mortified and Craig threw back his head and laughed.

'I'm afraid we're not. You'll have to put in a good word for me,' he told her.

Peggy smiled wryly. 'I doubt she'd listen to me.' She turned her attention back to her niece. 'I don't suppose you have much time for boyfriends at the moment, what with the new show.'

'It has been hectic,' Maeve agreed. 'Have you heard the show?'

Peggy's smile wavered. 'Yes, dear, it's very . . . interesting.'

'That's a tactful way of putting it,' Craig murmured.

Maeve glared at him. 'You don't like it?' she asked her aunt.

Peggy shrugged uncomfortably. 'I was never one for these talk shows, Maeve. I love a nice bit of music.'

'Right.' Maeve wished she'd go back to her friends. It was bad enough having Craig attack the show without her own flesh and blood joining in too.

'Have you seen your mum?' Peggy asked suddenly.

Maeve's expression was guarded. 'No.'

'She hasn't been well,' Peggy said gently. 'I'm sure it would really cheer her up if you dropped by.'

Maeve shrugged. 'I'm pretty busy at the moment.'

Peggy laid a hand on her arm. 'I know she'd love to see you.'

'I doubt that.'

Peggy smiled sadly. 'Well, I've said my piece. It was lovely to see you, Maeve.'

Maeve hugged her tightly. 'Yeah, you too.'

'It was nice to meet you, Craig.'

'And you.' He nodded at the older woman and when she'd gone turned curious eyes on Maeve. 'What was all that about?'

'Mind your own bloody business,' Maeve snapped.

Craig stared at her. 'Sorry I spoke,' he said grimly, drained his glass and stood up. 'See you around.'

36

Carrie opened her eyes as the front door banged. She glanced at the clock and groaned when she saw it was only seven o'clock. 'Thanks, Declan,' she muttered and buried her head under a pillow. After twenty minutes of twisting and turning, she gave up on sleep and threw back the covers. She may as well make the most of her morning and clean the house. After her shower, she pulled on her oldest jeans and a sweatshirt and went downstairs. As usual, Declan had left his mug and cereal bowl on the table for her to clear away. She grimaced as she saw that he'd spilt sugar on the floor – they'd be walking that around the house for days. She cleared away his dishes, scrubbed the worktop and swept the floor before making her own breakfast. She loved to have a leisurely breakfast, listening to the radio and leafing through the newspaper, but she could only enjoy it if the kitchen was clean. She put the kettle on and glanced critically around the room. The floor needed to be washed but then she'd let a lot of things go since she'd joined Forever FM. She'd never noticed before how little Declan did to help. She had happily taken care of the housework in the past because he worked a longer day than she did and had so much more responsibility. But things were different now, she decided as she spooned instant coffee into a mug. She was earning as much money as he was. It was time their relationship became an equal partnership. She went to the cupboard and took down the box of cornflakes that felt suspiciously light. 'Bloody hell, Declan!' She dumped the box into the bin and went to check the breadbin. There were two rather stale slices of white bread left; she put them in the toaster and made the coffee. As well as cleaning the house she was going to have to pay a visit to the supermarket. Now Declan could easily do that. Their local shop was open late most nights and it wouldn't take long if she gave him a list. At least it would take some of the load off her. The toast popped up and she scraped some butter across it and chewed thoughtfully. She'd never thought of looking after her home and Declan as cumbersome before but then she'd never enjoyed a job so much before. Even though she was a bit uncomfortable with the way *Secrets* had turned out, she still loved being involved. She smiled as she thought of the different reactions to her new job. Declan had become a lot more supportive because he liked the show and though he still grumbled things weren't as bad as they were. Her parents, however, had been disgusted with *Secrets*.

'Trash,' her father had said coldly. 'I don't know how rubbish like that is allowed on the airwaves.'

'It's very popular,' Carrie had said defensively even though she agreed.

Her mother had shaken her head sadly. 'It's a sign of our poor education system.'

Helen had stared at her. 'Ireland has one of the best education systems in the world.'

Her mother had given her a withering look. 'It doesn't appear that way. Imagine people wanting to listen to that kind of thing when they could be reading a book, or listening to some music or even going for a walk.'

'Don't be silly, Mum, everyone is interested in human interest stories.'

Her father looked at Helen over his glasses. 'Why?'

'Don't let it get to you,' Carrie had told her sister calmly later when they were alone.

'But doesn't it bother you?' Helen had asked.

'I'm used to it, Helen. They've never approved of anything I've done, why should they change now?'

She finished her breakfast, put her plate and mug in the dishwasher and looked around. She'd dust first then tackle the floors. When she'd finished, she changed into black trousers and a coffee-coloured pullover, applied her make-up and slicked her hair back with some wax. She smiled at the effect. Despite Declan's opinion, she loved the dramatic effect she could create with make-up. Her brown eyes looked huge, her skin tone was a healthy, even peach and her lashes looked incredibly long. She was particularly pleased with the apricot lipstick that was all the rage now because it really suited her. She smiled at herself and sat down to pull on her boots. Then she went downstairs, had a quick look through her fridge and the cupboards and slinging her bag over her shoulder left the house.

She was staggering back from the supermarket a couple of hours later, laden down with bags, when her sister pulled up beside her. 'Want a lift?'

'Oh, yes, please!' Carrie dumped the bags in the back and climbed in beside Helen. 'Were you coming to see me?'

Helen checked her mirror and then pulled out. 'No, I have a hair appointment in half an hour.'

Carrie appraised her sister's neat blonde bob. 'What are you getting done?'

'Just a trim. Oscar announced at breakfast that he's taking me out tonight.'

Carrie tried to imagine Declan surprising her, and failed. 'Anywhere nice?'

Helen indicated and then turned into Carrie's road. 'We're going to the opera and then having supper in the Four Seasons Hotel.'

Carrie's eyes widened. 'Oh, very nice. What's the occasion?'

'Nothing. We just haven't had any time alone together in ages.'

Carrie absorbed this piece of information in silence.

'Well, here we are.' Helen stopped the car.

Carrie smiled. 'Thanks. Have you time for a quick coffee?'

Helen checked her watch and shook her head. 'Better not.'

She helped Carrie with the shopping and then drove

away. Carrie waved and then went into the kitchen to unpack. It would be lovely to be taken to a nice restaurant – she could do without the opera! And it would be even nicer to go dancing afterwards. She and Orla hadn't been out clubbing since she'd started her new job. Now that she was out of the house five nights a week, she was afraid to suggest going out with Orla on the weekend too. If only she could persuade Declan to take her out. Occasionally, they did eat out, though it was usually only pizza or curry. Carrie didn't mind that, she was not a foodie like Helen. What bothered her was that they were always finished and back out on the street within an hour. Carrie knew for a fact that Oscar and Helen would talk for hours over their wine and coffee tonight. She sighed as she put the groceries away. There was no point in wishing her life away. She must concentrate on all the things she had to be grateful for. She thought for a moment and then decided that maybe it was time to get to work.

'Hi, Carrie.'

Carrie was halfway across reception before she spotted Linda sitting in the corner, flicking through a magazine. 'Linda, how are you?'

Linda put down the magazine and smiled up at her. 'Fine. How's the job going?'

'Great, thanks. I'm so grateful that you got me this position.' Carrie sat down beside her.

'I wasn't sure you'd still feel that way,' Linda remarked.

Carrie rolled her eyes. 'You don't like *Secrets* either, then?'

'I'm sorry, I didn't mean—'

'It's okay, Linda, none of us like it. Except Ben and Jonathan that is— Oh, sorry.'

Linda laughed. 'Don't worry, you're not telling me anything I don't already know. Do you mind working on the show?'

Carrie frowned. 'I feel guilty about it sometimes but if I'm honest I have to admit that I enjoy it too. It's really fascinating getting such an insight into people's lives.'

'Invasive too,' Linda remarked.

'But they ask to come on the show,' Carrie pointed out loyally.

Linda smiled. 'You sound like Jonathan.'

Carrie made a face. 'I'm not sure – is that a compliment?'

'I'll get back to you on that.'

'Linda, hi, sorry if I kept you waiting.' Jonathan crossed reception and bent to kiss her lightly on the lips. 'Hi, Carrie.'

'I'd better get on,' she said shyly. 'Nice to see you, Linda.'

'You too. 'Bye, Carrie.'

Jonathan led Linda back to his office. 'So, how are you?'

'Fine.' Linda smiled at him. 'Sorry I'm late.'

'Are you? I didn't notice. It's been a crazy morning.'

'Well, if you don't want to have lunch—'

He closed the door and took her in his arms. 'I've been looking forward to it,' he said, and kissed her. 'Although,' he sighed when he finally pulled away, 'I'm not sure it's food I fancy.'

'Don't even think about it,' Linda warned him, although her eyes were twinkling. 'We are going to a restaurant and we're going to eat food. I've had enough cavorting around like a teenager.'

Jonathan laughed. In the last few weeks, they'd been in car parks, lay-bys, even on the beach one day. 'But my car is very comfortable,' he pointed out.

'It is.' Linda agreed. She still couldn't quite believe this was happening. She'd never felt this way before – not even with Patrick. Even when they'd first met there had never been the excitement that she felt now. All the time, she thought about Jonathan; how he looked, how it felt when he kissed her, how he made her feel when he touched her—

'Are you positive that you want to eat,' he murmured now, trailing kisses down the side of her neck.

'Yes.' But she closed her eyes and leaned in to him.

He drew back and looked at her. 'You know I love you, don't you?'

Linda's eyes flew open. 'You don't have to say that, Jonathan.' She moved away from him and sat down.

He sat on the edge of his desk and took her hands. 'I know I don't have to. I want to.'

Linda refused to meet his eyes. 'Don't.'

'What is it, Lin? Don't you feel the same?' He raised one of her hands and kissed her wrist.

She shivered and closed her eyes again. 'It's too soon, Jonathan, I'm still married, for God's sake.'

'That hasn't stopped your husband,' he murmured.

'Thanks for the reminder,' she said grimly, pulling her hand away.

'Sorry. I didn't think it was still an issue.'

'It's not. Well, it is.' She sighed. 'Oh, Jonathan, we're having fun, enjoying each other's company, let's keep it that way.'

His eyes darkened. 'Is that all this is to you, fun?'

'Oh, Jonathan, please.'

'Right, sorry, let's forget about it.' He glanced at his watch. 'Come on, we'd better go.'

She put a hand on his arm as he opened the door. 'Are we okay?'

'Sure.' He smiled tightly. 'We're fine.'

Linda wasn't sure they were. All through lunch, Jonathan kept the conversation going, but it was impersonal as it had been in the old days when he was a client. She stared at him sadly as he talked about the problems he was having with the new mixing desks at the station. 'Jonathan?'

He stopped in the middle of a technical spiel and looked at her. 'Yes?'

'I didn't mean to offend you.'

His smile was guarded. 'Oh, Linda, you haven't offended me. I'm just a little' – he struggled to find the right word – 'disappointed.'

She frowned, unsure of what he meant and what her reply should be. When she didn't say anything, he switched on his cool, professional smile again. 'Excuse me for a moment.' Linda watched him weave his way through the tables to the door at the back of the room and sighed. She'd annoyed him again. He seemed to get irritated very easily if she didn't say the right thing or react the right way. Linda thought it was probably because he was used to dating younger women who'd hung on his every word and offered no conflicting opinion. 'But he knows what I'm like,' she murmured as she fiddled with her knife.

'Sorry, Madam?'

Linda started when she saw the waiter standing over her, a quizzical look on his face.

'Nothing.'

'Can I get you anything else?'

'Not at the moment, thank you.' The only thing worse than talking to yourself was being caught at it.

'What's funny?' Jonathan asked as he resumed his seat.

'The waiter thinks I'm a nutter and of course he's right. I wish you'd remember that too. I may say the wrong thing but I mean well.' She smiled apologetically.

He reached over and squeezed her hand. 'I know. Listen, I hope you don't think I'm rushing you but I have a very busy afternoon.' He looked round at the waiter hovering nearby and asked for the bill.

Linda hid her surprise. 'That's okay. I've a lot to do myself.'

'Fine.' He smiled at her.

'Fine.' She smiled back.

37

No matter what Maeve did she couldn't get the meeting with her Aunt Peggy out of her mind. And despite everything that had happened in the past, she was still worried about her mother. Several nights she had lain awake, the fingers of fear tightening around her heart. She was a child again wondering why her father had gone away. Why God had *taken* him away – everyone had told her that God had taken him – and why her mother had, in effect, left her too. Maeve owed her nothing, not even her concern. Which is why she was confused when she found herself driving towards the family home. She could still turn back, it wasn't too late, but despite the argument going on in her head, she kept driving. When she pulled up outside, she sat looking at the house for a while. It was much as she remembered it, although it seemed smaller to her now. But the red brick was still covered in a thin layer of ivy and the two large stone lions still flanked either side of the porch. But the garden that had been neglected since her father died was now neat and tidy, and snow-white net curtains hung at each window. Maeve felt the old animosity bubble up inside. Her mother couldn't be that sick if she was able to keep her home in such pristine order. The house had never looked this good when she'd lived here. She got out of the car and marched up the path. She still had a key but baulked at using it. After a moment's hesitation, she rang the bell. A pleasant, middle-aged woman with kind eyes opened it. 'Yes?'

Maeve stared. 'Er, I was looking for Mrs Elliot.'

'I'm afraid that she's not too well at the moment, not really up to visitors. Can I tell her who was asking after her?'

'Maeve. Her daughter.'

The other woman rolled her eyes and laughed. 'Oh, I'm so sorry, how silly of me, and she with that lovely big photo of you by the bed. I'm Bridget, by the way. Come on in, love.' She stood back and Maeve stepped hesitantly into the hall. It had been decorated since she was last here. The old-fashioned wallpaper had been stripped and now the walls were painted a pale apricot. The dark carpet had been removed and the floorboards had been sanded and polished till they shone. Maeve's mouth set in a grim line. 'Where is she?'

Bridget looked surprised. 'In bed, of course.'

Maeve frowned. 'Can I go up?'

'Of course.'

Maeve went slowly up the stairs, pausing when she reached the landing. The first door led to her old room – she wondered what her mother had done to that – the second was the bathroom and her mother's door was next. She moved towards it and knocked. There was no answer so she pushed it open and looked in. Her mother lay propped up in the bed, her eyes closed. Maeve stared at the frail looking creature that was her mother. She looked older, her face ashen against the white sheets and her thinning hair lay lifeless on the pillow. Maeve stood staring at her and wondering what she should do – her instinct was to turn tail and run.

'Are you just going to stand there or are you going to come in?' Laura Elliot opened her eyes and looked at her daughter.

Maeve started. 'I thought you were asleep.'

'To what do I owe the honour?' Laura's voice was cool.

'I met Peggy. She told me you haven't been well. What's wrong with you?'

'I got a bad flu and it developed into pneumonia.'

Maeve frowned. 'Is that all? Why do you need a nurse?'

Laura laughed. 'Bridget? She's not a nurse, she's my new neighbour. She just drops in to check on me.'

'Peggy led me to believe that it was more serious than that. And you do look terrible.'

'Thanks, but I'm sorry to disappoint you. I should be back on my feet in a couple of days. So why did you come, to make sure you were still in the will?'

'Mum! That's a terrible thing to say.'

Laura's eyes hardened. 'Well, what am I supposed to think? You haven't stepped inside this house in years and I can't remember the last time you called.'

'You could always have called me,' Maeve retorted. 'You could have visited.'

'Oh, yes, you'd have loved that,' Laura said drily.

Maeve crossed to the window and stared out at the little garden. 'Don't try and make me feel guilty, Mum. We both know that you never wanted me.'

'Don't be ridiculous, you're my daughter.'

Maeve whirled around, eyes blazing. 'Am I? You seemed to forget that when Dad died.'

Laura pulled nervously on the sheet. 'What are you talking about? What has this got to do with your father?'

Maeve shook her head in disbelief. 'What has it to do with him? It has everything to do with him! All you've ever thought about was him.' Maeve waved a hand around the room. Every surface was covered with photographs – nearly all of them of her father.

'You never had time for anyone else.'

Laura's eyes were bright with tears. 'I loved him.'

'But what about me, Mum?' Maeve wailed. 'He was dead, he didn't need you any more, but I did.'

'It was a hard time for me,' Laura stammered. 'But you were young. I knew you'd get over it.'

'I might have if you hadn't reminded me of him every minute of the day.' She ignored her mother's gasp. 'He was dead, Mum, but you still behaved as if he were more important than me. How do you think that made me feel?'

Laura stared at her. 'I've always done my best for you.'

Maeve nodded slowly. 'Really? I don't suppose you remember that Aunt Peggy had to bring me to buy

my first sanitary towels. That she was the one who
attended my school concerts and basketball matches.
She helped me pick my Debs dress. And she was the
one who played Scrabble with me on Christmas Day
while you stayed in your room.'

Laura looked shocked. 'It was very hard for me,
Maeve, you don't understand.'

'Neither do you, Mum!' Maeve yelled. 'Neither do
you!' She ran out of the room and down the stairs,
tears streaming down her face.

Bridget was still standing in the hall. 'I hope you
haven't upset your mother.'

Maeve smiled through her tears. 'No more than
she upset me,' she said, and left the house without
a backward glance. She drove around for about five
minutes before finally pulling in on the hard shoulder
and turning off the engine. Her hands were shaking
and she felt cold. Even after all this time her mother
didn't seem to realise how much she'd hurt her. 'She
still doesn't know me,' Maeve muttered as she mopped
at her tears with a tissue. 'And she doesn't even care.'
She started the car again and drove aimlessly for a
while. She wasn't due in the studio for a few hours
but she couldn't face going home. Within half an
hour she was in Blanchardstown – it hadn't been a
conscious decision but she realised that she needed
to see Craig, although he probably wouldn't want to
see her, she thought, feeling very sorry for herself
now. She was sitting in the car outside the garden
centre debating whether to go in or not when there
was a rap on the window. Craig was grinning in at

her. She pressed the button and the window lowered silently. 'Hi.'

'Hello. What are you doing out here? Can I interest you in a Christmas tree?'

Maeve smiled shakily. 'Maybe.'

Craig studied her carefully. 'I was just on my way out for a sandwich. Do you want to join me?'

She nodded gratefully and he stepped back as she climbed out of the car. They strolled towards the pub in silence, Maeve using the time to take some deep breaths and get her feelings back under control. They were sitting at a table and she'd taken a few sips of tequila before Craig said a word.

'Has this anything to do with your mother?'

Maeve stiffened. 'What are you talking about?'

'You're obviously upset. Are you feeling guilty about your mother?'

Maeve glared at him. 'I have absolutely nothing to feel guilty about.'

Craig sighed. 'Oh, Maeve, pull in those horns. You came to me, remember?'

Maeve looked away. 'I was just driving. I didn't realise I was even heading this way.'

'Interesting,' he murmured, his eyes twinkling. 'So you came here subconsciously.'

'Oh, leave me alone, Craig, I'm not in the mood for playing games.'

He turned his attention to the large ham salad roll in front of him. 'Sure you're not hungry? The food is very good here.'

She shook her head silently.

He smiled at her as he munched his food.

'What?' she said irritably.

'Nothing,' he said after he'd swallowed and taken a swig of his Coke.

'Are you still annoyed with me about last Saturday night?'

He frowned. 'If my memory serves, you were annoyed with *me* last Saturday night.'

'You were the one who walked out,' she pointed out.

'That's because you're a pain when you get bitchy.'

Maeve stared at him. 'I don't get bitchy.'

He nodded. 'Yes, you do. And cruel,' he added.

'I suppose this is about your beloved Aoife again,' she said with a twisted smile.

'You're not very nice to her,' he agreed. 'I suppose I shouldn't be surprised. If you won't visit your own mother when she's ill you're hardly likely to be nice to strangers.'

'You don't know anything about my mother,' she hissed angrily, tears in her eyes.

Craig's smile disappeared. 'I'm sorry.'

'I've got to go.'

'No, please, sit down, Maeve.' She hesitated, but he seemed genuinely remorseful.

'Please.'

She sat back down and drained her glass. 'Only if we can talk about something else *and* you buy me another drink.'

'I thought independent women like you bought their own drink. Okay, okay.' He got up hurriedly when he saw the look on her face. 'I'm going.'

Maeve smiled reluctantly as he went to the bar, and wiped at her eyes with his napkin.

'Are you all right?' he asked gently when he returned.

She nodded.

'Am I allowed to ask about your dad?'

'He's dead,' Maeve said flatly. 'He died when I was a baby.'

'That's sad – that you never knew him, I mean.'

Maeve laughed bitterly. 'I know everything there is to know about him, believe me.'

Craig shot her a quizzical look, but she shook her head. 'We agreed to change the subject,' she reminded him. 'So tell me about your love-life.'

'You mean Aoife?' He chuckled.

She rolled her eyes. 'Obviously.'

'I've just taken her for a drink a couple of times.'

'So you're not interested in her as a girlfriend?'

'Of course not! I'm just being friendly.'

'That's a really bad idea, Craig. I've told you that she fancies you.'

He raised his eyebrows. 'I thought you didn't like her.'

'Can't stand the girl,' Maeve said equably. 'But even she doesn't deserve to be messed around.'

'You're exaggerating.'

'Men and women can't just be friendly. She'll be crushed when she realises that you're not serious.'

He groaned. 'Shit. What am I going to do?'

She shrugged. 'Like I say, keep well away.'

'And what about the Christmas party?'

She laughed. 'Wear your chastity belt!'

He stared at her crossly. 'You're enjoying this.'

'I am,' she admitted, amazed that she could laugh after the morning she'd had.

He smiled. 'Why don't you come to the party, Maeve? You could protect me from her. We could pretend that we were in love.' He pulled her close and nuzzled her neck.

'Get off!' Maeve shoved him away, but not too hard. 'She'd never swallow that – no one would. We're always at each other's throats.'

'That's just an act,' he murmured. His eyes travelled over her face, resting for a moment on her mouth before coming back to look deep into her eyes. 'We love each other really.'

'Do we?' Maeve said lightly, unable to tear her eyes from his.

'Oh, yes. The problem is that we both like playing hard to get.'

'That is a problem,' Maeve agreed gravely. 'What do we do about it?'

'One of us needs to learn to be more submissive.' He leaned closer and she could feel his breath on her cheek and smell the spicy cologne that he always wore.

She pulled back and laughed nervously. 'Well, it won't be me.'

Craig chuckled, but the warmth had gone out of his eyes. 'There's a surprise! I'd better get back.'

Maeve looked startled at the sudden change in mood. 'Oh. But I haven't even bought you a drink yet.'

'Some other time.'

38

Carrie smiled as she looked around Orla's untidy sitting room. There were books and toys everywhere; Ethan's trike had been deserted in the middle of the room and half a yoghurt sat precariously on the edge of the sofa, a growing stain oozing from around the creamy spoon beside it. She took the yoghurt out to the kitchen and found a damp cloth. She was on her knees, rubbing at the stain, when Orla came down red-faced and breathless. 'Oh, don't worry about that, Carrie.'

Carrie sat back on her heels and smiled. 'All done. Is he asleep?'

Orla laughed. 'No chance, but I've told him that Santa is watching, so he's not allowed to cry.'

'I remember I used to be terrified to put a foot wrong coming up to Christmas in case Santa left me a bag of soot.' Carrie sat back up in a chair and reached for her drink.

Orla laughed. 'I haven't used the bag-of-soot line yet, but it's early days. So where's Declan tonight?'

'He's at a Christmas party.'

Orla raised an eyebrow. 'Weren't you invited?'

Carrie grinned. 'No, thank God, it's staff only. I

think the boss's wife must have told him how bored all the partners were last year – her included.'

Orla took off her shoes and tucked her feet underneath her. 'Well, I'm not complaining. It's nice to have some company on a Saturday night.' She rummaged through the papers and magazines on the table beside her and then tossed a leaflet to Carrie. 'Have a look and see what you fancy for dinner.'

'Where's Ray?' Carrie asked as she browsed through the menu.

Orla pulled a face. 'I think it's over between us.'

Carrie put down the menu and stared at her friend in dismay. 'Oh, Orla, what happened? He seemed so nice.'

'Yeah, he was really. But he couldn't cope with Ethan.'

'But I thought he got on fine with Ethan and Ethan certainly seemed to like him.'

'Oh, yeah, there was no problem there. It's just the administrative details he couldn't deal with.'

'Sorry?'

'He expected me to go places and do things at the drop of a hat, which of course I couldn't do. Or wouldn't do,' she added. 'I want to spend time with Ethan. I don't want someone else putting him to bed every night. And going clubbing on a weeknight when you've got a lively three-year-old dancing up and down on you at seven the next morning is not fun. Then there was the problem about him staying over.'

Carrie frowned. 'But you did let him stay over sometimes, didn't you?'

'Yeah, but I made him leave before Ethan woke. That really pissed him off.'

'So what happened?'

Orla shrugged. 'I told him that if he wanted to date me he'd have to realise that Ethan would always come first.'

Carrie sighed. 'So he decided he didn't want to date you any more?'

'It's looking that way.' Orla blew her nose loudly and held out her hand for the menu. 'Oh, to hell with him, Carrie. Give me a look at that, I'm starving.'

'It's a pity, though,' Carrie said as she handed it over. 'He was nice and I know you liked him.'

'That's immaterial now,' Orla said flatly. 'Chicken Moghlai for me, I think, and let's share some Aloo Saag.'

Carrie obediently allowed herself to be diverted. 'Lamb Korma for me and let's get some poppadums too.'

'Lovely.' Orla reached for the phone.

'What are you doing for Christmas?' Carrie asked after she'd placed the order.

'We'll probably stay here. It was okay going to Mum and Dad's when Ethan was small, but now I think he'll want to stay at home and play with his toys. I'll probably get them to come here for dinner – Ethan would love that. How about you?'

Carrie stared into her Guinness. 'Dunno.'

'Don't you all usually go to Helen's?'

'Yep, and God love her, even though she tries so hard to get everyone to have a good time there's always a row. I hate it. I'd love to stay in bed for the day.'

Orla's eyes widened. 'You can't do that. Anyway, what about Declan?'

'He can go to my sister's.'

Orla grinned. 'Well, her cooking is good.'

'And the booze is free,' Carrie said drily.

'Why do you stay with him?'

Carrie stared at her. 'What?'

'Well, I'm sorry, but you've done nothing but complain about him lately. Now don't get me wrong, I think you should have dumped him ages ago but I kept my mouth shut because you wouldn't hear a word said against him. But you've changed.'

'Yeah, I suppose I have. It's since I've got the job at Forever FM.'

Orla nodded in understanding. 'You don't want to be the mousy little girlfriend any more.'

Carrie looked affronted. 'Mousy! Thanks very much!'

Orla smiled. 'Sorry, but that's what you're like when you're around him. Completely different to the Carrie I know and love.'

Carrie frowned. 'Are you serious?'

Orla regarded her warily. 'Maybe I should have kept my big mouth shut.'

'No, it's okay, it's just I never realised . . .'

'You never do,' Orla said knowingly. 'It's only the people looking in from the outside who see all the cracks.'

They were tucking into their dinner, Ethan now fast

asleep, when Orla returned to the topic of Christmas. 'Why don't you and Declan come here?'

Carrie paused, a forkful of food halfway to her mouth. 'You don't want us!'

'Sure, the more the merrier.'

'But you and Declan—'

'Will get on fine if we've both had enough to drink,' Orla finished for her.

Carrie brightened briefly and then realised it was impossible. 'If we don't go to Helen's I'll have to go to Declan's mum's. The only reason I've managed to avoid it up until now is because I'm with my family.'

'Doesn't Declan ever expect you to go to his folks?'

Carrie grinned. 'Nah, he's glad of the excuse not to. His dad's an alcoholic and his mother won't allow a drop of drink in the house.'

Orla groaned. 'Ooh! Now that would be tough. So another year at Helen's then?'

Carrie nodded. 'Oh, well, at least I'll have Lily to distract me.'

'Yeah, kids are great when there's a lull in the conversation.'

'Sometimes the conversation doesn't even start in my family,' Carrie said ruefully. 'My dad snoozes behind the newspaper, my mother reads a book and the lads watch whatever adventure film is on. Helen, Lily and I usually end up in the kitchen.'

'At least you've got Helen,' Orla reminded her. 'Why does the girl insist on having all these family get-togethers if they're always such a disaster?'

Carrie sighed. 'She's afraid we'll just drift apart if she doesn't make the effort. She's probably right.'

'That's sad.'

Carrie smiled bravely. 'Hell, we can't all be like the Waltons.'

'Ice cream,' Orla announced.

'Sorry?'

Orla stood up and started to pack the cartons back into the bag. 'That's what we need now, ice cream.'

Carrie groaned. 'But I'm stuffed.'

'Rubbish, there's always room for a little ice cream.'

'Except you don't know the meaning of the word little.'

Orla grinned. 'That's why Ethan loves me.'

Carrie laughed as Orla carried the remains of their meal out to the kitchen. She stretched her legs and stared into the fire. Orla had a tough life as a single mother but Carrie envied her all the same. She seemed so complete, so together. Even the fact that Ray had left didn't seem to throw her. She'd always been like that, Carrie mused. While she liked the company of men they weren't necessary to her happiness. Unlike me, Carrie thought. Because the more she thought about it the more she was convinced that she'd stayed with Declan because it was preferable to being alone. But maybe she wouldn't be alone for long; after all, she wasn't bad looking and she was still only twenty-four – that wasn't old. Maeve Elliot was older than she was and she was still single and enjoying herself too, if you could believe the newspapers.

'Here we are.' Orla reappeared with two large bowls of chocolate ice cream.

'Oh, Orla, I'll never eat all that.'

'Sure you will. Now where's the remote? The film is coming on any minute.'

'What is it?'

'*Steel Magnolias.*'

'Oh, wonderful.' Carrie snuggled down with her ice cream. 'That film always makes me cry. Poor Julia Roberts.'

'No, it's her little boy that I feel sorry for.' Orla sniffed.

Carrie looked at her worriedly. Any sloppy films concerning children always depressed her friend. 'Maybe we should watch something else.'

'Oh, no, I'll be fine. It's hard to be upset for too long with Shirley MacLaine and Olympia Dukakis bitching at each other all the time.'

'They are brilliant,' Carrie agreed. 'Dolly Parton is good, too.'

'I'd love to be an actor,' Orla said with a sigh.

Carrie looked surprised. 'Really?' Orla had never been career-minded and had been the only one who understood Carrie's lack of ambition. She'd worked for the same travel agent since she'd left school.

Orla laughed. 'Yeah, think of all the clothes, the money and the men.'

Carrie swallowed a large spoonful of ice cream and licked her spoon. 'I'll take the clothes and the money but you can keep the men.'

39

Linda wandered around Jonathan's living room, blinking at the winter sun that streamed through the large bay window. Being in this room always reminded her of how cold and impersonal her apartment was. Jonathan must have read the same interior design magazines she had. The walls were painted a pale eau-de-nil, the ceiling, doors and windows were all brilliant white, and highly polished maple floorboards gave the room a warm glow. As the magazines recommended, a richly patterned rug lay in front of the large fireplace and some vivid cushions made a splash of colour against the black leather suite. Linda had been astonished when Jonathan had told her he'd done it all himself. Perhaps she should ask him to try his hand at her place. She paused by the fireplace to study the photo of Daniel with his mother. Jonathan had taken the photograph and Alison was laughing up into the camera, her arms cradling Daniel, their two heads close. Linda frowned at the picture and wondered why the marriage had failed. She also wondered why Jonathan had it on the mantelpiece in his living room. The first time he'd noticed her looking at it he'd explained that it was Daniel's home too and that it would be unnatural not to have photos of his mother about the place. Which seemed reasonable enough, Linda supposed, but she wondered sometimes did Jonathan regret leaving his wife.

'Where's Dad?' Daniel kicked his feet impatiently against the coffee table. 'We're going to be late.'

Linda smiled. 'No we're not. Anyway, how many times have you seen the Harry Potter film?'

Daniel grinned. 'This will be the third. Oh, but it's great, Linda. Especially the game of quidditch.'

'I can't wait,' Linda said gravely. At this stage she could probably act out the film herself, Daniel had talked about it so much. He'd first gone to see it with his mother, then with Jonathan and now he was insisting that the three of them had to go because Linda couldn't possibly go without a kid in tow. Linda was grateful that Daniel had accepted her presence in his father's life. He could easily have made it impossible for them – Linda remembered the hostility the day they'd gone to the zoo. But Daniel had thawed more each time they met and now they got on pretty well.

'Oh, Dad,' Daniel moaned.

'I'll go and see what's keeping him.' Linda went down the hall towards Jonathan's office, knocked tentatively and stuck her head round the door. 'Everything okay?'

Jonathan was about to answer when a loud sneeze overtook him. 'Excuse me,' he muttered as he pulled a hankie from his pocket.

'Are you okay?' Linda frowned at his red cheeks and bright eyes.

'I feel crap,' he answered and then sneezed three times in succession. 'We'd better go.'

Linda shook her head. 'The only place you're going is straight to bed.'

'But Daniel,' Jonathan protested.

'I'll look after Daniel.' Linda steered him out of the door and towards the stairs. 'You go on up. I'll bring you a drink and some aspirin.' She watched Jonathan climb the stairs and then she went back in to the sitting room. 'I'm afraid your dad won't be going anywhere today. I'd say he's coming down with the flu.'

Daniel's face fell. 'But what about the film?'

Linda smiled. 'Let me get him settled and then you and I can go.'

Daniel's eyes widened. 'Really?'

'Sure. I haven't seen it yet. Remember?'

'Wicked!' Daniel beamed at her.

'Now why don't you go up and say goodbye to your dad?'

Moments later, Linda went upstairs with a large bottle of mineral water, a glass and some tablets.

Jonathan frowned. 'I thought you meant a *real* drink.'

'This is better for you,' she told him. 'Now say goodbye to your son, we've got a film to go to.'

Jonathan looked surprised. 'Are you sure about this?'

'I've been looking forward to it. I'll drop him off at your mum's afterwards, okay?'

'Yeah, thanks.'

''Bye, Dad.' Daniel climbed up on the bed to hug him.

''Bye, Dan, be a good boy for Linda.'

'I will.'

'And Linda, he can have sweets or popcorn, but not both.'

Daniel rolled his eyes and Linda smiled. 'Okay. I'll call you later.'

'Thanks. Have a good time.'

Linda was amazed at how much she did actually enjoy herself. When they finally emerged from the cinema dark ominous clouds had obliterated the sun. Linda took Daniel to a nearby pizzeria and he talked nineteen-to-the-dozen between mouthfuls. It was raining when they came back out on to the street and by the time Linda had parked the car outside Kathleen's house it was coming down in a freezing deluge.

Kathleen drew them in and helped Daniel out of his coat. 'Take off that jacket and leave it by the radiator,' she instructed Linda, who stood dripping in the hallway.

'Thanks.' Linda did as she was told and then held her hands out to the warm, welcoming fire.

'Did you have a nice time?'

'It was great.' Daniel collapsed on to the sofa and stared blankly at the TV, his eyes heavy.

Kathleen looked at her sleepy grandson. 'You can watch that for thirty minutes and then it's bedtime. Would you like something to eat or drink, love?'

'Just a drink, please, Nan. I'm stuffed.'

Linda followed Kathleen out to the kitchen. 'Jonathan phoned earlier and told me what happened,' Kathleen told her as she poured fizzy orange into a Pokemon beaker. 'It was very good of you to take Daniel to the cinema.'

'I enjoyed myself,' Linda said honestly. 'The film was really good.' Kathleen looked doubtful and Linda laughed. 'I hate to tell you but I think he's going to take you next.'

Kathleen shrugged and put on the kettle. 'Oh, well, that's the price of being a grandmother, I suppose.'

Linda took Daniel's drink into him. 'Thanks, Lin,' he said, using his father's nickname for her. 'I had a great time.'

Linda tousled his hair. 'Me too.' She went back outside and sat down at the kitchen table. 'Just tea for me,' she said as Kathleen reached for the biscuit tin. 'I haven't stopped eating all day. So how was Jonathan when he phoned?'

'Barely recognisable.' Kathleen carried the teapot to the table and sat down.

'He may need an antibiotic,' Linda said thoughtfully.

Kathleen snorted. 'He won't go to a doctor. He's one of those tough guys who believe in sweating off a bug.'

Linda smiled ruefully. 'He didn't look very tough when I left him.'

'I'll make him some soup and take it over tomorrow,' Kathleen decided.

'Oh, that's a good idea. I've an early start and a lunch meeting too, so I won't be able to check up on him.'

'You've done your bit today, dear. I'll look after him tomorrow – if he stays out of work, that is.'

'He won't have a choice,' Linda assured her. 'Just don't go too close to him, we don't want you catching this dose.'

'And what about you, Linda, will you keep your distance too?' Kathleen's eyes twinkled at her over her cup.

Linda reddened. 'Kathleen.'

'I'm sorry, Linda, I shouldn't be embarrassing you. I'm very happy that you and Jonathan are so close.'

'You are? We are?' Linda looked surprised. With the number of women that had been in and out of Jonathan's life, Linda was surprised that his mother took any notice any more.

'He's very happy,' Kathleen confided. 'Happier than I've seen him since, well, you know.'

Linda didn't, but she smiled politely and nodded. 'I should be going.' She drained her tea-cup and stood up.

'Already?' Kathleen looked disappointed.

'I need a bath and an early night,' Linda said apologetically.

'Okay then. Daniel, come and say goodnight.'

Daniel followed them out to the front door and, standing on tiptoe, gave Linda a peck on the cheek. 'Thanks, Lin.'

Surprised and pleased, she hugged him. 'Thank you, that's the best film I've been to in years.' She winked at him. 'You'll have to take your nan.'

Daniel grinned. 'Yeah, I'll do that.'

Kathleen rolled her eyes. 'Thanks a lot!'

'Goodnight!' Linda hurried out into the cold rain and climbed into her car. She wondered briefly should she swing by Jonathan's but it was almost ten and he was probably asleep and she did have to be in work for seven thirty. She turned the car towards town with a sigh. A night alone in her apartment held little appeal. Since she had started sleeping with Jonathan she rarely spent a night alone and usually she went to his house. Just off Baggot Street, it was a short drive across town or a pleasant walk on a nice day. She switched the windscreen wipers on to a higher speed in an effort to clear the driving rain. It was a horrible night, but it had been a relatively mild winter so far so she couldn't complain. And in two weeks, it would be Christmas – the first one in years that she would spend in Ireland. She was still a bit nervous at the prospect. Jonathan had suggested they go skiing but though Linda was tempted, she felt she couldn't let her mother and sister down. It had been a difficult few months and they'd helped her through it, so she couldn't desert them now just because there was a new man on the scene. She was also a bit nervous of going away with Jonathan. It seemed such a serious thing to do, heralding a new stage of their relationship. But Linda still wasn't convinced that Jonathan loved her as much as he said he did. He was probably one of those men who used the word loosely, without thinking. It was the only answer and she wouldn't allow herself to think otherwise. That was the sure way to get hurt and she wasn't going to let that happen. She'd made

enough silly mistakes in the last few months because of
hurt pride. There was no way she was going to add to
the list by allowing herself to fall in love with Jonathan.
She must prepare for the day when she'd be alone once
more – it couldn't be far off. And as a sign that she was
prepared for that eventuality, she decided it was time
to decorate her new home.

40

Maeve sat at her desk in the silent office trying to concentrate on the script for tonight's show. It was the last week before Christmas and she was wondering if she should return to the programme – or even to the station – in the New Year. The phone call last night had knocked her for six and she still couldn't quite believe it. She'd been offered a job in a much larger, national station based in London and they wanted her to start as soon as possible. Though Maeve knew she should be thrilled, she just couldn't work up the enthusiasm. She had a week to make up her mind and as she ran her eye down the page, she thought that maybe her answer would be yes. Though a few of the *Secrets* shows so far had been quite good, she hadn't been happy with most of them, and some she was downright ashamed of. Ben had changed a number of them – with Jonathan's blessing – and more often than not the shows were about sex, violence or both. She would tackle Jonathan one more time, she decided, and then she would make her decision. Maeve turned the page and tried to focus but she kept replaying the conversation with her mother and then the rather strange lunch she'd had with Craig.

She couldn't make much sense of the latter, but the episode with her mother was par for the course. Her mouth settled into a grim line and her nails bit into her palms. Why had she expected things to be different? Laura would always be selfish and oblivious of her feelings; she had to learn to accept that and stop hoping for miracles. Maybe a fresh start in London was the answer. It would be a great opportunity, she convinced herself. The initial position was as a DJ on a music show but she'd have a foot on the ladder in a much bigger operation. If she worked hard, she'd have a better show within twelve months and Maeve was no stranger to hard work.

Carrie barged into the room and stopped short when she saw Maeve. 'Sorry! I didn't realise you were in yet.'

Maeve shrugged. 'Nothing better to do.'

Carrie flopped into a chair with a sigh. 'Lucky you. I've still got lots of Christmas presents to buy.'

Maeve smiled tightly. She'd bought Peggy a lovely cashmere top, but she was just sending her mother a hamper. That way she wouldn't have to go over there and pretend that everything was normal.

'Are you okay?' Carrie was watching her curiously.

'Yeah, sure, just daydreaming. Is Ben in yet?'

Carrie shook her head. 'He's off this week.'

Maeve frowned. 'It's the first I heard.'

'What is?' Karl asked as he strolled into the room and tossed his jacket on the back of a chair.

'Ben's skiving off for the week.'

He nodded as he lit a cigarette. 'Oh, yeah, he did

mention something about a family problem,' he said vaguely. 'Jonathan gave him compassionate leave.'

'I didn't know he had a family.' Carrie looked guilty. The man had been working with them for over a month now and she knew next to nothing about him. Though she'd mellowed towards him she was still afraid to get too friendly in case she upset Maeve.

Maeve's mind was working on a completely different level. 'Jonathan gave him compassionate leave? Is the man feeling all right?'

Karl chuckled. 'No, as it happens, Karen just told me he's down with the flu and will probably be out for the week.'

Maeve rolled her eyes at Carrie. 'It's probably just a cold. Men are such hypochondriacs.'

Karl touched his throat tentatively. 'Yeah, I feel a bit dodgy myself.'

'Tough, I'm not doing this show on my own,' Maeve retorted.

Karl winked at her. 'It's okay, darlin', I know you couldn't manage without me. Anyway I have some ideas as to how we can use this situation to our advantage.'

Maeve smiled slowly. 'Oh?'

'Well, for a start we can have our meeting now instead of seven o'clock tonight and that way the three of us can have a couple of well-earned hours off.'

Maeve grinned at Carrie's delighted expression. 'Sounds good.'

'That's not all,' Karl went on. 'This is a perfect

opportunity for us to run the show the way we want to run it.'

'Won't Jonathan be annoyed?' Carrie ventured.

'Probably, but it will be too late by then.' Maeve didn't care if Jonathan fired her, now that she'd another job to go to.

Karl looked at the schedule for the week. 'For a start I think we should axe a couple of these shows.'

Maeve nodded. 'Especially that one on incest.'

Carrie shivered. 'Oh, yes, I was dreading that one.'

'So what shall we do this evening?' Maeve sat up taller, her eyes bright and her personal problems forgotten.

Karl looked at Carrie. 'Is it too late to cancel?'

'Absolutely. The guest is probably on her way down from Donegal. But it's a great secret and it would make a good show if . . .'

Karl grinned. 'If Maeve doesn't savage her. Yeah, you're right, Carrie. You're going to have to be good, Maeve, if we're to convince Jonathan that the softly, softly approach can work just as well.'

Maeve looked at him. 'I can do that.'

'Great.' He looked down at the list in front of him. 'Let's air the show on euthanasia tomorrow night. Carrie, can you check if that guest can come in?'

Carrie nodded and scribbled in her pad. By lunchtime, they'd discussed the next three shows in detail and agreed to find something different for their final show before the Christmas break on Friday. They took a break and Carrie went out to fetch sandwiches, humming happily as she dodged the lunch-hour crowds.

This was definitely the best day she'd had since she'd started in the station – and that was saying something. She was impressed with the quality of shows that Karl and Maeve were coming up with and was chuffed that they'd included her in the discussion. Tonight's show should be great. The guest, Dee, had adopted a baby and even now, the girl – at twenty-two – still had no idea of the truth. The main reason for the secrecy was that the real mother was Dee's sister. The secret had been kept from everyone, and now Dee felt there was no point in telling the girl the truth. Carrie wondered idly if she was adopted. That would explain why she was so different from the rest of the family. Except, she smiled grimly, her mother would never have kept it a secret. She would have shouted it from the rooftops so that everyone would know that she wasn't responsible for the runt of the litter. Carrie paid for the sandwiches and forced her mind back to the show, aware that thoughts of her mother would only depress her. It was a good story and though she'd only spoken to Dee on the phone, Carrie was sure the woman would be a great guest. She was tough, very confident and unlikely to be intimidated by Maeve. Carrie hurried back to the office, her excitement building at the thought of the evening ahead. And she'd be able to go home for a few hours and have dinner with Declan – that should win her some Brownie points.

'Oh, good, Carrie, you're back, I'm starving.' Karl fell hungrily on the bag and rummaged for the giant-sized roll, oozing with ham and coleslaw.

'You're disgusting,' Maeve told him as she unwrapped her BLT sandwich. 'Thanks, Carrie. Is that all you're having?' She eyed the yoghurt incredulously.

Carrie smiled. 'I've decided I'm going to make dinner tonight.'

Karl grinned. 'Looks, intelligence and she can cook too. I think you're my ideal woman.'

Maeve winked at Carrie. 'Anything under sixty with a pulse is your ideal woman, Karl.'

Carrie giggled. She loved it when Maeve was in good form – she was so great to work with. The last few days she'd seemed positively morose and had snapped the heads off everyone around her.

'Now. Tell us more about tonight's guest,' Karl said, and listened carefully to Carrie as he munched his roll.

Dee sat in the chair across the desk from Maeve, her hands folded in her lap, her smile relaxed.

'Okay, Dee, I'll introduce you and then you just tell your story in your own way.'

'And then you'll ask me some awful questions, I suppose.'

Maeve shook her head. 'I don't plan to, no, but if I ask you anything you're not comfortable with just say so.'

Dee looked surprised. 'Okay.'

'Ready, Maeve?' Karl said in her ear. 'Five, four, three, two, one.'

'Good evening, listeners, it's Monday, 17th December, and you're listening to *Secrets* on Forever FM.

Tonight I'd like to welcome my guest who has travelled all the way from Donegal to be with us. You're very welcome, Dee.'

'Thanks.'

'Tell us a bit about yourself.' Maeve smiled encouragingly.

'I'm forty-four, I work part-time in a newsagent's and I'm married with two children.'

'Tell me about your children,' Maeve prompted.

'My eldest is twenty-three, he's getting married next year.' Dee smiled proudly.

'And you have a daughter too?'

'Yes, she's twenty-two.'

'My goodness, you had them very close together. Was that planned?'

Dee pulled a face at Maeve. 'You know it wasn't.'

Maeve shot her an apologetic look. 'I know, Dee, but our listeners don't. Tell them about your daughter.'

'She – oh, I can't keep calling her that, I'll call her Mary.'

'Fine. Tell us about Mary.'

'Mary is adopted.'

'I see. What made you adopt a child so soon after you'd had your son?'

Dee shrugged. 'It just seemed like the right thing to do.'

'Does your daughter know that she's adopted?'

Dee took a deep breath. 'No.'

Maeve reached over and squeezed her hands encouragingly. 'Why not?'

'It would only upset her and there's absolutely no need for her to know. As far as I'm concerned she is ours.'

Maeve frowned. 'She might be upset at first, Dee, but in the end I'm sure she'd realise how lucky she was to be adopted into a loving family.'

Dee watched Maeve warily, but said nothing.

'What's going on?' Karl hissed in Maeve's ear. She looked out at him and shrugged. No one had expected Dee to clam up. 'Go to a break,' Karl instructed.

Maeve did as she was told and then turned to look at Dee. 'Are you okay?'

'I don't know. Maybe this wasn't such a good idea.'

Maeve groaned inwardly. The last thing she needed was for Dee to walk out now. 'It's okay, Dee; remember, no one knows who you are. Apart from which this is a local station and all your relatives and friends are back in Donegal.'

Dee visibly relaxed. 'You're right.' She took a drink of water and smiled at Maeve. 'I'll be fine.'

Maeve nodded. 'Great.'

'Ready to go, Maeve?' Karl's anxious voice came through the headphones. She gave him a thumbs-up and he counted her in.

'You were telling us, Dee, that you don't plan to tell your daughter, Mary, that she was adopted.'

'Absolutely not.'

Maeve looked at the e-mail Carrie had sent her. 'Donna from Baldoyle sent us an e-mail, Dee. She points out that at some time in the future, for medical reasons, Mary may need to know her background and her family's medical history.'

Dee smiled bitterly. 'It won't be a problem.'

Maeve frowned. 'Well, it could be,' she said gently. 'What about when she has children? You hear all the time about how important family history is.'

'I know all that,' Dee told her.

'But she doesn't.'

'It won't be a problem,' Dee repeated.

Maeve stared at her. 'You're so sure. Why is that?'

Dee smiled at her, but her eyes were cold. 'Because my sister is Mary's mother and my husband is the father.'

'I still can't believe it.' Carrie sat in the chair between Karl and Maeve's desk, sipping coffee and shaking her head.

'As secrets go it was something else,' Karl agreed.

'I didn't push her into revealing it, did I?' Maeve chewed nervously on her lip.

Carrie shook her head. 'No, it's okay, Maeve. She told me afterwards that she'd decided during the break to spill the beans.'

'I wish she'd told me that!'

'It wouldn't have been as powerful if you'd already known,' Karl pointed out. 'In fact, Maeve, I think we'll keep you in the dark about our guests' secrets from now on.'

'What?' She shot him a suspicious look. 'You're beginning to sound like Ben.'

'No, think about it.' He leaned forward, his voice

urgent. 'If you didn't know what was coming next it would completely change the way you do the interview.'

Maeve frowned. 'But I could put my foot in it or really hurt someone.'

He shook his head. 'I'd steer you right.'

'I think it's a great idea,' Carrie said enthusiastically.

Maeve looked dubious. 'I don't know.'

'We have only this week before Ben and Jonathan are back to interfere. You don't know too much about the shows on Wednesday, Thursday and we haven't even decided on Friday's yet. Let's try it.'

Karl had never steered her wrong before and usually when he got one of his weird ideas, it worked. Maeve nodded slowly. 'Okay, we'll give it a go.'

41

'Here we go.' Linda arrived back with two hot whiskies.

Jonathan raised his eyebrows at the two glasses. 'Are you sick too?'

Linda grinned as she handed him his glass and climbed up on the bed beside him. 'Preventative medicine. That was a great show, wasn't it?' She was delighted that she could finally rave about a *Secrets* programme.

Jonathan frowned. 'It didn't quite follow the format we'd agreed. I should have known that Karl and Maeve would get up to something when I was out of the way.'

'But it was good,' Linda protested.

Jonathan shoved his glass into her hand and sneezed loudly. 'I suppose.' His voice was muffled as he blew his nose.

'So you wouldn't mind too much if Ben didn't come back?' she said lightly.

Jonathan eyed her suspiciously. 'Why wouldn't he come back?'

She shrugged. 'Oh, I don't know, I suppose he could get a better offer.'

'Linda, is there something you want to tell me?'

'You should get some sleep,' she said.

'Linda?'

'You're sick and shouldn't be worrying about work. And I should go.' She touched his cheek and stared into his eyes.

Jonathan kissed her fingers. 'I'd sleep better if you stayed.'

Linda's eyes twinkled. 'Are you sure of that?'

'Yeah. Eventually.' He took the two glasses from her and put them on the bedside table. 'Unless of course you're worried about catching something.'

'I think it's a bit late for that.'

Carrie was typing up the notes for Tuesday night's show on euthanasia when the call came. Her first reaction had been to hang up, but it soon became clear that the caller was genuine.

'I can't come into the studio. You're going to have to come and meet me.'

'I usually carry out all preliminary interviews with guests on the phone,' Carrie said hesitantly.

'But this is different,' the caller reminded her.

'I'm not sure about this,' Carrie prevaricated. 'I'll have to talk to the producer.'

'Then go and talk to him and call me back.'

When Carrie went in search of Karl she found him with Maeve. 'What is it, Carrie?'

'Oh, er, nothing important, I'll catch you later.' And she'd ducked back out of the room.

An hour later, he came in search of her. 'I'm

intrigued.' He leaned against her desk and gazed down at her. 'What did you want to talk to me about? Or, more importantly, what did you not want Maeve to hear?'

Carrie dragged him out to the stockroom and shut the door.

'I always knew you fancied me.' His eyes twinkled in amusement.

'Stop it, Karl, this is serious.' And Carrie told him about the phone call. He listened carefully as he paced the tiny room, stretching a rubber band between his long fingers. 'Wow, this is heavy stuff.'

Carrie nodded miserably. 'It is, isn't it? What on earth do we do?'

He shrugged. 'Call that number and arrange a meeting.'

'Do you think we should?'

'Absolutely. I think we have the topic for Friday night's show.'

Carrie stared at him. 'Are you doing this for the show or because it's the right thing to do?'

'Both.'

Maeve couldn't wait for the show to begin – she knew it was going to be their best yet. She wondered what Jonathan would think. He'd phoned this morning and mildly admonished Karl for changing the show, but he hadn't asked about what they had lined up for tonight.

'He was too miserable to care,' Karl said with a chuckle.

'Thank God for that,' Maeve murmured.

Carrie came in with the final scripts for the show and handed a copy to each of them. 'Shall I go and fetch Pauline?'

Karl glanced at his watch. 'Talk to her for a few minutes, Carrie, and don't bring her in until we've gone on air.' Maeve shot him a quizzical look. 'Trust me, Maeve, it'll help you do a more professional job.'

Maeve shrugged, went into her desk and put on her headphones. When Carrie returned with Pauline five minutes later, Maeve had already opened the show and was reading out e-mails and phone messages relating to the previous night's show. She smiled warmly at Pauline as she sat down and Carrie brought her some water. 'Well, thank you for all your messages, listeners, I think your support will mean a lot to Dee. And tonight, I'd like to welcome Pauline to the show. Hi, Pauline. Thank you for joining me on *Secrets*.'

'Hello.' Pauline smiled back nervously.

'Tell us a bit about yourself, Pauline.'

Pauline cleared her throat and took a sip of water. 'Er, well, I'm sixty-three, a widow and I have three children, although I live alone.'

'How long have you been a widow?'

Pauline sighed. 'Oh, it's more than eighteen years now.'

'Your husband died very young.'

'He was forty-seven.'

'What happened, Pauline?'

'He was diagnosed with lung cancer when he was forty-four. At first he put up a fight. After he'd had treatment and was in remission he gave up the cigarettes, watched his diet, exercised – he was very determined.'

'So he got better?'

'For a few months he was fine,' Pauline agreed, 'but then he went for his check-up.'

'And what did they discover?'

'The cancer was back and they thought it might have spread. They decided to operate.'

Maeve gazed at her. 'Was the operation a success?'

Pauline shook her head, smiling sadly. 'No, they couldn't do anything. They just sewed him up again.'

Pauline choked on a sob and twisted a handkerchief between her fingers. 'He was riddled with it. All they could do was control the pain. They wanted to keep him in hospital but he wanted to come home.'

'It must have been hard looking after him and minding three young children.'

'What could I do? I couldn't leave him in that place.' She shuddered. 'Anyway, my eldest was a teenager and she was a great help.'

'We'll take a break now, Pauline. Stay tuned, listeners, and hear the rest of Pauline's story.'

She pulled off her headphones and smiled at the other woman. 'Are you okay?'

Pauline wiped her eyes. 'Ah, yeah, I'm grand.'

Maeve went outside to have a quick word with Karl and Carrie. 'God, she's crying already and we haven't even got to the serious bit yet. I hope she doesn't break down.'

'She'll be fine,' Carrie said confidently. 'I think that was the difficult part for her.'

Karl nodded. 'Carrie's right, she'll be okay.'

'I hope you're both right.' Maeve ran back inside and put on her headphones. 'Okay, Pauline, we'll be back on air in a few seconds. Do you think you can do this?'

Pauline looked at her solemnly. 'Yes, I think so.'

Karl counted her in and with a last reassuring smile, Maeve welcomed the listeners back and recapped the story so far. 'So, Pauline, basically you brought your husband home to die,' she said gently.

Pauline sniffed. 'That was the idea, but it didn't happen that way.'

'What do you mean?'

'Well, the doctors had said that it would only be a matter of weeks, but he hung on for much longer and he was in terrible pain. Finally, he couldn't stand it any more. He wanted to put an end to it.'

'Do you mean he wanted to kill himself?' Maeve asked quietly.

Pauline nodded and then remembered she was on radio. 'Yes. But he was too weak to do it on his own.'

'So he wanted you to help him?'

'Yes.' The tears rolled silently down Pauline's cheeks. 'But I couldn't do it. I mean it went against everything I believed in.'

'What did he say to that?'

'He cried,' Pauline said, dabbing at her cheeks with a tissue from the box Carrie had left at her elbow. 'And then he got worse, steadily worse. I had to try and keep the kids out of the house as much as possible because he used to scream with the pain. It was like listening to an animal caught in a trap.'

'So what did you do?'

'I agreed to help him,' Pauline said simply.

Maeve took a deep breath. 'How?'

'Well, I was going to give him some of my own painkillers – I suffer from very bad migraine but my husband said that if they did a post-mortem they'd find out and I might end up in jail. We couldn't risk that, there were the children to think of. So instead, I filled his prescription for painkillers in three different chemists. That was enough to . . .' She shrugged.

'That was enough to kill him?' Maeve asked.

Pauline sobbed. 'Yes.'

'Would you like to take a break, Pauline?' Maeve asked gently.

'No, I'm okay. It was a Saturday night when we decided to do it. The children were staying with friends and there was just the two of us in the house. We had a wonderful evening. We listened to songs we'd loved when we first started dating, we looked through the old photo albums and then we had a drink.' Pauline paused to blow her nose, and smiled shakily. 'Well, I had a drink. He was only able to take the tiniest sip at that stage. And then I gave him the medicine, got into bed beside him and held him until, well, until he was finally at peace.'

Maeve became aware that her own cheeks were wet with tears. 'When did you call the doctor?'

'About seven the next morning. I told him that he was already dead when I woke.'

Maeve wiped her tears away. 'And did he believe you?'

Pauline smiled. 'I'm not sure, but he never questioned it. He signed the death cert and that was that.'

'Didn't anyone question his death?'

Pauline shook her head. 'He was so sick that his death came as no surprise. It was, as they say, a happy release.'

Maeve sighed. 'We'll take a break now. Our phone lines will be open for another fifteen minutes, so if you've any questions for Pauline, call us now. Also, you can e-mail us on *Secrets@ForeverFM.ie*.' She pulled off her headphones and looked at Pauline. 'How do you feel?'

'Strangely relieved,' Pauline said in surprise. 'It's nice to actually talk about it after all this time.'

'Have you never told your children?'

Pauline shook her head vehemently. 'And make them party to his death – absolutely not! As far as they're concerned their dad was sick and in pain and his death was inevitable.'

'I think you're incredibly brave,' Maeve said honestly. 'You obviously loved him very much.'

'He was my husband,' Pauline said simply.

Karl rapped on the window. 'Back in five, Maeve.'

Maeve hurriedly put on her headphones and took a sip of water before turning to the mike. 'Welcome back, listeners. Pauline, there are a lot of calls of support coming in but there are some listeners who believe that what you did was wrong. What do you have to say to them?'

'I probably would feel the same, but you never know until you're in the situation. Like I said, I refused when my husband first asked me to help him. I thought that he and I would both go to hell.'

'But you changed your mind?'

'When I saw how ill he was, the agony he was in, I just couldn't believe that God would punish us for putting an end to such suffering.'

Maeve glanced at the screen. 'Conor in Edenmore wants to know, Have you ever told anyone else about this?'

Pauline shook her head. 'No, I didn't think it would be fair to burden anyone else. I'm sure the doctor guessed, but he never said anything so neither did I.'

'And Nora in Portmarnock wants to know if you ever told a priest in confession.'

Pauline's cheeks reddened. 'Yes, but it was years later when I was on holiday in Spain and the priest didn't have a word of English!'

42

Linda listened to Maeve sign off the show and turned off the engine. Jonathan, now on the road to recovery, had begged her to go out and get curry and she'd heard most of the show while she was standing in line at his local takeaway. She took the carrier bag of food and let herself into the house. 'I'm back,' she called and went into the kitchen. After five minutes, when there was still no sign of Jonathan, Linda went upstairs. 'If you think I'm bringing you curry in bed, mate, you have another— Jonathan!' She stopped in the doorway at the sight of Jonathan sitting on the edge of the bed, his head in his hands. 'Jonathan? What is it? What's wrong?' She hurried over and sank to her knees at his feet.

He looked at her slightly dazed, his face wet with tears. 'Have you had some bad news? Is it your mother?'

'My mother,' he repeated. 'Yes, I suppose it is.'

Linda stared at him. 'Jonathan?'

He shook his head and looked up, his eyes focusing on her for the first time. 'Did you hear the show?'

'Some of it, but what's that got to do with—?' She stopped suddenly.

Jonathan nodded. 'Exactly.'

'What are you saying?' she whispered.

'I think my mother – no, I know my mother – helped Dad to—' He couldn't bring himself to say the word.

Linda took his hand and held it tightly. 'How old were you?'

'Fourteen, but don't tell me I'm imagining things.' He watched her steadily, his eyes dark with pain. 'She probably heard the show and it will have upset her. She might even think that I aired it deliberately.'

Linda shook her head. 'No, of course she won't, she knows you're out sick. Anyway, if it's true – and I'm not convinced that it is – she doesn't think you know, if you follow me.'

He smiled faintly and touched her face. 'I think so.'

'Are you going to ask her about it?' Linda sat up on the bed beside him.

He took her hand and stroked it. 'I don't know. I'm not sure I want to hear what she has to say.'

Linda frowned. 'Don't let this come between you, Jonathan. You're so close, and then there's Daniel to think of.'

'Why didn't she feel that she could tell me?'

'You heard what Pauline said. She kept her mouth shut in order to protect her family.'

'Yes.'

'But you still don't know you're right, Jonathan, not for sure. I think maybe you should talk to her. It will drive you nuts otherwise.'

He looked sad. 'But what if I'm right?'

Linda put a hand on his cheek and turned him to face her. 'Do you believe that your parents loved each other?'

He nodded. 'Oh, yes.'

'Then you know that if she did help him to die she did it out of love.'

'You're very wise.' He kissed her lightly on the lips.

'Come and eat some dinner,' she said, standing up.

'Yeah, okay.' He put on a dressing gown and followed her downstairs. While she reheated the food in the microwave, he opened some wine. He sniffed appreciatively when she put the plate in front of him. 'Lovely. One of the few things I miss about Alison is her cooking. She used to make a great curry.'

'Why did you leave her?' When he looked at her in surprise she put down her knife and fork and sighed. 'Oh, I'm sorry, Jonathan, please forget I asked.'

He smiled. 'Why?'

'It was a very personal question.'

'And don't you think that you're entitled to ask me personal questions?'

She shook her head. 'No, it's none of my business.'

'I'd prefer it if you thought it was.'

She stared at him.

'And now I'll answer your question.'

'You don't have to—' she started.

'I know I don't bloody have to.' He shook his head in exasperation. 'But I want to if you'll only shut up for five minutes.'

Linda reddened. 'Sorry.'

'Right.' He took a drink and nodded. 'Now. Firstly, I didn't leave Alison.' Linda opened her mouth to speak but he put a finger to his lips. 'Ah-ah, no interrupting. You're not the only one who thought that,' he said drily. 'I suppose it's because I've always been in the limelight, attending openings, first nights and Alison was never at my side.' He looked moodily into his glass. 'Although I begged her to come.'

Linda watched him steadily, biting her lip to suppress all the questions that were bubbling up inside.

'She wasn't interested, though. She had her own life. She was actively involved in the local musical society and her rehearsals and shows came before everything else.' Linda's eyes widened and he nodded. 'Yeah, I thought it was weird too. But then I didn't know at the time that she was sleeping with the director.'

Linda gasped. 'You're kidding – oh, sorry.' She put a hand to her mouth.

He smiled. 'So, you see, I wasn't the one to break up our marriage. Alison asked me to leave.'

She frowned. 'But she didn't get together with this other guy, did she?' From her conversations with Daniel, she had been pretty sure that he and his mother lived alone.

'No. He was married too and unlike her was not ready to walk out on his family.' Jonathan's mouth twisted in a bitter smile. 'She wanted us to get back together again, but I just couldn't. She'd killed any love I had felt for her. But it was hard. I felt that for Daniel's sake I should put it all behind me and try again.'

'Don't be so hard on yourself,' she said softly. 'You wouldn't have done him any favours if you'd gone back and the two of you were at each other's throats all the time.'

'That's what my mother said.' Jonathan sighed and looked at her over his drink. 'So now you know. Does it change things?'

'What do you mean?'

Jonathan pushed his plate aside and took her hands in his. 'I mean, Linda, do you think you might trust me now?'

Linda stared at him. 'But I do trust you.'

'You don't believe me when I tell you that I love you.'

Linda looked down at her hands in his. 'I suppose I just find it hard to believe.' She laughed nervously. 'That's more a reflection on my lack of confidence than a lack of faith in you.' She raised her head and looked into his eyes. 'I can't believe that I could be so lucky. That someone as wonderful as you could really love me.'

Jonathan was around the table and had pulled her up into his arms before she realised what he was doing. 'Oh, Linda, why don't you realise what a beautiful, intelligent, wonderful woman you are?'

She looked at him shyly. 'Maybe because no one ever made me feel that way before.'

He looked down into her face. 'Are you saying that I do?' he asked softly.

She nodded. 'Yes, Jonathan. I love you – God, I've wanted to say that for so long but I was afraid.'

He pulled her closer and kissed her long and hard. 'Never be afraid again,' he murmured when he finally stopped.

She shook her head, her eyes never leaving his. 'I won't.'

The following morning, the worst of his symptoms were gone and Jonathan decided it was time to go back to work.

'Are you sure you're up to it?' Linda asked, her eyes full of concern as he swung his legs out of bed.

He bent down to kiss her. 'For some reason I've never felt better.'

Linda smiled happily. 'We could always take the day off,' she suggested, running her fingers across his thigh.

'Don't tempt me,' he groaned. 'I need to get back in and have a word with my staff. Anyway, I was thinking of going to see my mother first.'

Linda stared at him. 'Are you sure you're ready?'

He shrugged. 'No, but I've got to do it. Now, I'm going for a shower. Why don't you go and put some coffee on?'

Linda frowned at him. 'Are you using me already?'

'Only for sex,' he promised.

She laughed. 'That's all right then.'

An hour later, they stood outside between the cars, holding each other. 'Will you be okay?' Linda asked.

'Yeah. I'll give you a call later.'

'Okay.' She stood on tiptoe to kiss him. 'I love you.'

He smiled. 'I love you too.' He stood watching as she drove away and then climbed into the BMW, his smile dissolving as he wondered what he would say to his mother. Though he'd been awake since six listening to Linda breathing steadily beside him, he still hadn't figured out how he felt about his mother. He knew he still loved her, but felt he didn't know her any more. They'd always been so close; he couldn't believe that she'd managed to keep such a secret for so long.

When he turned the key in the door, his mother was hoovering the hall. She smiled as she switched off the machine. 'What a lovely surprise, I wasn't expecting you.'

He kissed her cheek. 'I was just passing so I thought I'd cadge a cup of tea.'

Kathleen led the way into the kitchen. 'I think I can manage that,' she said and filled the kettle. 'Actually, I was going to call you about that show last night.'

Jonathan stared at her. 'Oh?'

She turned to smile. 'I thought it was wonderful, love. I cried like a baby when it was over.'

Jonathan swallowed hard. 'Why?'

She stared at him. 'Why? Because it was so moving of course. That woman, Pauline, was so brave. Dear God, listening to her reminded me of those last few weeks of your dad's life. I don't know how much you remember, Jonathan, but he had a terrible hard death.'

'I remember,' he mumbled, not taking his eyes off her.

She made the tea and sat down at the table beside him. 'Sometimes I think I let him down.'

'Why's that?'

She shook her head, her eyes filling with tears. 'He wanted to die,' she said. 'Oh, he didn't want to leave us, Jonathan.' She took his hand and held it tightly. 'But he was in such pain. I wish I'd been as strong as that woman on your show.'

Jonathan frowned. 'You didn't do . . . anything, did you, Mum?'

She shook her head and smiled a sad, distant smile. 'No, love.'

Jonathan let out a long sigh. 'Did he ask you?'

'Not in so many words. He just looked at me when I gave him his medicine and joked that if my hand slipped it would make life a lot easier for everyone.'

'What did you say?'

Her tears plopped on to his hand. 'I told him to stop feeling sorry for himself. Can you imagine me saying that to a dying man?' She wiped impatiently at her tears.

'Oh, Mum, don't be so hard on yourself. You loved him, he knew that.' He knelt down beside her chair and put his arms around her.

'How would you have felt if I'd done what Pauline had done?' she asked quietly after a few minutes.

'I don't know,' he answered honestly. 'But you didn't, so stop torturing yourself. You did everything you could for him.'

She sniffed. 'But what if he really did want me to, to . . . ?'

He looked steadily into her eyes. 'I don't believe that he did, Mum. I'm sure that every moment he had left with you was very precious to him.'

She touched his face tenderly and smiled. 'Do you really think so?'

'I'm sure of it.'

43

Maeve walked along Sandymount beach, kicking moodily at shells, and hurling the occasional pebble in the direction of the distant sea. She should be happy this morning; after last night's show she should be on top of the world. Maybe it would mean more if she had someone to share her happiness with. She'd thought fleetingly of calling Craig, but if he said anything else about her mother she'd probably scream at him. She sighed, and her breath came out as a white cloud in the cold air. Pauline's story had made her feel guilty about Laura. She'd never really thought about her father's death from her mother's side. It must have been difficult to lose her husband at such a young age. Maeve figured Laura was only about thirty-three at the time – just over three years older than Maeve was now. And having a small child to look after couldn't have been easy. Of course, Peggy had always been on hand to help. Her aunt had been wonderful. But nothing could make up for the lack of love and attention from her mother. Two joggers running past shot curious glances at her. Maeve wiped her eyes on her sleeve and turned for home. It was time to get ready for work.

*   *   *

'Jonathan's back.' Maeve and Karl looked up as Carrie arrived in, breathless and wide-eyed.

'What kind of mood is he in?' Maeve asked.

'Dunno.' Carrie flopped into a chair. 'Karen just called me to say he walked in five minutes ago, went straight into his office and closed the door.'

Karl lit a cigarette. 'Interesting.'

'It's a bad sign,' Maeve said darkly. 'He never closes the door when he's alone.'

'Maybe he needed to make a private call,' Carrie suggested.

'Maybe he's drawing up our letters of dismissal,' Maeve retorted.

The phone rang on Karl's desk. He smiled at the two of them. 'I think we're about to find out.'

But they had to wait until two o'clock that afternoon to find out what their boss thought of their unauthorised changes to the programme. They made their way up to the conference room where they sat for ten minutes before Jonathan showed his face.

'Tactics,' Maeve had murmured grimly, expecting the worst. When he finally arrived, Jonathan sat down at the head of the conference table and stared silently around for a moment. Karl stared back, a hint of a smile playing around his lips. Maeve met his gaze, a mixture of wariness and defiance in her eyes. Carrie kept her head down and played nervously with her pen.

'I wanted to talk to the three of you about last night's show,' he said quietly.

Maeve sighed irritably. 'Here we go,' she murmured.

'Did you say something, Maeve?'

She shook back her hair and stared him straight in the eye. 'The show wasn't working the way it was, Jonathan. So we changed a few things, so what? It worked. Last night's show was brilliant. Karen will tell you. The switchboard has been jammed all morning with callers saying how much they enjoyed it.'

Jonathan raised an eyebrow. 'I doubt if anyone could have enjoyed it.'

Karl's smile disappeared. 'I really don't think that's fair—'

Jonathan cut him off with a glance. 'Please let me finish.' Karl frowned and lit a cigarette. Jonathan turned back to Maeve. 'As I was saying, I don't believe anyone could have enjoyed the show but they were definitely moved by it.'

Maeve stared and Karl broke into a fit of coughing. Jonathan laughed. 'My God, have I finally managed to render you two speechless? It was a moving piece of radio, people, and I was very impressed.'

Carrie smiled widely at him. 'I knew you would be. It was amazing, wasn't it?'

'Amazing,' Jonathan agreed. 'However . . .'

Maeve rolled her eyes. 'I knew it was too good to be true.'

'However,' he continued, 'we had not agreed on that show.'

Karl nodded. 'No, you're right. But it was a choice between that and the incest case, which Maeve and

I were convinced would do nothing but shock and disgust our audience. Now, maybe that's what you and Ben are into' – he paused to glance at Maeve and she nodded – 'but we're not happy with that type of show.'

Jonathan frowned. 'Is this a stand of some sort?'

'I suppose it is,' Maeve watched him, her eyes grave.

'I see.' Jonathan sat back in his chair and frowned at the watercolour on the wall.

Karl stubbed out his cigarette and leaned forward on the table. 'Look, Jonathan, we know how important the listenership is, but we really think if you let us run the show our way it will be a success. We weren't trying to con you or take advantage.'

'Although we were taking advantage of the fact that Ben was away,' Maeve admitted.

'But only for the good of the show,' Carrie joined in.

Jonathan smiled slowly. 'You really are quite a solid little team, aren't you?'

Maeve scowled. 'Don't patronise us, Jonathan, we don't deserve that.'

'What do you deserve?' he countered.

'A chance,' Karl said quietly.

'Without Ben's interference,' Maeve added.

Carrie looked at her in alarm, but Jonathan was nodding. 'You've got it.'

Maeve shot him a suspicious look. 'Sorry?'

'You should be,' he told her. 'What you did was wrong, but,' he held up his hand as Karl opened his mouth to protest, 'I know you did it for the right reasons. And' – he smiled at them – 'it worked.'

Carrie smiled nervously at each of them. 'Well, that's great then – isn't it?'

'What about Donnelly?' Karl asked.

'Ben has decided that his talents could be put to better use elsewhere.'

Maeve's eyes widened. 'You fired him?'

'Of course not. He didn't feel happy here and I accepted his resignation.'

Maeve and Karl exchanged looks of astonishment. 'Now I want to talk about the next three shows. They are the last ones before Christmas and we need to go out with a bang.'

Carrie shot him a worried look and he sighed. 'Look, guys, I've told you I like what you're doing, so will you please stop treating me like the enemy?'

Maeve smiled reluctantly. 'I suppose we could go back to treating you like a difficult boss . . .'

'. . . Who's pigheaded and stubborn,' Karl mused.

'And short-tempered.' Carrie decided to get in on the act until she saw Jonathan's face. 'Sorry.'

'If we want to talk in detail about the shows, we're going to have to ask Maeve to leave the room though,' Karl said, pushing an A4 sheet towards his boss.

Maeve groaned. 'I really don't think there's any need for this, Karl.'

Jonathan looked curiously at the producer. 'Tell me more.'

When Viv called to try and persuade her sister to

meet her for a long, leisurely lunch she was amazed when Linda immediately agreed. 'Is everything okay?' she'd asked.

Linda laughed. 'Everything's fine. Look, meet me in QV2 in half an hour.' After she'd hung up, she went into Bill's office.

'Hi, Linda.'

'Bill, I was going to take the afternoon off, if that's okay.'

Bill looked mildly surprised. 'Of course, that's fine. Doing anything nice?'

Linda shook her head. 'Just meeting my sister for some lunch and shopping.'

'Well, enjoy yourself, you deserve it. I've just been going over the figures for last month and they're the best this year.'

'That's great, Bill.'

'Yes, and a lot of it is down to you, Linda, I do realise that. Why don't you treat your sister to lunch and give me the receipt?'

Linda flushed happily. 'Thanks, Bill, that's very nice of you. I'll see you tomorrow.' She went back to her desk to tidy up, gave Marie some CVs to file and went out to the loo to touch up her make-up. She stared at her reflection, not sure she recognised the confident, happy woman staring back at her.

Viv studied her carefully as she flopped down into the chair opposite. 'You're looking very well.'

Linda laughed. 'That sounds like an accusation.'

'It is. What are you up to? Is it sex or – lord, you're not pregnant, are you?'

Linda shook her head, still laughing at her sister's wide-eyed expression. 'Don't be silly. I'm just happy, I suppose. Work's going well – in fact, Bill told me I could buy you lunch and claim it back on expenses.'

Viv raised her eyebrows and reached for a menu. 'Better make the most of it then.'

'How's Mum?' Linda asked. She didn't want to discuss her love-life – at least not yet.

Viv put down the menu again and stared at her. 'Positively glowing. I think it's serious with Liam.'

It was Linda's turn to stare. 'Really?'

Viv nodded. 'They're spending a lot of time together and she actually asked me if he could spend Christmas with us.'

Linda's eyes widened. 'Crikey! He must be something special.'

'Yeah. I just hope we like him.'

Linda cringed. 'It would be awful if he turns out to be a complete prat.'

'Or doddery and senile,' Viv added.

'No, he couldn't be.' Linda shook her head. 'Mum's too hard to please.'

'Yeah, you're right.' Viv picked up her menu again. 'I want something very unhealthy – lot's of rich sauce, lots of butter.'

Linda smiled sympathetically. 'Having problems with the book?'

Viv grimaced. 'My heroine is a pain in the ass. I'm only halfway through the book and I want to kill her off.'

Linda chuckled. Viv was always like this when she was writing. She talked about her characters as if they were errant children who weren't behaving the way they should.

'What will you do with her?' she asked curiously.

Viv shrugged. 'Give her a disease, or a tumour or something – get her the sympathy vote.'

Linda burst out laughing. 'Maybe she just needs a man.'

'Of course she needs a man!' Viv rolled her eyes. 'That goes without saying. But he doesn't come along until chapter thirty-eight.'

'Oh, right, sorry.'

They ordered their food and a bottle of wine and Viv returned to the topic of Christmas. 'So do you think we should invite Liam?'

'I suppose so.'

Viv made a face. 'It will be a bit awkward, him and the three of us. Or worse, the two of us watching them canoodling over the turkey.'

Linda shuddered. 'Maybe we should invite a few more people.'

Viv's eyes twinkled. 'You could ask Jonathan.'

Linda thanked the waiter, who'd just brought their wine, and raised her glass to her sister. 'I could.'

Viv paused, the glass halfway to her lips. 'Work isn't the only reason you're in a good mood, is it?'

Linda's lips twitched. 'Like I already told you, Viv, I'm happy.'

Viv's expression sobered. 'Are you sure about this, Linda? It sounds like this is no longer just a bit of fun.'

'It's not,' Linda admitted. 'I love him and, I'm happy to say, he loves me too.'

'Oh, Linda.'

'Oh, Linda what?'

'Well, come on, you said yourself that he was bound to move on after a while.'

Linda smiled. 'That was before.'

'Before what?'

'Never mind, let's just say I know him a lot better now.'

'But, Linda—'

'Enough, Viv,' she hissed as their starters were set in front of them. 'Let's talk about something else. Like who are *you* going to invite for Christmas dinner?'

Viv glanced briefly at her before starting on her garlic mushrooms.

'What about Alec?' Linda liked the stockbroker that Viv had been seeing on and off for years.

Viv shook her head. 'Absolutely not.'

'But why?'

'Because I don't want to, that's why.'

Linda chewed on a piece of crab cake. Though Viv had always been more outgoing than she was, she'd never had a steady, serious relationship. 'I think you're afraid of commitment,' Linda said thoughtfully.

'Whatever,' Viv muttered, and carried on eating.

'If you and Alec have such a relaxed relationship then you should be able to invite him – casually like – to dinner.'

Viv stared at her. 'Oh, yeah, my mother playing footsie with her boyfriend on one side of us and you

and Jonathan gazing into each other's eyes on the other
– that should make it a very casual meal.'

Linda laughed. 'Rosemary is much too sophisticated to play footsie and I promise not to gaze into
Jonathan's eyes too often.'

Viv groaned. 'Oh, okay then, I'll ask him.'

'Excellent!' Linda smiled happily. 'We should get
on the phone over the next couple of days and tell
everyone about the drinks party on Christmas morning. I was thinking of saying any time between twelve
and three; what do you think?'

'I thought you didn't even want a party.'

Linda shrugged. 'Well, things have changed. I may
even invite some of my old friends.'

Viv laughed. 'You want to show Jonathan off, do
you?'

'Jonathan will be spending the morning with Daniel,
Alison and his mother,' Linda retorted. 'No, I don't
want to show him off. But because of him, I feel I
can face people again. Anyway, I owe Gwen and Sally
an apology. This would be a nice way to make up
for disappearing out of their lives for the last few
months.'

'You've missed them?' Viv said curiously.

'Of course I have. When Patrick left, I lost so much,
Viv. Now I want some of that back.'

'I'm glad for you, Lin, and I'm sorry if I've been
the prophet of doom about you and Jonathan. I really
hope that it all works out.'

'Thanks, Sis.'

44

The atmosphere all afternoon in the Forever FM offices and particularly in Maeve and Karl's office was positively triumphant. Carrie ran back and forth between Jonathan and Karl's desks with scripts until they both pronounced themselves happy. Maeve had gone home for a few hours, frustrated that they wouldn't tell her about tonight's guest. She grudgingly admitted that Karl was right and it would make the interview more exciting, but she still dragged her heels as she left, looking longingly at the script in Carrie's hand.

Carrie had held it tight against her chest and smiled apologetically. 'See you later, Maeve.'

'Yeah, seeya.'

When she'd gone, Carrie closed the door and sat down opposite Karl. 'Have you talked to Jonathan about Friday's show yet?'

He shook his head. 'Not yet.'

'Do you think he'll approve?'

Karl shrugged. 'Hard to know.'

Carrie nibbled worriedly on a fingernail. 'Maybe it would be best if he said no.'

'Why do you say that?'

'It's such a personal thing to go into on the radio.'

'But it's anonymous, remember?'

Carrie sighed. 'It's a big risk, Karl, and it could go horribly wrong. That would be a shame, considering that Jonathan has finally come around to doing things our way.'

Karl raised his eyebrows. 'Our way?'

She grinned. 'I'm part of the team, aren't I?'

'You certainly are, honey; I don't know what we'd do without you.'

'Thanks, Karl.'

He stood up and put his lighter and cigarettes in his shirt pocket. 'Right, I'll go and see Jonathan right now.'

'Good luck,' Carrie called after him.

Jonathan was humming happily to himself when Karl appeared in the doorway. 'Hey, Karl, how are you?'

Karl wandered in and sat down. 'Not as good as you.' He took out his pack of cigarettes and tapped one out.

Jonathan sat down behind his desk. 'You know you're not supposed to be smoking.'

Karl lit the cigarette and smiled. 'Didn't know you cared.'

'I don't, but you're going to get me in trouble one day.'

'I only smoke when I'm with you, Maeve and Carrie and you guys don't object.'

'Ben did.' Jonathan grinned.

'There, you see? I knew he didn't fit in here.'

Jonathan stretched out in his chair and put his hands behind his head. 'So what can I do for you?'

'I have a very different idea for Friday's show, that I need to run it by you.'

Jonathan raised his eyebrows. 'I'm flattered.'

'Don't be, I just don't want to carry the can if it backfires.'

'I thought we'd changed to the softly, softly approach.' Jonathan frowned.

'Yeah, but this one is a bit different and a bit complicated.'

'I'm listening.'

Linda looked around her apartment, pleased with the effect she'd created. An elaborate throw of crimsons and greens – very Christmassy – was draped across the sofa. Two large, soft velvet cushions in similar colours and patterns now sat in each chair. And there were green and red candles of various shapes and sizes around the room. Viv had insisted she buy them.

'Very important for atmosphere,' she'd told Linda. 'And candlelight hides a multitude of sins.'

As Linda turned off the main light, she had to agree. Her previously gloomy living room was now cheerful, cosy and warm. The buzzer rang and she hurried to let Jonathan in.

'Wow,' he said as he came through the door a few moments later. 'You've been busy.'

'I want to buy a nice rug too, but that will have to wait until the weekend. Do you like it?'

He pulled her into his arms and kissed the tip of her nose. 'Very romantic.'

She grinned. 'That's what I was aiming for.'

'Are you very hungry?' he murmured.

'Not very.' She took his hand and turned towards the bedroom. 'Perhaps we could work up an appetite.'

Jonathan turned her back around to face him. 'Where are you going? I want to stay where the atmosphere is.'

Linda sank down on to the sofa, pulling him with her. 'Then make yourself comfortable.'

A couple of hours later they strolled down to the Forum bar and ordered steak and chips. They talked idly about everything and nothing until finally Linda pushed her plate away and stared at him. 'Are you going to tell me about your mother or not?'

He shot her a sheepish look over the rim of his glass. 'You were right.' He finished his pint and signalled the waiter for another.

'What do you mean?'

'It was all in my head. Dad died naturally.'

'Oh, thank God – oh, sorry, but you know what I mean.'

Jonathan chuckled. 'I know what you mean.'

'How did she react? Was she terribly shocked that you thought that she'd—' Linda couldn't quite bring herself to finish the sentence. 'You know.'

Jonathan raised an eyebrow. 'You're not very articulate tonight, my dear.'

She glowered at him.

'She doesn't know that I suspected her,' he told her. 'She'd heard the programme and she thought that Pauline was very brave. It made her wonder if she should have done the same thing. So I was a total coward, told her nothing about my suspicions and explained that she'd done her best for Dad and that she couldn't have done more.'

Linda smiled at his downcast expression. 'You were not a coward, you did exactly the right thing. If you'd admitted your suspicions it would have devastated her.'

Jonathan sighed. 'I suppose you're right.'

'I know I am. Oh, I'm so happy you were wrong, Jonathan.'

'Me too.'

'So tell me, were your staff pleased that you liked the show?'

He laughed. 'Relieved would be a better word. I must say, I made them sweat a little before I told them. They were also very happy to hear that Ben had decided to leave.'

Linda grinned. 'So does that mean I'm forgiven for headhunting him?'

Jonathan scowled. 'I suppose you expect me to thank you.'

'No, just admit that I was right.'

Jonathan rolled his eyes. 'I'm surrounded by women who are always right. You, Maeve, Carrie – even my own mother.'

'Poor Jonathan.'

He took her hand and smiled tenderly into her eyes. 'I don't think anyone could call me poor tonight.'

'Well, then maybe this is a good time for me to ask you something.' Her eyes flickered nervously from his face to her plate.

'What is it?' he asked curiously.

'It's just that Viv and I had decided to make this a family Christmas; you know, spend it with my mother.'

Jonathan looked disappointed. 'Oh, well, I suppose we could see each other on Christmas Eve.'

'No, you don't understand. You see, Mum's seeing someone and Viv has a boyfriend – well sort of, and we thought that—'

'A sixsome – sounds great!'

Linda blinked. 'It does?'

'Sure. Viv and I get on well – at least most of the time.'

'She was very impressed with the show last night,' Linda said quickly.

'There you go, then, we'll have nothing to argue about. And your mum is great fun.'

'She can be quite . . . forceful,' Linda warned.

'You don't say,' Jonathan said drily. 'Look, I can cope with the Taylor women. What are the other two guys like?'

'Alec's nice, but I haven't met my mother's beau yet.'

'Has she had many partners since your dad died?'

Linda shook her head. 'No, that's why we're dying to meet this one. She's never shown any interest in dating before now.'

'He must be special.'

Linda grimaced. 'He'd better be.'

Jonathan looked amused at her concern. 'I think your mother can take care of herself.'

She smiled. 'You're right. It's a pity I didn't inherit that gene.'

'Oh, you're doing okay.'

She laughed. 'Only by accident. If it hadn't been for my stupid pride and your Sir Galahad impression, we'd never have got together. It was sheer luck.'

His eyes twinkled. 'Is that what you think?'

Linda looked blank. 'What do you mean?'

He took her hand and kissed it. 'Oh, Linda, you're so blind. I've always fancied you. Why do you think that you were the only one in Reeve's that I would deal with?'

'Because I was good?'

'You were, and you are, but there was a little more to it than that.'

'But I was married.'

'Tell me about it,' he groaned. 'When I finally fell in love again it had to be with a married woman.'

Linda stared at him. 'Are you joking?'

He looked solemnly into her eyes. 'No.'

'But what if Patrick and I hadn't split up?'

'Then I would have continued to take you to lunch and flirt with you. As it was, when you did split and you told me about your imaginary love-life it was as if all my birthdays had come together. Instead of having to be the supportive friend for a few weeks I was able to jump straight in – if you pardon the expression.' He grinned at her.

Linda shook her head in amazement. 'This is incredible.'

'Incredibly nice,' he corrected.

She beamed back at him. 'Incredibly wonderful.'

45

Carrie inspected her wardrobe. It was Friday, the day of the last *Secrets* show before Christmas and she wanted to wear something to suit the occasion. After selecting and rejecting several outfits, she finally settled on a long black chiffon skirt and a clingy green satin top. The skirt was close fitting and if she had to run for a bus, she would be in trouble, she thought, grinning at her reflection. But it was a bit special and suited her mood. After carefully applying her make-up, she fastened two silver chains around her neck, fixed large silver hoops in her ears and slipped three different coloured bangles up one arm. They weren't as expensive or as dramatic as the ones Maeve always wore but they were pretty. She hesitated as her thoughts turned to Maeve and she wondered if they were doing the right thing. Maeve knew absolutely nothing about tonight's show and no one knew how she'd react. Even Karl had seemed nervous last night and begged her to join him for a drink before she went home. Declan hadn't been too impressed when she'd rolled in after midnight, with several glasses of Guinness inside her.

She went downstairs and into the kitchen. Declan was still sitting at the table reading.

'Aren't you going in this morning?' she asked as she put on the kettle.

'I've a meeting offsite at ten,' he muttered, glancing up at her. 'What are you all dolled up for?'

Carrie shrugged. 'It's the last show today, so I thought I'd make a bit of an effort.'

'Won't you be home before the show?'

She shook her head as she put a teabag into a mug. 'No, I'll be too busy.'

He snorted. 'Too busy drinking with your producer.'

Carrie rolled her eyes. 'For God's sake, Declan, I only went for a quick drink with him last night. It's no big deal. Do you want more tea?'

He shook his head. 'No, but get me a muffin, would you?'

And what did your last slave die of? Carrie thought grimly as she opened the cupboard. She found the packet of muffins she'd bought in her lunch break yesterday – she still hadn't persuaded Declan to take over the shopping – and put them on the table.

Declan picked them up. 'These are blueberry.'

Carrie poured some cornflakes into a bowl and carried them over to the table.

'They're blueberry, Carrie,' Declan repeated.

'So?' She poured milk on her cereal and started to eat.

'You know I don't like blueberry.'

'It's all they had.'

'You could have tried somewhere else,' Declan complained.

Carrie put down her spoon and stared at him. 'Is this it?'

Declan continued to stare in disgust at the offending muffins. 'What?'

'Muffins. Is that all we've got to talk about?'

Declan looked at her in confusion. 'I was only saying—'

Carrie sighed and shook her head. 'I think it's time to call it a day.'

'What?' he said again.

'We're finished, Declan, over, finito, kaput.'

He stared at her. 'What are you talking about?'

'I'd like you to leave,' she told him patiently. 'I've always loved this house and I should be able to buy you out. Please let's make this as painless as possible.'

'This is because of that producer fella, isn't it?' He scowled at her.

'Don't be silly, there's no one else. I just don't love you any more.'

'But, but what will I do? Where will I go?' He looked at her like a baffled child.

'You could go home to your mum,' she suggested. 'Until you find another place.' Carrie had to suppress a smile at the look of total relief on his face.

'I suppose I could.' He stared at her for a moment. 'You know, Carrie, that if I go I won't be back. Are you sure this is what you want?'

'I'm sure.'

Maeve had also dressed carefully today, although she wasn't sure why. Jonathan had mentioned that they might have a few drinks after the show, but she didn't think she'd go. Julie had called yesterday to tell her about a party that was on tonight, although she didn't feel like going to that either. She'd missed out on a number of functions lately, which was not a good idea. Neither had she found a replacement for Paul Riche – somehow her heart wasn't in it.

'Where are you hiding yourself these days?' Julie had asked her curiously. 'It's ages since I've seen you. Have you got a man tucked away somewhere?'

Maeve smiled wryly now as she brushed her hair. There had been no man since Paul – unless she counted Craig. But how could she call a couple of innocent kisses a relationship? Craig wasn't interested in her. She was too hard, too ambitious, and too wilful for him. He obviously preferred weak and timid women like Aoife. She put down the brush and took off her robe. After she'd put on the cream silk bra and panties, she walked to the wardrobe and took out the coffee-coloured wool dress. She slipped it over her head, pulled on her black patent boots and long black wool coat. She examined herself in the full-length mirror in her bathroom and smiled faintly. She looked fine – she looked better than fine – although she wasn't sure why she'd bothered. Maybe she'd phone her aunt and invite her out to lunch. Peggy would enjoy that and it might ease her conscience. She'd been avoiding her aunt since her encounter with her mother. Time to face the music. She'd phone her as soon as she got into work.

*   *   *

Karl whistled when Carrie walked through the door. 'You look great!'

She smiled ruefully. 'I wish I felt it.'

Karl pulled a face. 'We did have one too many last night.'

Carrie laughed. 'I didn't have as many as you!'

'So if you're not hung over, why are you miserable?'

She sighed. 'Well, I've just finished with my boyfriend and I'm worried about tonight's show.'

Karl took a drag on his cigarette. 'Why?'

'I'm just not sure that Maeve will be happy about it.'

He smiled crookedly. 'I meant, why did you break up with your boyfriend?'

'Oh.' She grinned sheepishly. 'Because I bought him blueberry muffins and he wanted chocolate ones.'

Karl raised an eyebrow. 'Oh, I see.'

Carrie laughed. 'I know, it's nuts.'

'You don't seem too upset.'

'No, more annoyed with myself for putting up with him for so long. But this morning I knew it was over. The muffins were the final straw.'

'Muffins? Oh, good, I didn't get breakfast this morning.' Maeve swept into the room and shrugged out of her coat.

'You look gorgeous,' Carrie said reverently.

'Please don't tell her that,' Karl complained. 'She's hard enough to live with.'

Maeve made a face at him before looking appraisingly at the other girl. 'Thanks, Carrie; you're looking pretty ravishing yourself today. Maybe we *should* make Jonathan take us somewhere special tonight.'

Carrie glanced nervously at Karl. 'Er, yeah, maybe. I'd better go and get the post. Seeya later.'

'All set for tonight's show?' Karl asked casually.

Maeve rolled her eyes. 'How do I know? You won't tell me anything about it.'

Karl shook a finger at her. 'Not true. You know the guest's name is Fay.'

'Her fictitious name,' Maeve corrected.

'And that the secret concerns her husband and daughter.'

'That description covers about ninety per cent of the shows we've done to date,' Maeve said drily.

'True. Isn't it interesting that we have more women spilling the beans than men?'

'That's because men are used to living with lies.'

Karl raised his eyebrows. 'Ooh, we are bitchy today. Have you been dumped?'

'I've never been dumped,' Maeve said haughtily.

'Speaking of being dumped, Carrie's broken up with her fella.'

Maeve frowned. 'I didn't know they were having problems.'

'Not surprising, is it? We hardly know a thing about the guy,' Karl pointed out. 'Dermot, isn't it?'

'Declan. Is she okay?'

'Fine.'

Maeve grinned. 'In that case, we should definitely go out tonight and help her celebrate her freedom.'

Karl's eyes slid away. 'I suppose.'

'Our last *Secrets* show before Christmas – I can hardly believe it. It had better be good, Karl,' she warned him.

'It will be,' he said with false cheeriness, grabbing his jacket and moving towards the door. 'Seeya later.'

When she was alone, Maeve picked up the phone and called Peggy.

'Oh, hello,' Peggy said when she heard Maeve's voice. 'This is a surprise. Is everything okay?'

'Sure,' Maeve said brightly. 'Look, I know it's short notice but I thought we could have lunch.'

'Today?'

Maeve laughed. 'Yes, today.'

There was silence for a moment, then Peggy's voice again, sounding wary. 'Have you been talking to your mother?'

Maeve frowned. 'No, why? Is there something wrong?'

'No, no, of course not, I was just wondering.'

'So what about lunch?'

'Oh, I'm sorry, dear, I can't meet you today.'

'Oh.'

'I'm very sorry.'

'Oh, that's all right,' Maeve assured her. 'It was just an idea. Silly of me not to give you more notice. 'Bye, Peggy.'

''Bye-bye, Maeve.'

Maeve frowned as Peggy hung up. That had been a very strange conversation. Peggy had sounded almost nervous. Perhaps Laura had talked to her about her visit and Peggy was annoyed with her. That must be it.

On impulse, she picked up the phone again and dialled Laura. The phone rang out. 'Does that mean she's out or she's asleep?' Maeve murmured to herself. The phone rang and it was Karen. 'Jonathan wants to see you.'

'On my way.' Maeve fluffed her hair and made her way down the two flights of stairs to Jonathan's office.

Jonathan smiled as she walked in. 'Oh, good, you're dressed up. We're going to lunch.'

Maeve raised her eyebrows. 'We are?'

He nodded. 'Yeah, I need you to schmooze with some potential advertisers.'

Maeve groaned. 'Oh, no, Jonathan, not today. Take Karl.'

Jonathan laughed. 'He wouldn't be allowed through the door of Les Frères Jacques.'

Maeve grinned reluctantly as she thought of Karl in his battered leather jacket and frayed jeans sitting among the businessmen in the top Dublin restaurant. 'But I won't even be able to have a drink,' she complained.

'Nonsense. A couple of glasses of wine won't do you any harm. The show doesn't start till ten.'

'I know what these lunches are like,' she said darkly.

'You can excuse yourself if we haven't finished by three,' he promised.

'Oh, well, okay then.'

'Is she gone?' Carrie peered nervously round the door.

Karl waved her in. 'Yeah, Jonathan dragged her to one of his business lunches.'

Carrie sighed. 'Thank God; that should take a few hours. My nerves are completely shattered.'

'What time is Fay due in?'

'Nine thirty.'

Karl nodded. 'I think you and I need some distraction. Let's work on the first five shows for January.'

Carrie frowned. 'But shouldn't we be working on a script for tonight?'

'I don't think that will be necessary, do you?'

46

Maeve stood in the tiny ladies' room at Forever FM and cursed Jonathan Blake. Despite her good intentions, she'd had several glasses of wine at lunch and hadn't got back to the office until six.

'We have lots of ideas for the first few shows after Christmas,' Carrie had told her enthusiastically.

'Yeah, we thought we'd go through them with you now,' Karl added.

Maeve groaned inwardly. 'Just let me go to the loo first.' That had been fifteen minutes and five cups of water ago. She touched up her make-up and went back to the office. 'Would you make a large pot of coffee, Carrie?' she asked. 'I can't face the stuff from the machine.'

Carrie jumped to her feet. 'Sure, no problem.'

Karl dragged the meeting out until nine thirty when finally Maeve begged for time to get her act together before the show.

'Okay, then,' he relented and handed her a sheet of paper. 'We've had a lot of calls about last night's show so you can kick off with them. Carrie will bring Fay in after the first break.'

Maeve nodded. 'Fine, now can I please go and get ready?'

When the door had closed after her Karl and Carrie looked at each other. 'You'd better go to reception and wait for our guest,' he said quietly. 'And whatever you do, don't leave her alone for a minute.'

Carrie frowned. 'What about the phones?'

'I'll switch on the machine. Somehow I don't think we'll be taking many calls tonight.'

Carrie bit her lip nervously. 'Unless of course it all blows up in our faces.'

'It won't,' Karl said firmly.

'I hope you're right.' Carrie went out to reception to wait for Fay.

'Good evening, everyone, and welcome to the last *Secrets* show before Christmas. We've got a great show lined up for you tonight.' Maeve looked pointedly through the glass at Karl. 'But first I want to read out some of the comments about last night's show.' Maeve talked for ten minutes about Jake who had a penchant for women's undies. Some of the calls were hilarious – Dublin humour while often cruel could also be very funny. 'And finally, Martha says that Jake should buy his next suspender belt in Marks and Spencer as they're a lot more comfortable! Thanks for that, Martha, I'm sure that Jake will appreciate the tip. Okay, it's time for our first break and when we come back I'll be joined by tonight's guest, Fay.'

Karl dialled the green room. 'Carrie? Bring Fay up, but don't come into the studio until Maeve is back on air.'

When he hung up, Maeve tapped on the glass. 'Where is she?'

'Relax, she's on her way.'

Maeve drummed impatiently on the desk. When the last advert came on she looked nervously at the door. 'Jeez, Karl, she's cutting it fine. Are you sure she's here?'

'I'm sure.' The door opened as he started to count her in and Fay walked nervously to the chair opposite Maeve.

'. . . two, one. You're on, Maeve, good luck.'

Maeve stared at Fay in stunned silence.

'Come on, Maeve, you can do this,' Karl murmured urgently in her ear. 'You're a professional.'

Maeve glared at him, glanced once more at her guest and cleared her throat. 'Welcome back. I'm joined now by tonight's guest, Fay. Welcome to the show, Fay.'

'Thank you.'

'Maybe you'd like to start by telling us a little bit about yourself.' Maeve's voice sounded strained even to her own ears. She was vaguely aware that Jonathan had slipped into the studio and was sitting next to Carrie.

'I'm sixty years old, a widow and I have one daughter.' Maeve swallowed hard. 'And you have a secret.'

Fay's eyes remained fixed on Maeve. 'Yes, I have.'

Maeve glanced out at Karl, but he just gave her the thumbs-up. He obviously knew what was to come. She'd kill him for this. 'Go on.'

'I'm not a widow,' Fay said quietly.

'What?' Maeve stared blankly. 'I'm sorry, I don't understand.'

'I'm not a widow,' Fay repeated. 'I told everyone that my husband died as a result of a brain tumour nearly thirty years ago.'

'But he didn't die?' Maeve's voice was barely audible.

Fay shook her head. 'No, but I wish he had.'

'Maybe you should start at the beginning.' Maeve struggled to remain in control.

Fay's eyes were bright with tears. 'It's true about the tumour. He just keeled over one day – he was doing the garden at the time. I called an ambulance and they got him to the hospital within fifteen minutes, but it was still too late.'

Maeve closed her eyes for a second. 'But you said he didn't die.'

'No, but he was never the same again.'

'What do you mean?'

Fay sighed and tears rolled silently down her cheeks. 'He recovered consciousness after a couple of days – oh, I was so happy – but then, nothing.'

'What do you mean?'

'His eyes were open but he never said anything, never moved – never even smiled. And he's been like that ever since.'

Maeve stared at her in horror. 'But where is he?'

'He's in a nursing home in Clontarf. It's a very nice place,' she added. 'Not that he'd notice one way or the other. But they look after him well.'

'Go to a break, Maeve,' Karl said. 'Maeve?'

'Er, we have to take a break now. Back after these.' Maeve dragged off her headphones and threw them on the desk. 'Oh, Mum, why didn't you tell me?'

Fay took a tissue and wiped away her tears. 'I didn't want you to ever see him like that. I wanted you to think of him as the strong, wonderful man he once was.'

Maeve rested her head in her arms. 'Well, it didn't work. I've felt nothing but resentment for him for years.'

Her mother stared at her, distraught. 'But why?'

'We're back on, Maeve,' Karl said. 'Five, four . . .'

Maeve put her headphones on. 'Do you want to go on with this charade?'

Fay nodded miserably.

'Welcome back, listeners. Tonight I'm talking to Fay who has been telling us about the secret she's kept from her daughter for twenty-eight years. Did anyone else know what really happened?' Maeve asked.

Fay looked down at her hands. 'Just my sister.'

Maeve sighed. So, Peggy had betrayed her too. 'Tell me, Fay, how do you fake someone's death?'

Fay's eyes widened. 'I didn't! Of course, I didn't. When Andy – when my husband had his accident I moved house and I told everyone that I was a widow. No one ever questioned it.'

'But if he was still alive he must have got letters – from the taxman, the health board, how did you hide them from your daughter?'

'I arranged for all his mail to go to the clinic.'

'That was clever,' Maeve said with reluctant admiration. 'You obviously planned this very well.'

'Not really.' Fay shrugged. 'But when you – when my daughter – was young she didn't know any better. I only had to worry about details like that as she got older.'

'I see. And tell me, Fay, did it never occur to you that maybe your daughter would be happy to hear that her father was in fact alive?' She stared at her mother, her eyes cold and accusing.

Fay stared back steadily. 'Not for a minute. If she could see him lying there day after day, completely unaware of who he is, or who I am, she'd prefer to see him dead too.'

Maeve's eyes widened. 'So you go and visit him?'

'Of course I do, he's my husband! I go twice a week.'

Maeve closed her eyes briefly. More lies. She had thought her mother had a part-time childminding job. 'But you said he doesn't know you.'

'He's my husband,' Fay repeated as if that were explanation enough.

'And what about your daughter?' Maeve asked quietly. 'All the years you've been looking after a man that's practically dead, who's been looking after her?'

'Well, I have, of course.'

'Do you think that you had any love left to give her?' Maeve said baldly.

Carrie shot Karl a worried look. He'd said that this would be a wonderful reunion. He'd said that Maeve would thank them for this show. Right now, Carrie doubted that. Maeve's mother had aged ten years since walking into the studio.

'You think I've neglected her?' Fay looked crushed.

Maeve stared back, cold, unforgiving. 'Well, you tell me, Fay. Are you and your daughter close?'

Fay's eyes filled up again. 'No,' she whispered.

'Why do you think that is?'

Fay shook her head. 'I don't know.'

'Well, at a guess, I'd say it was because she was filled with jealousy and anger. As far as she was concerned, her father was dead. But all of her life, her mother has done nothing but talk about him – everything was always about him, wasn't it?'

'I – I – don't know,' her mother stammered.

'And I don't think she'd feel any differently if you told her the truth, do you?'

'Steady, Maeve,' Karl murmured, and she glared angrily out at him.

'My colleagues think I'm being a bit rough on you, Fay. What do you think?'

'I don't think so,' Fay replied, her eyes sad. 'You're right, I chose my husband over my daughter. I sometimes missed parents' day at her school or one of her basketball matches because I was with him.'

'But she didn't know that, did she?' Maeve pressed mercilessly. 'She probably thought that you just didn't care. She probably thought that you'd rather be dead than be with her.' Maeve was past caring now about the show, Jonathan or anyone else.

'No!' Fay stared at her horrified.

'Take a break, Maeve,' Karl said gruffly. 'Now.'

Maeve realised she was holding her breath. She let it out slowly and relaxed her hands, looking blankly at the angry red marks that her nails had made on her palms. 'We must take a break, folks, back soon with your questions for Fay.'

Jonathan came to the window and beckoned to Maeve. She took off her headphones and went outside. 'I never should have gone along with this show, Maeve, and I'm very sorry, but you can't go on like this.' He looked from her to the cowed woman sitting in the studio. 'It's just not right.'

'You should have thought of that before you contacted my mother,' she retorted coldly.

'She contacted us.' Karl came over and slipped his arm around her shoulders. 'She wanted to do this, Maeve.'

'She practically begged us.' Carrie put a caller on hold for a moment so that she could back Karl up. 'I'm so sorry, Maeve.'

'Can you go on?' Jonathan asked.

'I'll have to,' she said grimly.

'I'm not sure your mother can,' Karl said.

Maeve followed his gaze and felt tears prick her own eyes as she watched her mother sob quietly. Even though Laura's actions were misguided, she obviously thought that she'd done the right thing. 'I'd better get back. Are there many calls?'

Carrie rolled her eyes. 'You don't want to know.'

Maeve sighed heavily and went back inside. 'Are you okay?' she asked Laura.

'Not really.' Laura looked up at her through red-rimmed eyes.

'You don't have to go on if you don't want.'

'I want to,' Laura said, and blew her nose.

Maeve sat down and put on her headphones. She listened to Karl count her in as she surveyed the list of questions Carrie had shoved into her hand. The screen in front of her was full of e-mails too. Maeve's lips twisted into a bitter smile as she realised that there was a similar tone running through all of them. 'Welcome back to *Secrets*. I'm Maeve Elliot and my guest tonight is . . . Fay. Fay, all our listeners think I've behaved abominably towards you and that you don't deserve it.' She stared stonily at her mother.

'That's not true, they don't understand.'

Maeve's eyes widened in alarm and she shook her head.

Fay nodded slightly. 'You've made me see something that I hadn't realised before. I did neglect my daughter and I did it to spend time with a man who no longer needed me. But I realise now that *she* did.' She looked straight into Maeve's eyes. 'Thank you for that, Maeve. Maybe it's not too late for me to make it up to my daughter. Maybe it's time I told her the whole truth. Do you think she'd listen to me, Maeve?'

Maeve hesitated and then nodded slowly, her eyes bright with tears. 'I think she might.'

47

Jonathan, Karl and Carrie sat in a corner of The Kitchen, oblivious to the music and hum of voices around them. Jonathan leaned forward and emptied the last of the champagne into their glasses. 'Another of these.' He held up the bottle to a passing waitress.

Carrie took a sip from her glass. 'It doesn't seem right to be drinking champagne.'

Karl inhaled deeply on his cigarette.

Jonathan sighed. 'Do you think she'll forgive us?'

'No,' Carrie and Karl said in unison and then grinned at each other.

'Of course she will,' Karl said firmly. 'We've done her a favour.'

Carrie snorted and got some bubbles up her nose. 'I can't believe her mother? Imagine pretending that Maeve's dad was dead all this time.'

'Twenty-eight years,' Jonathan volunteered. 'It's weird all right.'

'She must be a bit nuts,' Karl added. 'You'd have to be to do something like that.'

'She seems sorry,' Carrie said. 'I thought she was very brave to face Maeve on air.'

Karl groaned. 'I was sure she was going to reveal her true identity towards the end.'

Jonathan rolled his eyes. 'So was I – God, Maeve would have killed us if that had happened.'

'I wonder where they went?' Carrie stared into her glass. 'I'd love to be a fly on the wall.'

'Well, at least they left together, that's a good sign,' Jonathan said, trying to convince himself that it would all work out just fine. He was probably in for another tongue-lashing from both Linda and his mother after tonight. He wondered if either of them had guessed the truth. 'Do you think people will realise that Fay was Maeve's mother?'

Karl shrugged and stubbed out his cigarette. 'I doubt it.'

'I wouldn't bet on it. Maeve came across as very angry.' Carrie pulled out her mobile. 'I've a friend that always listens to the show, let me see what she thought.'

Jonathan frowned. 'For God's sake, don't tell her.'

'Of course not.' Carrie dialled Orla's number and hoped that she wouldn't waken Ethan. 'Orla, hi, it's me. Sorry for phoning so late. Sorry? Yeah?' She grinned at the two men who were watching and waiting. 'Yeah, it was very emotional,' she said into the phone. 'Oh, good, I just wanted to see what you thought. We were afraid that Maeve came out looking like the baddy again. Yeah, true. That's great, okay. Declan? Oh, I'll fill you in tomorrow. Goodnight.'

'Well?' Jonathan asked impatiently.

'She thought it was a great show, but yes, she was

annoyed with Maeve at first. But, when she thought about the daughter growing up without a father and with a mother who was practically ignoring her, she changed sides. And now she thinks that thanks to Maeve there might be a reunion which would be great coming up to Christmas.' Carrie paused for breath and smiled. 'Orla's very sentimental.'

Jonathan let out a sigh of relief. 'That's great.'

'Bloody marvellous.' Karl grinned widely.

'It would be even better if Orla's right and there is a reunion,' Carrie said wistfully.

'Well, if nothing else, they'll have cleared the air.' Jonathan thought of his conversation with his own mother. 'And that won't do either of them any harm.'

Maeve perched awkwardly on a chair in the kitchen where she'd grown up. It was a lot more cheerful now, even given the current circumstances.

'More tea?' Laura asked.

Maeve shook her head. Since they'd got back, they'd hardly said a word and the silence was growing more uncomfortable every minute.

Laura stood up suddenly. 'Oh, to hell with this, I don't know about you but I could do with a real drink.'

'I'd kill for one,' Maeve admitted.

Laura opened a cupboard and peered in. 'There's no wine, but I have a bottle of gin.'

'Any tonic?' Maeve asked hopefully.

'In the fridge.' Laura took down two crystal tumblers and poured liberal measures of gin into them while Maeve fetched the tonic. 'Cheers,' Laura said shakily and took a gulp of her drink.

Maeve did the same. 'Oh, God, that feels good. I'd love a cigarette.'

Laura looked at her in surprise as she sat down at the kitchen table. 'I didn't know you smoked.'

'I don't.'

Laura chuckled. 'Oh.'

'Can I see him?' Maeve asked suddenly.

Laura stared. 'I suppose so. If you're sure . . .'

'Yes,' Maeve said, her eyes determined. 'You were so wrong to keep this from me.' Her voice was now sad rather than angry.

'Peggy said that too but I thought I was protecting you both.'

Maeve massaged her neck. 'How do you work that out?'

Laura sighed. 'He was a proud man, your dad. He'd have hated to think that your only memory of him was as a helpless, useless mess.' Laura shuddered, her face screwed up as if in pain. 'The doctors and nurses all told me that I should walk away from him – pretend that he had died. But I couldn't.' She looked back at Maeve. 'But neither could I drag a toddler along to a nursing home every week, with its smells and sickness and despair. Do you think that would have made me a good mother?'

'Maybe not, but you could have told me when I was older. I didn't really notice anything was wrong until I was almost ten. Then I began to wonder if you'd notice if I went to school one day and never came back.'

Laura flinched. 'Oh, Maeve, you were the only thing that kept me going. I'd have nothing to live for if it weren't for you.'

Maeve looked at her and wished she could believe it was true. She sipped her drink, her thoughts turning back to her father. 'He won't know me, will he?'

Laura smiled. 'He last saw you when you were a toddler – he used to call you his little princess. And now you're a very beautiful, successful young woman. He won't recognise you, no, but I know he'd be very proud of you.'

'Are you?' Maeve could have bit her tongue out. Why had she asked that? And what difference did it make now anyway?

'Of course I am.' Laura looked surprised. 'I have everyone driven mad talking about you all the time.'

Maeve shot her a look of pure disbelief. Laura smiled and stood up. 'Wait here.' She went into the dining room and Maeve could hear her rummaging through a drawer in the cabinet. 'Here we are.' She arrived back with a large scrapbook in her hand and set it down in front of Maeve.

'What's this?'

'Open it.'

Maeve did, and the first thing that caught her eye was the tiny piece that had appeared in *Hot Press* about her first show on Forever FM. As she leafed through the book, she realised it was all about her. Her mother had carefully cut out every article and photograph and pasted them in this book and occasionally she'd written something underneath. Beneath one photo taken at the People of the Year Awards she'd scrawled, 'Maeve looked lovely that night, the cameraman kept following her around!'

Maeve laughed. 'I think he asked me for my phone number actually.'

Her mother laughed too. 'Do you have a boyfriend?' she asked lightly.

Maeve shook her head. 'I just finished with a guy, but it was nothing special.'

Laura nodded. 'Paul Riche. I don't think he was really your type.'

'No,' Maeve agreed.

'You need someone who's strong and independent, someone who can stand up to you.'

Maeve scowled at her. 'You make me sound like some kind of ogre.'

'No, just a strong-minded woman who needs an equal. You could never respect a man that wasn't.'

Maeve was surprised at how well her mother knew her. And it was interesting that when she described Maeve's perfect man, Craig immediately came to mind.

'There is someone, isn't there?' Laura watched her.

Maeve glanced at her watch. 'Yes, but he's probably dancing with another girl as we speak.'

'Tell me about him,' Laura urged. 'I think a change of subject is exactly what we need.'

Maeve started slowly in stilted words, giving very brief details of the weekends she spent with FECC, Craig's business and their rather odd relationship. But between the drink and the emotional evening she'd had she soon found herself telling her mother everything about Craig.

'I don't think he's remotely interested in Aoife,' her mother said when she'd finished. 'He's just a fair-minded person.'

Maeve screwed up her face. 'Oh, he's that all right, he's always having a go at me for being bitchy.'

'You should call him.'

Maeve shook her head. 'No way, he'd probably just tell me to get lost.'

Laura shrugged. 'If he does, he does, but at least you'll have tried.'

When Carrie got out of the taxi and tottered unsteadily up the path, she half expected Declan to have locked her out. But after fumbling with the key for a few moments, she got it into the lock and it turned with ease. She was surprised to find that the alarm was on. After keying in the code she went into the kitchen to get a drink of water. She knew that no matter how much water she had she was going to have an awful hangover in the morning, but at least she could stay in bed. She groaned as she realised that she'd have to sleep on the sofa again. It was too much to hope for that Declan would have done the gallant thing and left her the bed. She had just finished her second glass of water when she saw the note on the breakfast bar. She picked it up and tried to focus on Declan's untidy scrawl.

Dear Carrie,
I've gone to Mum's – no point in prolonging the agony.
I'll be in touch about the house and about collecting the rest of my stuff.
Hope you have a nice Christmas, sorry it didn't work.
    Declan

Carrie read it three times before it sank in. 'Bloody hell,' she murmured, sitting up on a stool. 'He's gone!' She started to laugh, hiccup and cry all at the same time. 'Oh, God,' she gasped, dabbing at her eyes with a teacloth. 'What am I like?' She took her water and went upstairs, forgetting to put on the alarm again. As she reached the top stair she caught sight of her reflection in the full-length mirror. There was a stain down the front of her top where she'd spilled ketchup when she and Karl had gone for a hotdog, and her eye make-up was halfway down her cheeks. 'I look like I've been in a fight,' she muttered, and started to giggle again. When she went into the bedroom and saw the mess that Declan had left in his rush to leave, she stopped laughing. 'Messy bugger,' she growled as she kicked off her shoes and, without bothering to undress, she crawled into the unmade bed and fell fast asleep.

48

As agreed, but with some difficulty, Carrie arrived at Orla's house at one o'clock the next day.

Orla grinned at her white-faced friend. 'You look awful.'

Carrie winced and walked past her and through to the kitchen. 'Don't shout.'

Orla closed the door and followed her. 'You had a good night, then?'

'It was different.'

'Would you like some coffee?'

Carrie groaned. 'Just water.'

Orla's eyes widened. 'You must have had a skinful.'

'I was drowning my sorrows *and* celebrating,' Carrie explained.

Orla put a large glass of water in front of her and sat down. 'What do you mean?'

'I've split up with Declan.'

Orla goggled at her. 'You're kidding.'

Carrie shook her head and then instantly regretted it. 'No.'

'What happened? Did you have a row?'

Carrie chuckled. 'Sort of. He complained about his breakfast.'

Orla stared at her. 'Is that it?'

Carrie shrugged. 'Pretty much.'

'Oh, I am sorry, Carrie.'

'No, you're not!'

Orla grinned ruefully. 'Okay, I'm not. Just as long as you're all right about it.'

'Hey, like I said, I'm celebrating. The only thing I regret is that I didn't do it months ago. It's like a great weight has been lifted from my shoulders. And you've no idea how nice it was to have the bed all to myself last night.'

'He's gone already?'

'Yeah, it was weird. I told him that I'd like to keep the house and suggested that he could stay with his mother until he found another place. When I came home last night he was gone.'

Orla rolled her eyes. 'Back to Mummy. You've probably made the woman's Christmas. She'll spend the whole time waiting on him hand and foot.'

Carrie grinned. 'And telling him that he's better off without me.'

'Speaking of parents, how do you think yours will react?'

Carrie rested her head on her arm and groaned. 'Oh, God, I'd forgotten about them. This will be another failure that they can add to the list.'

'Don't mind them,' Orla said staunchly. 'I think you did the right thing.'

'The thoughts of having to listen to them nag me all over Christmas,' Carrie continued, and then raised her head to look at her friend. 'Unless . . .'

'Unless what?' Orla prompted.

'Could I take you up on your offer and spend Christmas here?'

Orla's eyes widened in delight. 'Yes, of course, Ethan will be thrilled. But won't you be in real trouble with your family if you do that?'

Carrie shrugged. 'Helen's the only one I care about and she'll understand when I explain the situation. No, I'd much rather spend Christmas with you, Ethan and your folks, if that's okay.'

'And Ray,' Orla said shyly.

It was Carrie's turn to stare. 'Ray? Are you two back together?'

'Yeah, we are. Would you believe, not only did he miss me but he missed Ethan too. And he's realised that we can't have as wild a social life as other couples.'

Carrie smiled. 'I'm so happy for you, Orla, but are you sure you've got room for one more for Christmas dinner?'

Orla laughed. 'Absolutely. In fact I could even squeeze in two if you meet a gorgeous hunk in the next two days.'

'The only hunk I'm interested in is your son. Do you think he'd be interested in an older woman?'

Orla put her head on one side. 'Do you know, I think he actually prefers blondes.'

Carrie grinned ruefully. 'Just my luck!'

Jonathan hung up the phone and went back into the kitchen where Daniel, Linda and his mother were finishing off a late breakfast. 'Everything's fine,' he told the two women when they looked up at him.

'I find that hard to believe,' Kathleen remarked.

'Of course, it's not perfect,' he admitted. 'But Maeve says they sat up talking for most of the night and they're meeting up again tomorrow.'

Linda smiled at him. 'That sounds promising.'

'Why was Maeve fighting with her mum, Dad?' Daniel asked.

Jonathan rolled his eyes at his mother over Daniel's head. He should know better than to talk about such matters in front of his son. He never missed a trick.

'Her mother used to give her a hard time about her homework,' Kathleen improvised.

Jonathan shot her a grateful look.

'But they've made up now,' he added. 'We'd better get going if we're to get all our Christmas shopping done.' He glanced at his watch.

Kathleen stood up. 'Just give me a minute to get ready.'

'You go on,' Linda told her. 'I'll stack these things in the dishwasher.'

'Thank you, dear.'

'Daniel, get your trainers on and go to the toilet,' Jonathan instructed.

When Daniel had reluctantly complied, Linda turned to Jonathan. 'What's your mum doing for Christmas?' she asked.

'I don't know.'

Linda sighed. 'Well, don't you think you should ask? It would be terrible if she were on her own.'

Jonathan frowned. 'What are you suggesting?'

'Well, if she's nothing better to do, she could always come to us. Although she might feel a bit out of it with three couples.'

Jonathan laughed. 'It's not as if we're going to spend the day smooching, now, is it?'

Linda smiled. 'I suppose not. So do you think she'd like to come?'

'Let's ask her.' He pulled her into his arms and kissed her. 'And thank you, you're very thoughtful.'

'I'm just sucking up in the hope of getting a good Christmas present.'

'But have you been a good girl?' he murmured, slipping his hands under her top.

'You tell me.' She shivered as his fingers trailed lightly across her stomach.

'Ready, Dad.' Daniel marched back in and they sprang apart. He looked at them in disgust. 'Oh, God, you're not kissing again, are you? Yuck!'

Jonathan grabbed him and started to tickle him mercilessly. 'You won't always feel that way, mate, trust me.'

Linda laughed and went to get her coat. Kathleen was just coming down the stairs, looking very festive in a short red wool coat and hat. 'You look lovely.'

'Thank you, my dear. I do love going into town at this time of year, don't you? Everyone always looks so festive and happy.'

'I like it if I'm just window-shopping,' Linda admitted. 'I hate it if I'm beating my way through the crowds, trying to get that last, elusive present.'

Kathleen laughed. 'Yes, I know what you mean. I did all my shopping weeks ago. It's the men that always leave it to the last minute.'

'It's not the last minute,' Jonathan protested. 'There's still two more days to go. Now come on, you lot, let's go.'

Kathleen and Daniel hurried out to the car, but Jonathan put a hand on Linda's arm as she went to follow. 'I've asked my mother to take Daniel for an hour, Linda, because I wanted to get you a special Christmas present and it's not something I'm comfortable buying without you.'

Linda smiled at the nervous look in his eyes. 'There's no need, Jonathan, I'll love it whatever it is.'

'No, really, you need to be with me,' he said firmly.

'Honestly, Jonathan, it's no big deal—'

'Oh, for God's sake, Linda, will you shut up!'

She blinked. 'Sorry?'

He smiled sheepishly. 'I'm trying to tell you that I want to buy you an engagement ring.'

Her eyes widened. 'Oh.'

He smiled nervously. 'Oh? Is that all you've got to say?'

She went up on tiptoe to kiss him. 'No, that's not all. I also want to say that I do love you but that it's rather unusual to buy a girl the ring before you've asked her to marry you.'

He groaned. 'God, I'm making a mess of this, aren't I?'

'Dad, come on!' Daniel waved furiously from the car.

'Just a minute, son,' Jonathan called back and went down on one knee. 'Linda Taylor, would you do me the honour of becoming my wife?'

She smiled. 'Well, I'm afraid you'll have to wait until my divorce comes through, but yes, Jonathan Blake, I'd love to marry you.'

'What did she say, Dad?' Daniel shouted.

Jonathan stood up, lifted Linda off her feet and swung her around. 'She said yes, son; she said yes!'

Maeve smiled as she put the phone back on the cradle. Poor Jonathan had obviously been expecting her to bawl him out, but she didn't have the energy to even raise her voice. It was after three when she got home and though she was exhausted, she couldn't sleep. She finally got up, put on the television and sat staring blankly at children's programmes, occasionally going out to the kitchen to replenish her coffee cup. Now, she decided it was time to shower and go into the office. She'd run out last night, leaving her desk a mess and she wanted to go in and tidy up. Her mother had asked her to come over this evening but she'd pleaded for some time alone. Tomorrow they were going to visit her dad and she needed to prepare herself for that. As she made her way into Forever FM through the heavy traffic that was customary for the last Saturday before Christmas, she tried to analyse her feelings. She wasn't happy, not really, but she did have a strange feeling of calm inside. Peace was a word that sprang to mind, though she wasn't a religious person. She used her keys to let herself into the offices – only a skeleton crew ran the station over Christmas, when they mainly used pre-recorded shows. The coffee machine was plugged out so she went to the kitchen, put on the kettle and rummaged in the cupboard for some instant.

'You'll need this.' Karl appeared behind her with a carton of milk.

'Jesus, Karl, you frightened the life out of me.'

'Sorry.'

'What are you doing here?'

Karl massaged his temples. 'Just putting my house in order before I go. My flight is at four.'

'I'd forgotten.' Karl was making a rare trip home to his family in Adelaide and would be gone for three weeks.

'Have you forgiven us yet?' he asked as she made the coffee.

'Nope.'

'Oh.' He took his coffee and followed her down to their office. On Maeve's desk was a teddy bear with a card tucked under his arm. Maeve reached for the card.

Sorry we interfered, Maeve, hope you have a peaceful Christmas. Love, Carrie.

Karl stared thoughtfully at the furry brown bear. 'She's a good kid.'

Maeve smiled grudgingly. 'Yeah.'

'So, how are things with your mother?' Karl stretched out in his chair and studied her.

Maeve sat down too and picked up the bear. 'Not bad, I suppose.'

'Are you glad that—?'

'That I had a very private conversation in public? Of course not!' Her eyes flashed.

He sighed. 'Yeah, I can't say I blame you. But she seemed to think that it was the only way she could get you to listen.'

'She was probably right.'

'What happens now?' he asked.

Maeve shrugged. 'Like they say, we'll take it one day at a time.'

An hour later, Maeve had hugged Karl, wished him happy Christmas and was back in her car, driving to Blanchardstown. She hummed along to The Pogues and Kirsty McColl on the radio singing 'Christmas Eve' and smiled at the Christmas trees and lights that seemed to adorn every house she passed. When she got to the garden centre she felt a moment of panic, but after giving herself a stern talking to, she got out of the car and strode purposefully towards the shop. She paused in the doorway, her eyes searching for Craig. Finally, she spotted him in the centre of a crowd, a pile of holly wreaths to his left and a mountain of Christmas trees to his right. She moved forward hesitantly, watching as Craig beamed at his customers, gave them instructions how to prolong the life of the tree and wishing them a happy Christmas. Finally there was a lull and he looked up and saw her. He came closer, a hesitant smile on his lips. 'Have you come for your Christmas tree?'

She shook her head. 'No, but I would like some mistletoe.'

Craig raised his eyebrows but obediently selected a piece and held it out to her. 'It's very good this year.'

'But does it work?' she murmured, and held it above her head.

His eyes widened. 'Are you coming on to me, Ms Elliot?'

'You did say that one of us should learn to be submissive.' She lifted her chin, looked him straight in the eye and took a step closer. 'So here I am.'

'Oh, Maeve.' He pulled her to him and kissed her hungrily.

Maeve dropped the mistletoe and wound her arms around his neck. When she finally pulled away she stared at him with a mixture of surprise and excitement. 'That was worth waiting for.'

He kissed her again, more tenderly this time. 'It was.'

'It looks like somebody's getting their Christmas present early,' said one of the customers, laughing.

A large woman with a blue rinse winked at him. 'I think I'll take a bit of that mistletoe, love.'

Debs laughed. 'I think we should put the price up!'

Craig grinned and bowed. 'Thank you, everybody, I'm afraid the show is over now.'

Maeve laughed as there was a chorus of 'aahs'.

'Now, Debs, if you don't mind, I'm going to take this young lady to the privacy of my van for five minutes.'

'Five minutes,' one of the men heckled. 'You'd want to do better than that, Craig, or she'll have ditched ye by Boxing Day!'

'Ha, ha.' Craig took Maeve's hand firmly in his and led her away. 'Sorry about all that,' he said when they were in the van.

She grinned. 'I quite enjoyed it actually.'

He looked at her thoughtfully. 'You look a lot better than I expected.'

Maeve frowned. 'Sorry?'

'I heard the show last night.'

She stiffened. 'You weren't at the party?'

He shook his head. 'There was no point – you weren't going to be there.'

'Aoife must be devastated,' she teased.

He didn't smile. 'Forget about Aoife. That was your mother on the show last night, wasn't it?'

She nodded. 'How did you know?'

'I know you, Maeve. I could tell from your voice.'

She closed her eyes briefly. 'Do you think anyone else would have been able to tell?'

He shook his head. 'Only those who know you well, and I don't think there are too many of them, are there?'

'No,' she admitted.

'How are things between you now?'

'Shaky.' She smiled sadly. 'We're not a very touchy-feely sort of family, but I think we'll get there.'

'Will you go and see your dad?'

She nodded. 'Mum's taking me to see him tomor-row.'

He squeezed her hand. 'That's going to be tough.'

'I don't know how I'm going to feel,' she said honestly. 'My father – the one I know from all the photos – was a vibrant, athletic man in his thirties. The man I'm going to see tomorrow is over sixty, can't communicate and can't do anything for himself. My biggest fear is that I'll feel nothing but pity.'

'Maybe that's what your mum was protecting you from.'

Her eyes flashed suddenly. 'Are you trying to tell me that she did the right thing lying to me all those years?'

'No, love, I'm just saying that perhaps she did it for the right reasons.'

Maeve smiled slightly.

'What?'

'You called me love.'

He kissed her on the lips. 'So I did.'

Maeve touched his cheek and kissed him back. 'What on earth is Freddy going to say? He thinks we hate each other.'

Craig laughed. 'Don't you believe it. Freddy realised we loved each other long before we did.'

Maeve pulled his head back down so that she could kiss him again. 'I wish he'd told us,' she complained. 'We've wasted so much time.'

He looked solemnly into her eyes. 'We've got the rest of our lives, Maeve. And from now on I'm not going to let you out of my sight.'

Maeve grimaced. 'I'm afraid you're going to have to. I'm spending Christmas with Mum and Peggy. I'd ask you to join us but—'

'I understand.'

'You won't be missing much,' she told him, her

eyes suspiciously bright. 'There'll probably be lots of arguing and crying.'

'And hopefully some laughing too,' he said.

She smiled tremulously. 'I hope so.'

Craig sighed. 'So I won't see you for three whole days?'

Her eyes twinkled. 'There's always Christmas Eve.'

'I won't be finished here until after seven,' he warned.

'I'll wait,' she murmured as she snuggled into his thick jumper. 'On one condition.'

'What's that?' he said into her hair.

'Make sure you bring the Christmas tree.'